I0823996

GONE IN THE NIGHT

Also by Joanna Schaffhausen

Detective Annalisa Vega series

All the Way Gone

Dead and Gone

Long Gone

Gone for Good

Last Seen Alive

Every Waking Hour

All the Best Lies

No Mercy

The Vanishing Season

GONE IN THE NIGHT

A Detective Annalisa Vega Novel

JOANNA SCHAFFHAUSEN

MINOTAUR BOOKS
NEW YORK

This is a work of fiction. All of the characters, organizations, and events portrayed in this novel are either products of the author's imagination or are used fictitiously.

First published in the United States by Minotaur Books, an imprint of St. Martin's Publishing Group

EU Representative: Macmillan Publishers Ireland Ltd, 1st Floor, The Liffey Trust Centre, 117–126 Sheriff Street Upper, Dublin 1, DO1 YC43

Printed in the United States of America. For information, address St. Martin's Publishing Group, 120 Broadway, New York, NY 10271.

www.minotaurbooks.com

Designed by Gabriel Guma

Library of Congress Cataloging-in-Publication Data

Names: Schaffhausen, Joanna, author.
Title: Gone in the night / Joanna Schaffhausen.
Description: First edition. | New York : Minotaur Books, 2025. | Series: Detective Annalisa Vega ; 5
Identifiers: LCCN 2025006969 | ISBN 9781250904171 (hardcover) | ISBN 9781250904188 (ebook)
Subjects: LCGFT: Detective and mystery fiction. | Novels.
Classification: LCC PS3619.C3253 G67 2025 | DDC 813/.6—dc23/eng/20250214
LC record available at https://lccn.loc.gov/2025006969

First Edition: 2025

10 9 8 7 6 5 4 3 2 1

For Becky DaSilva, treasured friend and editor.
When it comes to words, you are my touchstone.

PROLOGUE

Cyrus Merriman slipped off his wedding ring, the one inscribed *Love Always, Kara,* and put it in the pocket of his black wool overcoat before entering the bar. The place was loud, with people packed to the walls, and tacky—not the usual type of place that Cyrus frequented these days. Kara was away with her girlfriends on a ski weekend in Colorado and so Cyrus was undercover in his old life, the one he might have had if he hadn't gotten out of the South Side. He had hated his name while growing up in a hardscrabble neighborhood where every other kid was named Mike or Tony, while boys named Cyrus got called sissy and beat up on the basketball courts. Now his name was his secret weapon. Cyrus said *class.* Cyrus said *trust me,* and people did. He had parlayed his fancy name into a scholarship to Northwestern and then law school after that, where he fit right in with guys like Brett and Parker—names that belonged in the boardroom or the Supreme Court of the United States of America. *Supreme Court Justice Cyrus Merriman.* Now that was a name.

Cyrus ran his tongue over his teeth as he approached the bartender, a hipster-type with a pointy beard. "Four Roses, neat," he shouted over the din. He pivoted while the guy readied his drink and surveyed the pickings like a lion on the savanna. Women who wanted to be left alone traveled in herds, like the antelope, so Cyrus let his gaze wander to the ones left unattended. A sleek blonde in a tight white shirt looked promising, but the older redhead with the shot glasses lined up in front of her would be a sure thing. She had the curves and the face to still be sexy, but she'd also be a little needy here among the college-age set. Not that these girls went to college. They weren't like those feminist bitches Cyrus tangled with in school, unshaven freaks who hated men as their whole personality. No, the redhead would be grateful for a free drink and some male attention.

Cyrus accepted his drink and prepared to make his way toward the redhead when a woman in a black sweater and tight jeans bumped into him in her effort to flag the bartender. "Jimmy, another Bud, please," she said, putting her money on the counter. She didn't apologize for bumping Cyrus or even look at him. Still, he could smell the citrus and honey on her and the ass wiggle was meant to get his attention.

"I can upgrade you if you want," he said smoothly, leaning closer. He put a fifty next to her ten. She looked at the bill and then up at him. For a heartbeat, he thought he knew her. A former client, maybe?

"No, thanks," she said. "I've got to get back to the game."

Cyrus glanced at the televisions to see if anything exciting was playing but it was late November. No playoffs to be found. When he looked back, the woman was gone. He sipped his bourbon, idly fingering his wedding ring in his coat pocket. He felt eyes on him and looked over to see the redhead give him a smile. His for the taking, if he wanted. Instead he set out to find the woman who'd given him the brush-off. What was a conquest worth, really, without the chase?

He threaded his way through the crowd toward the pair of pool tables at the back and found the woman was bent over, wiggling her ass again as she lined up a tricky shot involving the three-ball and the corner pocket. "Go already." Her opponent, a bleary-eyed kid in a Cubs sweatshirt, leaned on his stick as he carped at her. He had a pack of Luckys sitting on the edge of the table, holding down the pair of twenties that constituted the stakes, and Cyrus would have bet both the bills that the cigarettes were the real source of the guy's impatience. He needed a fix.

"Can I have the winner?" Cyrus asked, holding up the fifty between his fingers. Maybe the woman would be impressed now.

The woman glanced back over her shoulder at him, her face speculative. She definitely saw him now. The kid snorted with amusement. "She ain't won nothing yet, buddy, so keep it in your pants."

He'd barely uttered the words when the crack of the woman's shot split the air. The three-ball spun across the table and into the pocket as she raised up with a satisfied nod. The kid's mouth hung open while she shifted to sink two more balls, clearing hers from the table. Onlookers hooted and hollered but the brunette kept going until she'd cleared the whole damn thing. She ended up right next to the Cubs kid, where she handed him the pack of Luckys. "You can go smoke now," she told him sweetly.

"She already smoked you," his buddy said, elbowing the guy and laughing.

The kid stormed off as Cyrus sidled closer to his target. "That was impressive," he told her as she folded the twenties and tucked them between her breasts.

"I won," she said, looking up at him from beneath mascara-coated lashes. "So you get to have me. If you still want."

"Oh, I want." Cyrus had yet to pick up a pool cue.

She eyed the fifty still in his right hand and then plucked it free. "You're waving this around so much it's clear you want to get rid of it. I'll get the drinks if you rack 'em up. Loser buys the next round."

So, she wanted to make him work a little, did she? Cyrus tugged at his shirt collar and grinned. "You're on."

She returned with two more bourbons. While they played, she said her name was Danielle and that she was from Michigan originally. He clearly didn't know her. She didn't tell him what she did for a living and he didn't ask. He didn't want to give the impression he cared. Cyrus considered this to be playing fair; the women knew he wasn't looking for love or any sort of real connection. He got the impression Danielle wasn't looking for romance either. She matched him drink for drink and there were stars in her eyes when she leaned into him and said, "Do you wanna get out of here?"

"Yes," he said immediately. He retrieved his coat from the nearby stool.

"I want to visit the little girls' room first. I'll meet you outside the rear door."

Outside it was colder than a witch's tits; the Chicago weather was threatening to snow but not quite pulling it off yet. Cyrus shuffled his feet to keep warm and he waited long enough to be annoyed. *Screw this,* he thought, ready to charge back into the bar and look for the redhead again. Then Danielle emerged with a smile and a wink. "Brr," she said, rubbing her hands along her arms with a shiver. "Hope you have a way to keep warm."

"Dozens of them." A few errant flakes swirled into her black hair, melting on contact, and he swore he could feel the heat radiating off her. "My car is that way," he said, jerking a nod to the lot he'd parked in down the block. "We could hang out and, you know . . . talk."

"Let's go for a walk first."

"A walk? I'm going to freeze my balls off."

"I hope not," she said with a giggle. She gave him a playful shove and he almost fell off the curb into the street. As he recovered his balance, alcohol singing in his veins, she tottered off in the opposite direction from his car.

"Wait," he called after her. "Where are we going?"

"I don't know yet."

They walked for a couple of blocks in what felt like an aimless pursuit, and he became irritated. He didn't come out tonight looking for exercise. Just as he was about to call it off, she yanked him into an alley and kissed him—her lips a shot of heat in the dark. He froze in shock for a second but then responded to her eager mouth. Yes. Yes, there were advantages to finding an older woman who knew what she wanted. He just had to get her somewhere warm and horizontal. "My car," he breathed again when they parted.

She yanked on the loose tie around his neck. "I'm not sixteen. I'm not doing it in a car."

"Then where?"

"My place is not far from here."

Cyrus hesitated. He didn't like going to the girl's place and seeing her family photos, her furniture, her stuffed animals on the bed, and a shopping list tacked on the refrigerator door. "Of course, if you have to get going we can forget it," she said, hurt by his silence. She squirmed away from him and escaped back to the lighted sidewalk.

"No. No, that's not it at all. I have work early in the morning." Tomorrow was Sunday so this was a big fat lie.

"Yeah? So do I."

Here again was his chance to ask: what kind of job did she have? He still didn't care. "Okay, then," he said. "Lead the way." The lighted sign at the corner market reminded him he'd left the condoms in the glove compartment of the car. He didn't want to double back. "Let me make one quick stop here," he said. A future Supreme Court justice could screw whoever he wanted, but he couldn't be leaving a string of babies in his wake.

"Do we have to?" She pouted. "It's freezing out here."

He noticed she'd put on only a sweatshirt. "Where's your coat?"

"Not in the habit of wearing it yet."

"Take mine." He draped his overcoat around her shoulders and she took the opportunity to twist her fingers into his shirtfront. They kissed again. "I'll just be a sec," he said, easing away from her.

She tugged him back. "Get some cigarettes too."

"You smoke?"

"Only after sex."

Hot damn, he was on fire. He hustled inside where the old man behind the counter had a space heater roaring at full blast. "Get me a pack of Winstons," he said to the man. "And the Trojans on the far left."

The man's expression didn't change as he did as Cyrus requested. Cyrus pulled out his wallet from his pants pocket and paid for the purchases in cash, all the while keeping his eye on the female figure just visible through the front door. The man looked too and saw Danielle's pacing. "Who says romance is dead?" he said philosophically as he handed Cyrus the paper bag with his items.

Cyrus returned to the night air, which had more snow swirling in it now. "Let's go," he said, casting his eyes around like he had any idea which direction to proceed.

She took his arm. "This way."

Maybe he'd drunk more than he thought because it grew dark and then darker still and he had no idea where they were. The wind picked up and he could smell the water. "Is that the lake?" She didn't seem like the sort that had waterfront property.

"Mm-hmm. Isn't it gorgeous?"

"It's a freakin' black hole right now. You can't see anything. Where's your place?"

"Not far. Come on, let's get closer. The city skyline is reflected in the water from over here."

He followed her the rest of the way and when they got to the fence at the edge, he had to admit the shimmering lights on the black water did make a pretty sight. Still, he had other priorities. "Okay, we've seen it. Can we go to your place now? Maybe have another drink."

"I think it's romantic," she said with a happy sigh. "Don't you think it's romantic?"

He eyed the skyscrapers with skepticism. "Sure, romantic."

"I want a closer look." She swung a leg over the fence. "Come on, it's fun!"

What, so he was a fucking gymnast now? No, thanks. "You're crazy," he told her.

"And you like it." She winked again and beckoned him to the other side. "Come see," she said. "You won't regret it."

He would have left then but she still had his damn coat, and it had cost him five hundred dollars. Far too much to spend on this broad. He heaved himself over the fence and balanced uneasily on the large rocks. She tittered at his wobbling and he grabbed the edges of the coat in revenge. "Happy now?" His breath came out in white puffs of booze-scented air.

"Very," she said. She kissed him and it went on long enough he felt warmth return to his face—and other regions.

"Let's go," he said, already leaning in the direction they'd come.

"Wait," she said. She pulled her hand free from his coat pocket. "What's this?"

It was dark but not black enough to hide his traditional wedding band. "Danielle, I can explain."

"You're married?"

The lake lapped furiously at the rocks, like it was angry on her behalf. She advanced on him and Cyrus retreated, his back against the fence. "I'm separated," he lied, holding up his palms. "It's bachelor central at my apartment." Technically true, even if it was only for the weekend.

"Yeah? If we called your wife, would she say the same thing? I bet not."

"Sure. She'd be real pissed if we woke her up at this hour, but why not?" He took out his cell phone, calling Danielle's bluff.

"I have a better idea." Danielle took his ring and tossed it into the water.

"What the hell?" He leaped after it in desperation but it was black and cold all the way down. "What the fuck did you do that for?"

"You don't need the ring. You're separated, remember?"

Cyrus saw red. He didn't think; just reacted. He grabbed Danielle around the throat and started to squeeze. "Who the hell are you? Trying to ruin my life when I don't even know you." She wheezed and struggled in his grip. It didn't take long to render a woman unconscious like this. He'd discovered almost accidentally when his first date went wrong ten years ago. The next day, he'd worried she might report him to the cops, but she never did. Danielle flailed her arms. She was still wearing his coat.

"You bitch." He squeezed tighter. "You had no right to do that. No right!"

She reached into his pocket and almost immediately he felt something sharp jab him in the gut. The shock made him drop his hold as he staggered backward. Danielle clutched her throat with one hand, coughing and doubling over as she heaved in deep breaths of air.

"What the hell? What did you do to me?" The world started to spin. He saw what looked like a small knife. She definitely hadn't pulled that from his pocket, so she must have had it in her sweatshirt this whole time. What, had she thought she was going to roll him? Take him back to her place and rob him? He should have choked her out when he had the chance. Maybe he still could. He lunged at Danielle again, but his vision blurred and he failed to grab her. He slumped onto the rocks, whacking his forehead as foam filled up his mouth.

Danielle plucked his wallet and cell phone and then rolled him over. "You think your wife will miss you?" She crouched down and wiped her mouth on the sleeve of his coat. She yanked open his shirt and he saw a flash of the knife again.

Stop, he tried to say. *You win. Just help me.* The swirling snow looked like a vortex sucking Cyrus away. *Stop. Help.*

"How many women have said that to you?" she asked when the plea formed on his lips.

He couldn't cry out as she cut him near his collarbone. *Not deep,* he realized, his pulse pounding. He'd expected she would slit his throat. She pocketed the knife and stood over him. Good. She was leaving and this whole horrible experience would be over. He'd tell Kara he'd been mugged. His eyes drifted closed as he rehearsed the story.

Wait. She wasn't leaving. He smelled cigarette smoke. The witch was actually standing over him smoking like they had just banged. He tried to move, to object, he couldn't move his mouth. He hoped someone saw this. A witness to come rescue him. There was never a damn cop around when you needed one.

Now he was moving. Almost floating. His heart leaped at the prospect of help and he used the last bit of strength to force his eyes open to greet his rescuer. *Her.* He didn't have time to be angry or to panic. His eyelids flickered one last time and he saw her smiling face as she rolled him into the icy cold water.

ONE

THE POLAR EXPRESS HAD DERAILED IN THE FRONT ROOM. At least that's what it looked like to Annalisa as she surveyed the Christmas chaos at her parents' home. Crumpled wrapping paper, bits of ribbon, boxes and toys scattered across the floor. She stooped to retrieve a shredded pile of tissue paper and her mother appeared tut-tutting at her shoulder. "Anna, you shouldn't be doing that. Not in your condition."

Annalisa rolled her eyes like she was sixteen again. "I'm pregnant, Ma. Not helpless. I can clean up easier than you or Pops can at this point." Ma battled arthritis in her hands and Pops had advanced Parkinson's disease that kept him mostly wheelchair-bound these days. At the thought of her father, she looked around but did not see him in his usual easy chair. "Hey, where is Pops, anyway?"

"Joyriding with your stepdaughter in her new sports car."

"What?" Annalisa cast a stricken glance at the window. Cassidy had only gotten her license a month ago, and the Chicago streets were winter-slick.

"Don't worry, Nick went along too for supervision," Ma replied.

"Was he strapped to the roof?" The little convertible didn't have a back seat.

Ma shrugged and pulled a bow from her fluffy white hair. "You know Nicky. He finds a way to get what he wants."

"You don't need to tell me." Nick had married Annalisa twice now. She wasn't sure how it happened exactly, but the second marriage seemed to be sticking. "I can't believe he gave a seventeen-year-old girl a red sports car." Nick had gifted Cassidy his used Mazda Miata and purchased a more family-friendly Toyota Camry TRD now that he and Annalisa were expecting a baby in April.

"Did you see how she jumped up and down when she opened the box of keys?" Ma said. "That's what he gave her. That happiness." She pinched Annalisa's cheek. "You never stop wanting good things for your kids. Never." She paused, considering. "Although we may need a forklift to get your father out of the seat when they return."

Two of Annalisa's older brothers, Vinny and Tony, were on the premises, along with their wives, kids, and one Goldendoodle named Sunny. "I think we'll be okay, Ma," Annalisa said. She heard childish shrieks of joy from outside and went to look for the source. The newest addition to the family, Greg Miller, was engaged in a snowball fight with Annalisa's two little nieces, Carla and Gigi. Annalisa watched them play with a wistful pang. Greg was set to marry Carla and Gigi's mother, Sassy, in the spring, but Annalisa couldn't help picturing her brother Alex out in the snow, playing with his girls. Instead, Alex had been in prison since Gigi learned to walk. Carla had nearly doubled in age, from four to almost eight. He'd missed so much of their lives and he would miss tons more. Gigi and Carla could be mothers themselves while Alex rotted inside his ten-by-twenty cell—where Annalisa had put him.

Her mother came up behind her and rubbed Annalisa's arm. "It's not your fault," she murmured as she watched the girls at play. "It's not your fault Alex isn't here."

"How do you do that?" Annalisa asked in genuine astonishment. "Are you psychic or something?"

"You'll know when you have your own." She smiled and touched Annalisa's swollen belly. Annalisa brushed her mother's hand away in a self-conscious gesture. She wanted this baby more than anything, but she was also terrified. Alex had been much-loved and dearly wanted, and look what had happened to him.

"How's work going?" her mother asked, changing the subject.

"Slow." The bigger Annalisa got, the fewer jobs she had working as a private investigator. Clients wanted to hire tough, no-nonsense Annalisa Vega—the ex-cop who took down the Lovelorn Killer. They didn't want a pregnant, waddling mother-to-be. Prospective clients came in, took one look at her stomach, and made polite excuses about how they had to "think it over" and they would "be in touch." Then she never heard from them again.

"Your father has a friend," Ma began, and Annalisa held up her hand to stop her.

"Please. No more of Pops's 'friends' who need to hire me."

"He's only trying to help."

"Last week he sent me a woman looking for her lost parrot." She sighed. "I'm going to find Sassy."

"Check behind the shed. She's out there smoking but she thinks we don't know."

"Smoking? Sassy quit that ten years ago, way before Carla was born."

Ma put up her hands. "Everything old is new again. What do I know?"

Annalisa put on her jacket and boots before heading out to the shed. Sassy dropped the cigarette the moment she saw Annalisa and started waving her arms in a frantic dance to clear the air around her. "What are you doing? Stay away from me."

"You look like a spider touched you," Annalisa remarked as she watched Sassy flail around to disperse the cigarette smoke.

"You shouldn't be breathing this stuff."

"Neither should you."

Sassy huffed out an irritated breath. “I know, I know. I’m quitting. I am.”

“No judgment,” Annalisa said as she scuffed at an icy patch of snow. “It’s just, I came out here for a pep talk on the benefits of motherhood, and here you are hiding from your kids and fiancé. Are you okay? With Greg and everything?”

Sassy leaned back to peek around the shed at her fiancé and two daughters having the time of their lives. “Sure, yeah. We’re great. He’s great. The kids love him and I love him. Doesn’t he fit right in with everyone?”

Annalisa hesitated. Greg blended with the Vega clan just fine, but there was no getting around the Alex-shaped hole in the family. “He’s funny, smart, and he’s wonderful with the girls. If you love him, we’ll love him.” She hoped she sounded convincing.

Sassy pursed her lips so hard they turned white. “Gigi called him ‘Daddy’ the other night.”

“What?” Annalisa couldn’t keep the horror from her voice.

“Yep. Right out of nowhere. But that’s not the worst part. After Gigi said it, Carla slapped her. Told her Greg wasn’t her father and never would be because they already had a father, even if he didn’t live with us.”

“Oh, no. Was Greg there to see this?”

“No, thank God.” Sassy took out another cigarette but didn’t light it. “But maybe it would be better if he had heard it. He should know what he’s getting into.”

“I think he does know.” Alex’s trial had been all over the news.

“Not—not the reality of it. Gigi’s fine but that’s because she doesn’t remember Alex, which is its own kind of awful, you know? She draws pictures for me to send him and we do video chats at visiting time, but to her, he’s a face on the screen. He may as well be Elmo. Carla remembers. She’s old enough to know what she lost.” Her face twisted and she let out a small sob.

“Oh, honey.” Annalisa moved to hug Sassy.

"She gets so angry sometimes. I can't blame her but it scares me and I don't know what to do about it."

"Therapy," Annalisa said. "Lots of it."

Sassy sniffed and pulled back, but her eyes were still watering. "We talked with a social worker a few times when Alex was arrested. The girls seemed okay then."

"That was three years ago. Maybe it's time for a tune-up."

"Yeah." Sassy stared at the ground. "Yeah, you could be right. Or at least a good night's sleep. I was up until two in the morning last night."

"Assembling a dollhouse from Santa?" Annalisa had seen the pictures already and Gigi wouldn't shut up about how it had a real, working elevator.

"No, Greg put it together, thank God. I was watching more of those true crime shows."

"Sass. You know better."

"I know, but I get sucked in." Annalisa knew very well why Sassy couldn't get enough of the true crime tales. She was looking for answers about what happened with Alex, trying to figure out why he'd gone off the rails as if somehow Sassy could have changed what happened. "This one was about that five-year-old Wisconsin girl who disappeared from a Christmas parade back in the eighties. Eve Collier?"

Christmas Eve. That's what they'd nicknamed the girl. Annalisa had been a child herself when Eve went missing, but she remembered her parents watching the news stories, how alarmed they had been for their own kids. Evie had accompanied her two siblings and her uncle to a Christmas parade in Madison, Wisconsin. The uncle went to change the baby's diaper and Eve disappeared while he was gone.

"They still haven't found her," Sassy was saying. "It's been almost forty years. Her parents are dead now, but the cops still have the case open and presumably her brother and sister are alive. Can you imagine? Not knowing what happened to your sister?"

Annalisa had lost Alex in a way, but she knew where he was: locked up in Illinois River Prison. She made a noncommittal noise and scuffed the icy ground with the toe of her boot. She didn't want to tell Sassy what every cop surely knew: whoever grabbed Eve on Christmas had probably killed her within twenty-four hours.

"The uncle couldn't live with himself," Sassy said. "He took his own life a few weeks after Eve disappeared."

Annalisa almost wished she could have one of Sassy's cigarettes. "Why do they run this stuff on Christmas?" she said, irritated by the networks for showing this garbage and Sassy for being unable to look away.

Sassy's reply hit Annalisa in the gut. "Maybe it's the one time of year people still hope for a happy ending."

One of Sassy's girls let out a happy shriek from across the yard. Annalisa summoned a smile. "Happy endings are possible, you know," she said to her sister-in-law.

"Sure. Look at you and Nick."

"We're more like a sequel," Annalisa replied, squinting.

"I guess that makes Greg a whole new book." Sassy let out a long sigh. "I went to see him a few weeks ago. Alex."

"In person?" Annalisa knew this was no small feat. Alex, probably in deference to Ma and Pops, had been transferred to Illinois River Correctional Center in Canton, Illinois. It was medium security—a coup for someone like Alex who had been convicted of murder—and a better overall environment than the rougher prisons closer to Chicago. But the trade-off was the distance. Illinois River was a six-hour round trip.

"I wanted him to hear about Greg from me, not anyone else."

"How did he take it?"

"Not great."

"Hmm, yeah. I guess I'm not surprised." Annalisa cleared her throat. "How's . . . how's he doing?" She got regular updates on Alex from her mother, but she didn't have much contact with him herself. A few cards. She put money in his commissary account for his birthday and Christmas, but she'd not been to visit since he got transferred two years ago. She loved him but there was a dead body between them now, each one standing on the other side of it. So, Sassy's next words came as a shock.

"He wants to see you."

Annalisa had to parse the meaning to understand what Sassy meant. "Me? Why?"

Sassy shook her head. "He didn't give me details. Just said it was important and he wanted you to come in person, not call."

"I don't get it. I mean, he knows about . . ." Annalisa gestured at her pregnant belly.

"He knows." She looked sideways at Annalisa. "He says congrats."

Annalisa held her stomach as she absorbed this news. She and Alex had said it all as far as she was concerned. "It's not a great time," she said aloud. "My business is down. I need to be hustling. I've had no new clients for weeks now."

"What about that woman with the missing parrot?"

"It was Pops again." Annalisa's jaw set as she thought of her father's meddling.

"How on earth did he kidnap a parrot?"

"He didn't. He sent one of his old buddies from the two-five—a sweet old lady named Bernice. I guess she was the captain's secretary back in the day, but I didn't know that when she hired me to find her parrot. She told me his name was Larry . . ."

"I'm sorry." Sassy cut her off with a hand on her arm. "The parrot's name was Larry?"

"Larry Bird. Yes."

Despite everything, Sassy threw back her head and laughed. "Oh my God. Does he dunk?"

Annalisa had to giggle too. "No, but apparently he sings Elvis."

"Get out of here."

"Yeah, when Bernice gave me the sad story about how Larry disappeared out of her open window, she told me he couldn't be far because his wings were damaged and he could only fly short distances. I scouted around Douglass Park because she thought he might flee to the nearest green space, but no one I talked to had seen a parrot. Bernice had mentioned she had bought Larry five years ago after his previous owner died and the son couldn't keep him. I wondered if Larry might have flown home, so to speak."

"Like those dogs in the kids' movie," Sassy said. "They found their way home."

"Yeah, parrots are smart, right? So maybe Larry did the same thing. Bernice agreed it was possible, so she gave me the son's contact info in Indiana. Kind of a long way to fly, but maybe Larry would try it if he felt motivated enough."

"The dogs did in the movie."

"So, I spoke to the son and he said he hadn't seen any trace of Larry. He was living in his father's house, so if Larry was headed home, that's where he'd go. I told him to keep a lookout, but in the course of the conversation, the son told me how sorry he was to let Larry go, how Larry had so much personality and made his father laugh all the time. He said that his father would play Elvis's 'Love Me Tender' on an old record player and the bird would sing along."

"No way."

"Yeah, so I got to thinking. Maybe that's how I find the bird. I pulled it up on my phone and wandered around the park for an hour, playing the stupid song over and over at high volume."

"You must have gotten some funny looks."

"I made sure to wear a hat and dark glasses so no one would recognize me."

"Did you find Larry?"

"Not at the park," Annalisa said darkly. "I went to Bernice's place to report on my failure and when she served me tea, I saw a few sunflower seed shells under the table. They hadn't been there on my previous visit."

"Oh no," Sassy said, seeing where the story was going.

"Oh, yes. I didn't ask her about the shells. I just took out my phone again and cued up Elvis—real loud. Sure enough, the bird starts warbling in the closet."

"She stuck him in the closet?"

"Yes. My father had paid her to pretend to have a lost bird."

"He's trying to help you. He knows you need work."

"Real work, yes. Not ridiculous, nonsense work." She flapped her arms in indignation, like Larry might have. "Before Thanksgiving, he sent me a former buddy of his who claimed his corner store got robbed. Nice old guy who walks with a cane—butter wouldn't melt in his mouth, you know? So I said sure, let me look at the CCTV footage and see what I can do. I watched it one time and it's obvious that the 'robber' is actually my dad's buddy in a wig and giant overcoat. He had the same damn limp."

Sassy laughed again. "At least it wasn't Pops himself doing the robbery."

"Don't even joke about that."

"I'm sorry." Sassy touched her arm. "So are you going to do it? Are you going to see Alex?"

Annalisa sighed. She didn't have anything better to do. "I don't know. Maybe."

The back door opened up and Ma stuck her head out. "Who wants hot chocolate?"

Carla and Gigi screamed with delight and raced for the door, with Greg trailing behind. He stopped when he reached the stairs and turned around, his face uncertain when he didn't see Sassy, who was still hiding behind the shed. Annalisa gave him a friendly wave. He lifted his hand in greeting and followed the girls inside.

"You are going to marry him, right?" she asked Sassy without looking at her.

Sassy slumped against the shed and put her hands over her face. "I don't know," she said. "Maybe."

TWO

Annalisa decided to visit Alex. She didn't tell Nick about her plan to drive to the prison. Nick wouldn't object to her visiting Alex, but he would insist on coming with her. These days, he didn't like her driving anywhere alone, even to her office. "What if you're in an accident and the airbag deployed?" he had argued last month, gesturing at her ballooning stomach.

"Then it would possibly break my nose, which is up here." She'd pointed at her face.

She sipped her decaf coffee and scrolled through the news on her phone like it was any other Tuesday morning. Nick entered, freshly shaved and showered, his shield on a chain around his neck. He left before she did most mornings these days because he was trying to pick up as much overtime as he could before the baby was born. "If Ramirez still needs help interviewing witnesses on that drive-by, I may be home late tonight," he said as he grabbed the thermos of coffee and microwaved breakfast sandwich she'd laid out for him.

He didn't ask about her plans for the day. Her schedule had become so boring it wasn't even worth small talk. She planned a three-hour drive to Canton, fifteen minutes to talk to Alex, forty-five minutes for lunch and then the three-hour return trip. She should beat Nick home with no problem. "I'll keep dinner warm for you."

"You mean you'll keep the pizza heated in the oven."

"I never claimed I'd cook." She looked up from where she'd been scrolling yet another baby name website. "Hey, what do you think about Tallulah for a girl? It means 'bubbling spring.'" He made a face. "What? I think it's cute."

"It's fine. It's just . . . I had an ex named Tallulah."

"Nick, if we rule out every girl's name because you dated someone with it, we'll have to move on to . . . I don't know . . . Svetlana or Hortense or something."

He winced and she slid her phone away in disgust. "Don't tell me you dated a Hortense."

"No, I arrested one. For murder. She poisoned her first husband."

Annalisa considered a moment. "Maybe he had it coming."

"Maybe. But she shot the second husband."

"Let's rule out Hortense then."

He grinned and leaned down to where she'd presented her cheek for his kiss. As he did so, a striped cat leaped out of nowhere and landed on Nick's shoulder. "Ow," Nick said as the claws dug into his shirt. Jack, their adolescent kitty, purred and ran his face over Nick's cheek. "What the hell is he doing on top of the kitchen cabinets again?" Nick grabbed him under his arms and the cat's lower half stretched out impossibly long.

"He's playing panther. Aren't you, cutie?" Annalisa scratched the cat's white belly with affection and he swished his tail in eager response.

"As long as he gets it all out of his system now." Nick set Jack on the floor. The cat immediately jumped onto Annalisa's lap—admittedly a trickier proposition these days. "Come April, he's going to have to share you."

"I'm sure he won't mind."

Nick gave her a look that said he questioned this idea, but he kissed her again and took his coffee out the door. Jack perched on her knee and rested his tiny chin on her rounded stomach, purring loudly. "Aw," Annalisa said, scratching him behind the ears, "you'll love the baby, won't you?"

The baby took that moment to kick, startling Jack. His ears flattened as he drew back with a hiss. He raised his paw and smacked her belly as hard as he could. Annalisa heaved a sigh as she stood up, forcing him down to the floor. "At least you didn't use your claws."

....

The drive to Illinois River Correctional Center took her down Interstate 55, which used to be part of the historic Route 66 connecting Chicago to Southern California. This included passing through Joliet, where the famous old prison stood. The foreboding limestone building had been everything from a home to convicts Leopold and Loeb to a featured setting in *The Blues Brothers* movie. Now it was a tourist trap where families could take selfies with empty cells and rusted, rotting prison bars. Barbed wire curled around the fences as a cheeky backdrop. Annalisa whizzed past the signs begging her to come for a fun visit, but prison wasn't fun for her.

At "The River," Annalisa had to show two forms of ID and lock her belongings away, including her cell phone, before she was allowed into the visitor area. A smattering of inmates already sat with their visitors at various tables, including one child in braids who couldn't be more than four. She colored with crayons, swinging her legs under the table, while the adults talked in low voices around her. Annalisa kept her head down and tried not to make eye contact. She never knew if she might encounter a felon she'd put away or if someone would recognize her as the cop who had stopped the Lovelorn Killer. Even as Alex's sister, she was infamous with prison guards whenever she had to visit one of the state lockups. The DOC staff checking her ID always took a second longer to look her over, wondering about the woman who would turn in her own brother.

Finally, the door clicked open and Alex came through it. No one else seemed to notice or care. He looked good, or as good as one could in prison-issued gray leisurewear and slip-on cheap shoes. Alex had entered prison a slightly doughy middle-school math teacher with black curls and an easy grin. The man standing across the room was leaner, his hair grayer now, short and stripped of any boyish charm. He smiled and raised a tentative hand in greeting. She wanted to wave back but her hands remained stuck in her lap, balled into fists. Alex took a visible deep breath, crossed the room, and took the seat opposite her. "Hey," he said. "Happy New Year."

"Not yet." The old year wasn't finished with them. It had three days left.

"Yeah, but I'm getting in early." If he got out early, Alex would maybe see Gigi graduate from high school. He'd be fifty years old. The state had sentenced him to life, but if he played his cards right, he might get away with half of one. He leaned over the table to be nearer to her, trying to peek at her stomach. "Mom told me about your news. Congrats. I'm sure Carla and Gigi can't wait. Boy or girl?"

"We want it to be a surprise." She didn't like to hear him say Carla's and Gigi's names, which she knew was irrational. He was still their father. But his actions meant they would be raised by Sassy and a data analyst named Greg. This was not supposed to happen. It was not supposed to be. "Why did you want me to come here?"

He sniffed and wiped at his nose. "Right to business, huh? No chitchat."

"Alex." She waited until he looked at her. He'd been her favorite brother. The one closest in age to her. Her playmate and her confidant.

Then he'd murdered someone she had loved. She still couldn't make sense of the two versions of him that lived in her head. "You and I can't do small talk," she told him. "You wanted me to come. Here I am. What gives?"

"You remember a guy named Joe Green? He did yard work for Pops sometimes."

The name rattled around in her head like a pinball, pinging off different memories. She recalled a man in a green outfit and a green truck and conjured up an image of him raking up their yard. *Mr. Green.* "Vaguely," she told Alex. "Why?"

"He's in here."

"What? In prison?"

"Yeah, they got him for murder, same as me. But Joe says he didn't do it, and I believe him."

"Everyone says they didn't do it." The words came out harsher than she meant them. Alex had owned up to what he did, but last time they had talked, he still made excuses. The alcohol. Pops's affair. Anything to move the blame off him.

"Yeah, but Joe's got proof he didn't do it. Well, sort of. I was hoping you could look into it for him. See if there is anything that can be done. Otherwise, he's probably going to die in here without ever seeing his kid again."

Annalisa decided to withhold her argument for the moment. "Who did he kill?"

"No one."

She shot him a look and rephrased, enunciating each word. "Who is he convicted of killing?"

Alex's lips thinned and he looked toward the window with the wires crisscrossing it. "His wife's lawyer—a guy named Cyrus Merriman. She was threatening to divorce Joe and take their kid. Joe admits he lost his temper and threatened the guy, but he didn't kill him. When they fished the lawyer out of Lake Michigan, the cops decided that Joe must've tossed him in there with no evidence to back it up."

"No evidence."

"Well, there was an eyewitness. But she's lying."

"Oh? You know this how?"

"Better for Joe to tell you himself." Alex turned and gestured at another inmate who had been talking with an older male visitor. The visitor left as Joe got up to join Alex and Annalisa at their table. Annalisa looked him over on his approach and did not recognize him as the guy who had worked in their yard all those years ago. He was tall, yes, but the man in her memory had a full brown beard whereas this guy was gray-haired and clean-shaven. "Annalisa, meet Joe Green. Joe, this is my sister Annalisa Vega."

"Thank you for meeting with me," Joe said as he took a seat.

Annalisa wished she could have kicked Alex under the table like they were kids again. He'd set her up, asking Joe to be in the room before she had agreed to anything. "I'm here to see Alex," she told Joe. "He's the one you have to thank."

Joe frowned at Alex. "You didn't tell her why she's here?"

"She's big into delayed justice." Alex's words had an edge to them. "Go ahead, tell her what happened."

Joe leaned back and stretched his long legs under the table. "Thirteen years ago, I thought my life was going pretty good. Wife and three-year-old son. Working construction and making decent money at it. Then my wife, Vanessa, starts acting kind of squirrely. Hanging up her phone the minute I walk in the room. She'd say she was talking to her sister, but I'd heard her talk with her sister plenty of times, and they didn't hang up unless the house was on fire. So I snoop on her phone. The number calling her is one I don't recognize. I decided to take off work and follow her one day to see what she was up to—where she went while I was out busting my hump to put a roof over her head. I saw this girl come to the house, someone I guess was a babysitter. She left Michael with this girl and drove across town to a parking lot, at which point she gets on her phone again. A few minutes later, a black Lexus rolls in with a guy driving it. Vanessa got out of her car and into his. They hugged and chatted for a while. He gave her some papers or something. Then they started kissing. It seemed like he wanted to go even further, but I guess she was in a hurry to get back to the kid because she got out of there. She drove off and he got on his phone to someone. I don't know what came over me. It was like a movie, like I left my body and watched myself get out of my truck, walk across the lot, and start banging on this asshole's window. I don't even know this guy and he's kissing my wife?"

"So you banged on his window," Annalisa said. "Then what?"

"Sorry. Yeah. I still get hot thinking about it, only now it's like a horror movie. I want to yell at myself: don't go over there! Stay in your truck. Don't touch that fucker or his fancy-ass car. I didn't even know this guy's name and now I'm doing life for murdering him."

"I gather his name was Cyrus Merriman and he was actually your wife's lawyer," Annalisa said.

"They didn't look like they were discussing the law when I saw them," Joe groused. "What kind of attorney holds client meetings in his car?"

"The Lexus was found abandoned in a city parking lot when Cyrus disappeared," Alex cut in. "It had Joe's fingerprints on it."

"I never said it didn't. I copped to banging on the car. I said if I saw the guy near my wife again, I'd blow his dick off."

"Did you own a gun?"

"Hunting rifle, yeah. I wouldn't have shot the guy, though. It was just talk."

"Alex says they fished him out of the lake," Annalisa said. "Was he shot?"

"No," Joe said. "He drowned. I guess someone hit him and tossed him in the lake."

"Why did the police think it was you?" Annalisa asked.

"Because I'd threatened him. Because I was home alone that night." He looked sheepish. "Vanessa and I had a huge fight about it and she went to stay with her sister in Bloomington. I sat around in my underwear drinking Bud and watching all the *Die Hard* movies one by one. Later, the cops would say Cyrus had a bite mark on him and that it matched my teeth." He touched his mouth now, as if still surprised. "But the kicker was this female witness. She says she was out walking her dog and saw me get out of my truck and drag Cyrus's body to the water."

"She didn't call the police?"

"She said she didn't see me throw him in. Thought we were two drunks sobering up in the night air. It never occurred to her that I was going to toss his ass in the freezing water because who would ever do such a thing?"

"Right," Annalisa said drily. "Whoever would?" Her rear end had started to go numb from the hard, plastic seat and the baby was doing a number on her bladder. She needed Joe to wrap up his story so she could go pee. So far, she had heard nothing that would cause any doubt that Joe had murdered Cyrus Merriman. "This is the witness you claim is lying?"

"Not me," Joe said. "I mean, yeah, I said she was lying at the time, but no one would believe me."

"What's her name?"

"Gwen Beaufort. She's this uptight skinny bitch with huge glasses."

Alex nudged Joe with his elbow to admonish him. "Joe. Language."

"Oh, yeah. Sorry." He blew out a frustrated breath. "It's just when a complete stranger decides to torpedo your whole life for no reason, it makes you kinda pissy."

"You never met this woman . . . Gwen Beaufort? You never met her before the trial?"

He held up his palm as though testifying. "As the Lord is my witness. I never even heard her name. I have no idea why she'd make up a story like that. My best guess? The cops fed it to her to sweeten their case. This Cyrus guy liked to party. He'd been out at the bars that night, according to other witnesses. Odds are he got drunk and fell in the lake all on his own."

"Mm," Annalisa said. "You said someone else had reason to doubt Gwen's story. Who is that?"

Joe hesitated. Alex put an encouraging hand on Joe's arm. "Go on," he urged. "Show her."

Joe pulled a folded piece of paper out of his pocket. "This is just a copy. I gave the original to my lawyer. Around five months ago, I got this sent to me in the mail here at the prison." He slid it across to her and Annalisa opened it to find a typed note. It read:

GWEN IS LYING. JOE DIDN'T DO IT.

It was signed with a stylized *B* at the bottom that looked like hand-drawn ink.

Annalisa let the paper fall down on the table. "That's it?" she asked. "That's your proof?"

"There was no return address. It's all I had to go on."

"Anyone could have sent that to mess with you," Annalisa pointed out. "Or you could have had someone send it on your behalf. Either way, it proves nothing."

"That's what my lawyer said when I showed him," Joe said, slumping in his chair. "Although after I called him like six more times, he said he'd send someone to find Gwen and talk to her. She stuck to her story. Except, I guess this new investigator was a little bit better than whoever my lawyer had working my case thirteen years ago. He went to Gwen's apartment building and talked to a few of her neighbors. And guess what?" He looked at Annalisa, expectant.

She spread her hands. "Tell me."

"Gwen Beaufort never had a dog."

Annalisa blinked. This was a weird wrinkle. The witness said she'd seen Joe taking Cyrus's body to the lake when she was out walking her dog. Why would she say that if she didn't have a dog? "Strange," she agreed aloud. "But still not proof of anything."

"I know, I know. My lawyer said unless there was new evidence that could have swayed the jury at the first trial, there's no way to appeal the verdict. So here I rot. All I can say is I hope that Detective Carelli is pleased with himself. He locked up an innocent man while the real killer—if there even is a real killer—goes free."

Annalisa jerked her head up at the mention of Nick's name. "I'm sorry . . . Detective who?"

"Oh, didn't I mention?" Alex had a gleam in his eye. Here it was, the shiv he'd been hiding in his sleeve. "It was Nick's case."

THREE

ANNALISA DID SOME MATH ON THE DRIVE HOME. Thirteen years ago, her first marriage to Nick had broken up and she'd dropped out of law school to become a cop. It would have been just before Nick moved back to Florida for a stint with the Jacksonville PD. In the meantime, he'd been sleeping with everything in a skirt. She knew Nick was a conscientious detective, but he had definitely been . . . she settled on *distracted,* around the time Joe Green was charged with Cyrus Merriman's homicide. Still, he'd have hardly been alone on the murder case. Other detectives, the forensic team that found the fingerprints, the forensic odontologist who had analyzed the bite mark on Cyrus's body, and the prosecutor who had put the whole case together and taken it to trial—they all collaborated to put Joe Green in prison. That redundancy was supposed to guard against mistakes, but Annalisa knew by now that mistakes, sometimes even deliberate cover-ups, could turn prosecution into persecution and the wrong person would be charged. Alex, of course, knew this as well as any man doing life for murder.

She gripped the wheel tighter as her thoughts turned to Alex. He must be feeling pretty smug right now, having thrown this little bomb into her lap. It was a delicious predicament from his point of view. Sure, she could walk away and not give Joe Green a second thought, the same way she could have let Alex's crime disappear into history undiscovered. But this was the turnabout in Alex's fair play: once she thought she had the truth, she couldn't let it lie.

To soften the coming blow to Nick, she picked up sushi from their favorite restaurant, something they hadn't done for months now since she couldn't eat much of it due to her pregnancy. They were also trying to save money given her income had dipped due to the lack of clients at her PI business. She realized as she handed over her credit card that Joe Green and Alex had not mentioned anything about how she might get paid for looking into his case. Joe did not exactly seem like he was sitting on a hidden million. Still, Annalisa stopped and added a six-pack of Nick's favorite IPA to her purchases, ignoring the thin-lipped silent judgment from the clerk who rang up her alcohol. She told herself she was treating Nick with wifely affection, not boozing him up for an interrogation.

Nick came through the door at seven-thirty and looked stricken at the sight of the spread on the kitchen table. Annalisa had gone all out with cloth napkins and candles. "It's not our anniversary," he said, not sounding totally sure. "What did I miss?"

"Nothing special," she told him as she patted his chair. "Just felt like giving you a nice dinner since you've been working so hard."

"All right, all right," Nick said like he was Matthew McConaughey. He washed up at the kitchen sink and joined her at the table, pausing to kiss her lips and pat her belly. "I hope you both had a good day."

"Mmm," she said as she picked up a California roll. She let him eat some food and crack open one of the beers before she told him the next part. "I went to see Alex."

Nick froze with his chopsticks in midair. "You went to the prison? That's a long drive. Why didn't you tell me you were going? We could have found time to go together so you didn't have to drive all by yourself."

"I can still drive, Nick. I'm pregnant. Not blind."

"Okay, okay." He ate another bite. "How's Alex?"

"He's good. They've got him teaching math." She knew this from her mother, not because Alex mentioned it.

"Puts his skills to good use," Nick commented. "I think teaching middle schoolers might be good training for a bunch of felons."

"I think the middle schoolers might be worse," she said and Nick laughed.

"Ours will be a perfect little angel. I'm sure."

Annalisa's smile faded. Alex had been a good kid. She reached for her water and drank it half down. "There's a guy on Alex's cell block right now who we used to know as kids. Joe Green." She looked at Nick to see if he recognized the name. His expression appeared blank.

"Yeah? What'd he do?"

"When we knew him, he did yard work. But he was charged with murdering his wife's lawyer. Seems she might have been plotting to leave Joe and take their son. Maybe even leaving him for the lawyer."

"Sounds rough." Not a flicker of recognition.

"Joe got charged with beating the guy up and tossing him in Lake Michigan."

The tiniest frown appeared on Nick's face. "When was this?"

"Thirteen years ago. The victim's name was Cyrus—"

"—Merriman," Nick finished for her. "I remember now."

"It was your case."

"One of the last before I moved, yeah. I had to fly up to testify at the trial. He's locked up with Alex, huh? Small world."

Yes, she thought. *Too small*. Like pinched shoes that hurt to walk in them. Aloud, she said, "What exactly did you testify to at his trial?"

"The usual. You know." Nick waved his chopsticks in the air. "He had no alibi. We verified he'd fought with the victim and threatened him before his death. Oh, and there was a witness."

“The woman with the dog.”

“Yes,” he said emphatically, pointing his chopsticks at her. “What a lucky break, huh? She just happens to be out walking her dog and sees practically the whole thing go down. God bless Fido’s tiny bladder.”

“Except,” Annalisa said carefully, “Gwen Beaufort didn’t own a dog.”

“Huh?” Confusion colored his features.

“Joe Green’s attorney looked into it recently. According to her neighbors, Gwen Beaufort never owned a dog.”

Nick did not seem perturbed. “Well, she had one that night.”

“You saw it?”

Nick sat back, looking at her full on now. He’d figured out this was no casual conversation. “As I recall, Ms. Beaufort came forward after Joe Green was named as a suspect in the investigation. She didn’t understand what she had witnessed. So no one interviewed her the night of the murder.”

“What you’re saying is that you never saw a dog.”

“I don’t remember. It was thirteen years ago. Why does it matter? There was physical evidence to back up her story. Means, motive, opportunity, forensics . . .” He ticked them off on his fingers. “Joe Green was guilty as sin. I get why he went after Merriman. The guy was a total player and he was making a move on Joe’s wife. I’d have wanted to take a swing at him too.”

Annalisa snorted. “I’m sorry . . . who was a player?” she asked, cupping her hand around her ear like she hadn’t heard him right.

Nick’s color heightened. “Yes, me, okay? That’s what I’m saying. I was kind of like Merriman back then. Why do you think I remember the case so well? Married guy plays around and pays the ultimate price for it. That kind of narrative makes you think.”

“It’s a narrative all right,” Annalisa agreed.

“You seem to believe there’s something wrong with the case. Are you saying I fucked up?”

"I'm not saying that."

"Because if you're saying I got the wrong guy, I hope you have evidence to back that up."

Annalisa looked down at her plate for a long moment. Then she pulled out the folded piece of paper with the note Joe had given her and handed it to Nick.

He read it and flicked it back at her. "That's it?"

"As I understand it, the case against Joe Green came down to three things: his fingerprints on the car, which could be explained by his earlier confrontation with Cyrus Merriman; his bite mark on the body; and Gwen Beaufort's eyewitness testimony." When Nick opened his mouth to protest, Annalisa held up her hand. "Plus, Green had no alibi. I get it."

"That's a strong case," Nick argued. "Even if you take away the fingerprints."

"What about if you take away the eyewitness? You and I both know that bite mark evidence hasn't held up well in recent years. People see patterns that aren't there. Dental bites aren't as unique as fingerprints. Remove the bite mark and suddenly the witness is the whole case against Joe Green."

"Sure, right, and if I had a wheel instead of legs I'd be a unicycle. You can invent whatever story you want but it doesn't make it true."

Annalisa picked up the note again, brooding over it. "That's what I'm afraid of. What if the person who sent this note is correct? Joe Green could be innocent."

"What reason would the witness have to lie?" Annalisa had no answer and her silence emboldened him. He threw down the white linen napkin she'd selected for their festive dinner and stood up. "And more importantly, what reason do you have to go mucking around in this case? You're not carrying a badge anymore, Vega. This isn't your turf. I get that you're bored at the moment. I'm sorry your business is slow, but maybe just enjoy the downtime rather than go manufacturing trouble." He left off the words "for me" at the end but the sentiment radiated from his angry posture.

"If the case is as solid as you say, then there's no harm in me looking into it for a bit."

"I wouldn't be too sure about that."

He stalked off with his dinner half eaten while Annalisa remained at the table. She'd bet Alex would be smiling if he could see her now. She reread the note and the signature *B* at the bottom. If she accepted the note was true, that someone believed Gwen Beaufort was lying about what she saw the night Cyrus Merriman died, who could it be? Annalisa pondered the possibilities and decided the most obvious answer would be Gwen herself. If she felt guilty for lying, she might send an anonymous note to correct the lie. After all, the *B* could stand for Beaufort.

....

ANNALISA AWOKE THE NEXT MORNING FROM A VIVID DREAM IN WHICH SHE'D BEEN A YOUNG GIRL AT HER PARENTS' HOME PLAYING HIDE-AND-SEEK AROUND THE NEIGHBORHOOD. She thought she was searching for one of her brothers, probably Alex, but when she moved aside the trash can in the alley behind the house, she found a girl around her own age sitting there. Annalisa was triumphant, prepared to shout, "I found you!" but the girl put her finger to her lips. "Come on," the girl whispered to her. "We can both hide."

Annalisa twitched herself awake, covered in a sheen of sweat. She reached for Nick on the other side of the bed but he was already gone. She curled around her swollen belly and wondered about the girl in the dream and whether she represented the unborn baby. Annalisa stroked her stomach, trying to convince the baby it would be safe to come out when the time came. Trouble was, she wasn't sure she believed it herself.

Jack leaped up on the bed and stuck his furry little face right up against Annalisa's, purring and meowing both. "You don't fool me," she told him as she hauled herself upright. "I know he fed you already." Jack curled in the warm spot she'd vacated, his tail swishing in indignation.

Annalisa showered, dressed, and went to her office, where as usual, no one waited to talk to her. Not even one of Pops's buddies came through her door with a made-up case for her to investigate. So, after a few hours of playing games on her phone, she scheduled a virtual visit with Joe Green and told him she would look into his case. "I can't thank you enough," he replied. "I don't have much, but I can pay you fifteen hundred dollars. I've been saving it to get another lawyer, but I know the lawyer won't be worth crap if I don't have new evidence."

"I don't guarantee to find any," Annalisa warned him.

Joe replied that he understood this and said he would contact his current attorney about getting Annalisa all the information available about the case. "Do you think you can find who sent the note?" Joe asked her, his gruff voice turning anxious.

"I don't know. To be honest, that's not my priority."

"I don't understand," Joe replied.

"From a legal perspective, it doesn't matter who sent it. It matters if it's true. If Gwen Beaufort is lying about what she saw and if we can prove that. So it makes sense to start with Gwen."

"She moved out of the city years ago. My lawyer told me."

"I have ways of finding her. What about your ex-wife? Vanessa?"

Joe's face hardened on the screen. "What do you need to talk to her for? She didn't even testify at the trial. She wasn't around when Cyrus got whacked—she was in Indiana with her sister."

"Look," Annalisa said. "If you didn't kill Cyrus Merriman, then someone sure wanted to make it look like you did. Your wife knew this guy. She was having an affair with him, yeah? So if anyone could lure him to the edge of the lake in the middle of the night, it might be her."

Joe looked dumbstruck by the idea. "You think she put Gwen up to lying about it then?"

"I don't know," Annalisa said. "But I sure plan to find out."

....

ACCORDING TO PUBLIC RECORDS, VANESSA GREEN LIVED ON THE SOUTH SIDE IN A TINY GRAY BUNGALOW ON KERFOOT AVENUE, ALONGSIDE A TIGHT ROW OF OTHER HOUSES THAT STILL BORE CHRISTMAS WREATHS AND STRINGS OF LIGHTS FROM LAST WEEK'S HOLIDAY. It was New Year's Eve day and Annalisa hoped to catch the woman at home. When she got close to the door, she heard a young child crying on the other side and then a woman's voice shouting. A teenage boy answered Annalisa's knock, holding a toddler on his hip as the scent of cigarettes wafted out from the house behind him. The girl had a tear-streaked face and a messy ponytail on top of her head that reminded Annalisa of Pebbles Flintstone. "Yeah?" The boy glanced over Annalisa with confusion because he obviously did not recognize her. He wore a grubby T-shirt with some sort of video game controller on it and bear-claw slippers on his feet.

Joe Green had a son with Vanessa, Annalisa knew, so this must be the boy, Michael. He would have been about the toddler's age when Joe went away, and now he was almost six feet tall. "Hi," Annalisa said with a friendly smile. "Is your mother in?"

He cast an uncertain look over his shoulder. "She's busy."

"Oh, I only need a few minutes of her time." Annalisa pulled out her card. "My name is Annalisa Vega. I'm a private investigator." She handed the card to the boy. Sometimes her name was enough to engender cooperation; a lot of people remembered the Lovelorn Killer and her role in solving the case. The kid's face remained blank as he studied the card. The toddler made a play for it, and he moved his hand out of her reach, causing her to scrunch up her face to scream again. "I said she's busy right now," the boy told Annalisa over the fresh round of shrieking. "Maybe try tomorrow or next week or something." He prepared to shut the door but a woman appeared behind him in a bathrobe.

"Can't you keep that kid quiet?" she demanded. "And why d'you have the door hanging open when it's freezing out? I'm not paying to heat the front yard."

"There's a PI here. Some lady wants to talk to you."

The woman moved fully into view so she and Annalisa could get a better look at each other. Vanessa Green was much younger than Joe; Annalisa guessed her to be about forty-five, but a hard forty of someone who had been working since she was ten. She was thin enough that the bathrobe almost wrapped twice around her but her overall appearance was like an unmade bed. Her stringy hair was somewhere between gray and pale blond, her flesh sagged on her face. Only her eyes, blue as sea glass, gave a hint that she might have been beautiful in the days that Joe knew her. "What do you want?" she asked Annalisa as she withdrew a pack of cigarettes from the pocket of her robe.

The toddler had stopped screaming at the appearance of her mother and started squirming to get to her. The boy tried to hand her off but Vanessa held up the cigarette like she had better things to do. "Give her some juice—but don't let her near my phone with it." The boy disappeared into the house while Vanessa lit her smoke and leaned against the doorjamb, making no move to invite Annalisa out of the cold. "What're you investigating?" she asked. She inhaled but turned her head so the smoke wouldn't land right in Annalisa's face.

"Your ex-husband."

"Joe? What's to investigate? He's in prison for life."

"For murdering your lawyer."

Vanessa's gaze turned sharp. "That's right. Long time ago now. Ancient history."

"Maybe not," Annalisa suggested. "If there were new evidence, he could get a fresh trial—or even be released with time served."

Vanessa appeared alarmed by this and she grabbed her robe closed at the neck. "What new evidence? Joe is right where he belongs. You need to take your investigation somewhere else."

"I promise I'll only take a minute." Vanessa hesitated, and in that second of hesitation, Annalisa figured out a new strategy to get inside the house. Vanessa had at least two kids that Annalisa could count, and that meant this woman had worked a lot of hours while pregnant. Annalisa placed a hand on her belly. "Please, I could really use a glass of water and to sit down for a bit. My feet are killing me."

Vanessa wavered, still reluctant. "No offense, but you don't look like a PI." Curiosity must have won out because Vanessa moved aside and admitted Annalisa to the cramped living area. The girl came over with a sippy cup and hugged Vanessa around the knees. Her disposition had improved with the juice, and she giggled as she played peekaboo with Annalisa around the folds of Vanessa's robe. She reminded Annalisa of Gigi, Alex's youngest, when she was a baby.

Vanessa fetched Annalisa a glass of water and indicated she could sit on one of the bar stools at the kitchen counter. Vanessa stood near Annalisa, continuing to smoke. "So who hired you? Joe? He sent a letter a few years ago, claiming he'd been set up. I threw it in the trash."

"You think he killed Cyrus."

She shrugged one thin shoulder. "The cops said he did it. They're the experts, right? I was at my sister's place at the time."

Annalisa looked around the place and took in the worn sofa, the Target-style décor, and the crack running up the wall by the fireplace. Cyrus Merriman had worked for a high-ticket law firm downtown, the kind of place where the attorney's hourly fees were the same as a car payment. Where had Vanessa gotten the funds to hire him? "Must've been easier to divorce Joe after he got convicted," Annalisa said.

"Ha. Still cost me a grand. I should've done like his first wife and left him in the middle of the night."

“I didn’t know he had a first wife,” Annalisa said.

“I never met the woman. She’s probably out there with her own war stories. If I did meet up with her, I’d buy her a drink and we could tell each other the truth.”

“What truth is that?”

Vanessa crushed out her cigarette in the nearby ashtray and scooped up her daughter. “That Joe Green is a lying, murdering sack of shit. Isn’t he, darling?” She bounced the toddler until the girl giggled.

“You’re that sure he’s guilty?”

“Let me tell you about Joe.” Vanessa blew her bangs out of her eyes. “Joe mooned around after his first wife took off on him. He came into the diner where I was working every day for breakfast and he seemed desperate for conversation. He was sweet to me, and good with my older daughter, Briana. She was seven at the time, and bored from sitting around at the diner all day. Joe would buy her food. The manager, he wouldn’t let me feed Briana for free. Had to come out of my paycheck. But Joe, he’d tell her to order whatever she wanted. He was like Santa Claus.” She gave Annalisa a look that was somewhere between defensive and pleading. “Who wouldn’t want to marry Santa Claus?”

“Sanna?” The toddler beamed and patted her mother’s face with excitement. “Sanna come?”

“He already came, baby. Remember, he brought you a dolly? Go find your dolly.” She kissed the girl’s head and set her down. “Look, I don’t know what story Joe told you, but he’ll say anything to keep a girl’s attention, you know? All of it’s horseshit.”

“What do you know about Gwen Beaufort?” Annalisa changed tactics, hoping Vanessa might be startled by the witness’s name after all these years.

“Who?” Vanessa sounded detached, her gaze in the direction her daughter had gone.

“Gwen Beaufort. She was the witness at Joe’s trial.”

"I don't know her. Never did." The answer seemed rote, like she'd had it prepared since the moment Annalisa walked into the house. "Look, Briana's here to watch the kids. You gotta go so I can get ready for work."

Annalisa turned to see a twenty-something blond woman coming up the walkway wearing an oversize gray sweatshirt emblazoned with the logo RUBY'S PLACE. The woman bounded in without knocking but stopped short when she saw Annalisa. "Hi," she said, friendly but also cautious around a stranger. She gave Vanessa an uncertain look. "Mom, I thought I was sitting for the kids tonight."

It was New Year's Eve. This girl didn't have a party to go to?

"She's leaving," Vanessa replied in a firm tone. She started herding Annalisa toward the door. *Ruby's Place,* Annalisa thought as she looked again at Vanessa's daughter. She knew the name. It was a women's shelter for victims of domestic violence. Did Briana work there? Annalisa halted on the threshold of the house. "Wait," she said, trying a stab in the dark. "Was Joe violent with you? Is that why you were leaving him?"

Surprise flickered over Vanessa's features. She reined it in quickly and returned to her fixed, thin-lipped expression. "Joe never laid a hand on me," she said as she began closing the door on Annalisa. "Goodbye now."

Annalisa stood on the stoop for a moment, pondering the conversation. She'd been overeager, she decided. Too desperate for real work that she'd jumped the gun and confronted Vanessa without doing more background first. Still, the Ruby's Place sweatshirt niggled at her—she'd seen it mentioned somewhere in the Cyrus Merriman news files. When she returned to her car, she searched first for Joe's name and the shelter and then after, Cyrus Merriman's. Cyrus's name returned a *Tribune* article written soon after his body had turned up on Montrose Point. There was a single line in the story: "Cyrus Merriman maintained close ties to Ruby's Place, where he performed pro bono work for women experiencing domestic violence."

Ah, Annalisa thought. This explained how Vanessa hooked up with Cyrus Merriman. He did legal work for the shelter. But then Vanessa had denied Joe ever hurt her, so how had she ended up at Ruby's Place? Maybe Vanessa didn't want to admit she'd been a victim, but she definitely had no love lost for the man. *Joe's right where he belongs.* Annalisa sat in her car wondering if she should return Joe's money and wash her hands of the case. If he was violent with Vanessa, then that only increased the odds that he'd killed Cyrus as well.

Annalisa looked up from her phone to see Vanessa, dressed now and heading for the train station. On impulse, Annalisa got out of the car and hurried after her. "Ms. Green . . . Vanessa, wait." She had to know the truth about Joe if she was going to continue to work on his behalf.

Vanessa looked back over her shoulder and scowled when she saw Annalisa huffing after her. "What now? I'm late for work. Leave me alone."

"Joe was violent, wasn't he?" Vanessa doubled her pace, and the baby weight made it harder for Annalisa to keep up. "You . . . you sought help from Ruby's Place and that's where you met Cyrus."

Vanessa halted and Annalisa stopped too, doubled over as she caught her breath. Vanessa advanced on her. "You think you're so smart, do you? Playing detective? You've got a husband, I see. A rich one by the looks of it." She nodded at Annalisa's diamond-studded wedding band. Annalisa closed her hand in a self-conscious gesture. Nick wasn't rich by any means, but he had splurged on the ring the second time around. He hadn't been able to afford an engagement ring for their first marriage. "Tell me," Vanessa asked, "does he know you're out here knocking on strangers' doors asking nosy questions?"

"He knows." Nick had certainly met this woman. He would have interviewed her back in the day. "I used to be a cop."

"Yeah? Good for you." Vanessa had about as much use for cops as she did her ex-husband. "But you're not a cop now, and that means I don't have to talk to you." She started off again and Annalisa followed.

"It's nothing to be ashamed of," Annalisa said as she loped alongside her. "That's why Ruby's Place exists—because there's such a need. Lots of women have been in the same position."

"Lady!" Vanessa stopped and held up her palm in Annalisa's face. "You don't know anything about me or my position. I told you—Joe never touched me, okay? Not one time."

"But Cyrus Merriman took your case for free."

Vanessa's lower lip unzipped in disappointment. At her fate, maybe. At Annalisa for guessing the secret. Annalisa expected an admission of the truth at this point so she couldn't believe what Vanessa said next. "Free? Honey, nothing in this life is free. Sure, Cyrus the big fancy lawyer would take legal cases for us poor girls, but he expected to be paid, all right. In BJs."

A fierce gust whipped down South Vincennes Avenue, sending Annalisa's hair in a whirlwind and she clawed it out of her face to stare at Vanessa with some horror. "You're saying Cyrus Merriman forced you to have sex with him? In return for his legal representation?"

Vanessa shook her head with pity and looked at Annalisa's ring again. "We all pay, right? Just in different ways."

FOUR

NICK PULLED JOE GREEN'S FILE. He had known and worked alongside Annalisa long enough to understand a key truth: if her internal alarm was going off about the Green case, he should pay attention. Of course, he remembered Joe Green, although he hadn't told Annalisa the reason why. He hadn't told anyone, not then and certainly not now. He had sat with Vanessa Green in her living room to tell her about Joe's arrest, but what he didn't say was that the Merriman case wasn't the first time he'd met her. He had been to the Green house the year before, when he wasn't yet a detective, in response to a domestic violence call. Joe Green placed the 911 call. He claimed Vanessa had threatened to kill him with a kitchen knife. Nick hadn't believed the story then and didn't believe it now. Men who abused women liked to make it seem like the woman attacked first. Both Vanessa and Joe had red marks on them the night Nick showed up. Joe had control of the knife. Who had started the fight? Joe said it was Vanessa, and Vanessa didn't agree but neither did she defend herself. Nick had no choice but to arrest her and to remove her from the house while her daughter sobbed. But Joe hadn't pressed charges. Nick had given Vanessa the card for Ruby's Place. *Please call them. They can help you.*

Given this history, it didn't surprise him a year later when Joe Green killed Cyrus Merriman. Violent men begat more violence. Nick had learned this at the tender age of eight when his father had murdered his mother while Nick hid in the closet. Annalisa would argue this was his blind spot, that he was quick to believe the worst of his fellow men, especially husbands. But Annalisa had a blind spot too: she believed the worst about cops. If he looked at Joe Green and saw an abuser, Annalisa looked at Joe and saw a guy possibly framed for murder by a lazy cop who fingered the easiest suspect. Only problem was, this time Nick was the cop.

She should know better from their years of working together. Annalisa was always the headstrong one, skirting jurisdiction and eschewing proper procedure in pursuit of whatever she believed to be the truth. *Justice first, screw the rules.* Nick liked rules. He'd grown up in chaos and now he played by the book. He'd been right about Joe Green; he knew it. Now he just had to convince Annalisa. He pulled up the computerized records from the Cyrus Merriman case and reviewed the photos. Sure, the bite marks on Merriman's body could be iffy. He'd been in the water six days before anyone found him. The fingerprints were solid—a ten-point match. But no question the case came down to Gwen Beaufort's eyewitness testimony. Nick reread her statement:

Just after two in the morning, I was walking my dog along North Eastlake Terrace when I heard a car engine to my right. I looked down West Birchwood in the direction of the lake and saw a red pickup truck idling near the barrier to the lake. The driver was a white man with a buzz-cut hairstyle. He got out of the truck and went to the passenger side, where he helped another man out of the seat. The other man wasn't walking properly and they stumbled in the direction of the water. I thought one or both of them must be drunk, and that the buddy was about to be sick and the driver didn't want him vomiting in the truck. I didn't think much more about it until I saw the news stories about Joe Green and Cyrus Merriman. The news had pictures of Joe Green and I recognized him as the driver of the truck. I didn't get a good enough look at the other man, but it could have been Cyrus Merriman. The size and shape are similar. I continued walking after I saw them heading for the water but I did make a mental note of the license plate because I thought the driver might be drunk driving. If I had seen him speeding past me or otherwise driving erratically while I finished my walk, I would have reported him. But he must have driven the other way because I did not see the truck again.

The plate number that Gwen gave them, Nick knew, matched Joe Green's truck. He pulled up the biographical information they had on Gwen at the time. Of course, they'd run a background check on her and she was clean. No arrests. Not even a parking ticket. She was single, twenty-eight at the time, and working as a freelance copyeditor. She'd lived nowhere near Joe Green or Cyrus Merriman, and there was no indication she'd ever met either of them. She lived in an apartment and Joe Green had worked as a landscaper. She hadn't had any legal trouble that would require Merriman's services. Still . . . the dog. What was that mystery about the dog that didn't bark? Now Nick had the case of the dog that didn't walk.

Annalisa maintained Gwen could not have been walking her dog that night because she didn't have a dog. Nick searched his memory for any hint of a dog but he recalled talking with Gwen at the station, not at her home. She'd come in voluntarily. He remembered her as buttoned-up, with a high collar and a blunt, chin-length cut, so sharp that it might have been a wig. She'd worn glasses; that was in the notes. She'd been wearing them the night of the murder and could see well enough to make the ID on Joe Green and grab the license plate on the truck. Gwen had struck Nick as someone who did her civic duty. She voted. She paid her taxes on time. She hadn't hesitated to come forward when she realized she had important information in a murder investigation. *This was a woman who would have registered her dog,* Nick realized. She would have paid the city for a license. He ran a records check and it came back empty. Gwen Beaufort had definitely never owned a dog.

Frowning now, Nick dug deeper in his search of Gwen and discovered she had moved to Eau Claire, Wisconsin, two years ago. He found a current number for her and gave her a call.

He knew his number would show up on caller ID as the Chicago Police Department and that alone might be telling if she refused to answer. But Gwen picked up on the second ring. "Yes?"

"Gwen Beaufort?"

"Yes," she said, mildly irritated now. Her face came back to him, pinched and pale, her jaw set with determination.

"This is Detective Nick Carelli from the Chicago Police Department. We spoke when I was investigating the death of Cyrus Merriman about thirteen years ago. Do you remember?"

"Yes," she said for the third time. She gave him nothing more.

Nick shifted in his seat. "I'm calling about your dog."

"My dog?"

"The one you said you were walking at two in the morning the night Cyrus Merriman was murdered." She didn't say anything in reply to this, and Nick shifted again. "The thing is, Ms. Beaufort, we don't have a dog registered in your name. Not ever."

Silence on the other end. Then a huffy sniff. "Let me get this straight: you are calling after thirteen years to ask me about a dog?"

The longer she went without explaining, the more Nick's concern grew. He'd had a mentor in his early days on the streets, one who taught him to be suspicious of witnesses found at the scene of the crime. *The thing you got to ask yourself is: out of all the places this person could be in the whole world, why are they here?* "Yes. Joe Green's case is up for review, and—" He didn't even have to finish his lie.

"I was dog sitting," Gwen cut in. "For my friend Miranda. She had a yellow Lab named Stanley. I'd tell you to go interview him to confirm, but Stanley died five years ago."

Dog sitting, Nick thought with relief. This made sense.

"I could send you an old picture of me and the dog," Gwen said. "If that would make you happy."

"It would, thank you." He couldn't wait to show Annalisa. "Let me give you my email address." A few minutes later, a picture of Gwen Beaufort, looking much like he remembered her, arrived in his inbox. She knelt on the grass, her arm around a dopey, grinning yellow Labrador retriever. Nick grinned back at the goofy animal and saved the picture for when Annalisa arrived to meet him for dinner. He also cued up the footage from Joe Green's initial interrogation. Joe never admitted to killing Cyrus, but there was something else in the video that Nick wanted Annalisa to see.

When she arrived at the station, he saw Annalisa before she noticed him. He stood at the coffee machine refreshing his cup while she looked for him at his desk, so he had a moment to study her unguarded. She looked expectant and eager to see him despite their spat from the night before, and he was amazed anew that they had found one another again after he'd worked so hard to screw it up the first time. Through his shirt, Nick touched the scar on his abdomen, the place where she'd literally saved his life. She'd left the police force, and while he understood why she'd had to leave it all behind, it meant she had left him too. He wondered now, as she eyed the desk that used to be hers, if she missed the thrill of the chase. PI work was often boring, as she had discovered. A cop's life never was. He wondered if she missed the strength of the badge behind her. He wondered if she missed him.

When she started snooping through his desk, he strode over to her. "Just the person I was hoping to see," he said.

"Me?" She actually looked surprised, and regret washed over him. She was pushing this Joe Green investigation because she was bored, not because she was out to get him. He had to remember that.

"Of course you," he said, squeezing her hands to show he meant it. "I have something to show you." He swiveled his monitor to present the picture of Gwen and the dog. "She was dog sitting for a friend," he explained. "That part didn't make it into her statement."

Annalisa stared at the picture for a long moment. "Can I read the statement?"

Nick looked at Zimmer's office but the commander was on the phone and not paying attention to them. Lynn "The Hammer" Zimmer liked Annalisa but she'd been clear: when Annalisa left the force, she lost all privileges in the squad room. She was a civilian now. "Sure," he said. He'd printed it out earlier so he had no reason not to let her take a quick peek. "But there's something else I want you to see."

Annalisa scanned Gwen Beaufort's official statement without comment. "Okay," she said when she had finished. "What's up?"

"Take a seat." He dragged over an empty chair so they could both look at his screen. Zimmer would definitely chew him out for this if she caught them now but Nick figured the risk was worth it to show Annalisa the truth. "This is footage of Joe Green's initial interrogation after his arrest." Nick remembered leaving the man to wait alone for more than an hour. It was an old trick cops liked to use to unsettle their suspects. Let them stew, wondering what evidence the police had, until they were so deep in their own heads they psyched themselves out and confessed. Joe Green hadn't fidgeted or paced or crushed his water bottle into a flat circle like other men Nick had questioned. No, Joe Green went to sleep face-down on the table.

Once again, Annalisa did not react beyond a slight tightening of her mouth. She'd been on the job long enough to know what a sleeping suspect meant: he was guilty. Innocent people practically climbed the walls, panicked at being arrested for something they didn't do. The guilty ones knew the jig was up and went to sleep. "This only means he was exhausted," Annalisa said finally. Her gaze traveled to Zimmer's office. She knew very well the chance Nick was taking by showing her this footage. "As long as you've got the video . . . do you mind showing me the CCTV footage from the night Cyrus Merriman disappeared? The one from the corner store."

Nick hesitated. "It doesn't show anything but him buying condoms and cigarettes."

"So then it's no big deal to show me."

He shot her a look. "You quit, remember? You decided you didn't want to do this job anymore."

"This is a closed case," she countered. "Not an active investigation."

Nick sighed and glanced at Zimmer. "Fine," he said. "One quick look."

Annalisa watched the short, grainy clip of Cyrus buying cigarettes and condoms at the corner market once and then she replayed it. "Okay, that's enough," Nick said as he moved to close the video.

Annalisa stopped him. "Did you search Merriman's home?"

"You know very well we did."

"I'd like to see the pictures. His car too."

"Vega, you've got to let this go. Joe Green killed Cyrus Merriman. There's no mystery here."

"So then there's no harm in letting me see the pictures."

Nick blew out a frustrated breath and opened the file with the pictures from the search of Merriman's condo. Annalisa clicked through each of them, her face close to the screen. Nick watched over her shoulder, glancing between the screen, to be sure he hadn't missed anything in Merriman's expensive condo, and Zimmer's office, to check that his boss was still occupied. What Nick mostly remembered about the search was Merriman's wife, Kara, and her stony silence as they had ransacked her home. Kara had an alibi—she'd been skiing in Colorado with her girlfriends—and returned home to find her life turned upside down. She'd been the one to report Cyrus missing, Nick recalled. He also remembered one odd detail, which was that Kara Merriman never cried.

Annalisa moved on to the pictures taken from Cyrus's abandoned Lexus. Out of the corner of his eye, Nick saw Zimmer get up from her desk. "Vega," he warned in a low voice, reaching for the computer mouse.

"Hmm?" Annalisa frowned at the screen and shifted the mouse beyond his reach.

"Vega, close it down. Close it now." He grabbed for the keyboard but he was too late. Zimmer's shadow fell across both of them.

"This is cozy," she said flatly.

"We were just going to go grab dinner," Nick said as he finally wrestled the mouse away from Annalisa. "Can we pick you up something?"

"Dinner, huh? Let's see what's on the menu." Zimmer grabbed Gwen Beaufort's printed statement from Nick's desk. "This is from thirteen years ago," she said as she noted the date on the paper. She scanned further. "From a closed murder case." She narrowed her eyes first at Annalisa and then at Nick. "What the hell are you two up to?"

"Nothing," Nick said quickly as he grabbed the statement back and made a show of putting it away. "Just settling a little curiosity. It's over. Done with. We're leaving now." He stood to leave but Annalisa tugged him back down to his chair.

"Joe Green's doing thirty to life for murdering Cyrus Merriman," Annalisa said. "And I'm beginning to think he didn't do it."

Nick turned to stare at her bug-eyed. Everything he'd just shown her backed up the original verdict. Joe killed Merriman. "What are you doing?" he asked in a low voice.

"Joe Green got an anonymous letter saying Gwen Beaufort lied in her statement about seeing him with Merriman the night of the murder."

"Which proves nothing," Nick argued. "We settled the dog issue."

"Right," Annalisa agreed. "But there's a new problem." She opened the folder where Nick had stuck Gwen's statement. "Gwen says she saw Joe Green's profile from where the truck was parked at the end of West Birchwood. I drove by the scene earlier today." She cast Nick an apologetic look for not mentioning this. "But at the time, I hadn't read Gwen's statement. It's possible Gwen could have seen Joe's face from where she was standing—not likely given the distance and the darkness, but plausible. But then she added in the license plate too."

"She said why she noted it," Nick said. "She thought the driver could be drunk."

"There is only room for one vehicle the size of a pickup truck at the end of that road to be parked sideways like Gwen said. For her statement, she needed it to be parked lengthwise to say she saw the driver's face. But if she saw his profile, she couldn't see the license plates on the truck." Annalisa glanced at Zimmer. "Her statement is too good to be true."

Nick took Gwen's statement from her and read it over again. "Seems thin," he said. "I don't know how she saw the plates. Maybe she was closer than she estimated to the truck."

Zimmer folded her arms. "I agree."

"There's more," Annalisa told them. She opened the video file of Cyrus Merriman in the convenience store the night of his murder. "Here's the victim buying two items: condoms and cigarettes. But if you look through the photos and lists of items from Merriman's home and car, he didn't have cigarettes or ashtrays anywhere. Merriman didn't smoke. What did he keep in his car? Condoms. They were found in the glove compartment of his Lexus after he disappeared. The Lexus was parked a few blocks from this store. So, wherever Merriman was headed after this, he wasn't going back to the car."

Zimmer moved closer for a better look at the screen. Nick started to sweat. "He spent the night cruising. We knew this already," he said.

Annalisa let the video play until the moment Merriman opened the door to leave the store. "There," she said, pointing at a figure barely visible off to the left. It was hardly more than a shadow. "See how Merriman isn't wearing a coat? It was freezing that night so he should have had a coat with him. Snow was falling. Whoever is standing outside has a large dark overcoat on—you can just make out the edges of it. From the length of it near the ground, I'd say it's Merriman's coat and it's being worn by someone much shorter than him. Probably a woman." She sat back, triumphant. "Merriman wasn't just cruising that night. He'd made a score. Whoever that woman was, I'd bet she was the person he was buying the cigarettes and condoms for."

"I'll be damned," Zimmer murmured. "We missed this?"

Nick's face turned hot. *We* hadn't missed anything. He had. He'd seen the shadowed figure on the CCTV footage and concluded it didn't mean anything, because Gwen's statement put the murder scene a mile away, with Joe Green's truck. "You're thinking what?" he asked Annalisa. "This woman was actually Gwen Beaufort? Or some other witness?"

"Gwen couldn't have seen what she said she saw that night. Beyond that, I don't know." Annalisa sat back in her chair, looking troubled. "But if Gwen didn't send Joe the note saying she's lying because guilt somehow got the better of her, I can think of only one person who would know for sure she'd made up the story."

"The person who knows what really happened," Nick concluded, his voice tight. He couldn't make himself say the words.

Annalisa had no such difficulty. "The real killer."

FIVE

CHARLOTTE HIGGINS USED A FADED PLASTIC CUP FROM CHICAGO'S LINCOLN PARK ZOO TO SCATTER SALT ON THE ICY CEMENT WALKWAY IN BACK OF RUBY'S PLACE. Bent over her task, she didn't notice Henry approaching until he was almost on top of her. "You should let me do that," he said and Charlotte raised up to meet his kind brown eyes. "The boss lady surely must have better things to do." In his hands, he held two steaming paper cups. "I'll trade you," he told her with a smile, extending one coffee to her.

"I'm about done," she replied as she accepted his offering and tossed the salt cup back in the bucket. "Besides, I don't mind. I like being out in the fresh air and sunshine for a while, especially when the kids are playing." She blew on the coffee and watched the kids zooming around the playground. Several were engaged in a competitive game of tag, while a pair of small boys had climbed the jungle gym to the very top, where they camped out in deep conversation. A trio of girls was trying to assemble a snowman from the meager few inches of fluffy snow they'd received overnight. At the swings, her assistant, Layla, and Danny the cook were pushing a pair of sisters high in the air. If you didn't look too hard, the cheerful scene could be from any elementary schoolyard. Pay attention, though, and Charlotte knew you would notice several of the kids wore clothes that didn't fit quite right: boots too big for their feet or mittens that kept falling off their small hands. A suspicious number of them had blue hats with the Chicago Fire logo, a welcome year-end donation from the local soccer team. Get up close and you'd see the bruises. Because more often than not, that was what sent the women running to the shelter—when the men turned their violence on the kids.

"Lord, bless his heart. He keeps trying." Henry nodded toward the swings, where Danny was nudging and flirting with Layla, clearly trying to chat her up. Layla gave him a polite smile but kept her eyes on the girl in front of her. "Think she will ever give him the time of day?"

Charlotte wrinkled her nose. In all the years she'd known Layla, she hadn't seen the other woman show any interest in men—or women. "We all have reasons for being here," she said lightly. "Even those of us who do it for a living." No one worked at Ruby's Place to get rich.

"Sure, but Danny's good people. He's not like the assholes who hurt women."

Henry was new. Ex-military. They had hired him for security at the shelter and to accompany the women to their court dates. Charlotte sensed he was arguing not only on Danny's behalf, but on his own as well. "I agree," she said. "But you have to remember—all the men look the same at first."

"Oh, hey. Would you look at that?" Henry grinned and pointed to where Layla laughed at something Danny had said. "I know it's freezing out here, but I do believe she's thawing."

Charlotte answered with a tight smile and cupped her hands around the coffee for warmth. She hoped many things for Layla, but romance was far down on the list. Layla was the longest tenured employee at Ruby's Place other than Charlotte, and Charlotte dreamed Layla might take it over one day. Layla currently handled all the paperwork—

helping the women file for restraining orders, get apartments, get new lives away from their abusers—and she was brilliant with all the details. But running the shelter meant adopting a mother warrior persona and Layla preferred to remain in the background whenever trouble started.

As if on cue, Karma came out the back door with a grim look on her face. Karma was always ready for battle, whether there was trouble or not. "Code Red," she said, and both Charlotte and Henry moved into action. Charlotte checked the security camera footage in the main office and saw a bearded man in a green army jacket banging at the front door. She switched on the intercom to listen and heard him yelling. "Maya, I know you're in there! I know these bitches brainwashed you. Come on, Maya, open the door."

"Karma, get Maya Ramirez and her children and take them to the basement for a tea party, please." Charlotte recognized their unwanted visitor as Ray Donovan, Maya's boyfriend and father of her two small kids. She kept her tone neutral even as Karma's eyes got big and round at the sound of Ray's threats filtering through the sound system.

"Do I tell them . . . ?" Karma asked, uncertainty etching her features.

"Tell them it's a fun surprise for new guests." The shelter kept extra toys and treats down there behind a metal door. Usually when the men showed up, security could make them go away, but rarely, they did breach the front door.

"I'll handle him," Henry said, touching the gun he had holstered on his hip. Charlotte watched on-screen as Henry went to the front door and told Ray to get lost. Layla appeared in the office and came to stand near Charlotte so she could watch too.

"Danny and I brought all the kids inside just in case," she murmured, hugging herself. "They're in the gym playing basketball."

"Good idea."

At the door, Ray didn't seem deterred by Henry's appearance. Henry was six foot six and a wall of muscle. Just his huge frame filling the door often convinced the men to move on, but Ray kept making threats. "I don't give a fuck who you are. Maya loves me. She loves me! I need to see her. I'm taking her and my kids." Henry denied Maya was on the premises and blocked him from entry, further enraging Ray. "Let me in or I'll come back with my buddies and we'll tear this whole place apart. You got me? We'll torch the whole thing."

Charlotte glanced over to see Layla's white face. She flipped off the audio. On the screen, Henry grabbed Ray's jacket and shoved him back from the doorway. Layla turned the audio on again. "It's important to document the threats," she whispered, clearly anticipating the restraining order. Maya had been reluctant to file one. They would show her this footage once Ray was gone in the hope that it would convince her. A restraining order meant they could call the cops the instant Ray showed up on-screen.

"I'll kill you," Ray screamed at Henry. "I'll fuckin' kill you all." But at least he was leaving. Henry stayed at the front door to watch him go. Karma reappeared in the room and looked relieved when she saw the screens no longer featured Ray anywhere.

"I'll tell Maya it's all clear," she said.

Layla whirled on her. "You see why we need the guns?"

Karma halted with a slight frown before drawing herself up to her full height, which was all of five foot four. "I never said we didn't need guns. I don't get why we need dicks to carry them." Karma would prefer the shelter to be women and children only, and she objected to Henry's hiring.

"All clear," Henry said as he returned from his mission. Karma pivoted and left without a word. Henry raised his eyebrows at her chilly departure. "Something I said?"

"No, it's not you," Charlotte said. The adrenaline hit her then and she gripped the edge of the desk so the others wouldn't see her shaking. "Layla, could you help Danny with getting lunch set up? I'll be along in a minute. Henry, please take over in the gym so Danny can get back to the kitchen."

They left her alone and Charlotte shut the door behind them before sagging into her desk chair. A man showing up like this unexpectedly never failed to fray her nerves. No matter what they looked like, she only saw her own tormenter—his red face and roaring mouth, his huge hand raised to hit her. She opened the desk drawer to check her own gun and took a deep breath at the comforting sight of it. *Never again,* she vowed. Never again.

A sharp knock at the door made her jump. "Just a minute," she called, hoping whoever it was could not detect the quaver in her voice. She needed to collect herself before joining the others.

Karma stuck her head in the office. "Sorry to bother you, but there's a call for you on the kitchen phone."

"The kitchen phone?" This unusual development was enough to shift Charlotte's attention away from her thundering heart. "It must be about a food delivery," she decided. "Give them to Danny or just take a message." The kitchen phone had been the main line years ago, but it was switched when they upgraded the whole system in 2018. Now Danny and the others only used the old landline to coordinate grocery shipments.

"The lady didn't say anything about a delivery," Karma told her. "She said it was about your cousin Ida."

Charlotte froze. "Ida? Are you sure?"

"That's what the lady said. You want me to tell her you're busy?" Karma looked Charlotte over skeptically, like she could see her sweat.

"No, no. I'm coming." Her heart lodged in her throat, Charlotte trailed her fingers along the wall for support as she walked down the hall and around the corner to the kitchen. Danny looked up from making sandwiches and greeted her with his customary smile.

"Hey, boss. I've got one with extra pickles for ya."

"Thank you, Danny," she replied automatically, her gaze fixed on the phone receiver that Karma had laid on a chair. Charlotte picked it up and wound her hand around the curly cord. "Hello," she said, bracing herself for the voice on the other side.

"Charlotte? It's Gwen Beaufort."

"Yes." Charlotte closed her eyes. She'd imagined as much. Cousin Ida had been their code years ago.

"Listen, I don't know why, but that cop called me. The one who investigated Cyrus Merriman's death. Nick Carelli?"

"I remember him. Yes." She'd followed the case in the news and seen his name. "What did he want?"

"He's checking my statement." Gwen paused. "I get the feeling he knows."

Charlotte did an internal assessment. She looked at where Layla and Danny were loading the sandwiches up on trays to serve to the women and children. What could Nick Carelli know? Nothing had changed. "What did he say, exactly?" she asked Gwen. Gwen gave her a rundown of the conversation and Charlotte relaxed a fraction. "So you sent him a picture with the dog? And he didn't call back after that?"

"No. But it's really strange, right? Why's he messing around with the case after all these years? Something's up. You don't think . . . you don't think Joe Green could get out, do you?"

Charlotte closed her eyes. "No," she whispered into the phone. "That can never happen."

SIX

AT TWENTY WEEKS PREGNANT, ANNALISA HAD UNDERGONE AN ANATOMICAL SCAN TO MAKE SURE THE BABY WAS DEVELOPING ALL ITS PARTS CORRECTLY. Nick had sat with her while the technician ran the wand over her belly, holding Annalisa's hand, both of them wide-eyed as they took in the impossibly tiny head, the little waving arms, and the kicking legs. No, they didn't want to know the sex. They wanted to be surprised. Annalisa was indeed surprised when the sonographer had asked to speak to her alone. Immediately, she'd panicked about the baby. "Is something wrong? Is my baby okay?" She felt vulnerable lying there with cold gel on her exposed belly and couldn't imagine why the woman would kick Nick out of the room.

"The baby is fine," the technician had assured her, pulling up a stool. "I want to ask about you. Are you safe at home?" Her gaze traveled to the bruise on Annalisa's arm.

"Oh, that," Annalisa had said. "Yes, I'm fine. I tripped over the cat and hit my arm on the kitchen counter."

Annalisa thought about that moment now as she sat parked outside Ruby's Place with Nick in the passenger seat. He'd asked after she left the exam room what the private meeting was about and she'd fibbed to him. *She just wanted to make sure I didn't have any questions*. Nick had never been violent with her, not even in their troubled first marriage, but she knew about his parents' tragic history. She didn't want him to think she worried for even one second that he might turn into his father. "Have you ever been inside?" she asked him now, nodding at Ruby's Place. The shelter was unmarked with no signage of any kind. Just an opaque door, an intercom, and a solid brick wall.

"No. I've written them a bunch of checks over the years. Referred some victims. But . . ." He trailed off, squinting at the fortresslike building.

"Same," she said.

He shook his head. "I've wondered sometimes how it might have gone different if my mom went to a place like this. If she could've gotten free." Annalisa stretched over and squeezed his hand in wordless support. His jaw tightened but he didn't pull away. "What you said about Cyrus Merriman makes me sick. He was coming here pretending to help these women with their legal troubles, meanwhile just abusing them some more . . . It makes me wish I'd tossed him in the freezing lake."

"I take it nothing like that came up in your investigation." She kept her observation as neutral as possible but Nick heard it as an accusation anyway. He took his hand from hers and shoved it in the pocket of his leather coat where she couldn't reach.

"No. Background on Cyrus Merriman turned up rampant infidelity, but nothing else."

Rampant infidelity, Annalisa knew, Nick was happy to overlook. She bit her lip, hesitating before pressing onward. "And Joe Green? Nothing there about domestic abuse?"

He shook his head, silent.

"If he'd been violent with Vanessa, you'd think it would have come up at trial," Annalisa reasoned. "It would support the idea he could attack Cyrus too."

"Vanessa didn't testify. She didn't have to. The case was strong enough without her." There was something else he wasn't saying, Annalisa could tell. She waited while he battled whatever voices were raging in his head. "I sent her here," he muttered at last, slouching in his seat.

She almost didn't catch the words. "What?"

"Vanessa Green. When I was a patrol cop, I responded to a call at the house, maybe a year before the murder. But it was Joe Green who called. He said Vanessa had tried to kill him." He turned to Annalisa, pleading for understanding. "You know how it is. Sometimes the one who calls is actually the abuser."

Yes, Annalisa had seen this multiple times. The abuser would claim self-defense and calling the cops was part of the ongoing threat. *Retaliate against me and I'll have you thrown in jail.*

"So I gave Vanessa the card for Ruby's Place," Nick continued. "But I don't know if she called."

"But there were no more calls to the Green house?"

"None. I double-checked."

"Hospital records?"

"I don't have access. I think the prosecutor looked into it casually at the time of Joe's trial and there was nothing obvious. Neighbors didn't complain about fighting or anything like that. No one had seen Vanessa with clear injuries."

Annalisa rested her hands on the wheel and considered his words. "How hard did you check Vanessa's whereabouts?"

Nick looked surprised, then annoyed. "You must think I am a total idiot."

"No, I—"

"She was out of town with her kids, staying with her sister. Yes, I checked, and the sister vouched for her."

Annalisa drummed her fingers on the wheel. She wondered about that sister alibi. If Joe had abused Vanessa and Cyrus had extorted her for sexual favors, then Vanessa was the one person who seemed to have motive to get rid of both of them. Plus, whoever was waiting for Cyrus outside the corner store that night was a woman. "We're not going to find out anything more sitting out here in the car," she said at length. "Let's go in."

At the door, Annalisa rang the buzzer and a woman's voice answered on the intercom. "Yes?"

"Hi, I'm Annalisa Vega, a private investigator, and this is Detective Nick Carelli. We'd like to speak to someone about a case we're investigating." There was silence and Annalisa waited, but no one appeared at the door. "Maybe show your ID to the camera," she murmured to Nick, and he took out his shield to show it off. Still nothing. Annalisa tried the buzzer again.

"We can't help you," the woman's voice said curtly. "Please leave."

Annalisa and Nick exchanged a look. Nick shrugged. "She's right. They don't have to talk to us."

Annalisa rang a third time. When the intercom engaged, she didn't give the woman a chance to speak. "Listen, we're not after any of your guests. We're trying to find out more information about a lawyer who worked here years ago. Cyrus Merriman."

The woman did not answer. A minute later, the door clicked open and a woman in tight jeans and high-heeled boots appeared. "Cyrus Merriman is dead," she told them bluntly.

"We are aware," Nick replied.

"Like, ages ago."

"We know that too," Nick said.

"He was a piece of shit." Her chin rose and she gave Nick a challenging look. "Did you know that part? Because a lot of people didn't."

"That's why we're here," Annalisa said gently. "To find the truth."

The woman eyed Nick's holster. "We don't allow men with guns in here."

"I'm a cop."

"Then you're a cop who can wait out here on the sidewalk." She looked at Annalisa. "You carrying?"

Annalisa spread her coat to show she was unarmed. Nick rolled his eyes. "Just a sec," he muttered, and he went to lock his gun in the car. He jogged back and rejoined the women. "Okay now?"

"Joyous," she replied, deadpan. She let them both inside. "My name's Karma. I do admin work for the shelter. The one you probably want to talk to is Charlotte Higgins."

"But you knew Cyrus Merriman?" Annalisa asked as Karma led them down a hall. Children's drawings were tacked up on bulletin boards, alongside informational flyers about job training events and self-defense classes.

"I knew him," she said, her voice even.

"And did you think he was a piece of shit at the time?" Annalisa inquired.

Karma halted and turned to face her. "No, he seemed nice. But then they all do at first, right?" She shot Nick a glare. "Only when he turned up dead did the girls start telling the truth about him. That's how they get away with it. Everyone's too scared to talk. Everyone thinks they're the only one it's happening to. Besides, even if he was a shitty human being, Cyrus Merriman was a great lawyer. He got women their kids back. He got them money and freedom. For some people, he was worth the price." She walked on and Annalisa and Nick followed.

"What about Joe Green?" Annalisa asked her.

Karma didn't hesitate. "Never met him." She reached the main office and knocked on the partially open door. "Charlotte? I've got the po-po here to talk to you."

"Oh, I'm not . . ." Annalisa began but Karma cut her off.

"Please. I know who you are. Maybe you've gone private, but we all know the truth. Once a cop, always a cop." She walked off in dismissive fashion and the woman behind the desk rose to make excuses.

"I'm afraid Karma doesn't care much for the police," she said, her tone clipped. "It's not personal."

"Believe it or not," Nick said, "we're on your side."

"Is that so? I could have Karma come back here so you could explain that to her. She couldn't call the police when her boyfriend broke her arm. She couldn't call them because he was the police. Then there was Dudley Porter—perhaps his name rings a bell?"

Annalisa didn't recognize the name Dudley Porter but she knew Charlotte wasn't going to like that answer. Men, of course, could be victims of domestic abuse too, and they were even less likely to seek help than the women. She ventured a guess. "Did the cops not believe his story?"

"You might say that." Charlotte gave them a tight, humorless smile. "We sheltered Dudley Porter's first fiancée when he attacked her because she'd smiled too much at the mailman. The police arrested Dudley but he was out again in less than a week. We didn't hear more about him, though, until his second fiancée showed up here with bruises matching Dudley's fists."

"I'm sorry," Annalisa murmured.

"Did the arrest stick that time?" Nick wanted to know.

"Alas, no. There was a third fiancée. Her name was Maggie, short for Magnolia, like the flower. She was referred to us by the previous girlfriend but she never made it here. Dudley shot and killed her outside their home." She gestured at Nick. "At that point, yes, the police did arrest him and the prosecutor negotiated a sentence of fifteen to thirty years in prison. One for the win column, right?"

Nick looked away, taking a minute to collect himself, and Annalisa stepped in between them. Charlotte Higgins had a soldier's stance, protecting the victims. Annalisa understood the urge to fight, to scream and rage over the many injustices. In Chicago, someone died too soon nearly every day. All the murders were awful. But the cops couldn't bleed over every one or they wouldn't live to carry on. "We know you do invaluable work here. Work that the police can't do. Both of us have referred women to your shelter many times, and you've provided them with a real sense of safety. By doing so, you help the victims feel strong enough to press legal charges and the law can step in again. The women who come here . . . they need both sides. Both kinds of help."

Charlotte's posture relaxed somewhat. "I suppose that's fair. Please, won't you sit down? Tell me what brings you here."

"Cyrus Merriman," Annalisa said as she took her seat, and Charlotte frowned at the name. Annalisa put Charlotte Higgins at about her own age, maybe a few years older. She had wild red hair and a turtleneck sweater so big she might still be hiding bruises. Her demeanor had shifted to cautiously cooperative but Annalisa knew she wouldn't hesitate to toss them out if she didn't agree with their mission. Annalisa explained what they had learned about Cyrus's abuse of his female clients.

"That matches with the stories I heard after his death," Charlotte said when Annalisa had finished. "Obviously if we had known he was coercing sexual favors from the women we would have reported it to the authorities and ceased all contact with him. It's agony, of course, thinking that we furthered the abuse by referring the women to Cyrus Merriman in the first place. We let a predator in the door. Now we only work with female attorneys."

"Isn't that kind of sexist?" Nick asked.

She gave him a pointed look. "We do whatever we have to do to ensure our clients' safety. Now, I'm afraid I didn't know Cyrus Merriman very well—obviously. May I ask why you're inquiring about him? He's been dead for many years now."

Annalisa took out a copy of the note Joe Green had received and handed it over to Charlotte. "Someone sent this to Joe Green, the man convicted of murdering Cyrus. Gwen Beaufort was the key witness at Joe's trial."

Charlotte took much longer to look at the note than anyone would need to read the two short sentences. When she was done, she set it carefully on the coffee table. "Interesting. And you think this witness was lying? That Joe Green didn't kill Cyrus?"

"We're looking into that possibility."

"Joe Green had a wife named Vanessa," Nick said. "I referred her to this shelter about a year before Cyrus was murdered. Cyrus was doing some legal work regarding her divorce, and we wondered if Ruby's Place was the one that connected them."

"I'm afraid I can't tell you that. All our records are confidential, as I'm sure you understand."

"Look," Nick said, "I get that Cyrus Merriman was not a nice guy. What he did to the women here was terrible and I'm sorry we didn't get a chance to nail him when he was alive. But someone murdered him, and Joe Green is currently in prison for the crime. We'd just like to know if that's the right outcome here."

Charlotte gave him a shrewd look. "It was your case," she said. "Wasn't it?"

"You remember it?" Nick sounded surprised.

"Cyrus worked for us. We followed the headlines." Nick looked at Annalisa and she wondered if he was thinking the same thing she was. Gwen came forward as a witness only after the case was in the news. Charlotte observed their silent exchange and she rose from her chair. "Detectives, if all you've got is this strange message, I'm afraid I can't help you. I don't know anything more about Cyrus Merriman. But as for Joe Green and his prison sentence, well . . ." She went to her desk and hit a buzzer. "You say you want to know if it's the right outcome, and I'd have you consider that it is."

Karma returned to the office and Charlotte handed the anonymous note back to Annalisa. "You can keep it," Annalisa told her. "I have copies."

"No need." She shoved the note at Annalisa. "Karma will show you to the door. Goodbye."

Annalisa reread the note as she walked out. "You know what's odd?" she remarked to Nick. "The *B* at the end. Whoever sent the note went to a lot of trouble to keep their identity hidden, so why write anything at all as a signature?"

"Maybe it's trying to throw us off. Maybe the *B* doesn't mean anything."

Karma leaned over and peeked at the note as they walked toward the main door. "That's not a *B*," she said. "It's a rune."

"A what?" Nick stopped walking so Annalisa halted too.

Karma grabbed the paper without asking. "I mean, it is kind of a *B*, like an early *B* from the ancient Germanic languages. See how it looks like two sideways triangles on top of one another? It's a Berkanan. It represents rebirth, wisdom, sanctuary, and healing. I'm surprised that Charlotte didn't tell you this herself."

"And why is that?" Annalisa asked.

Karma handed the note back to Annalisa with a shrug. "Because she has one tattooed on her leg."

SEVEN

I DON'T LIKE IT," NICK SAID AS HE DROVE ANNALISA TO HER OFFICE.

"Which part?" she replied.

"Any of it."

"Come on, we may be getting somewhere. If one of the women at the shelter killed Cyrus Merriman—possibly with justified cause—and Charlotte Higgins knows about it, she could have sent that note. She would know that Joe Green didn't kill Cyrus, and maybe she's feeling guilty that he got convicted, but at the same time, she doesn't want to reveal who the real killer is and get that woman in trouble."

"And if that's the truth?" Nick changed lanes like he was still driving a sports car. "What are you aiming at here, Anna? We both suspect Joe abused his wife. We know Cyrus preyed on the women he was supposed to be helping. If it's really some poor abused woman who pushed Cyrus into the lake, maybe because he wouldn't keep his hands off her, what are you gaining by hunting her down all these years later? Who wins here? Not that woman, who probably gets arrested now. Not Cyrus—he's dead. Okay, so Joe gets out of prison, but are you sure that's a good thing? Nobody wins except you." He looked sideways at her. "You get the satisfaction of being right. Again."

"Is that what you think? This is about my ego?"

"I think that's part of it, yeah."

"Well, as long as we're tallying the possible fallout, let's not forget about you." She folded her arms and sat back in her seat. "If Joe's not the killer, then you arrested the wrong man."

He looked incredulous. "You think that's why I want you to drop this? Because I'm afraid I screwed up?"

"No one wants to admit they messed up." She glanced at him. "You, maybe more than most."

He snorted. "That's rich, coming from you. I've screwed up plenty in my life and I'll be the first to tell you all about it. But I didn't pressure Gwen to make that witness statement. I didn't put Joe Green's prints on Cyrus's car. I didn't sign off on the bite mark analysis. If this case blows up, it won't be because of me."

It would be because of me, Annalisa realized. If she pressed to reopen the investigation and it turned out Joe was innocent, the story would be about her—and how she would do anything to show up her fellow cops, even her own husband. Nick had stood shoulder to shoulder with her through the worst of the fallout after Alex and Pops were arrested. Now she was rewarding him with another potential public stoning.

Nick pulled into a spot near her office building, the car idling, and squinted past her. "I know this is what you wanted," he said. "Freedom to chase whatever questions you find interesting, damn the rules and the consequences."

"Hey, I live those consequences every day," she replied.

"Yes." He dropped his chin in acknowledgment. "Maybe that's why you're so eager to dole them out to everyone else." He leaned over and pressed his face to hers. "Not all of us are as tough as you, Vega."

She held his face with her hand for a moment before releasing the seat belt from across her rounded belly. She wanted a fair world for their child, one where justice mattered. Nick wanted safety. Both of them had good reasons, so this wasn't a matter of who was right and who was wrong, more a question of priorities. "I'll think about it," Annalisa murmured to him.

He pulled away with a small smile. "I'll see if Pops can rustle you up a more interesting case."

"Oh, no. Don't even joke. Next thing you know he'll have his former commander in my office asking me to find his missing dog."

"I didn't know Bill Rivas had a dog."

"Yeah, it died ten years ago." Annalisa got out of the car and watched him pull away, standing on the sidewalk until his taillights were out of sight. Nick had hidden his childhood trauma behind an easy charm and a series of one-night stands that he hadn't bothered to give up when he married Annalisa the first time. He'd loved her but not enough to show her his scars. But then again, she'd had some secrets of her own. Only when the whole thing fell apart did Nick and Annalisa show each other the pieces of themselves they'd been hiding, and somehow, those unseen parts matched. She'd picked truth and justice over family once; maybe this time she could make a different call.

As if the universe were listening, it sent her a sign in the form of three sealed boxes sitting outside her office door. She checked the label and found they were files from Joe Green's attorney. Inside was a terse note. *Copies of everything,* he wrote to her. *Good luck.* She riffled through the contents and discovered he'd sent everything from photos of the crime scene and the autopsy report to the interview transcripts and eventual plea agreement. Annalisa had nothing better to do so she studied the autopsy report and the grisly accompanying photographs.

Cyrus Merriman had been a handsome man while alive, with good skin, classic Roman features, and a thick head of dark hair. Italian heritage, Annalisa guessed, despite the generic last name. He looked like Nick, the kind of guy who needed a second shave at five o'clock in the afternoon. In death, Cyrus looked gray and swollen, like a wax museum figure gone wrong. He'd been found in an $800 suit with a

Rolex watch attached to his wrist—still keeping the correct time, the medical examiner had noted—so no one had murdered Cyrus in a robbery. He had no wallet or phone, but these could have fallen out as his body moved with the currents. Cause of death was listed as drowning and manner of death read homicide, an easy call when the victim was found fully dressed in the lake in December. The cold temperature of the water preserved the body fairly well, but it did take some damage from sea creatures and banging against the rocks. Cyrus had all manner of scrapes, nicks, and discolorations. Annalisa took out the photo that showed the close-up of the bite mark near Cyrus's collarbone. She saw several purplish gouges that could have been made by teeth. Or, she supposed, by a hungry fish. This was the problem with bite mark evidence. It was rather like those dot-to-dot puzzles kids had to do in elementary school: the pattern you saw at the end depended on how you connected the dots.

Annalisa was still squinting at the photos when a woman appeared in her doorway. "Ms. Vega, I presume?"

Her visitor was about Pops's age, seventy-five or perhaps older. *Here we go again,* Annalisa thought, pinching the bridge of her nose. "Yes," she said, forcing a smile as she rose to greet the woman. "That's me. And you are . . . ?"

"Effie Christos." Her voice had the slight crackle of the very aged, but her gait was steady as she entered the room. The woman took off her leather gloves, and Annalisa got a better look at her coat, which appeared to be ankle-length cashmere. If the Birkin bag she carried on her arm wasn't a knockoff, this woman had money. From the way Ms. Christos looked around at Annalisa's disheveled office with a faint hint of judgment on her face, she'd correctly concluded that Annalisa did not.

"How can I help you, Ms. Christos?" Annalisa gestured at the chair in front of her desk for the woman to take a seat.

"Mrs. Christos, please. Or call me Effie." She brushed it lightly before assuming a regal, stiff-backed posture, her bag perched next to her on the chair. "I lost my Theodore last year, but we were married for more than half a century."

"My condolences."

"Thank you." She inclined her head. "In a way, Theo is the reason I'm here."

Oh, no. Annalisa hoped Pops didn't send her a freak, someone who thought she was a mystic who could commune with the dead. "Yes? What sort of help are you seeking?"

Effie twisted her hands in her lap, her loose skin wrinkling like crepe paper. "First, I need to know that I can count on your absolute discretion."

"Of course," Annalisa replied.

"My diamond-and-sapphire engagement ring has gone missing. As you might imagine, I'd like it returned."

Gone missing, Annalisa thought. An odd turn of phrase. "You mean you lost the ring or you suspect it was stolen?"

"Someone took it from my bedroom dressing table last week." Effie didn't sound angry, only regretful. Her thin lips pursed as she steeled herself. "It can only be one of four people, but I don't know which one. The trouble is that I don't want it to be any of them."

"Go on," Annalisa said. If Pops had sent this lady, he'd found a better actor than the rest of them. "Tell me about this ring."

"Theo gave it to me, of course. My father didn't approve of him. He wanted me to marry Nathaniel Huntzberger—you know, the fish stick king?"

"I'm afraid I don't know the brand." Ma would never have dared serve frozen fish sticks.

"Oh, they go by Freddie's Fish Sticks in the stores. I guess they aren't as popular now as they were during the sixties and seventies when everyone was on a budget. Frederica was Nathaniel's mother and the supposed genesis of the recipe, but I knew the woman and she probably boiled her toast for all she grasped about the culinary arts."

Annalisa suppressed a smile. "And the ring?"

"Right," Effie said, holding up one finger. "Theo was in real estate back then, selling commercial properties. Daddy felt I should be with the man buying the property, not selling it. I wasn't allowed to see Theo but of course we carried on privately. In public, he dated my best friend, Portia. I thought she was in on the scheme, you see, but I guess she fell hard for Theo. When he landed the deal that allowed him to afford the ring, he gave it to me, not her. It took him almost every cent he had but it convinced Daddy that Theo had prospects. He consented to the match."

"It sounds like it was a good one," Annalisa remarked, "if you lasted more than fifty years."

"I didn't care about the ring or his prospects," Effie replied, her gaze misty. "I just wanted Theo. I had my own money, and I guess that's what Daddy worried about—that Theo was a gold digger. Well, he found gold, all right. He made a killing in the 1980s real estate boom and ended up overseeing seventeen regional offices. I wish Daddy had lived to see it. Maybe now that Theo is gone to the other side, he's met up with Daddy and explained things to him. I don't know." She gave a philosophical sigh. "I expect I'll be finding out myself before too long."

"Oh, no. Are you ill?"

"No, I'm as healthy as you can get for eighty-three, but I attended six funerals for friends last year, and then there was Theo, of course. I understand the odds. I'm making sure my affairs are in order and my attorney advised me to have the ring appraised. I sent it for professional cleaning first, and that is why I had it set out on my dresser. I was going to take it to the appraiser in the morning."

"But the ring disappeared?"

"Only five people were in the house that day. Myself; my housekeeper, Matilda Linetti; and my three bridge club ladies: Portia Parker,

Louise Gamble, and Helen Huntzberger. Yes, Helen's the one who married Nathaniel and enjoyed all those marvelous fish stick royalties. The ladies came over for lunch and an afternoon of cards. Portia and I set Louise and Helen, three games to two. When the festivities were over, I went to my room for a rest and discovered the ring was missing. I searched all around in case it had somehow fallen to the ground, but it was nowhere to be found. One of the others must have taken it."

"Did you report this to the police?"

Effie looked aghast. "Good heavens, no. Matilda's been with me for four decades now. She's like family. So are the other ladies. Theo and I didn't have children. Most of my relatives are gone. I can't imagine one of these people would take the ring because they all know how much it meant to me, but all I care about is getting the ring back. I don't want any of them arrested." She leaned closer. "You won't arrest them, right?"

"No, ma'am. I don't do that anymore."

Effie relaxed. "Good. Then we can do business. I'm prepared to pay you whatever you need to make this case your top priority."

Annalisa did not reply that she had no other priorities worth mentioning. Joe Green had offered to pay her, but no money had come through yet. She quoted her usual fees and Effie took out a checkbook. "That's fine, and I'll double it if you can get the ring back to me in a week."

"Is there a particular rush?"

"I can't sleep. I can't sleep knowing one of the people I love most in the world did this to me. I want to know who it is. I want to know why."

"We can go over the afternoon in detail," Annalisa said as she accepted the check, "but I have to point out one obvious suspect: your friend Portia. She's the one who hoped that Theo might give her the ring, right? Maybe now that he's gone, she took it back."

Effie's wrinkled face became fixed with pain. "I dearly hope not. Do you ever have cases like this . . . where you need the answer but you don't want to know it at the same time?"

"Yes," Annalisa said with sympathy. "All the time."

"Well, I appreciate you taking time away from your current project," Effie said, frowning at the photos on Annalisa's desk. In her surprise to have a visitor, Annalisa had failed to gather them up. The top ones showed the close-up pictures of Cyrus Merriman's clavicle where the apparent bite mark had been. If you didn't know what you were looking at, it could have been abstract art. Effie narrowed her eyes. "What is that?"

"That's a subject of debate." Annalisa slid the photos together into a pile but Effie was quick for an older gal, and she snatched the top one for a better look.

"It looks like a sideways *B*," she said and handed the photograph back to Annalisa.

Annalisa tilted it at the same angle Effie had held the picture. Damned if Effie wasn't correct. Draw the dots in the right way and you could make the rune symbol from the anonymous note that Joe had received. What had Karma called the rune? A Berkanan.

EIGHT

Charlotte walked the halls of Ruby's Place as she did each night, checking locks, pausing to say hello to those who still had their dorm-style rooms open. She kept a small apartment on the top floor, but she was rarely in it, preferring to be visible to the women and their children. A symbol of safety. She patrolled the grounds like a guard dog and, though Karma wouldn't approve, kept the gun locked in her desk drawer. Charlotte's friend Jane had nagged her repeatedly about getting out and finding her own space. *You may as well be a nun, cloistered away in that place,* Jane said. Charlotte felt this was true in more ways than one. Although she wasn't especially religious, she felt Ruby's Place like a calling, a reason to be on this earth. Also, she was celibate.

"Do you just not like men?" Jane had asked her one night over tacos and sangria at their favorite Mexican restaurant—Charlotte's suggestion, to prove she could leave Ruby's Place if she wanted. "I mean, I wouldn't blame you, I guess, given the kind of men you deal with. But they are not all like that." Jane had been married for years to a teddy bear of a man named Vince. *He literally wouldn't hurt a fly,* Jane told her when they got engaged. *I have to kill all the bugs in our house.*

"I like individual men," Charlotte had replied. "As a species, I don't trust them."

"They're the same species as us, Char."

At that moment, Charlotte had one of her young women in the hospital with three broken ribs. "No," she'd said. "I don't think they are."

She completed her first- and second-floor rounds, and on the third floor, a tiny boy in footie pajamas toddled out into the hall. He had a stuffed elephant tucked under his right arm and his thumb in his mouth. He curled into the wall at the sight of Charlotte, as though she might hurt him for being out of bed at this hour. Charlotte's heart hurt to look at him cowering. The only way to stop the cycle of violence was to get these boys out while she could, so they could grow up to be like Vince, who cried at his own wedding and let Jane deal with the bugs. Charlotte crouched down to greet the boy. "Brennan, that's a nice giraffe you have there."

Brennan overcame his fear to defend his stuffed friend. "Elephant," he corrected her, holding out the blue-gray terry-cloth creature for Charlotte to inspect. "They gots a big nose. See?"

"Oh, yes. I see I was wrong and you have indeed a very handsome elephant. Sometimes grown-ups make mistakes. Where's your mom?"

"Inna bathroom."

As if on cue, his mother emerged with her toothbrush and face towel from the shared bathroom down the hall. "Brennan, what are you doing out of bed? You know it's time to be sleeping."

"Marfy had a bad dream." He hugged the elephant to his small chest.

"I'm sorry about this," his mother apologized to Charlotte. Charlotte remained crouched with Brennan.

"It's all right. Everyone has bad dreams on occasion." She looked to Brennan. "You need to tell Marfy a happy story about a time when you felt good. Then he'll have nice dreams, okay?"

Brennan nodded at her, his eyes huge and wide. He glanced over his shoulder as his mother shepherded him back inside their shared room. "Bye," he mouthed at Charlotte, and she gave him a little wave as she rose to her feet.

She walked on until she found Layla in the library, working on a laptop. "It's late," she told the other woman. "You should be going home." She knew even as she said the words that Layla wouldn't leave. They had much to discuss.

"Karma has finally convinced Maya to file a restraining order against Ray," Layla said. "And to file for custody of the kids. But she's afraid. She's worried that because Ray has a job and she doesn't, that a judge will give the kids to him."

"Then we need to find Maya a job."

"That's what I'm doing." Layla turned her screen around so Charlotte could see the search results. "There's a nursing home that needs a health aide starting immediately, which seems promising."

Charlotte barely heard her. She noticed the other open tab on Layla's screen, the one for Illinois River Prison. "Checking up on Joe Green?" she asked.

Layla snapped the computer closed, looking embarrassed that Charlotte caught her looking. "Karma told me about the two detectives that were here. About the note."

Charlotte looked sharply around the room. "Karma isn't here, is she?"

"No, she left at eight."

"Good. I don't want her any more mixed up in this than she already is." Charlotte rubbed her temples with both hands, trying to dull the ache that had started to form there. Keeping the women safe meant she couldn't let her guard down, ever, and the physical toll of the constant vigilance weighed on her.

"She said they asked her about Cyrus Merriman," Layla said. "But I don't think they know what he did to her."

"They'll find out eventually about the connection—he was her lawyer, after all."

"Someone's making trouble for us," Layla said. "Whoever sent that note."

Charlotte brooded. She'd recognized the rune signature on the note, of course, and knew its meaning. The question was who else knew the significance. Someone wanted Joe Green out of prison and they were happy to set Charlotte on fire to achieve that aim. She wondered if Joe Green had manufactured the note himself, if he could have seen her tattoo or learned about it somehow. "I talked to Gwen," she told Layla. "She's sticking to her story."

"But the detectives must suspect something if they're poking around after all these years."

GWEN IS LYING. JOE DIDN'T DO IT. The note was half right and half wrong. Someone thought they had the true story, but they'd only countered with more lies. Where did it end? Certainly not with Charlotte, who'd had to tell another lie that afternoon when Detective Carelli and his PI wife came snooping around. She'd let them think she found out about Cyrus Merriman's mistreatment of the women only after his death. She hadn't said how she'd learned the truth about Cyrus. "Suspicion is one thing," Charlotte said to Layla. "Proof is another. Let's not overreact. Whoever sent that note is trying to force a mistake. If we behave as if everything is normal, then it will be. All the same, you tell me if that detective tries to speak with you, okay?"

Before Layla could answer, the floorboards creaked behind them, and both women startled and turned around. Danny Romero, the shelter's chef, stood there looking chagrined. "Sorry," he said. "Didn't mean to scare you." He held two mugs in one beefy hand and a plate of fresh-baked cookies in the other. "I thought you might like a little snack." He walked over and carefully placed the hot coffees down in front of them. "Cream, no sugar for you," he said to Layla. "And black decaf for the boss lady."

"Those cookies look amazing," Layla said, leaning over to give them a close inspection. "Thank you."

"Oatmeal cherry coconut," he replied with a beaming smile. "My mom's recipe. Go ahead, try one." He cast eager eyes to Layla, who obliged him by nibbling at the edge of one cookie.

"Mmm, delicious," she said. "I wish I could bake like you, Danny."

"I could show you sometime," he said shyly. "If you want."

"Sure," she said. "Sometime."

Danny's face fell. Charlotte could tell he didn't believe her. "Thank you for the treat," she told him, laying an affectionate hand on his arm. "You're very kind to think of us. Now you should be getting home, no? It's quite late."

Danny shrugged. "No one to get home to," he said. "I'm prepping tomorrow's lunch. Just holler down to the kitchen if you need anything."

"I will. Good night, Danny." When he'd gone, Charlotte looked at Layla, who regarded the cookies in front of them with a pained expression. "I'd say you could shoot him down by telling him once and for all that it's never going to happen, but I think you actually like him."

"I like him," Layla said faintly. "I think he's an actual nice guy."

"I agree. Danny's been with us for three years and been nothing but wonderful." Charlotte had to watch her words here. They put so much emphasis on survival in this place; maybe sometimes they forgot to live. "Still, if you're looking for companionship, Danny might not be the best choice." *Not for you,* she added silently. *Not now.*

Layla crossed her legs and angled her body away. "Usually you're so hot for me to get a life. Now you tell me to cool off. Make up your mind, Charlotte."

"I'm just trying to protect you."

"From Danny?" Layla looked incredulous. "The staff loves him. The women who come here love him. The children follow him around and beg him to play with them. Maybe you love him too, huh? You want him for yourself."

"Ha," Charlotte said. "As if."

"What's that supposed to mean?"

"Look around. I don't have time for a personal life. This place would fall down if I left for more than a few hours." Layla looked stricken, and Charlotte wished she could snatch the words back. "Wait, I didn't mean—"

Layla stood up abruptly, cutting her off. "I guess my work doesn't matter then. I guess Karma's nothing around here either. Or Danny or Henry. It's your baby and we're just the hired help."

"I didn't mean it that way." Charlotte hated to upset Layla, never wanted to make her angry. She lived her whole life in service of these women. Couldn't they see that? When the coming storm arrived in all its fury, Charlotte would be swept away before she let it take them. "You and Karma mean everything to me. Today's little visit from the police should remind you of that."

The fight drained out of Layla. She hugged herself and looked away. "Sometimes I wish he'd killed me." The words came out so soft that Charlotte barely heard her. She rushed to embrace Layla, to hold and shush her.

"Never say that. Never."

Layla returned the hug with tentative arms. She laid her head on Charlotte's shoulder. "I won't talk to Danny anymore. Not if you don't want."

"Oh, honey." Charlotte stroked the back of Layla's warm head. "Danny is fine, I'm sure. But his brother is a cop. Did you know that? His uncle too."

Layla pulled back, her blue eyes clouded with concern. "He wouldn't bring them here. He wouldn't."

Charlotte held Layla's face in her hands for a long moment. "We can't take that chance."

"Danny's family is not what we have to worry about," Layla said as she broke free. "Not that cop either. It's his wife."

"The pregnant lady?"

"You don't know her? She found that old serial killer a couple years ago. The Lovelorn guy."

Now that Layla mentioned the story, Charlotte did remember Annalisa Vega's name. "I don't see what that has to do with anything. She's not even a cop anymore, you know."

"So what's she doing here? Who hired her? Did you even ask?"

Charlotte's face went hot. She hadn't asked. "It doesn't matter. They've both gone now and as long as Gwen sticks to her story, they don't have anything to go on but that anonymous note."

"Right," Layla said with a nod. "The note. Someone wants Joe out of prison."

"Well then we know it wasn't any one of us who sent it," Charlotte said lightly. "Right?"

Layla stared at her for a long moment and then rubbed her temples with both hands. "I think I will be going home now. See you tomorrow, okay?"

Charlotte let her go without further argument. She moved to open the laptop and navigated to the tab that showed Joe Green's prison contact information. She knew she shouldn't go see him. That would be too dangerous. Charlotte wondered about the note and who could have sent it. Then she pondered a question she hadn't considered in more than thirteen years: who really killed Cyrus Merriman?

NINE

Annalisa awoke from the same dream again, the one where she played hide-and-seek with the blond girl in her neighborhood. It always ended the same, with Annalisa finding the girl just as a truck drove past in the alley behind them. She couldn't figure out why the truck mattered; even the more residential portions of Chicago were still part of a city and trucks drove past the Vega home all the time. In the dream, she tried to turn to see the truck and who was driving, but she couldn't make out the face. She blinked awake and was relieved to see her own cozy bedroom.

She ignored the pleading from her bladder, which felt like it had shrunk to the size of an acorn during her pregnancy, and chose to stay in bed a few minutes longer. Gray January light filtered in through the windows and she hid from it by burrowing closer to Nick. Sleepy, he put a comforting arm around her and she questioned again whether she wanted to risk this sense of peace and safety for the answer about whether Joe Green had killed Cyrus Merriman. "Are you going to go look for that rich lady's diamond ring?" His voice was a rumble beneath her ear. "How much is it worth, anyway?"

"More than you and I will ever see, most likely, unless we start a fish stick empire. In any case, yes, Effie said she was having another bridge game this afternoon so I could come by and meet all the suspects."

"Maybe one of them will be wearing the ring. Easy case."

"I never get that lucky."

"You get lucky all the time," he said, his hand wandering under her T-shirt. "We've got the evidence right here."

"Yes, and he or she is doing the two-step on my bladder." She heaved a put-upon sigh and got up to use the bathroom. When she returned, Nick had already left the bed. She found him making eggs and toast in the kitchen. Jack wound figure eights between her legs, meowing loudly until she picked him up. He nestled into her as she scratched his chin in an absent gesture. "Nick, I meant to ask you: did you ever interview Joe Green's first wife?" Charlotte at the shelter had made a point about repeat offenders, and Annalisa figured if Joe had been violent with Vanessa, he'd probably knocked around the first one too. After all, she'd pulled up stakes and left him without a word, which often signaled trouble.

Nick turned from the stove with a perplexed expression. "I thought you were done with all that."

"I never said I was dropping it."

He frowned and returned to his cooking. From the tense set of his shoulders, she figured he wasn't going to answer her and decided to take a shower. Just as she set the cat down and turned to leave, he surprised her by saying, "No, I didn't talk to her. She'd been gone for years and Joe had no contact with her. The case was about his current wife, Vanessa, and her relationship with Cyrus. The previous wife didn't matter." He didn't look at her as he explained, moving the eggs around in the pan.

"The thing is, I looked it up, and Joe wasn't married before."

Now he did turn around. "Maybe it was a common-law thing. You could ask Joe if you want to know so bad."

"I will ask him. But I want to know the answer first. Do you remember her name?"

"Kathy? Karen? I don't know. Like I said, I never actually spoke to her." He paused and took a deep breath. "But if you want, I can check my notes. Her name might be in there somewhere."

She flashed him a smile. "That would be great."

....

PERSEPHONE "EFFIE" CHRISTOS LIVED IN A MANSION IN THE GOLD COAST NEIGHBORHOOD, THE KIND OF PLACE THAT HAD STONE LIONS OUT FRONT AND ORNATE CHANDELIERS IN THE KITCHEN. An older woman in a black dress and white apron answered the door and admitted Annalisa to the white-marbled atrium. "Mrs. Christos will be right down," she told her. "She said to show you to the parlor." Along the hall, they passed a half-dozen big fancy rooms decorated with heavy, expensive furniture. The estate was straight out of Clue; Annalisa counted a billiard room, a library, and a conservatory with a glossy white grand piano. The parlor was more intimate, with rich mahogany bookshelves, a tufted peacock-blue sofa, and gold-framed artwork on the walls. Wherever the missing ring was, Annalisa would bet it was gorgeous because the Christos family obviously had killer taste.

The woman who answered the door gave her a shy smile and gestured at Annalisa's stomach. "When are you due?"

"Early April."

"That's nice. You'll have good weather for the baby. My Bobby was born during a hailstorm in December and I think winter lasted six months that year. I hated bundling him up to take him out, but he screamed if he stayed inside too long so there we'd be, promenading around the park, me in my earmuffs and him with just his little eyes and nose peeking out." Her smile crinkled the edges of her brown eyes. "Can I get you something to drink while you wait? We have coffee and tea, as well as a selection of seltzer waters and fresh juices."

"Thank you, I'm fine."

At that moment, Effie Christos entered wearing a rose-colored sweater and flowing beige pants. "You've arrived. How wonderful. The others will be here shortly. In the meantime, I can give you the grand tour."

Annalisa once again eyed her surroundings and imagined there were a million places a ring could be hiding in a home this large. "That would be helpful, thank you."

"Matilda, could you please prepare a tray of treats for everyone to enjoy? Remember, Portia likes the blueberry scones."

"Of course." Matilda turned to go and then faced Annalisa again. "Can I offer you something to drink? We have coffee, tea, and some wonderful fresh juices."

Annalisa gave her a quizzical look. "No, thanks. I'm fine."

Matilda smiled and nodded again before leaving the room. As she left, Effie turned to Annalisa and said, "She's been having some memory problems, the poor dear. I've had her see three specialists and they all say the same thing: there is nothing to be done. But most days, she copes just fine living here with me. We keep each other company."

"Matilda lives here?"

"Oh, yes. As I mentioned, Matilda has been with us for decades. She and Bobby moved in when he was just three years old. There's a small separate apartment on the top floor. I can't show you that part without Matilda's permission. It's her private space. Shall we start with my bedroom? That's where the ring was when it disappeared."

"Of course, yes. Please lead the way."

As they walked, Annalisa inquired about Matilda's son. "Is Bobby local? He might be some help if his mother's health is declining." She and her two brothers took turns spelling their mother on Sunday afternoons so Ma didn't have to look after Pops 24/7.

Effie's face stretched in a thin, sad smile as they mounted the carved wooden stairs. "Bobby died at twenty-six. He was killed overseas in a military training exercise."

"That's terrible. I'm so sorry."

"She forgets sometimes that he's gone. I'm not sure if that's a blessing or the worst kind of curse. Anyway, the bedroom is down this hall." She led Annalisa to a spacious room with an antique four-poster bed at the center. At one end, the sheer curtains let in filtered light through the three massive windows, allowing Annalisa to see the crown molding and delicate floral wallpaper. Classic, tasteful, feminine. She wondered if it had changed at all since Theo's death. "The ring was sitting here on my dressing table," Effie said. "Still in the box that it returned with from the cleaners." She picked up the box to demonstrate it was empty.

Annalisa made a half-hearted search of the area, but she figured Effie had no doubt been down on her own hands and knees looking for the ring already. "Who had access to this room?" she asked.

"Why, anybody. The door isn't locked."

"You say Matilda is having some memory issues. Could she have come in to clean and mislaid the ring?"

"Oh, I doubt that very much. She was busy in the kitchen, making pie—blueberry for Portia—and getting the sandwiches ready."

"But she knew the ring was here?"

"Yes," Effie replied, drawing out the word with a quaver. "I like to have Matilda's input on my outfits so she helped me get dressed that morning. We chitchatted and she remarked that it didn't matter what the appraiser said about the ring's value: since it came from Theo, it was priceless. I had to agree."

"Okay, let's talk motive then. Which of the three bridge club ladies could have had a reason to take your ring?"

Effie gave a helpless shrug. "That's just it. I can't think that any of them would do this. We've been friends for years. Yes, Portia dated Theo ages ago but then she married Stephen and had four kids with him. Helen buried Nathaniel fifteen years ago, and she's been the merry widow ever since. Believe me, she has more jewels than the Queen of Sheba. She wouldn't need mine. Louise . . ." She paused with a frown. "Louise's husband, Stanley, died two years ago after a long illness. Alzheimer's. What a terrible way to go. I thank God daily that Theo and I were at least spared that. Losing your partner before you lose them. He lingered for a decade and the expenses did add up. I think Louise has struggled some—I know she's moved in with her son and daughter-in-law—but I can't believe she would think stealing my ring would help any."

A sonorous bong rang through the downstairs and Effie moved toward the door. "That will be the ladies arriving now. Come, I'll introduce you."

"Do you plan to tell them why I'm here?" Annalisa asked as she followed the old woman back down the stairs.

"Unless you think I shouldn't."

"It's liable to make them defensive."

"They should be defensive," Effie replied tartly. "One of them stole my ring." She fixed a smile to her face as they arrived on the ground floor. Annalisa could hear voices in the front atrium and she followed Effie in the direction of the sound. "Ladies, you all made it despite the chilly weather. And all so promptly too."

"We know how fussy you are about time," said one with carefully styled, dyed black hair. She wore a huge fur coat and carried a carved wooden cane. "Don't worry, it's fake," she said about the coat when she saw Annalisa looking. "But it's convincing, isn't it? Looks so real. It's amazing what they can do with synthetics these days. You could never tell it wasn't actual mink fur, although I swear the cost is the same."

"We need not tell, Helen, because you always do it first," another lady replied as she handed off her own pink wool coat to Matilda. She turned to Annalisa. "Before the afternoon is over, she'll also have apprised you of her handbag, her new car, and the new pinky ring she's got on her left hand."

Helen looked delighted. "You noticed! I wore it just for you, Portia, darling."

Annalisa noticed that Effie had been correct in her assessment of Helen's jewelry collection. The woman sported a ring on nearly every finger. Maybe someone with a yen for sparkly jewels might have coveted Effie's ring all these years, but surely with her money, Helen could have afforded to buy something similar. But it was her cane that made Annalisa knock Helen off the likely suspect list; she didn't see how Helen could have navigated the stairs to the bedroom and back in such a short time that she wouldn't arouse suspicion.

Matilda went to store the coats while Effie introduced Annalisa. "Ladies, please welcome Annalisa Vega, who is observing us this afternoon. She's a private detective."

"I know you," said Portia, pointing a finger at Annalisa. "You caught the Lovelorn Killer a few years ago." Annalisa picked up a hint of a British accent in the woman's speech.

"The who?" asked the fourth lady, looking Annalisa over in appraising fashion. By process of elimination, Annalisa knew this had to be Louise, the woman who had fallen on financial hard times due to her husband's illness.

Portia waved her hand. "You know, that serial killer preying on women back in the 1990s. Dreadful stuff."

"Ohh, I remember him, yes," Helen said. "Nathaniel hired a bodyguard who went everywhere with me for two years." She paused with a slight frown and put a ring-studded finger to her chin. "I wonder why we let him go if the killer wasn't captured until recently."

"Because you were sleeping with him, dear," Effie replied airily, "and your husband didn't like it."

"Fair enough, I suppose," Helen said with a regretful sigh. She leaned heavily on her cane. "Shall we adjourn, then? I'd like to get off my feet."

"Not so fast," Portia said, her gaze shrewd. "Effie hasn't told us why a private detective is here to observe us play cards."

"My diamond-and-sapphire ring, the one that Theo gave me, has gone missing," Effie said. "Annalisa is here to help me track it down."

"We can help you look," Helen offered. "Can't we, gals?" She began casting around as if the ring might be lying near the front door somehow.

Portia wasn't fooled. "Effie thinks one of us nicked the ring. That's right, isn't it? Otherwise, why would we be here? Helen's got a bad leg and I'm having cataract surgery next week so I can't see worth a damn. We're not here to join the search."

"I'm feeling fine," Louise volunteered, holding up her hand. "I can look for the ring."

"I'm hoping we can retrace our actions from last week," Effie explained. "That may reveal where the ring has got to."

"You mentioned you were having it appraised," Louise recalled.

"Let's go to the drawing room, shall we?" Effie said, extending her hand to indicate the way as if these women hadn't been to her home a hundred times. "We can all work on our recollections from there."

"I remember Matilda made a blueberry pie that was scrumptious," Helen said as they walked. "Is there any more of that lying around?"

"Scones today," Effie told her. "With tea, jam, and clotted cream. Portia should feel right at home."

"Are you from England?" Annalisa had the chance to ask.

"I lived in London from age four to twelve," Portia explained. "My father was a diplomat. But I was born in Illinois like the rest of them."

"She fancies herself half British," Helen said. "I say one-quarter at the most." She took what appeared to be her standard seat at the card table, and the others followed suit, taking out their chairs and settling into place.

"My grandmother was English," Portia replied.

"And my father played the ponies, but that doesn't make me a Clydesdale." Helen shuffled the cards like a pro. "Must we play the same hands as last time? I'm not eager to lose again."

"No need to repeat the same cards," Annalisa told her. "Just the sequence of events."

Louise sorted her cards as she considered. "We had lunch first," she said. "But it was earlier in the day and I've already eaten today so I don't think we need to repeat that part. Then we played three rubbers, with Portia and Effie defeating Helen and me."

"The cards beat us, Louise darling, not Portia and Effie."

Matilda entered carrying a tray with a teapot and a plate of cookies and scones, which she set on a nearby serving table before pouring tea for each of the ladies. "Do you need anything else right now?" she asked Effie.

"No, thank you, Matilda, this all looks lovely."

As Matilda left the room, Helen put down her cards and picked up a cookie. "We were talking about Ruth Bernstein and her broken hip, remember?" she said to the others. Annalisa, who had been stalking slowly around the room, halted at the familiar name.

"Ruth broke her hip?" Annalisa asked. "I didn't know that."

"She fell last month," Helen explained.

Portia looked suspicious. "You know Ruth?" she asked Annalisa.

Effie answered for her. "It was Ruth who recommended Annalisa to me. You may remember Ruth lost her cat, Duchess, last year. Annalisa is the one who found her."

Portia regarded Annalisa with grudging respect. "That was kind of you."

Annalisa made a mental note to contact Ruth and see how the old woman was faring. "It's always a matter of logical deduction. So, you discussed Ruth. What else?"

"Effie asked me if I would donate Stephen's old golf clubs to a charity fundraiser for Ruby's Place," Portia said. "I told her to ring me and give me the details."

"My granddaughter had a baby," Louise said to Annalisa. "I'm a great-grandmother. I showed everyone the pictures." She was already moving for her purse to get some photos.

"Yes, we all admired the baby," Effie said. She ticked off some more topics they covered: the yo-yoing weather; it had been near sixty degrees that day, almost a record for Chicago in December. Then snow again two days later. Portia's arthritis. The new mayor and how only 20 percent approved of his performance, despite voting him in only a few months ago. Annalisa made some notes while they talked, but she didn't hear anything in the discussion that provided a clue about the ring.

Matilda returned to freshen the tea. "Oh," she said, surprised to see Annalisa. "Did you want a cup too?"

Annalisa was beginning to think it might be easier to accept a beverage. "No, thank you."

"The scones are delicious, Mattie," Portia told her, holding one up and waving it. "You're a wonder."

Matilda smiled with pride. "I love to bake."

When she had gone again, Annalisa asked the most important question: "Did anyone leave the room at any point? Besides Matilda, that is?"

Helen gave a throaty chuckle as she studied her cards. "Honey, we have the bladders of octogenarians. We all visited the facilities at least once. Are we bidding now or what?"

Portia stopped putting cream on her scone and pointed her butter knife at Effie. "I knew you suspected us. I knew it! You think one of us sneaked upstairs and took your ring instead of visiting the toilet? Why would we do that?"

Color heightened Effie's papery cheeks. "I don't know why! That's why I've brought Annalisa here—to find out."

"Honestly, you must be sick. I think you've taken leave of your senses, accusing us like this." Portia pushed back from the table and hustled out of the room shockingly fast for an old woman.

"Boy, you made her mad," Helen told Effie with a low whistle.

"I should go talk to her." Effie started to get up, but Annalisa stopped her.

"No, let me." She wanted to question Portia alone. Finding the other woman in the maze of a house took her some time, but she eventually located Portia in the library. Portia had removed a handkerchief from her purse and was dabbing gently at her eyes.

"Oh," she said, sniffing with embarrassment when she saw Annalisa. "Don't mind me and my nonsense. A terrible display of sentimental poppycock. I must look guilty now, mustn't I? Running off like a silly schoolgirl. Tell me, does Effie sincerely believe I took that ring?"

"She can't believe anyone would take it," Annalisa said. "That's the problem."

"My guess? Matilda misplaced it and then forgot what she did with it. Her memory isn't what it used to be."

"That thought has occurred to me," Annalisa confessed. "But I know Effie has searched high and low around the house and that Matilda denied she has the ring."

"Maybe Matilda thought it was a sausage and stuck it in the fridge. Lord knows I found my cell phone in there one day last month and I don't even have memory issues." She paused with a frown. "At least I don't think I do."

"You were there when Theo gave Effie the ring," Annalisa said. "Isn't that right?"

"Not in the room with them, no. That would have been awkward."

"Because you were seeing Theo at the same time?" Annalisa knew she was being forward, pressing an old woman about her salacious romantic history like this, but she sensed Portia could take it.

Portia gave Annalisa a thin smile and a tight nod of acknowledgment. "Effie has told you much about our complicated history. Yes, I loved Theo. He loved me too, although Effie always conveniently forgets that part of the story. But there are chapters Effie herself is unaware of because Theo wanted it that way and once he picked her I would never have done anything to interfere."

"But Theo's gone now," Annalisa pointed out.

"Yes. As is my Stephen. Isn't it funny what a fuss we made over these men in our younger days when we were destined to outlive them all? The four of us—Effie, Helen, Louise, and me—we're the marriage that lasted longest."

These ladies are my family now, Effie had said. Annalisa wondered if finding the truth about the ring would be worth destroying Effie's most precious relationships. Then she guessed that was the point Nick had been trying to make with her. Truth wasn't the only variable that counted.

Portia squared her thin shoulders and reached over to squeeze Annalisa's arm. "You come see me tomorrow morning. Shall we say half nine? We'll have tea, and I'll tell you everything you need to know about Effie, me, Theo, and that ring. I think you'll be satisfied that I didn't take it."

"I don't have any reason to suspect you did."

Portia narrowed her eyes and tilted her head. "Then you're not a very good detective. Come on, let's get back to the others before Effie sends the hounds after us." She returned to the drawing room, but Annalisa detoured to the kitchen to talk to Matilda. She found her at the sink washing up some dishes.

"I'll dry, if you like," Annalisa said as she took up a towel.

"Bless your heart," Matilda replied with a smile that crinkled her eyes. "Mrs. Effie has a dishwasher, but I guess I'm old-fashioned enough to prefer the old way."

"My mother feels the same." Annalisa noted a pair of rings lying on the counter next to the sink. "Are those yours? They're lovely."

"The gold one is Bobby's class ring from college. I had it resized after he passed away. The other is a gift from Mrs. Effie for my birthday some years back—rubies, on account of I was born in July. I told her it's too fancy but she insisted."

"She has a lot of nice jewelry."

"Oh, yes. Mighty fine pieces. But her favorite is that ring Mr. Theo gave her for their engagement." She handed Annalisa a teacup and looked over her shoulder. "She thinks maybe one of the ladies took it. Don't tell her but I know which one."

Annalisa paused her wiping and glanced at the doorway. No one was coming. "Who was it?"

"The white-haired one. I didn't remember it until I saw her again. Oh, what's her name?" She balled one wet hand into a fist and bopped it on the edge of the sink. "I know it. I know I do."

"Louise?"

"That's right." Matilda's face brightened. "I saw her with the ring last week when the ladies were here for cards, and I asked her why she had Mrs. Effie's ring. She said she wanted to donate it to a charity auction for Ruby's Place. Don't misunderstand me—I love Ruby's Place. They helped me enormously when Bobby's father started with his violent rages. Got me safe. Got me the job here with Mrs. Effie. But I don't think Mrs. Effie would want that ring going anywhere, even somewhere as special as Ruby's Place." She looked uncertain. "Don't you agree?"

"I do," Annalisa assured her. She heard Helen's loud voice say something that made the others laugh from the nearby room. Matilda's story didn't make sense to her. No way Louise would have tried to donate Effie's ring without discussing it. Still, Annalisa would have to ask her about the incident. Her phone buzzed in her pocket, and she finished drying the cup and excused herself before checking the text. It was from Nick.

According to my notes, Joe Green's first wife was named Jessica. But there's something weird. Call me.

She ducked into the nearest empty room, one with a large dining table and a tall china cabinet, and called Nick immediately. "What is it?" she asked when he picked up.

"If you wanted me to feel like I fucked up, then congratulations," he said.

She closed her eyes, pained. "That is not what I wanted."

"As you found, there's no official record of Joe and Jessica Green's wedding, so I don't think they were formally married. But there is also no record of Jessica Green after 2005. No driver's license. No work history. No public record whatsoever. That's around when Joe started saying she left him, right?"

"Yes, I think so. You're saying you think she fled and went into hiding? That he was that dangerous?"

Nick's answer was grim. "I'm saying: what if she never left at all? What if she's dead?"

Annalisa sagged against the wall. This was a possibility she had not considered: that Joe Green was in prison for murder—just not the one he was officially accused of. "That would explain the frame-up," she said to Nick. "If someone knew the truth."

"That someone would have to be Gwen," he said. "The witness."

"Or she's lying on someone else's behalf. We still don't know."

"I can't believe I missed this. I should have followed up on Jessica Green back then."

"It didn't seem important." She braced herself on the wall and listened to the old familiar sounds of the station house filter through the phone on the other end. Nick said nothing. She knew he was beating himself up and that there was nothing he could do from his position.

He had no body, no new evidence. The commander would never allocate precious department resources to re-investigate a man who was already in prison for murder. If the truth about Joe Green were to come out now, Annalisa would have to be the one to pursue it. “Still want me to drop it?” she asked finally.

Nick took a long time with his answer. “No,” he said.

TEN

LAYLA LOOKED AGAIN IN THE REARVIEW MIRROR TO MAKE SURE THEY WERE NOT BEING FOLLOWED AS SHE MANEUVERED THE LITTLE BLUE KIA INTO A FREE SPACE OUTSIDE MAYA'S APARTMENT BUILDING. Maya saw her looking and turned in her seat to check as well. "What are you worried for?" she asked Layla. "Ray has to be at the courthouse for the hearing. That's what you said."

"Yes, and that's where we have to be too." Layla didn't feel comfortable with any deviation in the plans. "We have to meet your lawyer and make sure everything is in order."

"You said the paperwork was good and I trust you." Maya glanced down at her outfit. "Do you think I look okay? For the judge, I mean."

"You look great."

"The jacket is too big." She indicated the blazer the shelter had loaned her along with a blouse and skirt; only the airy scarf around her neck belonged to Maya. She touched it in a self-conscious gesture. "I grabbed this when I ran out with the kids . . . you know, to hide the bruises. Ray never let me wear it because he didn't like me wearing red. He said red was for sluts trying to get men's attention."

"Well, I think it's a great color on you," Layla told her.

Maya managed a conspiratorial smile. "You know what? I think I'm going to wear red all the time now."

"I love that," Layla said. "But right now we need to hurry."

"I just want to grab a few things for the kids. I'll be in and out, real quick. I promise."

Layla tamped down her objections. Part of the healing was getting the women to feel in charge of their lives again, to make their own decisions after months or years of being worn down by an abusive partner. She didn't want to override Maya in this fresh stint of independence, and Maya was correct that the risk seemed low. "Go ahead. Be fast."

Maya flew out of the car, keys in hand, and disappeared into the building. Layla dug out her phone and watched the minutes tick by. The lawyer sent a text. *In room 222, as arranged. Where are you?* Layla responded: *On our way!* She kept glancing up from her phone at the front door, expecting Maya to reappear, but Maya did not show. After nearly ten minutes, Layla got out of the car and went into the building after her. She knew Maya and Ray shared apartment 313 and so she took the stairs to the third floor. At the door, she knocked loudly. "Maya? Maya, it's Layla. We have to go."

No reply.

Layla put her ear to the door and heard nothing on the other side. The fine downy hairs on her arms rose up. She tried the door and it opened with a loud creak that vibrated her bones. "Maya?" she called again, more hesitant this time. Eerie silence answered her. Maybe Maya had taken the elevator down and was waiting for Layla at the car. She took a few small steps into the apartment. The blinds were drawn. Empty beer bottles and fast-food trash lay scattered around the front room. Dread blossomed inside her like a corpse flower. "Maya?" Her voice sounded high and fearful to her own ears. "Are you in here?"

She edged toward the kitchen, and when she came around the island, she discovered Maya splayed out on the tile floor. Maya lay crooked like a broken doll, her hands on her chest as if reaching for her neck. Around her neck, the red scarf had been tightened into a garotte. Layla knelt next to her, calling her name, trying to loosen the horrible cincture. Maya did not move and she did not seem to be breathing. "No, no, no," Layla said, repeating the word like a mantra as her numb fingers worked at the knot in the scarf. She called 911 and started CPR, still chanting "No, no, no" with each chest compression. The EMTs eventually had to pull her away. Only when the police came, after Maya had been taken away in an ambulance, did Layla realize the attacker could have still been in the apartment the whole time. He could have come for her too.

The cops put her in the back of a squad car outside, like she was the criminal, with one of them standing guard and blocking the window so she couldn't really see what was going on. Her cell phone buzzed with another text from the lawyer. *You're too late. It doesn't matter now. Ray didn't show so the hearing has been postponed until next week.* Layla knew she would have to call Charlotte and explain everything, but she didn't have the words. Her brain was full of static and she feared if she opened her mouth she'd just start screaming.

She sat rigid in the hard leather seat, clutching her phone and staring out the window at the backside of the uniformed officer. Eventually a dark-haired man about her age climbed in the car with her. "Ms. McCoy," he said. "I'm Nick Carelli, a detective with the Chicago PD. I'm so sorry for what you've been through today."

Layla recognized him as the cop who had come to the shelter asking questions about Joe Green. She recoiled when he stuck out his hand to shake hers, and he immediately pulled back. "How's Maya?" she blurted. "Is she going to be okay?"

His face darkened and she knew the truth before he said a word. "I'm afraid the doctors at the hospital were unable to revive her. I'm sorry."

Her kids, Layla thought. *Someone will have to tell her kids.* She tried to bolt from the car, but the detective grabbed her arm.

"Wait a second."

"Let go of me!"

He released her and she didn't flee. Just curled like a cornered animal against the door of the car. "I know this is upsetting," he said. "Is there anyone I can call for you? A friend or family member?"

"Shouldn't you be out looking for him?" He gave her a blank look. "Ray Donovan, Maya's husband. The man who did this."

"You saw him?" Detective Carelli's voice became animated and his posture strengthened. He was ready, she saw. Like a loaded gun. All she had to do was point him in the right direction and he'd go off. It would be easy enough to lie. *Yes, I saw him.* She remained silent and Detective Carelli leaned closer, practically vibrating as he waited for her to say the words. "Ms. McCoy? You saw Ray Donovan at the scene?"

She opened her mouth prepared to swear to it. Somehow the truth came out instead. "No. I didn't see him." She whispered the words, full of sorrow. These huge, violent men with their angry fists and their tempers fearsome enough to destroy a whole household; when it came time for justice, they shrunk down to slip through the cracks. She looked at Nick Carelli with wet eyes. "But it was Ray who killed her. You know it was. He said he'd do it and that's why she was going to get a restraining order today. She was about to be free."

"We'll find him. If he did this, he will pay."

He sounded so certain, and she shook her head as tears filled her eyes. "The law only helps you after you're dead," she murmured to the window. Charlotte had told her this once, years ago, half-drunk in the middle of the night. She had never repeated it but she didn't have to; Layla lived the truth of it every day.

ELEVEN

KARMA TOOK IT HARD. "I'm the one who talked Maya into the restraining order. I'm the reason she's dead." She paced the length of Charlotte's office, clawing at her own face like she couldn't exist in her skin any longer. Charlotte tried to calm her, to take her hands and make her see reason.

"The restraining order was the right move."

"How can you say that? Maya is dead!" Karma raged at Charlotte because that's who was in front of her. Still, the force of her anger blew Charlotte backward. "Why do we always do this? We act like a piece of paper is going to stop these men. We hide out here in this fortress while they get to walk the earth like kings. How is that fair?"

"I know. It's awful." Charlotte had been Karma once, bleeding emotion all over the carpet, tearing her hair out for missing some sign. "But it's Ray Donovan's fault and his alone. You did nothing wrong."

"I can't. I can't stand it. He killed her and did they arrest him? No, of course not. He's walking free while his kids have to shelter here like he's a nuclear bomb. Why can't someone stop him?"

"They will," Charlotte said, trying for a certainty she did not feel.

The cops had an unmarked car sitting outside in case Ray decided to show up looking for his kids. Inside, they had Henry, who refused to go home. "I'm not leaving until that asshole is caught," he'd said to Charlotte when she urged him to get some rest. They were all exhausted, walking zombies powered by caffeine and adrenaline.

"I'm not going to stay here cowering like a trapped animal. I'm not going to take it anymore. I'm going to do something."

"Karma, wait . . ." Karma fled the office but Charlotte didn't chase her. She went instead to her desk and checked the locked drawer to see that her gun was there. The sight of it gave her no peace. She shut the drawer and opened a different one instead, the one with the good gin. She took it to the kitchen where Danny was wiping down the stainless-steel counters. They already gleamed so it was clear that he, too, didn't want to leave.

"Evening, boss," he said when he saw her.

"Do we have any cranberry juice?" she asked, holding up the half-empty bottle of Dorothy Parker.

"Sure do." He produced an unopened bottle from the pantry and Charlotte poured two glasses. They clinked without any kind of toast, but Danny held his glass up to stare at it. "Man, times like this I wish I'd been a cop like my brother and my uncle. Then I could be out there looking for him. I'd pound his face into the ground so hard he'd be tasting cement for the rest of his life."

More violence, thought Charlotte. Karma had compared Ray to a nuclear bomb, but he was more like a stick of dynamite in a shed full of TNT. One explodes and then the rest go off, one by one. The only way to prevent it was to snuff out the first stick. The alcohol sang in her veins and she set down the glass on the counter. "Have you seen Karma?"

"No. I know Layla's been sitting with the kids. Maybe Karma went up there."

Charlotte thanked him for the drink and went up to find Layla just coming out of the children's room. "They're asleep finally," she said, leaning against the wall. The hall was totally silent; all the women and kids were holed up in their rooms like the threat was meant for them. Layla rubbed at her tired eyes. "I kept telling them it was going to be okay, that they would be safe, but I can't really promise that, can I? We don't even know what will happen to them."

"Foster care."

"We can't keep them here?"

Charlotte gave her a pained look. "They need parents, Layla. A family. We're a lot of things, but we're not that."

Layla took on a wounded expression. She didn't have family, not really. Ruby's Place was as much a home to her as anywhere, but she had to know it was not suitable for raising little kids. "I just want to do something to help them," Layla said.

"You are." The echo of Karma's words—*I'm going to do something*—reminded Charlotte of her purpose. "Has Karma been up here recently?"

"I haven't seen her. Why?"

At that moment, Henry opened the door from the stairwell and appeared in the hall as part of his rounds. "All quiet?" he asked, nodding at the children's room.

"For now," Layla told him.

Charlotte pressed him on the matter at hand. "Have you seen Karma?"

"I just passed her a little bit ago. She was in the office."

"My office?" Charlotte started to run, and Layla and Henry came after her.

"What is it?" Henry called as they reached the stairs.

"I hope nothing." Charlotte hurried as fast as she could. Her skin tingled in the patches where she'd been burned, places that usually lacked any feeling at all. She knew it was imaginary, a remnant of the terrible night her ex-boyfriend tried to set her on fire. She'd lied and said it was an accident when the house went up in flames. She'd covered for him with the EMTs, the doctors, the social worker, and the police. He'd been so relieved, so kind to her during her recovery in the burn unit. He had no idea she'd been planning her escape.

Charlotte reached the office and went immediately to her desk. The drawer with the gun in it sat pried open and empty. She bit back a groan as she collapsed into the chair. "Karma, no . . ."

Layla knew the stakes right away. "I'll call her." She had her phone out ready to dial.

"What is it?" Henry wanted to know. "What's going on?"

"My gun is missing."

He looked shocked. "You have a gun?"

Her chin lifted in challenge to him. "Working here, wouldn't you? I keep it locked in my desk. Karma forced it open." She saw now the screwdriver sitting amid the papers on her desk. "This is bad. This is very bad."

"She wouldn't do something foolish," Henry said. "Would she?"

"Karma can be arrested just for possessing a gun," Charlotte replied. "She shot her boyfriend eight years ago."

"She what?" Henry gaped.

"Don't worry," Charlotte said darkly. "He lived. It was his gun. He'd taken her hostage and he'd played Russian roulette with her a dozen times, each time Karma figuring this would be the shot that killed her. When she finally got the gun from him, she did what she had to do to get out of there."

"It was self-defense then," Henry said.

"Not according to the cops. He was holding her prisoner in their own apartment. Karma didn't have any bruises or other injuries. She pled out and got ten years, but served only three." Somehow, this counted as a win. Her ex took three years of Karma's life instead of stealing the whole thing. "But she's still on parole. She can't possess a weapon."

"And you think what? She's going after Ray Donovan? But no one knows where he is," Henry pointed out. "I checked with one of my buddies a little bit ago, and he said Donovan's still in the wind."

"Karma's not answering her phone," Layla reported with wide eyes. "What should we do?"

Charlotte wasn't going to play phone tag in the hopes everything would work out okay. "I'm going to go look for her. Go to the places she'd be searching for Ray."

"Look for her where?" Henry spread his arms. "Ray Donovan could be anywhere in this whole damn city. Or he could be halfway around the world by now."

Layla and Charlotte exchanged a look as Charlotte got her coat and keys. Henry's job was to keep the women and children safe. Layla and Charlotte's job was to heal them, and that meant listening while they poured out all the secrets they'd been keeping during their abuse. The bars their abusers drank at before coming home to knock them around. The friends and relatives who saw the signs but didn't intervene. Maya had told many stories about Ray and his behavior, enough to guess at some places he might be hiding out.

"Be careful," Layla said. "Call me if you find her."

"Wait, I'll go with you." Henry moved to follow Charlotte out the door, but she stopped him with a hand on his chest. He looked startled by the physical contact, which she usually avoided.

"Thanks, but you need to stay here with everyone else. I'll feel better knowing you're looking after them."

Henry hesitated before reaching for her hand. "But who will look after you?"

"I'll be fine." This was her life's credo, no matter how painful. *I'll be fine.* She left them and went out in the biting cold to her car, which had a fresh round of frost on it. Not a night to be out if you could help it. Charlotte scraped away the thin layer of crystals and then shivered in her seat as the old engine chugged to life. She consulted her phone and entered a few possible addresses to try, none of them nearby. Ray Donovan came from the city's ripped backside, far from the shiny skyscrapers and gleaming vast lake.

Charlotte drove the cold and empty streets, leaning over the wheel to look in the shadows for any sign of Karma. A lone figure, buried under dirty blankets, slept up against an apartment building. Male or female, alive or dead, it was impossible to tell. *What happens to some people,* Charlotte thought, a pain in her chest. Any other night, she would have stopped and offered a ride to the nearest shelter, but the person she most wanted off the streets right now was Karma.

Charlotte continued her search, cruising by the all-night corner stores and the cousin's house that Maya had mentioned. A man in a knit cap made eye contact with her. *Not him*. Charlotte drove on, telling herself she was only looking to find Karma. She did not think about what could happen if she found Ray Donovan first.

TWELVE

Jack did not like it when Nick worked late, which was why 2 a.m. found him sitting on Nick's pillow, complaining loudly to Annalisa. "I know, bud," she said as she tried to pet the cat. "I miss him too." Jack flattened his ears and stalked away to the end of the bed, swishing his tail so she would know how offended he was that she didn't fix it. Exhausted as she was, she could not sleep. She picked up her phone from the bedside table and stared at it for the hundredth time. Nick had not sent any news since his last text, shortly after eight. *Home late. Don't wait up.* She knew the case and knew the job; Nick had to interview anyone who might be able to prove Ray Donovan murdered Maya and anyone who might know where Ray was hiding out. The problem was there were no witnesses to question, which meant plausible deniability for Ray's friends and family. *Ray would never do this. He's innocent. You're looking for the wrong guy.* Abusers were often charming and likable at work or with their friends. No one could imagine what happened behind closed doors at home. When the truth came out—if it ever came out—these violent men left a trail of bewildered people in their wake. *He was the nicest guy. He'd give you the shirt off his back.*

Annalisa put the phone down and tried to sleep for the baby's sake if not for hers. Pregnancy, she'd learned, meant the baby came first even in her own body. Don't eat enough food for two? The fetus would start eating your insides, leaching minerals and nutrients. She was used to being able to put off sleep, put off hunger, anything in pursuit of a case, but now any extra reserves she had went only one place.

Nick stumbled in close to three, shedding layers of himself until he climbed under the quilt with her nearly naked. He smelled like the street, like cold and sweat, and she wrapped herself around him as Jack slithered in between, purring with contentment. She could feel the tension in him and knew this meant that Ray Donovan remained at large. She rubbed his back and listened to the thundering of his heart. He held her in a fierce embrace, his face buried in her hair. "Tell me," he said in a desperate voice, "tell me we're not crazy." His hand curved around her swollen stomach and she knew what he was asking. What a world to bring a baby into, one where a father would murder his children's mother, leaving them essentially orphans.

She put her hand over his. "Ours will be different." Even as she said the words, she wondered if every parent told this lie. Maybe not a lie. A willful ignorance. A wish and a prayer.

"I loved my father," he confessed under the cover of darkness. "I loved him even when I was afraid of him. Even after he . . . did what he did."

"I know." She squeezed his hand. "I still love Alex."

"That's what scares me." He rested his head heavy on hers. "Love isn't enough to save you."

"No," she replied. "I think maybe it's the only thing that can." She stretched up and kissed his forehead. "And think of all the beautiful things we can show this baby. This time next year, it will be their first snow. First taste of Ma's pasta sauce."

"First taste of ice cream." He had started to relax.

"Yes, chocolate," she agreed. "Oh, and there will be picnics in the park and bedtime stories. Christmas morning around the tree."

"Baseball games," he said in a sleepy voice, snuffling her hair. "Cubs fan."

She smiled, closing her eyes and snuggling in with him. Nick had already bought a tiny hat in Cubbie blue. "And the lake," she murmured. "How blue it is. The way the sun shines on it and makes it like an ocean of diamonds." She fell asleep then, and this time when the girl came to her in her dreams, they stood at the water's edge.

Let's get a boat, the girl said. *We can sail away from here.*

Why do you want to leave so bad? Annalisa asked her. She loved her Chicago home.

I don't belong here, the girl replied. *I need to find my home.*

They walked on, looking for the girl's house, but ended up back at Annalisa's parents' place where Ma had supper waiting on the table. Annalisa asked Ma if her friend could stay to eat with them, but when she turned around, the girl was gone.

....

NICK GOT LESS THAN FOUR HOURS OF SLEEP BEFORE HE HEADED OUT ON THE HUNT AGAIN UNDER THE PALE JANUARY SKY. Annalisa sat bleary-eyed in the kitchen, wishing for a real cup of coffee. She decided against making breakfast for herself. Instead, she ventured to the diner where Vanessa Green worked. If anyone might know the whereabouts of Joe's first wife, Jessica, it would be Vanessa. Annalisa took a seat at the counter and waited for Vanessa to make her way over.

"Oh, it's you," Vanessa said, unsmiling as she slapped a menu in front of Annalisa. "What do you want?"

"To ask you a few more questions about Joe."

"No, I mean what are you having?" Vanessa nodded at the menu. "I don't have time to chat."

“I’ll have the avocado toast and a side of hash browns. Decaf coffee.”

“Great, thanks.” Vanessa moved to swipe the menu from Annalisa, but Annalisa held it fast.

“What can you tell me about Jessica? Joe’s first wife.”

“I told you I never met her. She skipped out on him.” She tried again to take the menu, but Annalisa wouldn’t let her.

“He never said where she went? Did he talk about her at all? Did he mention if she had family that she might have gone to stay with?” Annalisa wasn’t even sure this missing woman was alive, but if she was, her family would be the best route to finding her.

“He didn’t say and I didn’t ask. Happy now? I need to get back to work.” She did grab the menu then and Annalisa had only one trick left to prevent Vanessa from walking away.

“I’m worried he killed her,” she said.

Vanessa froze and turned around. She glanced at her manager, a woman younger than her with a blond ponytail, and licked her lips in a nervous fashion. “Why . . . what makes you say that?”

“No one can find her. Joe said she left him but there’s been no trace of her since then.”

Vanessa edged closer to Annalisa once more. “I—I never thought he killed her. I haven’t thought about her in years. Joe didn’t mention her much.”

“Did he have pictures of her?” Annalisa didn’t even know what she looked like.

Vanessa shook her head. “No, Joe isn’t the sentimental type. He had some of her clothes, I think. She wasn’t a big girl.” She shook her head. “Jeez, I haven’t even thought about any of this crap in years. You want to know something funny?”

“What’s that?”

“The last person I know who was looking for Jessica was Cyrus Merriman.”

Annalisa blinked. "Your divorce lawyer?"

"Yeah. He thought the same thing that you did . . . that she might help us dig up some dirt on Joe."

"Do you know if he found her?"

Vanessa shrugged. "No clue. He died and then it was all over."

Annalisa thought it was interesting that Vanessa said Cyrus died and not was murdered. After all, her husband Joe was convicted of the crime. Annalisa did not know what to make of the fact that the last person to look for Joe's first wife ended up dead. If Joe had killed her, and Cyrus was onto him, that would give him yet another motive to have tossed the lawyer into the lake. Annalisa scooted forward on her stool. "Please," she said. "I really need to find this woman. Anything you can tell me about her would be helpful. Any tidbit Joe might have mentioned about her past, like where she was born or where she went to school . . ."

Vanessa looked blank for a long moment; then she scowled. "It's always the same, right? You cops only care when we're dead."

"I'm not a cop."

"You were until like ten minutes ago. Like I've told you and told you, I don't have any information. I can't help you."

"If Joe did this, if he hurt you and maybe hurt Jessica too, then why are you protecting him?"

"Honey." Vanessa gave her a pitying look. "I'm not protecting Joe. I never was. Look, either you're right and this lady Jessica is dead or she's alive somewhere, living her best life and she doesn't need the likes of you coming around to harass her. Either way, I want no part of it."

....

ANNALISA PONDERED THE CASE AS SHE DROVE TO PORTIA'S HOUSE FOR THEIR MEETING. She'd hoped that Joe's first wife, Jessica, might be the key to unlocking the strange puzzle as to why Gwen Beaufort would give a false statement implicating Joe Green. If Gwen knew Jessica, it could explain her willingness to perjure herself. The fact that Cyrus was murdered just as he started asking questions about Jessica only deepened Annalisa's conviction that she needed to find out what happened to the woman.

Portia's penthouse on East Superior Street wasn't as grand as Effie's estate but it featured sprawling city views and the crystal expanse of the lake visible in the distance. Annalisa tried not to gawk out the floor-to-ceiling windows as Portia had tea and shortbread cookies served by her housekeeper—a younger version of Matilda from Effie's place. "It's herbal," Portia assured her. "No caffeine."

"Great," Annalisa replied with a fixed smile. She would kill for some caffeine. She took a polite sip and put down her delicate porcelain cup. "Thank you for seeing me. As you know, Effie is terribly upset about her missing ring. Anything you can tell me about it may help in tracking it down."

Portia pulled out a plain white envelope the size of a letter and held it protectively on her lap. "You have to understand," she said. "Theo never wanted Effie to know. He'd be turning over in his grave right now if he knew I was speaking to you about this."

Annalisa knew the price of family secrets. "I understand," she said sincerely. "I won't tell Effie anything she doesn't need to know."

Portia hesitated a moment longer before handing Annalisa the envelope with a resigned sigh. "I wish you could have known Theo. He was a lover, through and through. When the doctors diagnosed him with an enlarged heart, we joked that we'd known it all along. He had this big booming voice but I don't think I ever heard him say a cross word with it. Those last few weeks, when he hadn't much strength left and it was clear this was the end, he cared more about us. He worried about Effie and wanted to make sure we looked after her."

Annalisa slid the letter from the envelope. The handwritten scrawl was difficult to read, and after a minute or so of her squinting, Portia plucked it from her fingers and read it aloud.

"'Dear Ducky,'" she began and then turned to Annalisa to explain. "He called me 'Ducky' because I picked up the word during my time in London. I'd say 'that's just ducky' and Theo thought it was hilarious. Anyway, it continues . . . 'I'm afraid that eighty-two years is going to be the limit on my story so you'll have to continue on without me to the end. Knowing you has been one of my greatest joys, and if I had a thousand lifetimes, I'd want you there with me for every one of them.

"'Please look after Effie. Tell her that my heart may have failed but my love for her never did. I will be waiting with Stephen for you on the other side. We'll have champagne and strawberries ready—but please forgive us if we enjoy a cigar or two in your absence. Until then, I remain . . .'" Portia teared up, her voice becoming emotional. "'Your Theo.'"

"It's a lovely letter," Annalisa told her as Portia wiped her eyes. "Theo obviously held you in great affection."

"As I did him. But you see: we both loved Effie more." She folded up the letter and put it back in the envelope, giving it a gentle stroke with her fingertips before setting it aside. "Yes, Theo and I saw quite a lot of one another when Effie's father forbade her to be with him. Yes, I loved him."

"Loved him as in wanted to marry him?"

Portia froze with her mouth open. She probably hadn't been asked this question in decades. She gave a little shrug. "It didn't matter what I wanted. Theo wanted Effie. I loved Effie. I never would have tried to interfere. In fact, it was the opposite."

"You helped get them together?"

"I would offer cover sometimes so they could meet up. But no, it was me who suggested the solution." She gave a meaningful pause. "The ring."

"The ring convinced Effie's father to let her marry Theo," Annalisa recalled.

"My idea." Portia put a hand to her chest. "Effie's father was concerned that Theo was a hustler, only after her money. If he knew Theo had money of his own, then his objections to the match would subside."

"But Theo didn't have a lot of money back then." A thought occurred to her. "Did you buy the ring?"

Portia let out a musical laugh. "No, dear. Helen did."

"Helen? Helen Huntzberger?"

"She was Helen Showalter back then, only hoping to be Mrs. Huntzberger. But you see, Effie's father wanted her to marry into the Huntzberger clan. He set her up with Nathaniel."

"Ah," Annalisa said as the pieces came together for her. "So Helen fixes things for Effie and Theo by purchasing the ring, thereby clearing the way for Helen to become Mrs. Nathaniel Huntzberger. Very clever."

"Thank you." She sipped her tea. "I thought so. Theo was hesitant at first, but Helen and I worked on him together until he saw reason." She eyed Annalisa with a probing look, as if wondering how much more to say. "There was only one small problem left."

"What's that?"

"How to afford the ring. Don't misunderstand me—Helen's family was quite well off. Not 'Fish Sticks' wealthy, but they got by. They wouldn't, however, be letting Helen waltz off with a huge sum to buy a fancy ring, only to hand it over to some middle-class cad to woo his girlfriend. Helen had limited finances. Money was a man's domain back then. We weren't even allowed to have credit cards unless our husbands signed off on them."

"So?" Annalisa prompted. "How did Helen get the ring?"

"It's fake." At Annalisa's shocked look, Portia clarified. "Well, the sapphires are real, I believe. But the large diamond in the center? No, it's fake. Helen had limited funds, but she did have great connections.

She knew someone who could make an incredibly believable facsimile for a fraction of the cost. She traded one of her own real pieces for two faux rings: a copy of hers and the one that Theo gave to Effie. Theo paid her back over time."

"And no one ever told Effie?"

Portia looked horrified. "No, of course not. Effie loved that ring and spoke often of Theo's grand gesture for her. We would never tarnish Theo in her eyes. He would have bought the ring for her if he could have. Indeed, he later gifted her other more expensive pieces. But the engagement ring is the one she loved the most because of what it signifies."

"Effie was set to have that ring appraised when it disappeared."

"Yes," Portia said with regret. "A qualified jeweler would definitely know the difference and the secret would come out."

"Maybe," Annalisa ventured, "maybe someone who knew the secret took the ring to stop Effie from finding out the truth."

"Well, it wasn't me. But I dare say I considered it."

"Really? You'd leave your friend wondering forever what happened to her ring?"

"The way I see it, she can miss either the ring or the foundational love story that goes with it. Theo was perfect in her eyes. I wouldn't want to be the one to take that from her, not now, when all she has left are the memories." She leaned closer to Annalisa. "I asked you here today to tell you the truth in the hopes that you won't want to be that person either."

"You're asking me to lie to her."

"Not at all. I don't know where that ring went. Neither do you. All I'm asking is that you leave things as they are."

THIRTEEN

RAY SPENT THREE DAYS HOLED UP IN THE BASEMENT LIKE A RAT BEFORE HE COULDN'T TAKE IT ANYMORE. Yeah, his buddy Jimmy was doing him a solid by letting him crash there, but the basement was foul. Rotting cardboard boxes. Dust and mouse poop. The place was freezing cold and he had only a sleeping bag to keep him warm. Jimmy smuggled him food at least once per day. Any more than that would make his wife suspicious. She'd already told the cops she'd turn Ray in if she so much as glimpsed his ass on the streets. She'd have a conniption if she knew he was camped out under her kitchen floor. At least Jimmy believed his story about Maya's death. *I swear I didn't do it, but the lazy-ass cops are going to hang me for it. I need someplace to hide out for a bit and make a plan. Get some cash together for a lawyer who can help me fight this bullshit.*

Ray stood on tiptoe, his fingers scrabbling along the dirty sash, to peer out the basement window at the dark street. The house was quiet. He didn't see any signs that the cops were watching the place, but he couldn't be sure until he went outside. Fuck it. He had to get out of this dungeon for a while. Get some real food. Find some booze. Jimmy had given him two hundred bucks toward finding that lawyer. Ray's real plan was to get to Mexico. He had a grand stashed in the apartment but no way he could get to it right now, not when it was still taped up as a crime scene. He had to buy time for things to cool down. The cops would move on to other problems. Then he could get his money and get the hell out of town.

Ray unlocked the basement door and tugged it until it came free. It groaned and he winced, momentarily freezing while he listened to see if he woke anyone upstairs. The family slept on the second floor, so when he did not hear footsteps after a minute or two, he figured it was safe. He hugged the outside wall at first, scanning the street for signs of life. He saw a few parked cars but none with a radio antenna that might signal an undercover unit. He relaxed and started walking. He knew there was a 24/7 convenience mart about four blocks away, and he already planned to get six hot dogs and a six-pack of Bud. Before entering, he pulled his knit cap down to his eyebrows, hunching his shoulders to look smaller.

The old man at the counter barely reacted when Ray walked in. He had his eyes closed, listening to some radio program on his phone in a language Ray did not recognize. He peeked at Ray through slitted eyelids but otherwise made no move. Ray went to the refrigerated section at the back and considered buying lunch meat to hold him over the next day. It would certainly stay plenty cold in the freakin' basement. He grabbed some sliced turkey and a bag of bread. The electronic doorbell beeped, signaling a new customer, and Ray instinctively moved to hide. He peered around the rack of chips and exhaled with relief. A woman. Not young or old—maybe she'd even be kind of hot if it weren't for the fluorescent lights. She was dressed in jeans and a black jacket and didn't seem to be looking for him, so he knew she wasn't a cop. Ray walked to the front.

"Gimme six of those," he said to the old man at the counter, indicating the hot dogs rolling on the heater. He kept his head down, avoiding eye contact.

"Only four hot ones," the man replied as he moved to get Ray's order. "If you want more, you have to wait."

Ray shifted his feet, trying to decide. His stomach rumbled. He hadn't eaten since that morning when Jimmy brought him a breakfast sandwich and a soda. "I'll wait."

The woman picked up a half gallon of milk and a bag of chips. "You trying for an early grave?" she asked him as she joined him near the counter.

"What's that?"

"Hot dogs are the worst food you can possibly eat. Fatty, salty . . . all those nitrates and preservatives. They'll give you colon cancer, you know."

"Yeah?" Ray had like a billion other more important problems. "What do you care?"

"I'm a nurse. It's my job to care about people." She eyed the hot dogs the old man was preparing for Ray and then looked back at him. "I'll say you must work it off, though. You're plenty fit."

She said it in an admiring way, and Ray puffed up a little. He made sure to work out every day and he had the abs to prove it. Maya never appreciated the effort he put into looking good for her, all those hours at the gym. She wanted him home with the kids. *The kids.* He went a little stricken at the thought of them. Who would get the kids now? Probably Maya's bitchy cousin. She'd poison the kids against him, tell them all sorts of lies.

"Hey, you okay?" The woman looked at him with concern. "You kinda got all pale there for a second."

He hunched up again. "Just hungry. Worked a lot of hours today."

"Yeah? I just got off shift myself and I'm about to make dinner. Nothing fancy. Just pasta and salad. You're welcome to join me if you want. My apartment's not too far from here."

He looked at her with suspicion. "You're inviting me to your place? No offense, lady, but you don't even know me."

She shrugged and made an expansive gesture. "I told you. I like to take care of people. You seem like you could use it." She pointed at him. "No funny stuff, though. I know self-defense."

Just the part where she called it "self-defense" almost made him laugh. This lady was an idiot. He could probably snap her in two if he wanted. But that wasn't his priority now. No, he saw a different kind of opening. Maybe he could sweet-talk her a bit, get her to let him stay at her place for a day or two. Hell, maybe there was even a way he could use her to get to his money. Or take her money. Ray was open to anything at that point.

"You live nearby?"

"About a mile. My car's outside."

Even better, Ray thought. No way the cops would be looking for him at her place. "You know what?" he said. "You're on. As long as I can buy the wine." He gave her his best smile and damn if she didn't blush. He legit had a shot at this. "Bottle of merlot," he told the guy at the counter. He nudged the woman with his elbow. "Red wine is good for you, right?"

"So they say. Half a glass won't kill me either way."

They finished their purchases and Ray shoved a hot dog in his mouth on the way out the door. He didn't care if she thought it was gross. He was starving. He looked around the cold, dark street. "You said you had a car?"

She tilted her head. "This way."

He ambled after her, already imagining her warm apartment. He could sleep on a couch. Or maybe a bed. Her bed. *Make nice,* he told himself. "Hey, I'm Mike, by the way," he told her, extending his free hand.

She smiled and took it. "I'm Jessica."

FOURTEEN

NICK HAD CONSUMED SO MUCH COFFEE THAT HIS LEG TOOK ON A PERMANENT BOUNCE, HIS TEETH GRINDING AND HIS VISION BLURRY AS HE SCROLLED THROUGH THE OVERNIGHT REPORTS LOOKING FOR ANY TRACE OF RAY DONOVAN. It had been three days since Maya's murder, and any second his boss, Lynn Zimmer, would yank him off the case in favor of something fresher. Nick had pressed every person Ray Donovan even said hello to on the street for information as to his whereabouts—friends, coworkers, relatives all swore they had not seen him. Nick had even interviewed Ray's barber. The things you tell the person who cuts your hair, he thought. It was almost like visiting a priest. But the barber had no leads that Nick hadn't already run down, so now Nick was deep in the haystack, mucking around with straw up his ass as he searched through a hundred burglary and robbery reports. If Ray was truly on the run with only the clothes on his back, he'd need to get food and money from somewhere.

"No luck?" Zimmer's voice startled him from his intense concentration on the computer screen.

"I'm close to nailing this SOB. I can feel it."

Zimmer hummed a non-reply as she cleared away a stack of empty paper cups from his desk so she could lean against it facing him. She ducked her head to try to make eye contact with him, but he avoided it by keeping his gaze trained on the screen. "A woman in Pilsen reported that someone broke into her house and stole her husband's coat and boots, along with fifty bucks from her purse," he narrated for her. "Could be Ray Donovan."

"Could be a lot of people. It's cold out there. Lots of hungry folks. Speaking of, when's the last time you ate something?"

Nick wagged his finger at the screen. "Also, a couple got mugged in the parking lot of the Super Mall by a man with a knife. The description roughly matches Ray Donovan. I've got a call in with the responding officer."

Zimmer twisted to look at the screen. "This says the suspect is a thin man in his thirties, with light brown skin and a crooked nose. Ray Donovan is a jacked-up white boy who's only twenty-five."

"But they're both about six feet," Nick argued. "And witnesses are unreliable on details."

Zimmer waited a beat and then switched off his monitor. When Nick leaned forward to protest, she held up her hand. "Look, I know how bad you want this guy. I do too. But you've been pounding the pavement nonstop for three days with nothing to show for it. Wherever Donovan is holed up, he's staying put. We've got his face all over the media; all units have a BOLO. He'll pop out sooner or later and then we can nail him. In the meantime, I've got other cases piling up."

"What about the kids? Ray and Maya have two little kids and they could be in danger." A boy and a girl, ages six and four. Nick had been only eight when it happened to him. Was it better to be younger? he wondered. Better to have less memory of before?

"DCFS will look out for the kids. I think they've found a cousin who will take them. She lives in Sacramento and already has two of her own. Maybe that'll be good for them—cousins to help take their mind off things."

“Sure,” Nick muttered. Zimmer didn’t know what it was like. How even if you landed somewhere good, with someone who took care of you, you knew you weren’t supposed to be there. They hadn’t planned to take you in. Nick’s grandmother had just moved into a retirement community in Florida when he ended up on her doorstep with his little blue suitcase in hand. The place didn’t allow kids and so she’d had to move out, losing thousands in the process.

“Give it until the end of the day,” Zimmer told him. “If you haven’t turned up Ray Donovan by then, go home, get some rest, and we’ll start fresh tomorrow.” She clapped him on the shoulder as she left and Nick felt the gesture like a slap. The woman from Ruby’s Place had accused them of only showing up afterward to arrest the guy, and Nick couldn’t even manage that much. He scrubbed his face with both hands and then reached forward to turn on the monitor again.

His phone rang. “Carelli,” he said absently, his eyes on the next burglary report.

“Hey, it’s Gary Miller. Marine Unit just pulled a body out of the lake. Male, white. About six feet, one eighty pounds. Description matches the perp in your domestic case. You want to come have a look?”

Nick was already out of his chair. “Tell them I’m on my way.”

He got the specific address and raced down to East Marine Drive, where a bunch of officers clustered at the scene while a news helicopter buzzed overhead. The day was cold but bright enough that Nick needed sunglasses, which he welcomed to hide his tired eyes. He parked and walked over to the scene where the body had already been zipped up inside a bag for transport to the nearest morgue. An ambulance idled nearby, its lights flashing. “We’ve been waiting on you,” one of the guys said. “Think you’ve got a late Christmas present here.”

Nick unzipped the bag enough to see the victim’s face. Ray Donovan. He gave a short nod and closed the bag once more. “Get him out of here.”

“Should’ve left him in there to rot,” one of the guys muttered as they prepared to load Ray’s body into the back of the ambulance. The helicopter swooped low and then disappeared now that the show appeared to be over. Nick walked to the shoreline. He thought about Maya and how she'd been about to get her own place. She'd been about to start a new job. About to enroll in cosmetology school. Maya had been about to be so many things. He looked out at the water, vast and blue. The brilliant sunlight danced across the surface, and Nick thought Annalisa was right: it did look like diamonds.

....

NICK DID NOT GO HOME, INSTEAD CHOOSING TO SPEND THE AFTERNOON WRITING UP THE INTERIM REPORT ON MAYA'S MURDER. They didn't yet have proof that Ray had killed her, despite the fact that it was obvious he had. Ray lived in the apartment where Maya was killed, so his DNA was everywhere. The forensic unit took samples from the scarf around Maya's neck, but it would probably take weeks to get those results back. If, as they hoped, Ray had left skin cells on the scarf, then the case would be final. At least Ray had saved them the cost of a trial by throwing himself into the lake.

Nick hit "save," about to wrap up his shift, when he got a call from the morgue. They had done a preliminary work-up on Ray Donovan. "Drowning, right?"

"Seems probable. You'll have to wait on that. But there's something odd that you may wish to come take a look at sooner rather than later."

Nick checked his watch. He was dead on his feet. "Can't you just tell me?"

"Your victim has a mutilation."

"Say what?"

"Like I said, you probably want to see it for yourself."

Resigned, Nick reached back and grabbed his jacket. "I'll be there in twenty."

Twenty-five minutes later, he stood with the assistant medical examiner staring at the naked body of Ray Donovan. Zimmer had been correct in her assessment: Ray was a jacked white boy. Toned and fit, with a mountain lion tattoo on his bicep. All those hours in the gym, Nick thought, only to end up like this. He had expected to find the body with its dick cut off or missing a finger or two. "He looks fine to me," he said.

"Help me roll him over."

Nick made a face as the ME handed him a pair of gloves. He held his breath as together they rolled Ray onto his side. Nick's heart about stopped when he saw the weird *B* carved into the back of Ray's side. What had Annalisa called it? A rune. "Oh, shit," he breathed.

"Does it mean something to you?" the ME asked.

Nick pulled back and Ray rolled over again, face up, his eyes unseeing. Just like he hadn't seen it coming. But then again, Nick hadn't seen it either. He held back another string of curses. He took out his phone and called Annalisa.

"Joe Green didn't kill Cyrus Merriman."

"What? How do you know for sure?"

"Because we've got another one." Could there be more? He was almost afraid to check because he feared he already knew the answer. Whoever sent that note to Joe Green had signed it with the rune, the Berkanan, the same way they signed their other handiwork—like the body lying cold on the metal slab fifteen feet behind him. Nick knew of only one psychopathology that operated like this with taunting notes and a desire to mark their victims. He swallowed hard and lowered his voice so the ME wouldn't hear him. "I think we're looking at a serial killer."

FIFTEEN

It took Nick four days to unearth three more potential victims, men pulled from the chilly Lake Michigan at various times over the past thirteen years: Travis Jenkins, Jamal Wellman, and Mike Loggia had all been classified as accidental drowning victims, although Jamal Wellman's family had always maintained that he hated the water and never would have gone near it willingly. All three had autopsy photos showing what looked like the Berkanan carved into their skin. Ironically, Travis Jenkins's name came up in one of the many "Possible Serial Killer Stalks Chicago" headlines that the media generated every April. The arrival of spring never failed to surface a bunch of bodies on Chicago shores, most of them drowning victims who had not been previously recovered, but whenever the cops pulled multiple bodies from the lake in the space of one week, people always started rumors of a serial killer. Now, it seemed, they had really missed one.

Nick gave Annalisa the names of the men but not much more than that, so she had to compile what information she could from news stories and public records. They all had been arrested at least once, for crimes ranging from assault to drug possession. Social media posts suggested that the most recent one to be found, Mike Loggia, had a girlfriend named Kelly Carver at the time of his death. That was three years ago, and from the pictures of her with a toddler girl, Kelly had moved on quickly.

"Are you going to interview her?" Annalisa asked Nick at the breakfast table.

"Ray Donovan is the priority," Nick replied. "He's the most recent victim."

Annalisa put raspberry jam on her toast as she considered how quickly Ray had moved from wanted murderer to victim. "Going to be hard to trace his movements," she said, "given that he was hiding out before he died. Something or someone must have lured him out. I'd reinterview his closest associates. They might be willing to talk now that he's dead."

Nick paused with his coffee halfway to his mouth. "I know how to do my job."

"I know, but—"

"You win, okay? It's an official case. There will be all kinds of headlines again for you if you want them. 'Detective Annalisa Vega Unmasks New Serial Killer.' Chicago PD somehow totally missed it."

He was exhausted. He was crabby. She tamped down her hurt and replied calmly. "I just miss working with you," she said. "That's all. It feels like old times, talking about a case again."

Nick's mouth twitched and his expression softened. "Yeah," he said gruffly as he reached for her hand. "I know what you mean." He squeezed her once and pulled back. "Are you going to tell Joe Green the good news? I mean before the press gets hold of the story. Right now, it's just me poking through old records, but Zimmer is making noises about setting up a task force." Fewer journalists on the crime beat meant they could keep these kinds of stories quieter now; if there wasn't a big public crime scene, no one paid attention anymore.

"Yes, I am going to see him today, actually." She planned to make the drive to confront Joe in person rather than through a computer screen. She wanted to see his reaction when she asked him about his first wife, Jessica.

"Joe's been locked up for all the murders but Cyrus's," Nick said. "No way he did those other crimes, which makes it more likely he's telling the truth that he didn't kill Cyrus either."

Annalisa gripped her coffee cup and said nothing. If the facts remained unchanged, Joe Green would get his fondest wish: he would be released, thanks to Annalisa's digging around in the case and a fresh body washing up on the beach. She knew Nick was correct about the timing, that Joe couldn't be involved in the later murders of the male victims, but she still wondered about Joe's missing first wife, Jessica. She wondered who hated Joe enough to put him behind bars in the first place.

....

JOE GREEN APPEARED IN THE VISITING ROOM WEARING A DRAB SWEATSHIRT THAT SUITED HIS NAME. The gray stubble dotted his face, and as he took the seat across from her, Annalisa looked at his hands. They showed age spots and a scar near the left thumb; his right pinky stuck out at a different angle from the others, suggesting it might have been broken and not healed correctly at some point in the past. These did not look like threatening hands, but then again, Joe was practically an old man now. The state might have freed him anyway simply because it did not make financial sense to keep him locked up when he had a low chance of reoffending. "You've got to be yanking my chain," he said when Annalisa told him of the latest developments. "A serial killer?"

"Maybe. The police are investigating now."

"So this *B* symbol. The rude?"

"Rune."

"Yeah, what the hell does it mean? It's like the killer's signature or something?"

"It means starting over, rebirth." Annalisa speculated that the killer was removing problematic men from the earth and "starting them over" in the next life. Karmic recycling.

Joe held a copy of the note in front of him, squinting at it. "So then this letter I got came from the real killer? I'll be damned. Why's he writing to me?"

"Maybe to gloat. He or she knows you didn't kill Cyrus Merriman but you still took the fall, so it's possible they relive that rush by contacting you. Or maybe they legitimately feel bad that you went to prison for a crime they committed."

Joe scowled and tossed the note at Annalisa. "Then where the hell were they during my trial? Why'd they let me rot in here for thirteen years before saying anything? I think it's that first thing you said—they're rubbing my face in it. But joke's on them, right? I'll be getting out of here."

"Too soon to say."

"The hell it is. First thing I'm doing, I'm calling my attorney and then I'm calling the press."

Annalisa widened her eyes, alarmed. "You can't do that. Right now, the killer doesn't know the police are onto them. If you broadcast it, you could cause them to flee or go underground or any number of actions that mean the real killer is never caught. Remember, a judge is only going to let you go if they have solid evidence someone else did the crime. That means finding the actual murderer."

Joe crossed his arms and looked away from her. "You better find him then."

"Or her."

He snapped his attention back to Annalisa. "You think a woman did this? Cyrus, he was a pretty big guy. How's a woman supposed to get the jump on him and toss him in the lake?"

"I don't know. But Cyrus abused plenty of women. One of them might have wanted revenge and to stop him from harming anyone else."

Joe stretched to pick up the discarded note, which he scrutinized once more. "Then you'd better talk to Gwen Beaufort, right?"

"Why do you say that?"

"She's the one who made up the lies about me, about seeing me with Cyrus. We all know by now that can't be true. So why'd she make up the story? I'm thinking she could be covering for someone. Maybe even herself." He jabbed at the table with his finger. "I'm still paying you, right? I want you to find that woman and make her admit what she did to me. Maybe you even catch a serial killer in the process."

"Sure, I can talk to Gwen." It would require a road trip to Wisconsin, but Annalisa had the same curiosity that Joe did. If he was indeed framed, then Gwen was critical to that frame. Annalisa did not believe Joe's theory that Gwen was their serial killer; Gwen lived six hours away from Chicago and Ray Donovan was murdered last week in the city. It seemed unlikely that she drove down to ice Ray and then returned to Wisconsin, but it was technically possible. "Listen, I wanted to ask you about your first wife."

Joe narrowed his eyes. "Jessica? What about her?"

"Her name came up a couple of times in my investigation—"

"What? How? Jessica was long gone by the time I got arrested."

Long gone. That could mean left or left for dead. Annalisa gave what she hoped looked like a casual shrug. "Someone didn't like you, Joe. Someone framed you for Cyrus's murder. Jessica seems like someone who might fit that bill. She left you, right? You didn't part on great terms?"

"We split up. I think that says it all."

"Why'd she leave?"

"She didn't exactly leave a lot of details in her note. It said, 'I need to be on my own for a while. I'll call when I'm ready.'" He spread his hands. "She never called."

"Nothing about where she went? She might have stayed with friends or family . . ."

"Search me. She didn't say and I didn't ask."

"You never went looking for her? Not once?"

He gave her a blank look. Annalisa chewed her lip and thought about her divorce from Nick, how messy and prolonged it had been with the yelling, the crying, and the one weekend it looked like they might call the whole thing off and get back together. She remembered the shabby little apartment he'd moved into with its view of the neighbor's brick wall and a stove that probably dated from the 1960s. She'd gotten her hair done and spent half her paycheck on a hip-snug pair of designer jeans before going over to drop off the last of his stuff. The idea that Joe's ex left him a note and walked out without ever seeing or talking to him again did not compute.

He shifted, looking uncomfortable. "Why all these questions about Jessica? You really think she's the one who set me up? It makes no sense. We'd been split up for years by then. I was with Vanessa. If anyone hated my guts then, it was her. Jessica was younger than me and I guess she got tired of the old man coming home at night with an aching back. She wanted to get out. She wanted to party."

"Who would she be partying with?"

"Whoever she could find. Look, I went to see a friend of hers a few days after Jessica split on me. Beth something. They used to swim together at the Y. I thought maybe Beth would know where Jessica went and how to get in touch with her. But not only did Beth not have any idea where Jessica was, she didn't even know she was with me in the first place. Can you imagine?" He seemed boggled by it all these years later. "She was pretending to be someone else the whole time. Anyway, I thought she'd get it out of her system and then come back home to me and my steady paycheck. She never did."

He seemed philosophical about it. Win some, lose some. Annalisa ventured a guess. "There's no trace of Jessica anywhere. Maybe she moved away." She paused and looked Joe straight in the face. "Maybe she's dead."

Joe didn't blink. But he almost smiled when he replied, "Maybe she is."

....

Annalisa needed a road trip buddy to Eau Claire, and she asked Sassy to join her. Nick was swamped at work with the revelations about a possible serial killer, and Annalisa believed she'd have an easier time getting Gwen to talk if she came without any cops. Sassy jumped at the chance for a break. "Ma and Pops volunteered to keep the kids for the weekend," she said.

They took Annalisa's Civic and left Sassy's minivan with the booster seats in it for Ma and Pops, not that they were likely to drive anywhere. *That thing has so many Goldfish crackers living in it I am surprised the mice have not moved in,* Ma confided in Annalisa the last time she drove Sassy's car.

"I warn you," Annalisa said as they started off, "I need to stop every fifty miles to pee."

Sassy snorted in reply. "I wish I could tell you that goes away after the kid is born."

"Stop. You're physically hurting me."

"Okay, okay, you might make it seventy-five miles afterward if you're lucky. But then you have to contend with the kid's tiny bladder. Remember what happened with Carla? She learned that 'I need to go potty' stopped the car while we searched out the nearest public restroom. Then she'd hop out at the gas station and ask for snacks instead."

"Oh my God," Annalisa said. "I'd forgotten that she took recreational bathroom trips to a whole new level. Alex once brought her down to see the police station and we showed her where people get their fingerprints done. Carla spotted an open holding cell and made a beeline for the metal toilet bowl, exclaiming loudly that she had a new potty to try. Alex grabbed her just as she was pulling down her little pink pants."

Sassy chuckled and sipped from her travel mug of coffee. "Alex joked he should've just left her locked up there until she was eighteen. Funny, huh, what you remember?"

Annalisa's smile faded. "Yeah, funny." She looked sideways at her friend. "How are things with Greg?"

"Good. I guess." Sassy picked at the rubber edge of her mug. "He keeps asking to take me up in his little airplane. He flew, you know, in the navy."

"I know. You don't want to go up?"

"He says it would be fun. He says it's amazing and peaceful up there, but all I can think about are the stories of small planes crashing and killing everyone on board. I'm the sole parent now. It's all on me. What if Carla and Gigi got orphaned because I had to pretend to be a bird?"

Annalisa did not point out that riding in the car with her was almost certainly riskier than going up in the plane with Greg. "What did Greg say when you told him this?"

"Oh, he said he's flown more than ten thousand hours with no problems. He says we would pick a totally calm day and the plane is inspected regularly for safety, and that flying is statistically the safest form of travel." She got quiet for a moment. "I know all that. But he also said it's not all on me anymore. That he loves the girls and will be there for them no matter what. I can see that he loves them. The other day, Gigi was giving her stuffed animals a spa day, you know, doing their fur at her toy salon? Greg was down on the floor with her making noises for the blow dryer and Gigi could not stop laughing." She choked back a sudden sob and reached over to grab Annalisa's arm. "That's what you'll find out when you have one—there is no sound on earth sweeter than your child's laughter."

Annalisa gave Sassy an answering squeeze. "But?" she said gently.

Sassy sniffed back her emotion, wiping at her eyes with her sleeve. "Greg wants it to be simple, but it's not. The girls have a father. He's gone but he's not forgotten—not by Carla, not by me, not by you or all the rest of the family. I see him in the way Carla takes over the room with her antics, making everyone laugh. I see him in the way Gigi can eat a whole bowl of salsa with a spoon. He's part of us and he always will be."

"You still love him."

"I hate that it's true. But yes, I've loved him since I was thirteen. If that's true even now, after everything he's done, after everything he's put the family through . . ." She shook her head. "Maybe nothing will change it. Not even Greg."

"Do you love Greg?"

"Yes," Sassy replied without having to think about it. "I look forward to being with him. I love the sound of his car pulling up to the house because I know when he walks through the door he will have a smile and a kind word for all of us. He cooks. He does his own laundry. If I don't snap him up, some other woman will."

"How is he not married already?"

"He was married for eight years. His first wife died of cancer. Her name was Lily and she taught piano. Greg still has it in his house. Carla takes lessons, as you know, and she loves playing on it so much more than our little electronic keyboard she practices with. I tried to stop her the first time because I saw it was making Greg tear up to see her playing Lily's instrument, but he said no, let her play."

"Oof, that's rough."

"Yeah." Sassy stared out the window at the flat, barren scenery. "We have that in common, I guess. We both love someone who's not around. Problem is, my ex is coming back one day. What happens when Alex gets out?"

Annalisa dreaded and longed for that day in equal measure. She had dreams sometimes about embracing Alex again. She hardly dared hope to get her brother back. "That will be years from now," she told Sassy. "What are you going to do in the meantime?"

"That's just it." Sassy replied to her reflection. "I don't know."

....

THANKS TO AN EARLY START, THEY PULLED INTO EAU CLAIRE BY MIDAFTERNOON, EVEN ACCOUNTING FOR NUMEROUS STOPS DUE TO ANNALISA'S BLADDER. "I understand why I'm here," Sassy said as she parked the car. "You need someone to share the driving. But what's with the six crates of canned vegetables in the back seat?"

"Plus six more in the trunk." Pops had a buddy in the grocery business who was able to get Annalisa a deal on the slightly dented cans. When she'd explained her plan, Pops kicked in an extra hundred bucks to her donation fund. She eyed the combination homeless shelter and soup kitchen they had pulled up next to and nodded her head at it. "Let's see if we can make a big splashy donation." Armed with a ton of vegetables and a check for five hundred bucks in her purse, Annalisa fixed a smile on her face and entered the shelter.

The women running the shelter were predictably excited to see Annalisa and her many cans of vegetables, especially when she topped it off with the cash donation. They ferried the boxes of vegetables from the car to the soup kitchen like ants at a picnic. A middle-aged blond woman wearing a sweatshirt that read LOVE LIKE JESUS hugged Annalisa and Sassy before saying, "Let me get our director, Gwen, to come say hello real quick. She'll want to thank you personally for your generosity."

"Oh, sure. I'd love to meet her." Annalisa's tone remained enthused and helpful, like this hadn't been the plan the whole time. Sassy suppressed a smile and turned away to admire some children's artwork tacked up on the wall.

Gwen Beaufort did not make them wait long. She came downstairs and greeted both of them with warm handshakes and effusive thanks for their donation. “I’d like to help you further,” Annalisa said. “Is there somewhere we could talk?”

“My office.” Gwen smelled a recurring donor and led them both upstairs with a smile. “Can I get you anything? Coffee? Tea?”

“No more coffee for me, thanks,” Sassy said, making a face. She’d refilled her travel mug at every stop.

“We’re fine,” Annalisa told Gwen as they made themselves comfortable on the worn leather couch.

Gwen fetched a clipboard and handed it to Annalisa with a pen. “If you’d like to fill this out, we can put you on the mailing list so you stay up to date with all the news from the shelter.”

“I will in a minute.” Annalisa put the clipboard aside. She’d given Gwen her full name and Gwen didn’t seem to recognize her. But then again, Gwen had left Chicago years ago. She probably didn’t get much news from the city. “Your work here is impressive,” she told Gwen. “I read that you serve more than a thousand meals per week.”

“That’s right. We have folks coming from surrounding towns too. There’s such a need right now in the winter months when people have to choose between heating their homes and feeding their families, which is why we count on support from our gold-tier donors—”

Annalisa cut her off before she could launch into her donor spiel. “That’s a really beautiful picture you have,” she said, leaping up and grabbing a photo from Gwen’s desk. It showed two girls, one a teen and the other elementary age, against a woodland backdrop. “Is this your daughter?”

“No, it’s me and my sister Natasha when we were kids.”

“It looks like it could be the UP.”

“It is,” Gwen said, giving Annalisa an appraising look as she took the picture and put it back on her desk. “We camped there every summer growing up.”

“Us too. So pretty.” She held her belly. “I can’t wait to take this one when he or she gets old enough. Do you and your sister still go camping?"

"Ah, no." Gwen's chin dropped to her chest. "She passed away when I was only twelve."

"Oh, I'm sorry," Annalisa said.

"Me too," Sassy added.

"Yes, well, never mind my personal story," Gwen said, taking a breath and forcing a smile. "What can I tell you about the shelter? We currently have more than three hundred clients, and forty percent of them are children."

"That's incredible," Annalisa said, looking around at the various accolades for the shelter on the wall. Gwen shaking hands with someone who looked like the mayor. A front-page write-up in the *Leader-Telegram*. "You know, this reminds me of a shelter in Chicago called Ruby's Place. Do you know it?"

Gwen closed her mouth. She looked from Annalisa to Sassy. "What is this? First you ask me about Natasha and then you bring up Ruby's Place. What's going on here?" Annalisa said nothing, using the silence to encourage Gwen to fill in the blanks however she wanted. "Is it Kevin? Did something happen?"

"I don't know who Kevin is," Annalisa said honestly. Sassy backed her up with a shrug.

Gwen regrouped. "Wow, okay. Maybe I jumped to conclusions but . . ." She chewed the inside of her lip for a moment. "No, the vibe is off. Most donors can't wait to hear about our work here. The two of you couldn't care less. What gives?"

"Tell me about Kevin," Annalisa suggested.

"So it is about him." Gwen sank into the armchair. "Kevin was Natasha's husband. He took my beautiful, talented, proud sister and turned her into someone afraid of her own shadow. When she finally got up the courage to leave him, he hunted her down and shot her in the street. He knew he was probably giving up his own life by doing so, but he didn't care. It was worth it to him to have her dead. The prosecutor assured me he wouldn't get out. Not ever. Please tell me he's not getting out."

"As far as I know, he's not." Annalisa rejoined Sassy on the couch. "We're not here about Kevin, although I'm very sorry to hear about your sister. Is that how you knew about Ruby's Place? Natasha was a client there?"

Gwen nodded and bowed her head. "They tried to help her. It didn't work. One of the detectives on the case, a woman, told my parents that when one person is willing to trade their life to take yours, there is little anyone can do to stop it. Can you imagine? Wanting someone dead so badly you'd sacrifice yourself to make it happen?"

Annalisa thought of her rooftop confrontation with the Lovelorn Killer and the realization that only one of them would make it out alive. "It makes you think," she said. "What you would give your life for—what you would give up to get justice for someone else."

Gwen looked at her with wonderment. "Who the heck are you?"

In answer, Annalisa took out her copy of the note that Joe Green had received saying Gwen had lied in her witness statement. Gwen looked it over and her mouth tightened. "I already talked to the police about this. It's bunk. I stand by what I said. I know what I saw." She folded the note and tried to hand it to Annalisa, but she refused to take it. Let Gwen hold it and live with it for a while.

"I went to the intersection where you say you were standing. It's not possible to read the license plate from the angle you had. You couldn't have seen Joe Green's truck."

"Obviously I did see it," Gwen said, snippy now as she tossed the note in Annalisa's lap. "So you're wrong."

"I don't know why you lied," Annalisa continued, her voice neutral. "I don't know if you had a specific reason for targeting Joe Green or if you piled on when the news reports named him as the suspect in the case."

"I've been over this with the cops. I did not know Joe Green before that night and I have no motive to make up a story against him. He was there. He was guilty. I wasn't the only evidence at his trial, you know. The police had physical proof it was Joe who killed that man."

Annalisa shook her head slowly. "No, the rest of the proof has evaporated. It's just your statement now."

Gwen appeared startled. "No. No, that can't be right. You're trying to trick me. Who are you, coming here to tell me this stuff?"

"I'm a private investigator hired to look into the case."

"Hired by whom?" When Annalisa didn't answer right away, Gwen's voice rose. "Who hired you?"

"Joe Green."

Gwen stood up. "I want you both to leave now."

"Ms. Beaufort, please listen." Annalisa scooped up the note and unfolded it again. "You see this symbol at the end? It's a Berkanan. It's been found on five male victims so far, including Cyrus Merriman. Joe Green couldn't possibly have killed the others because he's been in prison all this time. There's a killer out there who knows you lied. That doesn't worry you? Whatever reason you had for making up the story, it's time to tell the truth—for your own sake, if not Joe Green's. If you come forward now, they'll be less likely to file perjury charges against you."

"I told you what I saw," Gwen repeated, her posture rigid. "Maybe I was closer to the truck that night than I remembered, but I saw Joe Green's license plate, and you can't prove I didn't. To prove perjury, you'd have to establish both that my statement is not factually true and that I had an intent to deceive the court. You can do neither. So, goodbye now." She held out her arm to indicate they should leave. Sassy moved to go, but Annalisa stopped her.

"Whatever it is you're afraid of, I can help you," she said to Gwen, her voice low and urgent.

"Sure. Right. What are you willing to sacrifice? Isn't that the question?"

Annalisa considered this for a long moment. "I did trade my life for the truth, in a way. I put my own brother—my favorite brother—in prison. I could have looked the other way. Someone else would have gone down for the crime, as Joe Green has, and no one would ever have known. But I knew the truth." She stepped closer to Gwen. "And now so do you."

Gwen shook her head, denying what Annalisa was saying.

"Yes. Maybe you thought Joe Green was guilty when you gave that statement. But someone else killed Cyrus Merriman—someone who has gone on to claim multiple other victims. I don't know if you're covering for that person or not, but you should know they are very dangerous." When Gwen didn't say anything, Annalisa advanced a step closer, keeping her voice soft. "Maybe you didn't know Joe Green. Maybe you just knew what he was capable of. Maybe you knew Vanessa, his wife. Or . . ." Annalisa licked her lips. ". . . maybe you knew Joe's first wife. She seems to have disappeared."

"Stop it. You're rambling on, making a fool of yourself. I didn't know Joe or Vanessa or Jessica. I told what I saw. I happened to be walking my friend's dog that night, and believe me, I wish I hadn't been. I should have kept my mouth shut. I never should have gotten involved." She was trembling by the end and Annalisa saw the genuine regret on her face. Gwen wished she could take it all back.

"Maybe so," Annalisa said. "But you are involved now. The police are looking for answers and soon they're going to want some from you. Joe Green, too, if he gets out."

Gwen went pale at the thought of this and pressed her lips into a thin white line. "I want you both to leave." She said the words in a vicious whisper.

Annalisa put her business card down on the edge of the table. "If you want to talk, this is how to reach me." She and Sassy left the office and returned downstairs, where the female volunteers at the front gave them a cheery wave.

"You all come back soon!"

Annalisa answered with a tight smile and a finger wave. She didn't think Gwen would be welcoming her back, no matter how many vegetables she brought with her. Outside on the chilly street, Sassy clutched Annalisa's arm with excitement. "Did you catch that? She said she didn't know Joe's first wife, but then she said her name was Jessica. She knows her. She knows her!"

"That's why I wanted to come here in person rather than calling on the phone." It wasn't the same without the weight of a badge behind her, but her physical presence while she asked the hard questions often rattled the interview subject into making a mistake, as Gwen had.

"So what do we do?" Sassy asked, breathless as they climbed into the car. "Do we tail her? Bust her on the lie?"

In an ideal world, Annalisa could subpoena Gwen's phone records to see if she got in touch with Jessica Green, but even if she was still on the job, she wouldn't have enough cause to get a warrant. Not yet. "We're going to get a hotel room for the night," she said as she started the engine. "Then we'll find dinner."

"That's it?" Sassy was disappointed. "She gave us a hot lead and we're not going to do anything with it?"

"She gave us more than that," Annalisa said. "Did you catch her textbook definition of perjury? She may not be an attorney, but that woman knows her way around the law."

"I don't see why that matters."

"Me either—yet. Let's get the hotel room and I'll do some digging."

"Okay." Sassy settled back into her seat with a sigh and dug out her cell phone. "It'll give me a chance to call home and check on the kids."

Her phone buzzed in her hands and she emitted a surprised gasp. "Oh, no . . ."

Annalisa glanced over, trying to glimpse the phone's screen as she drove. "Trouble with Ma and Pops?"

"No, worse." Sassy turned the phone around to face her. "It's a news alert from the *Sun-Times*. The serial killer story is out."

SIXTEEN

CHARLOTTE STOOD AT HER APARTMENT WINDOW LOOKING OUT OVER THE LIGHTS OF THE CITY. The buildings and wide streets stretched on as far as she could see, melding into one hulking, architectural monster that swallowed any one human being. At supper earlier, the whole shelter had buzzed with the news that Ray Donovan might have been the victim of a serial killer. *That's karma for you,* one woman said, and Charlotte had excused herself from the table. A car sped by below her, the engine gunning, and Charlotte tracked its white stripe down the street until it roared around the corner and out of sight. Karma was still missing. So was Charlotte's gun. Charlotte had been to Karma's apartment a half-dozen times, had left her voicemail messages and sent emails that all went unanswered.

Danny had volunteered to get his law enforcement family members involved. "We can file a missing persons report," he said. "Then every cop in the city will be on the lookout for her."

"No." Layla had objected before Charlotte had a chance to answer. "No cops. If you get the police involved, Danny, I swear I'll never talk to you again." She'd stormed out leaving a bewildered Danny in her wake.

"I'm just trying to help."

Charlotte had rubbed his arm. "I know you are. But you have to understand: around here, the police don't help." It was sweet, really, that he thought the cops would be on the lookout for one ex-con woman, that he believed they'd be concerned for her safety.

A knock at her apartment door broke Charlotte from her ruminations. She checked her watch and saw it was after nine, which usually meant there was some sort of problem with one of the women or children. She hurried to the door and found Henry standing on the other side. He had a bottle of Pinot Noir in one hand and two glasses in the other. "I hope I'm not intruding," he said. "I thought you could use a little break."

Charlotte glanced at the wine. Her ex would get loaded up every time he'd hit her—the alcohol gave him an excuse for why it was never his fault. The sour smell of booze meant she would be backhanded across the mouth. She rubbed the burn scar on her arm through her sleeve as she let Henry into her living area. He was ex-military, smart, and trained to spot a deserter. If he started asking difficult questions about Karma, Charlotte would be hard-pressed to answer. As Henry poured the wine, she pondered how no matter how independent she was, how deeply she buried her past, she never seemed to escape this place where she needed to appease a man. That she had to fear what he might do.

She accepted the glass and forced a smile. "This is kind of you, Henry. Thanks."

"It's nothing fancy. What shall we toast to?"

Her heart was racing but she raised her glass to his. "To peace."

He looked pleased at the suggestion. "To peace," he echoed, clinking their glasses together. Charlotte took a small sip. On the counter, her cell phone buzzed and she rushed to check it, hoping it would be a message from Karma. No, just a political candidate urging her to donate. *Every dollar counts in the fight.* Charlotte shoved the phone in her pocket and returned to Henry.

"Everything quiet downstairs?"

"No trouble whatsoever." He eyed her. "You're still worried about Karma."

"She'll turn up."

He set his glass down, his brow wrinkling. "I confess I got worried when I heard they'd pulled Ray Donovan's body from the lake. From the way you went racing after her the other night, I wondered if Karma might have put him there—no pun intended. But now they're saying it could be a serial killer, and we know that can't be Karma."

"Right," she agreed automatically. She picked up the wineglass and clutched it. "How ridiculous even to think so."

"Oh, maybe not so ridiculous."

"Karma's five feet four inches tall. Ray Donovan was a muscleman. The victims—they're all large men. No way she could have overpowered them."

"She shot her ex, right?"

"These men weren't shot."

"No, but a gun might convince them to go for a swim. You have to admit, Karma is not the biggest fan of the male gender. Half the time, she looks at me like she'd like to shoot me in the nuts."

She set the glass aside and gave him a hard look. "You've really thought about this." He was more dangerous than he seemed. Maybe Karma had been right: don't hire any men. She tried to think of anything she could say to nip his curiosity in the bud. "Even if what you're saying is true, Karma couldn't have killed all those men. One of the victims, Travis Jenkins, was killed during the time Karma was in prison."

Henry looked surprised. "So you've thought about it too."

"No, I—"

"Enough to do the math," he pointed out.

"Karma's a victim." She enunciated each word. "Not a killer."

"I believe you," he said, but his gaze was speculative. "I've seen what the women here go through to get free—what they're willing to risk. I only know the vague details of Karma's case, but if she shot her ex, I'm sure he had it coming."

"She might have walked if she'd kept her mouth shut and asked for a lawyer right away. But she confessed everything." Karma had thought the cops would be on her side once they heard the whole story. Once they'd seen the bruises. Maybe they were sympathetic, but she'd admitted to attempted murder, and that's how they booked her.

"Well, if there is anything I can do to help find her, let me know."

"That's kind of you but it won't be necessary."

He heard the dismissal in her words because he frowned. "I won't go to the cops. I get it. At Ruby's Place, we have to look after our own." His brown eyes seemed sincere. "I want to help you, Charlotte. You just have to let me in."

How lovely it would be, she thought, to share the burden. She lived with the dread of what might happen if it all came out, what would become of Ruby's Place and the women and children sheltered within its walls. She'd thought she was protected. She'd tossed her secrets into the deep like the bodies in the lake, but like the bodies, they seemed to be washing up on shore. "I think," she began to say but then her phone rang. She dug it out and saw an unfamiliar number, a sight that usually made her ignore the call, but this time she felt a need to answer. "Hello?" she said, her voice cautious.

"Charlotte?" Karma sounded tired and afraid, but at least she'd called.

Relief washed over Charlotte and she pressed the phone closer to her ear. "Karma, thank goodness you're all right. We've been worried about you."

"I'm in trouble," she said in a small voice.

Charlotte's gut clenched at the news and she closed her eyes. "Where are you? I'll come right now and get you."

"You can't. I think I'm about to be arrested."

SEVENTEEN

ANNALISA LAY IN THE HOTEL BED, SCROLLING ON HER PHONE WHILE SASSY USED THE EN SUITE BATHROOM. She hoped Nick would get back to her with her question about Gwen's schooling, but so far, no reply. She couldn't fault him. No doubt he was caught in the media tornado now, with everyone wanting to know about the possible serial killer. She decided to run a search of her own and discovered that Gwen had been enrolled in law school at Northwestern University, the same school Cyrus Merriman attended. Were they there together? The dates seemed to line up but she couldn't be sure.

Sassy came out with her toothbrush still in her mouth. "You know what I was thinking in the shower? What if Jessica Green and Gwen Beaufort decided to do a *Strangers on a Train* scenario . . . you know, where Jessica kills Cyrus for Gwen because of something he did to her in law school, and then Gwen frames Joe Green for the murder to take care of Jessica's problem?"

"I think you've been watching too much true crime."

"Aw, come on. It's a good idea." Sassy waved her toothbrush at Annalisa. "Two guys fixed with one murder. You gotta admit, it's pretty brilliant."

"But then who killed the other men?"

Sassy looked perplexed, then annoyed. “Okay, so maybe that’s not the answer.” She stomped back into the bathroom to ponder some more while Annalisa picked up her phone again.

She had an email from Effie dated yesterday asking how the search for the ring was going and whether she had learned anything useful from her talk with Portia. Annalisa had delayed answering it because she didn’t know what to say. Portia had kept the secret about the fake ring for decades. She claimed she hadn’t waylaid the ring to prevent Effie from finding out, but Annalisa suspected someone else might have, meaning that any further investigation risked Effie learning that her husband had lied to her. Nick would love this predicament. *Some answers aren’t worth the cost,* he had argued. She now had to agree maybe he had a point.

Like he knew she was thinking of him, Nick called. Annalisa curled on her side and welcomed the sound of his voice in her ear. “Hey,” she said. “How are you holding up?”

“I’m still at work and afraid to go home. The press is growing like a tumor out there.”

“Sorry,” she said with sympathy. “Do you know how the story got out?”

“Oh, yeah. Joe Green and his attorney, who has found a new enthusiasm for the case now that it’s guaranteed a national spotlight. They have already started the drumbeat for Joe’s release.”

“That takes time.”

“Not if the governor steps in, which is what Joe’s lawyer is agitating for. He says Joe’s wasted too many years in prison for someone else’s crime and he should be released immediately, even if the state wants to put him through another trial. I’ll tell you, though, the worst call I got today was from Kara Merriman—Cyrus’s wife. She thought the whole thing was settled, that Joe Green murdered her husband, and now she finds out from the news that maybe it was a serial killer. She was ripshit we didn’t tell her, and I don’t blame her for that.” He took a deep breath. “Anyway, I had a spare two seconds and I ran that search you wanted.

Cyrus Merriman and Gwen Beaufort were both in the class of 2011 in law school at Northwestern, but only Cyrus graduated."

Annalisa rolled over onto her back and stared at the ceiling. "I wonder if Cyrus had anything to do with Gwen not finishing her degree. We know he was basically a human wrecking ball when it came to women."

"That could explain why she decided to sweeten the evidence against Joe," Nick agreed. "But it doesn't get me any closer to finding the killer." Annalisa heard his desk phone ring in the background. "Hang on a sec," he told her. The sound grew muffled as she heard him speaking on the other line. "Hey, I've got to run," he told her when he returned.

"Hot lead?" She missed the thrill of the chase.

"I'm not sure. They've got Karma Bryant detained at the twelfth district station."

It took Annalisa a moment to place the name. Karma had recognized the Berkanan symbol on the note Joe Green received. "You mean the woman from Ruby's Place? What happened?"

"I don't know, but they're holding her on a possible attempted homicide."

....

CHARLOTTE CRASHED THROUGH THE DOORS OF THE POLICE STATION WITH HER HEART IN HER THROAT. She had to get to Karma before Karma spilled everything. Henry, who had insisted on driving her, followed close behind as Charlotte begged the man at the desk for any information. "Karma Bryant," she demanded with her fists on the counter. "I need to see Karma Bryant."

"Karma Bryant," the young male cop repeated as he checked his computer. "Yes, she's here."

"Where?" Charlotte tried to see beyond him in the chaos.

"She's being interviewed by Detective Carelli at the moment. You can wait over there." He indicated the row of chairs against the far wall.

"No, I have to talk to her right now."

"Are you her lawyer?" His expression was skeptical.

"No, I'm her friend."

"Friends wait over there." He pointed at the chairs again.

"I'm her lawyer." Charlotte turned with surprise as Henry stepped forward. "Henry Holmes, esquire. All questioning needs to stop until I've had a chance to confer with my client."

The young cop looked Henry up and down before getting on the phone. "Yeah, it's Gonzalez at the desk. I've got a man here saying he's Karma Bryant's lawyer. Wants to talk to her." He kept his eyes on Henry like Henry might make a break for the back rooms. He uh-huh'd his way through the rest of the conversation and then hung up the phone. "I'll show you to room three," he told Henry. He pointed at Charlotte. "You still get to wait over there."

Charlotte gripped Henry's arm as he moved to leave. "Tell her to keep her mouth shut," she said in a low voice.

Henry looked determined. "Either they're charging her, or we're walking out of here."

Charlotte took a seat in one of the uncomfortable plastic chairs. Layla had texted three times, asking for an update. *Maybe I should come down there too.*

NO! Charlotte texted back a forceful response. The last thing they needed was Layla getting involved. *I'm handling it. Hopefully Henry will have her released soon.*

....

Charlotte could barely believe it when Henry reappeared five minutes later with Karma next to him. She looked terrible—pale, her hair a mess, and what looked like blood drops down the front of her gray sweatshirt. Charlotte almost gasped at the sight.

"It's my blood," Karma told her, tearing up. "He hit my face and I got a nosebleed."

"Shh." Charlotte moved to hug her. "Just keep quiet," she said in Karma's ear. "You can tell me everything later."

At that moment, Nick Carelli appeared from the back to join them, and Charlotte stiffened with renewed fear. This wasn't his precinct, which meant he'd come specifically for Karma. He didn't look enthused about it, she had to admit. His shirt was a wrinkled mess, his dark hair lank like seaweed against his scalp, and he sported a thick stubble across his cheeks. Charlotte had seen the news reports saying he'd unearthed a serial killer, but he did not seem like he wanted congratulations. "I remember you," he said, shaking his finger at Henry. "You're the security guy from the shelter. You're not a lawyer."

Henry drew himself up to his considerable height. "I know enough about the law to say you can't keep Karma here unless you're formally arresting her. Are you arresting her?"

Nick tilted his head at Karma, who shrank inside her clothes. "Not yet."

"Just what is it you think she's done?" Charlotte asked. Best to find out how much the police knew—or at least what they were willing to admit.

"Patrol unit responded to a 911 call saying a man was running down the street, being chased by a woman. He was hollering that she was trying to kill him and the 911 caller said she had a gun."

"I told you: he tried to rape me," Karma snapped. "I was walking out of the bar and he followed me. He pinned me up against the dumpster and tried to pull my pants down. I kicked him in the nuts and that's when he hit me in the face. So yeah, then I took out the gun."

"You admitted all this?" Charlotte asked her, worried. "You gave a statement?"

"I had no choice. They were going to hold me on gun charges because I have no permit and it's not my gun."

"We're keeping the weapon," Carelli said.

"It's my gun," Charlotte told him brusquely. "I loaned it to Karma. I have all the appropriate paperwork."

"That's great for you, but she's got nothing. We picked her up and she didn't even have any ID on her. No cell phone. Nothing. Like she was out there on the streets as some kind of ghost. She's lucky we're not filing weapons charges. The DA may still change her mind on that."

"And this man, the one who attacked her, are you bothering to question him?"

"He denies it. Says she's the one who followed him out of the bar. She threatened him with the weapon, and he tried to get the gun from her—that's when he bloodied her nose—and when he failed to gain control of the weapon, he started running." Nick folded his arms. "We have people looking for any CCTV footage that might shed light on the actual events."

"Well, if you find any, then we can talk again. Right now, we're leaving." Charlotte took Karma by the elbow and went to leave, but Detective Carelli moved to block them.

"Funny thing. The rune symbol that is carved into the victims—the Berkanan? Karma told us you have it tattooed on your leg."

Charlotte felt it like a burn. She'd gotten the tattoo years ago to cover some of the scars left by her abuser. To reclaim her body as her own. *Rebirth*. "What of it?" she said to Carelli.

"Odd coincidence, don't you think? First that message to Joe Green has the rune on it, and then Maya Ramirez comes to your shelter for help and her boyfriend ends up dead with your tattoo carved on his chest."

Charlotte's heart beat so fast she thought she might pass out in front of him but she kept her voice steady. "I don't have any explanation for that."

"I don't either," he said. His flinty gaze pinned her like a butterfly.

"Yet." He eased to the side and let her pass by with Karma, and Henry followed them out of the station. They walked like they were tiptoeing out of a haunted house.

In the car, Henry drove while Charlotte sat in the back with Karma. "Where have you been?" she asked the other woman. "We've been looking everywhere for you."

Karma hunched deeper into her seat and turned her face toward the window. "I was staying with a friend."

Charlotte didn't ask who. She also didn't ask Karma why she'd been out at a bar with a gun, but with no cell phone or ID. She feared that she already knew the answer. Henry met her worried gaze in the rearview mirror. "Thank you," she told him. "For your help back there."

"Don't mention it." He paused. "She's going to need a real lawyer, though, and quick."

Charlotte agreed with this assessment. Nick Carelli struck her as a smart detective—the news reports made it seem like he'd missed a serial killer at the time of Cyrus Merriman's death, but he was also the one bringing forth the evidence now. Charlotte wondered what else he might find. One thing was for sure: now that Karma was on his radar, it wouldn't take him long to notice the name in Karma's earlier arrest records and the plea deal when she shot and wounded her ex-husband. Her attorney was Cyrus Merriman.

EIGHTEEN

ANNALISA COULD DO NOTHING MORE FOR JOE GREEN AT THAT MOMENT, SO SHE DECIDED TO SPEAK TO LOUISE GAMBLE ABOUT EFFIE'S MISSING RING. Matilda the housekeeper said she had seen Louise with the ring the day it disappeared, and initially Annalisa had dismissed this as confusion or an invented narrative. Now, she suspected Matilda had been right all along. Her hunch was confirmed by Louise's dismayed expression when she opened the door to her son's house and found Annalisa standing on the doorstep. "I was afraid you'd get to me eventually," she said.

"Portia told me the truth about Theo's ring. She and Helen both know the origins, so I imagine you do too."

Louise's mouth tightened. "Oh, I didn't know for a long time. Helen only told me now because she had no other choice. Come in, won't you? It's cold." She led Annalisa to a cozy den where she was apparently in the middle of knitting. "I'm making a sweater for my new granddaughter."

"That's sweet."

"Do you knit?" Louise asked, eyeing Annalisa's belly.

"No, I never learned."

"Your mom?"

"No, I'm afraid she doesn't knit either."

Louise frowned like Annalisa's baby might go naked. "If you give me your address, I can send you a blanket and some hats."

"That's really generous of you to offer, but—"

"Every baby needs hats." Louise lowered herself into the easy chair and picked up her work on the pink and white sweater. "Sit, sit," she pestered Annalisa. "Get off your feet."

Annalisa needed no further urging. "I talked to Matilda and she said she saw you with Effie's ring the day it went missing."

"She caught me coming out of the bedroom. I have no idea what made her come up there. She had been downstairs making the pies. But I practically bumped into her in the hallway. She saw Effie's ring in my hand and there was no way I could deny it. I told her Effie was thinking of donating it to the charity auction."

"What did Matilda say?"

"I could see she didn't quite believe me. Effie's the spryest one of the lot of us; if she wanted the ring, she would have gone to the bedroom and gotten it herself. I was busted. Helen asked me to retrieve the ring from upstairs when she learned Effie was having it appraised. She would have gone after it herself but, you know." She paused her knitting to gesture at her left leg. "Bad knees. So that's why she looped me in. Portia and Helen would distract Effie and I would retrieve the ring."

"And then what was the plan after that?"

"Helen wanted to see if she could have one made for real."

Annalisa sat back. "For real? How much would that cost?"

Louise shrugged. "Helen has more money than God since Nathaniel died. Who knew fish sticks paid that well? But the jeweler would need to see the ring to be able to copy it well enough to fool Effie."

"So did you give Helen the ring?"

Louise looked chagrined. "No, my escapades as a cat burglar lasted exactly two minutes. Once I saw that Matilda wouldn't believe my story, I knew she would go running to Effie to ask her about it. We'd have to put the ring back and try again later. I gave the ring to Matilda and asked her to put it back in the bedroom for safekeeping. As far as I know, that's what she did. I saw her enter the bedroom."

"Did you see her come out?"

"No, I returned downstairs. But Matilda adores Effie, and she knows Effie loves that ring. She would never take it and upset Effie like that."

"Maybe Matilda knows the secret too."

Louise considered for a beat but then shook her head and resumed knitting. "No, the only ones who could have said anything to her would have been Theo himself or Effie if she figured it out. As far as we know, she never did. Theo wouldn't breathe a word. He took that secret to the grave." She paused again to give Annalisa a stern look. "And you better not tell her either."

"Effie hired me to find the ring."

"And I'm sure she'll pay you even if your search proves fruitless. Effie is good to her word."

"It's not about the money. It's about the truth."

Louise's expression turned melancholy. "The truth is Theo's love for Effie. The ring is immaterial. You're married, I take it? That's a pretty nice ring you have on too. But I'm betting it means more to you than the price would indicate."

Annalisa held out her hand to examine the diamond-studded band Nick had given her. "It's lovely," she agreed. "But it's just a symbol. I'm sure our relationship could stand it if I found out the stones weren't real."

"Is that so? You're comfortable with him lying to you?"

Annalisa shifted. Louise had her there. Nick had lied early and often in their relationship. They rebuilt with a new foundation of honesty. She had to admit if she discovered he'd deliberately kept the truth about the ring from her, she would wonder what else he might be hiding.

"Aha!" Louise said, reading her face. "Not so easy, is it?"

No, not easy, and in fact, somewhat harder now that they no longer worked as a team. There were things Nick didn't tell her, like when she asked how his interview with Karma had gone and all he said was "Fine." Or the things she didn't tell him, which is that she went to the Y to find out if Jessica Green and Gwen Beaufort could have been there at the same time. The computer records system had been overhauled five years ago, and no one could provide her with a definitive answer. Gwen Beaufort, it seemed, was forgettable. But not Jessica Green.

"A pretty redhead," said the old guy at the membership counter. He had to be near seventy but he was still buff under his tight T-shirt. "But she never smiled."

Annalisa thought about how women were trained to smile for men and mentally gave Jessica props that she wouldn't play along. But then the man said something else. "She came almost every day at lunchtime to do her laps, like clockwork for months. Then one day, she just quit showing up. She had half a year left on her membership, but she didn't ask for a refund or anything."

"Do you think she might have moved?" Annalisa had asked.

"Maybe. But I'll tell you what. The last day I remember seeing her, there was a man who showed up here looking for her. He didn't have a membership so he wasn't allowed back in there to get her, but he parked himself in that chair over there and watched the door like a hawk. When Jessica came out, she froze like she wasn't happy to see him. I asked her if he was bothering her, and she said no, it was fine." He shook his head. "It never set right with me. I felt uneasy, you know, watching him go off with her. Maybe a husband or boyfriend, but old enough to be her father."

Jessica had no living family, Joe had said when she asked him.

Annalisa had shown the man a photo of Joe from around the time he got arrested. "Was this the man you saw?"

He put on his glasses and took the phone from her to study. "Maybe." He pronounced it like "mebee." Then he shrugged. "Maybe not. I remember her more than him, you know? Mostly I remember the feeling I got looking at him. Not good."

"You'll see one day," Louise told Annalisa, pulling her from her thoughts. "The things you miss. I lost Stan after a long illness that slowly robbed him of his personhood, erasing finally the memory of how to breathe. But he called me Lulu till the end, which was a childhood nickname my sister gave me when she couldn't say 'Louise,' and Stan took it up too." The knitting sank to her lap, her face sagging with it. "They're all gone now—Mom, Dad, Margaret, and Stan. There is no one left to call me Lulu."

Annalisa would have no choice now but to follow up with Matilda if she wanted to uncover the truth about the ring. In the car, she went to turn the engine on but halted when the baby gave her a particularly strong kick. "Okay," she said. "I'll find a snack. How does a sliced apple with peanut butter grab you?"

She didn't get an answer from her stomach, but her phone rang and the call ID read Nick Carelli. "Hey," she said. "How's it going?"

"You may want to turn on a TV or a radio."

"Why? What's happening?"

"The governor showed up this morning in person. He wanted a walk-through of all the evidence we have in the serial killer case and how it relates to Joe Green. He saw pretty quick that the whole case rests now on Gwen's statement saying she saw Joe's truck, and Joe with Cyrus by the lake, the night of the murder."

"What did you tell him?"

"We told him Gwen's standing by her statement, which is true. But then he looked at the photos of the Berkanan symbols on the victims, and he seems convinced the marks on Cyrus Merriman are the same as the others. Oops, I gotta go. He's scheduled a press conference right outside."

Annalisa turned on her car's radio to WBBM, and sure enough, they were carrying the governor's news conference. After a few introductory remarks, he got right to the point. "My background is in law. We learned in school that the law may be written in black and white, but interpreting and applying it always involves a certain amount of gray. That's because there are human beings involved—the accused, the prosecutors, the police, and the defense attorneys—and none of us is perfect. Even the judges have to make . . . as you might say . . . judgment calls. I've reviewed the trial transcript for Joe Green's case and I've looked at the emerging evidence suggesting that Cyrus Merriman may have been the target of a serial killer. Now it's my turn to make a judgment. There is not yet sufficient legal cause to overturn the verdict in Joe Green's case. However, there is substantial new information that, if it had been uncovered at the time of his trial, may very well have altered the outcome. Given these new findings, I am ordering Joe Green be released pending further investigation. If, as I suspect, the results prove that he did not kill Cyrus Merriman, then the city of Chicago and the state of Illinois will owe Joe Green a large apology. He can start with me."

NINETEEN

Annalisa traveled the three-hour journey to the prison the next day when Joe Green was to be released. The press mobbed the parking lot, reporters angling for the best shot. Annalisa couldn't have gotten an audience with Joe if she tried, but she wasn't there to see him. Alex meandered into the visiting area with his hands in his pockets, looking perplexed at the sight of her. "I don't usually get visitors on the weekdays," he said as he took a seat across from her. "Did you come to see the show?" He gestured outside to where the three-ring circus waited for Joe to emerge. "Now that he's leaving, suddenly everyone can't get enough of him. He may well have grown old and died in here without anyone caring he was innocent, and now he's going to be walking around a free man. He's like a miracle man around here." He gave her an appraising look. "I guess that makes you the miracle worker."

"Don't give me too much credit."

"The way I hear it, you've uncovered another serial killer. Tell me, what's your secret?"

"You put me onto the case, remember? Maybe you're the one with the secret."

He deflated in his seat. "Not anymore. I'm clean like crystal." He looked up at her from underneath charcoal lashes. "How are the girls? How's Sassy?"

"They're good." She eyed him. "Sassy's still on the fence about getting married."

"Yeah?" He rubbed his thumb in a crack along the edge of the table. "Ma says he's a good guy."

"I checked. He is."

Alex gave a wry smile. "Can't be too sure, huh? Not after the first time."

Annalisa took a deep breath. This is what she came to talk to him about. "I was thinking it would help Sassy to have your blessing."

"What? Are you crazy? I'm supposed to sign off on some other guy sleeping with my wife and raising my kids? No way. I won't object—it's not like I'm in the position to do anything about it from in here anyway. But I'll be damned if I give her my blessing." He slouched like an angry teenager.

Annalisa took in his gray prison attire and the bars on the windows. He'd been in here for years already and would do at least ten more, maybe longer. From where she sat, Alex was already damned. She offered him the only hope of salvation. "Don't you want Sassy to be happy?" she said, her voice plaintive.

Alex faltered and looked at his hands. "Of course. It's all I ever wanted from the time we were kids."

"Well, then?"

"I was supposed to be the one who made her happy. Me, not him."

"And whose fault is it that you're in here and he's out there?"

"It's mine. I know it. Don't you think I'd give anything to be able to go back and change that night? I dream about it sometimes. It's so vivid but also like I'm watching a movie. I'm outside of myself—me, my age now, knowing what happens. I see myself getting loaded and heading over there to confront her and I start screaming at myself not to do it. But it's like I'm behind a soundproof wall. I can't hear me." He looked haunted by the end, his eyes dark and his face pale. "I didn't go over there planning to kill her. You have to believe me."

"I know." Annalisa's reply was gentle. "But you did."

He dropped his chin in a single short nod. He spread his hands in a gesture of surrender. "I worry that when I get out of here, there won't be any life to go back to. Everyone moves on while I'm standing still."

Pops was ill enough with Parkinson's that there was a good chance he wouldn't live to see Alex released. Ma, who knows? No one could see the future. Annalisa had never imagined they would be sitting like this now in a prison. That she would be remarried to Nick and expecting a baby. She'd wanted a large family, like the one she'd grown up in. Now she hoped for something better. She heard a commotion outside and so did everyone else in the room. One by one, they all got up and hurried to the windows, trying to glimpse the show. From this vantage point, Annalisa could just see the reporters flocking at the main gate.

"Get back," the guard ordered everyone. "Get away from the windows."

Annalisa saw the light fade from Alex's eyes as he returned to his seat. Hope, she supposed. That's what Joe represented to everyone at the prison. Alex was wrong that she was a miracle worker. But she was his sister. She reached over and took his hand. "I'll be there when you get out," she told him, giving him a soft squeeze. "I promise."

His quick answering smile was lopsided, a flash from their childhood. "You remember when I brought a laser pointer to school and Brock Devlin got ahold of it and convinced the principal he was under a sniper attack?"

"Brock got suspended, and Ma and Pops grounded you for a month as his accomplice."

"You argued for a reduced sentence. You said I didn't know what Brock would do with the laser when I gave it to him." He paused. "But I did know. So did you. We all knew what kind of kid he was."

The kind that would end up here, Annalisa thought. Aloud, she said, "I must've made a good argument because if I recall correctly, you got off with just a week."

"This is what you find out when you have a kid," he told her. "The punishment is worse for the parents."

"Hey, do you remember a girl from our neighborhood? She had kind of stringy blond hair and we used to play hide-and-seek?"

"Doesn't ring a bell. Why?"

"I've been having dreams about her. I can't figure out who she is or why she won't leave me alone."

"Ask Ma and Pops. They knew everyone in the neighborhood."

"Yeah, I'll do that." She glanced outside to where the Joe Green show looked like it might be wrapping up. "I should get going. Long drive back and all."

They hugged a quick goodbye and Annalisa went to retrieve her belongings so she could begin the journey back to Chicago. She checked her phone and there were no messages from Nick. Her attention on the screen, she didn't notice as she walked through the doors that the press was still waiting there. A throng of cameras rushed to greet her as people shouted questions all at once.

"Annalisa! Annalisa, Joe Green tells us you're the one who proved his innocence. That you found another serial killer."

"Annalisa, how does it feel to be cleaning up your husband's mistakes?"

"The Lakeside Killer has been active for more than a decade without anyone catching on before now—is this another Lovelorn Killer?"

Annalisa shielded her eyes. Beyond the crowd of microphones and digital recorders, she could make out the tall shape of Joe Green loping toward the shiny town car driven by his lawyer. He glanced back over his shoulder and she swore she saw him smile. "No comment," she said, setting her jaw. She tried to push through the wall of bodies. She wanted to catch Joe and ask him whether he'd followed Jessica to the YMCA all those years ago. But by the time she got free, the dark sedan was speeding away, carrying Joe off to his new life as a free man.

Berkanan, Annalisa thought. *Rebirth.*

....

KARMA SHOWED UP FOR WORK ON TIME, MEEK AND EAGER TO PLEASE. Charlotte saw no trace of her usual temper, but Henry worried. "Are you sure she's safe to be around the kids?" he asked as they watched through the window of the gymnasium door. On the other side, Karma led a group of about eight children in a series of games.

"I'm glad she's here where I can keep an eye on her," Charlotte replied.

"Any luck getting her an attorney?"

"I'm waiting to see what the CCTV footage shows—if indeed there is any to be found."

Henry glanced to where Karma and the kids had the parachute raised high over their heads. "She'd better hope it shows self-defense."

"It will." Charlotte feigned a certainty she did not feel. She bent down and rubbed absently at the tattoo hidden beneath her jeans. She liked to show it to the women who came into the shelter and explain its deeper meaning. *Your past doesn't define you. You can be reborn.* She wore it as a reminder of what she had overcome, but someone had taken it too literally. Kill the past. Become the future. She thought back to the moment Vanessa Green had come into the shelter more than thirteen years ago with her two kids in tow. Could they help her? Of course. Of course they could. Vanessa would have seen the news that Joe was getting out. What had she said? *Joe can never get the children. I'll kill him first.* The boy would be a teenager now. Would Joe try to come for him? Everything they had tried to cover up was coming undone. Once Nick Carelli started digging, there was no telling what he would find and what he would tell Joe. "I'm going to see if Danny needs any help getting supper together," Charlotte said.

Danny was the only one of them not on edge. He whistled a cheerful tune as he palmed and rolled meatballs into shape, setting each one in a large bowl like he was forming a nest. “Hey, boss,” he greeted her. “A crowd-pleaser on the menu tonight.”

“The kids will be thrilled.”

“Yeah, I’m almost sorry I’m going to miss it.”

“Oh?” Charlotte asked, more out of politeness than actual interest. “You’re leaving early tonight?”

“Rob’s covering for me.” His grin split his face, cheekbones riding high. “Layla finally agreed to go out with me. It only took like one year of asking. Don’t worry—I know to behave myself. I’ll make sure to take good care of her.” His smile faded as his face grew earnest. He knew he needed Charlotte to sign off on this union too. “Promise,” he added, like he was a teenage boy heading out to prom.

Charlotte barely heard him. “I’m sure you’ll do fine. Please excuse me.” She went in search of Layla and found her doing paperwork in the main office. She looked oddly calm, considering the circumstances, and greeted Charlotte with a gentle smile.

“I’ve found an apartment for the Ortiz family. They can move in on Monday.”

“That’s great, Layla. Thank you.” Charlotte drew up a chair next to the small second desk. “I just came from the kitchen. Danny is over the moon at the prospect of your date.”

Pink tinged Layla’s cheeks and she looked down at her laptop. “We’re just going for pizza and then bowling.”

Layla spoke the least of them about her life before the shelter. Unlike Charlotte and Karma, she didn’t have outward scars. Her abuser had wounded her on the inside, in places that were the most difficult to heal. Charlotte scooted closer and kept her voice low. “Do you think that’s wise?” she asked. “I mean given the timing and everything that’s going on. That detective, Nick Carelli, he’s still poking around about Karma.”

“That’s her problem, isn’t it?” Layla stood up abruptly, leaving Charlotte blinking in surprise. They were all vulnerable now that Joe Green was getting out—Charlotte, Karma, Layla, Gwen, and maybe especially Vanessa, whose attempt to flee all those years ago set this whole thing in motion.

Layla stood with her back rigid at the filing cabinet, rummaging for nothing in particular. "It was stupid of Karma to go out like that alone. She could have been killed."

Charlotte stood up and went to join her at the cabinet. "It wasn't a great idea, I'll grant you. But she was trying to protect us. To protect you." She tried to brush a lock of hair from Layla's shoulder, but the other woman shrugged her off.

"I'm tired of being protected. I want to live."

"And any other time I would support that. But right now, we need to be cautious." Charlotte couldn't shake the dread she felt at the prospect of Joe going free. They had put him there and lived with the lie for thirteen years. Now that he was out, the universe was unbalanced again, and she feared that one or more of them would replace him on the inside. Layla's strange equanimity in the face of their nightmare made Charlotte wonder. "Did you send Joe Green that anonymous note?"

Layla whirled, looking horrified. "I want nothing to do with that man. Ever."

"I know. I know. But someone did." *Someone knows,* she thought. She felt so guilty at times that she imagined she could have written the note in some fugue state.

Layla remained unruffled as she closed the file drawer. "It must be the killer, no? That's what the news is reporting."

"Yes. And that doesn't worry you?"

"No. The killer targets men." She smiled. "And Danny will be safe with me."

....

THAT NIGHT, THE NEWS CHANNELS ALL FEATURED JOE GREEN'S SHORT PRESS CONFERENCE IN FRONT OF THE PRISON. His lawyer, Eugene Lynch, did most of the talking. Joe said he was grateful to the governor for his freedom and he hoped that maybe now the authorities could truly find out who had killed Cyrus Merriman. The attorney hinted at a lawsuit to come. Joe looked uncomfortable at the prospect and the attention. He kept his head down and shuffled his feet like he couldn't wait to get away.

When the news report shifted to Annalisa coming out of the prison, she gasped at the sight of her own face. Nick turned his back to her in bed. "Can you turn that down? I need to get some sleep."

"I didn't go there expecting the press to talk to me."

"Sure." He punched the pillow with his fist. On the TV, Nick's face flashed as the chyron underneath said DETECTIVE MISSED A SERIAL KILLER. Annalisa turned off the television. She cuddled up against Nick from behind, their growing child trapped between them, and his body gradually relaxed its rigid posture. But they didn't sleep. They lay curled like two question marks in the dark.

....

ACROSS TOWN, CHARLOTTE WATCHED THE NEWS IN HER PRIVATE APARTMENT, CHEWING HER NAILS AND WORRYING. She heard a knock at her door and saw the shadow underneath the crack. Henry, probably, offering tea and sympathy. She wanted neither so she did not answer it.

....

VANESSA GREEN REFUSED TO WATCH JOE'S FACE ON-SCREEN, BUT SHE HAD NO CHOICE BUT TO SEE IT IN HER OWN HOME. Their son, Michael, looked just like him. "I don't remember him," he said of his father. His young face wrinkled in worry beyond his sixteen years. "Is he going to want to see me? Do I have to meet him?" Briana had started having nightmares again since that horrid private detective woman came around asking about Joe. *You said he'd never get out*. Vanessa had been ready to run until the moment that Cyrus Merriman turned up dead and answered all her prayers. Now, she thought, she wouldn't run. She would stay and fight.

....

KARMA DIDN'T WATCH THE NEWS. She went out into the cold night, walking the empty streets while she still could. She swore she could hear the detective's footsteps behind her and turned around twice, imagining she glimpsed him in the shadows. The Berkanan promised a second chance, but Karma felt like she could never be free of what she'd done. A halfway crime. Her ex remained free, living in Poughkeepsie, New York, probably with some new woman under his thumb. Now Joe Green was out too, walking the same streets as Karma. Maybe this time she could fix things for good.

....

JESSICA GREEN SCROLLED THROUGH THE NEWS ON HER PHONE. Joe got national headlines, his face everywhere; all those eyeballs on him and still no one could see him for what he really was. Like back when she was little and they put missing kids' faces on the milk cartons, their sweet faces everywhere and yet nowhere all at once. She'd read somewhere that the milk carton campaigns had failed to bring home even one child. That one boy who started it all, Etan Patz, had been dead from the first afternoon he vanished. And that little blond girl in Madison who had vanished from the Christmas parade was never recovered. What was her name? It was harder to remember with each passing year. It was easier to disappear than anyone liked to think. Jessica studied her reflection in a compact mirror as she put on lipstick. She would worry about Joe later. Right now, she had a date to keep.

TWENTY

HIS LAWYER TOLD HIM TO LAY LOW. Don't talk to the press. That was fine with Joe; he wanted nothing to do with the limelight. He was nobody's hero. But he hated being cooped up inside the hotel room. One room, four walls. It was bigger than a cell, and the bed sure as hell was more comfortable, but even a palace can be a prison if you're not allowed to leave. So, Joe went out. He felt like a toddler learning to walk again and wished it were spring so he could feel the grass under his bare feet. The sharp blue winter sky hung huge over his head. People rushed past him on the streets in a hurry to get somewhere else. Doors opened and he waited for permission to walk through them.

The same lawyer who set him up with the hotel room also gave him a prepaid credit card to boot. Joe knew the man smelled a multimillion-dollar lawsuit. Wrongful imprisonment. The bill started at one million per year, and Joe had done thirteen and change. He liked the idea of the money, but he didn't want to spend even one more day in a courtroom to get it. He thought about those millions as he walked down the Magnificent Mile. After scraping by, working hard building other people's houses or raking their yards, how would it feel to be able to go into any of these fancy stores and buy whatever he wanted? Money talked pretty loud if you knew what to say with it. How about that $1500 he'd saved up to hire Annalisa Vega? Best money he'd ever spent. He'd been nervous when Alex first suggested the idea. Alex swore that once Annalisa started digging, she wouldn't stop for anything, and this is what Joe feared. But no. She had stopped in precisely the right place.

He went to Millennium Park, where he spread his arms and turned around in a slow circle, his face to the sun. He never imagined he'd be free again. He bought a hot dog from a street vendor. He studied his face in the Bean. Prison had made an old man of him—gray and hairless. He'd thought he landed there because the cops got lazy, pinning Cyrus Merriman's murder on him because he was the most convenient target, but the note he got suggested maybe it was a frame-up from the start. The note was maybe from the real killer, Annalisa said. Well, let her look for him. That should keep her busy. Cyrus Merriman wasn't Joe's problem anymore, and whatever Vanessa might have told him back then, Merriman had taken it to his watery grave. Joe was free at last.

He tried to behave and do what the lawyer wanted. He spent the afternoon in the hotel watching movies and ordered a steak dinner through room service. But he'd been eating, sleeping, and even pissing on another man's schedule for thirteen years. He would keep his own time now, thank you very much. He looked at the simple Timex piece around his wrist, which had been given back to him upon his release, along with the pants and shirt he'd been wearing when he was arrested. Where had they been keeping his stuff all these years? The watch had stopped, he saw now. He flicked it hard and put it to his ear. Nothing. He wondered about that credit card and what the limit was. He could buy a new watch, a better one—or hey, what about one of them fancy new cell phones? They were new on the market when Joe went away. Now they seemed to be everywhere.

Joe took his credit card and went down to the hotel lobby. He spotted a single mom with a brown-haired girl about nine years old. She reminded him of Briana. She looked bored as her mother tried to negotiate something at the front desk. Joe ambled over to her. He'd always been good with kids. "Hey," he said, taking a seat on the velvet bench. "You want to see a magic trick?"

She wrinkled her nose but came closer. "You're not going to pull a quarter out of my ear, are you? Because that's lame."

"The lamest," he agreed. "No, I can make a pencil float in my hand. You have a pencil?"

She checked her little backpack and furnished him with a pencil. While she was searching, Joe affixed his own pencil under his useless watch. Then he took the girl's pencil in his hand and slipped it so the other pencil held it in place in his palm where the girl couldn't see. "Abracadabra, hokum pokum, eenie, meenie, miney, moe . . ." She giggled as he waved his free hand over the pencil. Then he opened his palm and the pencil appeared to float in his hand.

"Wow," the girl said. "That's cool. Can you show me how to do that?"

"Sure," he told her. He glanced up at the mother, who had noticed her daughter talking to a stranger. He tried to give her a reassuring smile. She was attractive—honey-blond hair, tailored clothes. He didn't see a wedding ring.

"Natalie," the mother said as she strode over to them. "Don't be bothering this nice man."

"I wasn't. He's showing me a magic trick."

Joe stood up and extended his hand to the woman. "Joe Green, at your service. Sorry if I overstepped. She looked ready to run for the hills. I know how it goes with the little ones."

The mom shook his hand but didn't offer her name. She still looked wary. "You have grandkids?"

Oof, Joe thought. He really had gotten old. But Mike, his son, would still be a teenager. If he had a kid already, that would be bad news. "Sure," he fibbed. "Don't see 'em as much as I'd like." He just needed to keep her talking, win her confidence.

"Wait a second," the woman said. "I know you. You're that man who just got released from prison." The little girl's eyes grew round.

"Yes, ma'am. They locked me up for someone else's crime."

"That's what the news said." She looked sympathetic now. "It's just awful what happened to you, but what an incredible story—to be freed because they think there's a"—she covered the girl's ears—"serial killer on the loose. I heard that even Oprah wants to interview you."

Joe hadn't heard any such thing. "It would be a pleasure to speak with her. I hope my story can, you know, bring hope to others who might be locked up for something they didn't do."

Natalie, the girl, squirmed away from her mother and reached for Joe's hand. "Show me how to do the trick now," she said.

"If it's okay . . ." Joe risked a glance at the mom.

"Oh, of course. I'd like to see it too." She smiled and Joe knew he had her. He went through the trick for them, all the while plotting his next move. The hotel had an upscale hamburger joint attached to it. He'd offer to buy them dinner and milkshakes to celebrate his newfound freedom. Who could resist?

"That's clever," the mom said when he'd finished his demonstration. Joe straightened up and prepared to ask her name and make his pitch. Right then, a man entered the lobby from outside, his eyes searching. He looked like one of the J.Crew mannequins Joe had seen earlier on Michigan Avenue. He smiled when he spotted Natalie and her mom, and Joe held back a beleaguered groan. Of course, there was a dad.

"Honey," the woman said, light in her eyes. "Meet Joe Green—the man from the news."

Joe shook the man's hand. He even learned the woman's name—Stephanie—but it didn't matter anymore. *You have to give it time,* he coached himself as he said goodbye and went out into the cold night air. *The perfect situation isn't going to land right in your lap.* He'd had to spend a couple of months courting Vanessa, buying little treats for Briana and bringing Vanessa roses he'd picked from some client's garden. *Ease back*, he thought. *You'll find the one you're looking for soon enough.*

The restless feeling inside him didn't subside and he gave up on the idea of shopping. The stores would be closing soon anyway. He walked instead, eventually finding himself down by the water near the planetarium, not that he'd ever been inside. He sat on the cement steps that led directly into the cold black lake. The chill from the concrete seeped into his bones as the wind roared off the water and into his face, like it was screaming at him to leave. Ever stubborn, Joe didn't listen.

With the wind whistling past his ears, he didn't hear her come up behind him. In the dim light, she cast no shadow. She appeared sitting beside him like she'd been beamed there from another world. He glanced at her once, then again as recognition set in. *Well, shit*. This was no coincidence. She had to have been following him. He lost track of her years ago, but of course she knew exactly where to find him. The news had practically drawn her a map. "Been a long time," he offered when she did not say anything.

She had her hands in her coat pockets. Her eyes fixed on the choppy waves in front of them. "Bet you thought it was all over," she said without looking at him. "That you'd never see me again."

He grunted. "I'd hoped." He looked sideways at her. "You look good."

"No thanks to you."

"Look, what is this? You saw the news, is that it? You think I'm getting a big payment now and you want in on the action?"

For the first time, she looked him dead in the face. "I'd be entitled."

Like hell. She'd been free as a bird while he did hard time. He opened his mouth to tell her off but then shut it again. If she went to the press, he'd be finished. She read his mind and gave a thin smile.

"I've kept your secret, if that's what you're wondering."

"Yeah? Thanks, I guess." The wind picked up again, shearing him through his coat. Maybe he should get the hell out of the city. Go somewhere warm. "I've got no money, if that's why you're here. Maybe there'll be a payout down the road, but maybe not." He shrugged, philosophical. "I just want to get on with my life."

"That's too bad," she replied.

He didn't understand what she meant. Was she mad he didn't have money to pay her off? "You can run along then. Go back wherever it is you came from."

"I can't." She squinted into the wind. "You saw to that."

"Aw, come on now . . ."

"Did you like my note?" She was watching him again, gauging his reaction. "The one I sent you in prison?"

He'd gotten no mail from her. He'd have damn sure remembered it. "I don't know what note you're talking about."

"'Gwen is lying. Joe didn't do it,'" she quoted to him.

His jaw fell open. "That was you? You knew the whole time I didn't kill Merriman and you let me rot in prison? For thirteen damn years? Where the hell were you at my trial when that lying witch set me up?"

"I kind of hoped they'd kill you." She let him parse that for a moment. "I've heard that happens in prisons, especially to men like you. Once it became clear they wouldn't ever be bothering with that, I had to do something."

"You got me out." So there it was. She did want the payoff after all. "I always knew you were a smart one."

"Smarter than you," she agreed, taking her right hand from her pocket.

Joe saw the glint of a switchblade. "Now wait a minute—"

She shoved the knife through the gap in his coat and right between his ribs. He gurgled at the shock of it. Blood filled up his mouth and he tried to get up. She stabbed him again. He thought back to the moment he'd first seen her, how pretty and delicate she was and how he had to make her his. Here at last was payback. *Should've bought the watch,* he thought as she rolled him into the waves.

TWENTY-ONE

Joe Green's body turned up right away, the current bumping him repeatedly against the concrete wall as though the lake was an angry toddler with an unloved doll. Annalisa heard the call on the scanner and went to the scene with the rest of the looky-loos, but she was no longer allowed inside the perimeter. She had a small set of binoculars in her pocket, which she used to scan the faces of the men down at the lake's edge. She located Nick, looking grim as he stood over the black bag that contained the latest body. Nick knelt down and unzipped for a closer look. Annalisa knew he had to be searching for the Berkanan. Nick had a tell: when he expected one thing and got another, he would blink rapidly for a couple of seconds. Annalisa saw the blink and turned away. *No Berkanan,* she thought. Not unless it was hidden somewhere else on the body, and the divers said Joe had been found in all his clothes. Even his wallet had been left in his pants, making it easy to identify him even if he hadn't been all over the news. Maybe it was an accidental drowning. Maybe Joe, unused to freedom, tied one on and fell into the lake. This was more or less how most bodies ended up there. Annalisa turned around again and searched out Nick among the crowd.

He was on the phone, walking away from the body. She could see the set of his shoulders and the purpose in his stride. No, this wasn't an accident. Someone had killed Joe Green only days after his miraculous release. The obvious suspect would be whoever had put him behind bars in the first place. Gwen Beaufort? She was all the way up in Eau Claire. Vanessa Green? She had wanted to be free of Joe badly enough to endure Cyrus Merriman's sexual abuse, although she denied that Joe ever laid a hand on her. Annalisa knew she should walk away at this point; her client was dead. Only problem was, she had a terrible feeling someone had engineered it that way, and that Annalisa had been part of the plan.

She took out her phone as she walked away from the crowd and back toward her car. Moments later, she had Joe's lawyer, Eugene Lynch, on the line. "Is it true?" he asked her, and she heard the news playing on the TV in the background. "Is it Joe?"

"Looks that way."

Lynch answered with an epithet. His multimillion-dollar lawsuit had drowned in the lake the same as Joe. "He has a kid, right? Mike or Ben or something? Maybe the kid would be entitled to lost wages, at least."

"Glad we're keeping our eye on the ball here," Annalisa said as she climbed inside her car.

"He's dead. Murdered, maybe? The reports aren't clear." Lynch sounded like he didn't give a crap either way. "I obviously didn't kill him, so I don't know how I can help you anymore, Ms. Vega."

"You rented him the hotel room, right? I want to get inside."

"Why?" He sounded suspicious.

"Because I feel used. Frankly, so should you. We fought to get Joe Green out of prison just for someone to kill him three days later. I don't think that's a coincidence, do you?"

"You're telling me his killer wanted him set free so they could murder him?"

"It looks that way to me."

"It could be a random mugging for all you know. This city . . ." He let his voice trail off. The muffled sound of the TV had switched to a different murder. "It'll kill you soon as look at you."

"The city didn't put Joe Green in the lake. A person did, and I'm guessing it's the same person who put Cyrus Merriman there. Someone who plans to keep right on killing. Give me five minutes in Joe's hotel room. That's all I need."

"Fine," he said with a resigned sigh. "I can meet you there at five."

"No, it has to be now." She had maybe a couple of hours' head start on Nick at the hotel room because he would want to be with the body at the morgue. First order of business would be to try to confirm it was the same killer. Next, he would be at the hotel trying to trace Joe's movements. Annalisa had to be in and out before he got there.

"I can't meet you now. I have a client coming in thirty minutes."

"Move the meeting," Annalisa told him as she started her engine. Before he could object, she continued, "Look, someone used both of us to free Joe Green, and that person is most likely the same someone who murdered him. I'd like to know who that is in case they ever come calling again. Wouldn't you?"

Silence as he digested this. "I'll meet you at the hotel."

Eugene Lynch was a small, balding man in a big trench coat. He got the front desk to issue him a new key card and they rode up together in the shiny elevator. "Joe asked me if the gold was real," he said, nodding at the trim, his smirk showing what he thought of the question. *What a rube.* "You would have thought I booked him a room at Versailles."

Annalisa ignored the lawyer as she took the card and located Joe's room, 1134. Donning latex gloves from her pocket, she tucked her hair in a hat and put disposable booties on her feet. When Lynch tried to follow her in, she held up her palm. "You wait out here."

"It's my room."

"It's now a crime scene." She knew how to leave the room virtually untouched. Lynch would muck around like the entitled asshole he was.

Joe Green had kept the room tidy. Annalisa guessed he didn't have many belongings to create a mess. She checked the closet and found exactly one suit hanging there. Toothbrush, toothpaste, and shaving kit in the bathroom. She found an opened bottle of Jim Beam at the counter of the kitchenette, and one glass beside it. There was no sign of any disturbance, no indication Joe had any visitors here, and certainly nothing to indicate he'd met his killer in this room. She checked the trash and found it empty. The maids must have been by already. She snapped a few pictures with her phone to document the scene, right down to the lone gray suit in the closet. When she glanced down to make sure she'd gotten the shot she needed, she noticed a safe at the foot of the closet.

She knelt to study it and guessed from previous experience the digital lock would require a six-digit code to access. She tried Joe's birthday, which she knew from her earlier research into his case. Nothing. She tried the date of his release and that failed too. On a whim, she tried 123456 and the lock released. She rolled her eyes as she opened the door. *What a rube.* Annalisa snapped a shot of the mostly empty safe before examining the contents. Not much there. Joe had a single manila envelope that contained a few photos—a posed shot of him and his son Michael as a baby, with proud Joe holding the one-year-old on his lap. Another of what looked like Vanessa's daughter, Briana, eating pancakes at the diner years ago. The camera sure loved her, zooming in to capture her little cheeks and the sweet pink bow of her mouth. She'd been happy in this picture, Annalisa noted. Maybe that's why Joe had kept it. To prove he'd been part of a loving family at one point in time.

The third photo was more of a mystery. It was a faded, old-time Polaroid that showed three kids, a redheaded boy and two girls, posed in front of a nondescript brown house with a tan station wagon off to the side. The boy was the eldest, perhaps eight, with a kindergarten-aged sister and the curly-haired toddler holding her sister's hand. No leaves on the trees. Kids in pastel dress clothes. Annalisa guessed maybe it was Easter and that if she could zoom in she might see crocuses just popping out of the ground near the children's feet. As it was, she could make out no distinguishing characteristics in the kids' faces. They were Caucasian and looked to be well cared for, but the setting could be anywhere from the Mississippi River on east. Annalisa knew the boy couldn't be Joe. He had been born in 1958, and from the clothes and the model of the station wagon, this shot seemed more recent, perhaps taken in the 1980s sometime. Maybe, Annalisa reasoned, he had other family someplace. She took photos of all the pictures and then also snapped a shot of his social security card, which was the only other item in the envelope.

After she had replaced everything where she found it, Annalisa went back into the hall where Eugene Lynch stood scrolling through the messages on his phone. "It's blowing up," he told her. "Media wants to interview me." He looked her up and down. "Did you find anything worth telling them about?"

"No," she replied.

"Great. Let's check out."

She stopped him with a hand on his arm. "You can't release the room yet. It's still part of a crime."

He sighed, heavy with regret at his lost millions. "You're damn right it is."

Annalisa saw the cops had already arrived in the lobby by the time they got down there. She let Lynch try to settle his bill as she slipped out the side door before anyone spotted her. She did not want Nick to know she was running a parallel investigation. If she crossed paths with him, he'd be furious, and rightly so. This was their fundamental difference: Annalisa's first allegiance was to the truth, not her people. Not even Nick. Still, she didn't want to look like she didn't trust him to run a competent investigation or to set him up for more on-the-job ribbing—*Little Nicky's wife has to check his homework!*—so she parked around the corner from Vanessa Green's front door. She'd tried the restaurant first and been told that Vanessa hadn't been there for three days. The house looked like it was under siege: all blinds drawn, no movement heard within.

Annalisa knocked and waited. When she got no reply, she knocked again. "The police are coming, Mrs. Green," she called through the door. "You're going to have to talk eventually. Joe's dead now. Don't you think it's time the truth came out?"

Finally, the door cracked open and Vanessa peered at her with one wild eye. "You don't get to come here and talk to me about truth. I know who you are. You're married to that cop. The one who screwed up the first investigation. Now he's the one that let Joe go free."

"No, ma'am, if you want to lay blame for that, it's on me."

The eye narrowed. "Like you say, Joe's dead. There's nothing anyone can want from me."

"I only want a few minutes of your time," Annalisa said. "Then I'll go."

Vanessa's little girl wound around her legs and peeped up at Annalisa with a winsome smile. "I have a new stuffie. Wanna see?" She produced a small stuffed dog to show Annalisa.

Annalisa crouched down with effort. "Oh, he's nice."

"She," the girl corrected with a sniff. "Her name's Elsa."

"I like her. Do you ever watch *Bluey*?"

Vanessa gave a mirthless laugh. "Constantly."

"I have some *Bluey* stickers in my pocket." She had picked them up at the checkout line at the grocery store and been saving them for Gigi. The girl's eyes grew round when Annalisa pulled them out partway.

"Can I?" she asked her mom. "Please?"

Vanessa hesitated and widened the door. "Come in," she said. "Five minutes."

Annalisa gave the stickers to the child as she entered, and the girl ran off into the back of the house with her new prize, stuffed dog forgotten on the floor. Vanessa bent to pick it up. "Her dad got her the dog," she said as she placed it on the counter. "She wants a real one and I've told him if he gets a puppy it damn well lives at his place. He says we could share it like we share Julie." She snorted and looked to Annalisa to see what she thought of this idea.

"I'm guessing you have Julie most of the time," she replied.

"Bingo. Men don't know what it is to look after a living thing. How damn tiring it is. Or maybe that's the truth—they do know, and that's why they don't want to do it." Vanessa pulled out a stool and perched on the edge. "Okay, your five minutes are ticking. What could you possibly want to ask me about poor dead Joe?"

"He kept a few photos," Annalisa said. "Would you mind taking a look at them?" She showed the woman the snapshots she had taken. Vanessa frowned at the one of Joe and their son Michael. She looked at the one of Briana for a long time, until tears appeared in her eyes.

"She was a pretty little thing," Vanessa whispered. "Sassy too. Look at her mugging for the camera. You're saying Joe has this picture?" She shuddered and tried to give the phone back to Annalisa. "They say the devil does like to admire his handiwork."

Annalisa called up the mystery photo of the three little kids and showed it to Vanessa. "What about this one? Do you recognize it?"

Vanessa glanced once, disinterested. "No. Sorry. Was there anything else?"

"The restaurant says you haven't been at work for a few days."

"You've been checking up on me?"

Annalisa couldn't believe she had to spell it out. "Ms. Green, your ex-husband is dead. There is a violent killer on the loose. If it turns out he was murdered, the police are going to do quite a lot of checking up on you."

"I didn't kill him," she said, her voice hollow. It was not a convincing denial. "I should have, maybe. But I didn't."

"Why should you have killed him?"

The tendons in Vanessa's skinny neck stood out but she shook her head. "No good comes from rehashing it now," she said, her voice tight. "Joe's gone. Maybe this was the ending we were supposed to get the whole time."

"You said Joe never laid a hand on you. But you went to Ruby's Place looking for shelter."

Vanessa turned a whiter shade of pale. "Who told you that?" she asked as she jumped up off the stool. "What did they say about me?"

Julie, the toddler, ran back into the room giggling. She had put the *Bluey* stickers all over her shirt and her face. "Look at me! Look at me! I'm Bluey." She did a little dance and ran to Annalisa's legs. "Do you gots any more?"

"Julie!" Vanessa's voice was strident. "What did I tell you about taking stuff from strangers? Only if I say okay."

Julie stiffened at her mother's sudden rage and her tiny bottom lip stuck out. "She's not a stranger," she argued, gesturing at Annalisa. "I knowed her two times."

"Get in your room. Get in your room now." Vanessa banished the girl, and Julie ran sobbing from the room. Vanessa turned her steely gaze to Annalisa. "You can go too. And don't come back here."

Before Annalisa could react, a door opened at the back of the house and Vanessa's older daughter, Briana, emerged holding a sniffling Julie in her arms. "Mom, what did you do to her?"

"Stay out of this," Vanessa said, keeping her eyes on Annalisa like they had guns drawn.

"She's just a little kid," Briana protested from behind her mother. "She doesn't understand."

Vanessa did not turn around. "That's why we're here. To protect her."

Vanessa couldn't see the way that Briana's face hardened, but Annalisa could. "This is about Joe," Briana said to Annalisa. "Isn't it?"

Something clicked for Annalisa at that moment. Whether it was the way Briana's arms tightened around the little girl as she asked about her dead stepfather or the way Vanessa looked sick at Joe's name on Briana's lips, Annalisa couldn't say. But she got it. *I'm not protecting Joe,* Vanessa had said. *I never was.*

"It was the children," Annalisa said, her voice barely above a whisper. "Wasn't it?" She recalled Vanessa's story of the way Joe wooed her by being sweet to her daughter. But Joe hadn't been using Briana to get to Vanessa. No, it was the other way around.

Vanessa clasped a hand over her mouth to stifle a sob. Briana came to her side. "Mom," she said. "It's okay."

"No, it's not. It never will be."

"Joe abused you?" Annalisa asked softly.

Briana turned her head away. For a long moment, she said nothing. Then she gave a short nod. Vanessa took the clingy toddler into her own arms. "You see now why I didn't want him to get out."

"Of course. But . . . you didn't say anything when he was on trial." There was nothing in the files or news reports she had seen that even hinted of Joe's proclivities. "They could have prosecuted him for the abuse, they could have . . ."

"They could have made Briana tell the whole dirty story. They would have put that on her record too, you know, what happened. She would've been in all the news stories—maybe not by name, but Joe had one stepdaughter so it wouldn't have been too hard to figure it out. It's his shame, you get that? Not hers." She spat out the words. "Joe going away for Cyrus's murder was an answer to our prayers. He was gone and Briana was safe. No need to tell the whole world what a damn fool I was, falling for his lies. No need to put Briana through more hell. So now I'm asking you—please do the same. Walk out of here and leave us alone."

Annalisa swallowed. “Someone killed Cyrus Merriman. Someone who is apparently still out there.”

“Killing men like Joe.” This, from Briana. “Excuse me if I don’t weep.”

Annalisa looked from Vanessa to Briana and back again. “Joe went missing from his hotel last night. I hope you both can account for your whereabouts.”

“We were here together,” Vanessa said. “All night.”

Briana hesitated for just a fraction of a second before nodding along. “That’s right. All night.”

Annalisa could see she would get nowhere by pressing further without evidence. “Okay,” she said, making peace. “If that’s how you want to play it. I’ll see myself out.”

Vanessa followed her to the door, Julie’s face buried in her neck. “You tell your husband that Joe got what was coming to him. Tell him I failed to protect my kids one time but I won’t fail again.”

Annalisa turned around in the doorway. “The people at Ruby’s Place . . . they knew what Joe was, right?”

“They’ve known plenty like him. You cops, you’re always looking for the broken windows or the bullet holes—someone standing over a dead body with a gun or a knife. You don’t see the guys like Joe whose threats will choke you out as sure as any jungle vine. You wanted him out of prison so bad? Well, congrats, you won. His death is on you, not me.”

TWENTY-TWO

ANNALISA SAT ON THE SOFA WITH HER FEET PROPPED UP, LAPTOP RESTING ON HER PREGNANT BELLY. Nick's daughter, Cassidy, came into the room with Jack on her heels, the young cat mewling loudly. Cassidy had a plate in one hand and a dish towel in the other. "I'm trying to clean up and he won't leave me alone," she said to Annalisa with faint exasperation. Jack sat at Cassidy's feet, still complaining.

Annalisa did not look up from her work. "He wants you to sit down."

"Huh?"

"He wants you to make him a lap." She gestured at hers, which was full with both a computer and a growing baby. "Mine is not sufficient anymore."

"Can he wait until I finish the dishes, at least?"

Jack reached out one white paw and tapped Cassidy's leg. Annalisa caught the motion out of the corner of her eye and smiled. "I think that's a no."

"Fine," Cassidy said with a great sigh. "It was time for ice cream anyway. You want any?"

"No, thanks." She was probing around for any additional information she could get on Joe Green, especially anything that might link him to other victims. Cassidy returned to the kitchen to put down the plate and fetch a bowl of chocolate-chip ice cream. She had barely sat down next to Annalisa when Jack leaped onto her lap like a puma from the jungle. He began purring and kneading her legs in satisfaction while Cassidy rolled her eyes. "When Dad asked me to stay over tonight, I thought it was to help you."

"You are helping me." Jack had Cassidy to nag so he left Annalisa alone.

"Does it bug you at all? That Dad's out looking for a serial killer and you're on the couch with me and the cat?"

Annalisa paused her scrolling. "I'm glad someone as smart and capable as your father is on the case." People always wanted to give her credit for solving the Lovelorn Killer case, but Nick had spotted the perpetrator before she did.

Cassidy scratched Jack's ears with one hand as she scooped ice cream with the other, the bowl in the crook of her arm. "The news makes it seem like he screwed up," she ventured in a hesitant voice. "That he arrested Joe Green for a murder that the serial killer did."

"If that's true, it's because the killer wanted it to happen. Your father was set up the same way Joe was set up." Annalisa recalled Briana's haunted eyes as she'd hugged her baby sister. *Excuse me if I don't weep.* She thought about Julie and Julie's absent father. Maybe the new baby was Vanessa's second chance. Her do-over. The father didn't matter; it was the mother who had to atone.

Annalisa's baby kicked, making the laptop jump. Cassidy startled with a laugh. "Oh my God," she said. "That's hilarious."

"Yeah," Annalisa said. "Ha ha." She put her hand on the side of her swollen stomach and wondered if the baby could feel the laptop at all or whether it was simply trying out its new legs. *Look out, world,* it seemed to say. *Here I come, kicking and screaming.* The kid might be ready but Annalisa was not.

"It must be hard," Cassidy offered, glancing at Annalisa's screen where she had been looking at sex offender databases for anyone who matched the general description of Joe Green or who might have been active around the same time and been part of the same network. "Looking at that stuff all day."

Annalisa closed the computer. "Sometimes it is. But I'd rather know the truth, even if it's difficult."

Cassie eyed her laptop. "And that's the truth?"

"Hmm? Yes, unfortunately. Men like Joe Green are out there and we can't pretend they aren't. If we don't see them, we can't stop them. But . . . they aren't the whole truth. Most people want to be good. They try to be helpful and kind. They want a better life for their kids."

Cassidy put the bowl aside and snuggled closer to Annalisa. "So you think that people make a choice then? Which one to be, good or bad?"

Annalisa considered. "I don't think it's one single choice. At least I hope it's not." Her cell phone rang from its place on the coffee table, and the caller ID said it was the county morgue. Annalisa stretched futilely to reach it before being rescued by Cassidy. Jack protested as he was shifted off the warm lap. "Thanks," Annalisa said before taking the call. "Vega."

"I can only give you the highlights," said her source on the other end. "It'll all be in the press tomorrow anyway."

"I appreciate the head start, Ed." Ed Cameron, one of the assistant medical examiners, had been one of her "friendlys" on the job and he apparently saw no reason to change their relationship as long as she kept him in good scotch. Now she was counting on him to tell her the details of Joe Green's autopsy. "What did you find?"

"Stab wounds," Ed said. "Three of them in the chest and abdomen. He was still alive when he went into the lake, though, because we found water in his lungs."

"So cause of death was drowning?"

"Yes, although he would have expired from the penetrating trauma in short order if he didn't get immediate medical intervention."

"Murder weapon?"

"A thin blade about an inch wide and four to five inches long. Your killer is strong. He or she achieved full penetration into the thoracic cavity."

Maybe it was a man they were looking for after all. "Got it," Annalisa said, making some notes on her laptop. "One more question, doc. I gotta ask: did he have the Berkanan anywhere or not?"

Ed made a noise like he was sucking on his lip. This was clearly information that would not be in the morning papers.

"Come on," Annalisa wheedled. "Did Joe Green get murdered by the same killer as the rest of them?"

"I can't tell you that," Ed snapped. "I told your husband the same thing."

"But the Berkanan . . . ?"

"The body had surface abrasions from hitting the seawall." He gave a meaningful pause. "No other distinguishing marks."

Annalisa hung up with Ed and mused on what she had learned. Either Joe Green had a different killer from the rest of them or the killer hadn't branded him with the Berkanan for a reason. Perhaps it could be as simple as running out of time. Or maybe Joe had never been a real target but was clean-up somehow; the killer thought he'd remain behind bars and when he was released, they had to make a move. Stabbing usually suggested a personal motive, or at least that the killer wanted to be up close and personal with the victim while he died. Someone strong, Annalisa thought. Determined.

She heaved herself up again so she could retrieve the laptop. She would have to be equally determined. She had one more clue on Joe Green and that was his social security card. When she entered it into her database, she got a surprising hit. So shocking that she picked up her cell and called Nick right away.

"Hey," he said, his voice warm when he answered. "How are you? How's Cass?"

"We're making insufficient laps. Jack's got a call into the ASPCA for animal abuse."

Nick chuckled. "Wish I was there."

"We do too. Hey, I was poking around and . . . did you know there was a missing persons report filed on Joe Green up in Wisconsin? Way back in 1986."

Nick got quiet. "Yes," he said at length. "I do recall something like that."

"Did you look into it?" The report would have predated Joe's arrest for Cyrus Merriman's murder by several decades, but it was strange enough to warrant some investigation.

"We asked him about it. He said it was a misunderstanding. He left town without letting his buddy know beforehand. It didn't seem related to anything, and obviously, at that point, Joe Green wasn't missing anymore. He was sitting in our interrogation room. Why?"

"Just curious."

"Hmm. Have Jack tell you what happens to cats with curiosity."

"Funny," she replied.

Nick sighed. "Look, I've got to go. We're looking at like a thousand CCTV cameras to see if we can figure out who got to Joe Green the other night."

"Still think it's the same killer?" She kept her voice light. She didn't want to rat out Ed for helping her, so she didn't admit that she knew Joe's body didn't have the Berkanan.

"Not sure yet." He hung on the line like he wanted to say more so Annalisa waited. He lowered his voice before continuing. "I didn't want to mention anything earlier because I wasn't sure there would be much to report, but I had the lab do an analysis on the anonymous note Joe received in prison."

Annalisa closed her eyes as she thought of how many times that note had changed hands. "Anything?"

"Nothing useful on the note. But Joe saved the envelope and the techs were able to raise a DNA profile from where the sender licked the flap. Female."

"Interesting."

"Yeah. Anyway. I've got to get back to watching video before my eyeballs fall out. I'll probably crash here for a few hours and then get back at it. You cuddle the cat sufficiently so he can't turn us in to the authorities."

She smiled. "Try Visine. And coffee. Just don't get confused about which one is which." They'd had a killer a few years ago who poisoned her husband with eye drops in his coffee. Annalisa hung up with Nick and went to her photos to look at the mysterious picture of the three kids that she'd found in Joe's safe. The date on his missing persons report was 1986. The picture looked like it could have been taken in 1986. Did Joe have a previous family with three other children? The math worked out to possible. Nick said it was a buddy who reported him missing, not family, and Annalisa feared she knew the reason why.

She looked up the location mentioned on the date of the report, Fitchburg, Wisconsin, and saw it was a suburb of Madison. The only way to find out more would be to go there herself and poke around. She found a one-way, same-day ticket for the next day for only $109. She felt a slight guilty flush as she clicked "buy" on the ticket; no one was paying her expenses any longer. But Effie had given her a bunch of money to look for the ring, and now Annalisa had a pretty good idea of where to find it: in the housekeeper's belongings. She had to work up the courage to go over there and explain to Effie that her forgetful housekeeper had misplaced the ring and then let the chips fall where they may, appraisal-wise. In the meantime, a hundred bucks and twelve hours in Wisconsin seemed like a small price to pay for the truth.

TWENTY-THREE

Annalisa left a full bowl of water and kibble for Jack and a note for Nick. *Gone to Madison for the day. Back late.* She had grabbed an early flight so it was only 8 a.m. when she touched down at Dane County Regional Airport in Madison, Wisconsin. The airport was in the process of a big modernization project to add extra gates, but this effort had not reached the interior, which still looked straight out of the 1970s with its brown leather seats, drop ceiling panels, and striped carpet. Annalisa filled her travel mug with water from the public fountain and grabbed a taxi to the police department. She explained to the desk sergeant that she wanted to speak with someone in missing persons. Eventually she got to speak to a gray-haired man with a wide tie and mustache who could have been from the 1970s himself. He cheerfully introduced himself as Detective Don Johnson—no, not that guy, but ha ha, people do get them confused all the time—and pulled out a form to take her report. "So, you're here to report a missing person," he said, his pen poised at the ready.

"Ah, no. I'm following up on an old report from the 1980s."

His seat creaked as he sat back with a sigh. "The reward is still good," he told her. "If that's what you want to know. Twenty-five grand. The city sure thought it was a lot of money back then, and I guess it's still a healthy chunk of change, but the amount hasn't gone up in all these years."

"I'm sorry?"

"The reward money." He looked confused now. "For that little girl, Eve Collier? When folks come in here asking about a missing person from the 1980s, it's always her they want to know about."

It took Annalisa a moment to place the name. "The girl who went missing from the Christmas parade."

He looked relieved that they were back on the same page, his head bobbing like a turkey's. "Right. You betcha. Terrible thing, what happened. We spent weeks looking for her and got nowhere. What kind of world is it, I ask you, where you can't turn your back for one second without your kid going missing? Tore that whole family up. Everyone knows the uncle killed himself because he felt so bad—he was the one supposed to be watching her—but the parents went to an early grave too. Heart attack took the dad six years later, and the mom passed on from cancer a few years after that. Eve's brother and sister, they only got each other now. My wife's cousin, she knew the sister from school, and she says the girl left home at age eighteen and never looked back. Can't say I blame them. Nothing here now but bad memories." He looked to Annalisa to support his assertion and she nodded.

"It's terrible," she agreed. "But that's not why I'm here. I'm here about a different missing person. Joe Green? I have his social security number if that helps." She showed him the picture she'd taken of Joe Green's card.

Detective Johnson put on his glasses to inspect her phone and then he frowned at her. "What are you doing with a photo of this fella's social security card? Is he a relative of yours?"

Annalisa explained that she was a PI, that Joe had been her client, and that he was recently murdered in Chicago. Detective Johnson listened with his fingers peaked together, his face adding deeper lines the more he frowned. "A serial killer, you say? I think I heard something about that on the news."

"No one is sure of the link yet," she replied. "It's possible someone from Joe's past caught up to him. That's why I'm here."

"How come it's you and not the Chicago PD?"

"They're working the serial killer angle."

He flashed her a pitying look as he pulled his keyboard over. "Seems like the more exciting end of the investigation if you ask me. I've been on the job thirty-five years and we've never had a serial killer in these parts. One man murdered his family and then took off for Canada, but a serial killer? Only on TV and the movies."

He sounded envious and Annalisa wondered how he would have felt standing on the roof with the Lovelorn Killer. "I'm also curious if you have any reports on Joe outside of the missing persons file."

He paused from entering Joe's information into the computer. "Like what sort of reports?"

"Oh, anything." Her experience told her that pedophiles did not change. Joe had been an adult man in his late twenties at the time of his "disappearance," which gave him plenty of years to rack up some victims.

Detective Johnson had never learned to touch-type. He slowly entered Joe's details and hit "enter" with a big flourish, sitting back to watch the results roll in. "There you go," he said, gesturing at the screen. "That report was closed fourteen years ago. Joe was found like you said—up in Chicago. Says here a Detective Nick Carelli called to check on the report. You heard of him?"

"We've met."

"Carelli said Joe Green was in custody over in Chicago, and seeing as how that meant Joe was alive and well, we closed out the case." He gave a short nod of satisfaction.

"Who reported him missing?" Nick had said a buddy filed the report, not Joe's family.

"Uh . . ." Detective Johnson clicked for more info and leaned closer to the screen. "Says here the initial report was filed on December 23, 1986, by Otis Long. He and Mr. Green were friendly since they had served together in Vietnam, but Mr. Long had been unable to get in touch with Joe Green for a couple of weeks. He finally went into Mr. Green's apartment through an open window by the fire escape and found him gone."

"Was there an investigation?" Annalisa wanted to know. "Did you contact Joe Green's family, for example?"

"Says here no family."

"Hmm." Annalisa wondered if this was the truth, or if it was a story Joe Green told his war buddy.

"Lookit," Detective Johnson said, turning to face her. "I'll be honest with ya. Probably the most they did back then was put out a BOLO on Green. He was a grown man who moved around a lot. Says in the report he had a problem with alcohol and was intermittently homeless. Not judging. It's a sad story with some of the vets, but it's not an uncommon one. It looked like Green couldn't pay his rent so he moved on without telling his buddy where he was going—which was Chicago apparently—and he wasn't exactly missing per se. Not the kind of situation that gets the whole force out, if you know what I mean. Besides, if you look at the timing here, everyone in the city would've been tied up in the Eve Collier case."

"Oh? The two cases happened at the same time?" She stretched closer for a look at the screen.

"Well, sort of, yeah. No one is quite sure when Joe Green turned up missing, but the report came in just a week after little Eve disappeared.

But you can see where the priority would've been with the girl and not a grown man who's free to move on his own accord."

Annalisa's skin prickled with an equal mix of dread and excitement. What were the odds that a pedophile would disappear at the same time as a five-year-old girl? Joe Green had gone after Briana, who was about eight at the time he targeted her. Five would have been right in Joe Green's sweet spot. "Do you know if Joe Green was at the Christmas parade when Eve went missing?"

"Lessee . . ." He poked around on the computer. "No telling one way or another. Coulda been, I suppose. Half the city was there. Or he may already have left town by then."

"And no other reports on Joe Green? Nothing in the system?"

"Right. You wanted me to check on that. Uh, I've got two counts of public drunkenness—disturbing the peace and whatnot. A couple of counts of loitering. That's not unusual for the itinerant folk. They hang out on the benches and we roust 'em. Nothing serious in here, though. Why'd you ask? The fella's dead now, isn't he?"

"The loitering charges . . . they wouldn't happen to be near a school or a playground?"

"Hmm. Well, now that you mention it, two of them are right by a city playground. But again, that's pretty standard. The homeless folks tend to congregate in the public parks."

"I see." Annalisa took out her notepad. "You wouldn't know how I could get in touch with Otis Long, would you? The friend who filed the missing persons report on Joe Green?"

Detective Johnson seemed dubious. "I got a phone number here, but I don't know that it'll be any good." He gave it to her anyway.

"And Eve Collier's brother? You indicated he was still around?"

"Keith? Yes, I think so. He's the name listed here in case there's any new developments. Needless to say, there haven't been any developments. Keith knows how it is. He doesn't even bother calling to check up on the case anymore. I think he accepted that Eve was dead a long time ago, but the baby sister always wanted to keep looking. I think that was the reason they had a falling out and why she left town. Couldn't shake the idea that her sister was out there somewhere, lost and needing help. Keith, he's more sensible. He did the research. Kids who are grabbed like that, they're usually dead within twelve hours. The ones who survive are taken by family members—like a divorced dad or something—and that wasn't the case here. But without a body, I guess the sister kept clinging to hope. Since we're talking almost forty years by now, I imagine even she's given up." He jotted down Keith's number and gave it to Annalisa.

"Thanks. One more thing." She called up the photo Joe had of the three kids in front of the brown house. "Does this picture mean anything to you?"

Detective Johnson took the phone and squinted at it. "Well, sure. That's the Collier kids. Keith, Eve, and the baby sister . . . shoot, what was her name?" He set the phone in his lap as he thought about it. "Charlotte. Her name was Charlotte."

TWENTY-FOUR

KEITH, THE ELDEST OF THE COLLIER CHILDREN, DID NOT WANT TO MEET WITH ANNALISA. She reached him by phone at the number Detective Johnson provided, but his reception turned chilly when she brought up Eve's name. "I don't give interviews about my sister."

"I'm not a reporter. I'm a private investigator. I may have a lead on what happened to Eve." She wanted to meet with him and show him Joe's picture. It was a long shot, but maybe Keith would remember seeing Joe at the Christmas parade.

"You found her?" Keith was skeptical.

"No, but—"

"Then leave me alone."

"I may know who took her."

Keith's end of the line went silent. "Who?" he said at last, his voice like sandpaper.

"A man named Joe Green." Joe had a photo of the family, which suggested that Eve's abduction wasn't random and that he'd been familiar with the Collier family.

"I don't know him." Keith sounded certain.

"He might have done landscaping for your family." That's how Annalisa knew him, after all. She imagined Joe in the Colliers' yard, watching Eve play. Easy enough to go inside, perhaps for a glass of water or to use the bathroom, and sneak a family photo from the album. A trophy to keep even after Eve was gone.

"I don't remember any landscaper. My dad mowed our lawn. This man, Joe Green, has he been arrested or something? Why do you think he's connected to the case?"

"He's dead," Annalisa admitted. "Murdered in Chicago. But he had in his possession a photograph of you and your two sisters."

"Two sisters," Keith repeated as if surprised to be reminded of that fact.

"Eve and Charlotte." Annalisa had to tread carefully here. If, as she suspected, Charlotte had ended up running Ruby's Place, that would explain how she'd come into contact with Joe Green. "Are you in contact with Charlotte at all? I'd love to speak to her."

"Ha, no. She left right before she turned eighteen. Ran off with some older guy who promised to help her look for Eve." He sniffed. "I bet he promised a lot of things. I tried to help her when he turned abusive, told her she could come home at any time, but she wanted nothing to do with me. She could never accept the truth—that Eve died a long time ago."

"Do you know where Charlotte went? Where she's living now?"

"She sends me a Christmas card. The return address is some shelter in Chicago. When I got the first one, I thought maybe she was living there, like homeless or something. I actually drove down to find the place and they wouldn't let me inside. They acted like I was the criminal. Maybe to Charlotte, that's what I am."

"Why would you say that?"

"You really don't know anything about my sister's case at all, do you? You think you're the first one to call, the first one who thinks they have some hot lead? Putting up that reward money was the worst mistake the city ever made."

"I don't follow."

"Uncle Doug was covering for me when Eve disappeared. Charlotte needed a diaper change and she was being fussy. Uncle Doug took her off to the restrooms and he told me to watch Eve, that I was to hold her hand and not let go. But some of my friends from school were there buying popcorn from a nearby stand and they saw me holding hands with my sister. They looked so grown up, you know, using their own money to buy the popcorn—no adult in sight. They laughed at me for having to stay with Eve and made kissy noises at us. So I . . . I let her go. I searched my pockets to see if I had enough money to buy popcorn. I would have shared it with Eve. I would have. But in the moments I was distracted, she slipped away."

Annalisa closed her eyes against the horror of it. "I'm sorry."

"So you see, it was my fault. Uncle Doug took the blame, but really, it was me who was responsible for what happened to Eve. He killed himself, you know." Keith sounded almost envious. "A few weeks after Eve disappeared, it became clear to everyone she wouldn't be coming home. That she was probably dead. The press went after him. Even my parents, in their grief, banned him from the house, when really it was me they should have sent away."

"You were just a kid."

"I knew better. I knew I was supposed to hold her hand and I let go anyway." He took a deep, steadying breath. "So you can see, then, why Charlotte might not want to see me. The papers have one story of what happened to Eve, but Charlotte knows the truth."

....

ANNALISA HAD BETTER LUCK WITH OTIS LONG, JOE GREEN'S FRIEND WHO HAD REPORTED HIM MISSING. He worked as a barber in the city and insisted Annalisa do a stint in his chair while they talked. "You have so much hair," he marveled as he took down the pins and her thick, dark hair fell in waves around her shoulders.

"They tell me it will fall out after the baby comes."

"You could lose half of this and still be gorgeous." He spritzed her down with a water bottle. "Boy or girl?"

"We're waiting to find out." She thought of the nursery at home with its white walls. They had a crib assembled and some tiny yellow onesies folded on top of the dresser. *You should paint now,* Sassy had cautioned her. *Pick something neutral if you want, like pale blue or green. But you and Nick will be walking zombies once the baby is here.* Annalisa knew Sassy had a point, but she couldn't commit to a color or a decorating scheme. What if she picked green and the baby hated it?

"Waiting, huh?" Otis said as he combed out her hair. "You want to be surprised? Well, I've got some news for you: it's all a surprise. You can find out boy or girl, but you spend your whole life waiting for them to show you who they're gonna be."

"You have kids?"

"Four of 'em." He gestured at his wall of pictures. "Two boys, two girls. All grown now with kids of their own but darned if they don't surprise me still. My oldest, Gus, we tried to get him into sports growing up. I played football in high school and loved it. Gus, he collapsed like a lawn chair every time someone threw him a ball, like he would die if he had to touch the thing. But last month he won some axe-throwing contest at his work. Axe-throwing?" Otis shook his head like he couldn't believe it. "I've had folks working here that I hesitated to trust with scissors. I sure wouldn't be handing them an axe. Anyway, never mind me rambling on. You wanted to ask me about Joe."

"You reported him missing," Annalisa said, meeting his eyes in the mirror.

"Long time ago. I'd given up hope of ever knowing what happened to him when one day after almost thirty years gone by, a police sergeant called me up. He told me Joe had turned up in Chicago, and I looked into it. Joe was arrested for killing his wife's lawyer or some such horror. I wrote him a letter in prison but he never answered it."

"Did that surprise you? That Joe was arrested for murder?"

"Oh, Lord, yes. Joe was a happy drunk. A dreamer. Always planning for a better time when he'd kick the bottle for good and turn his life around. A time or two, he'd get sober and I thought he'd make it. Then he'd reward himself for his new job or his new place by visiting the bar and the whole thing would start again. My wife told me to stop taking Joe's calls, but I couldn't. Not after what he done for me."

"What did he do?"

"Joe Green saved my life. We were both kids together in the war. Barely eighteen. We weren't assigned to the same unit but we met in a hospital ward in Thailand because we both had the same injury—broken leg. You step into the rice paddy wrong and snap your femur. Happened to a bunch of guys. Me and Joe, we'd play cards to pass the time and hobble around together. Later, when we got better, we got assigned to this base where they would bring the jeeps for cleaning and repair. Joe was a good mechanic. He could listen to the engine once and know immediately what was wrong with it. Me, I did what Joe told me. But the condition of some of these vehicles, let me tell you, was utterly foul. Blood, guts, puke—pardon my language—but they stunk to the heavens and part of our job was to clean them off. I was out there by the edge of the jungle with the hose, preparing to clean up a particularly nasty specimen, when out of the trees comes a huge tiger. Guess he smelled the jeep. But once he saw me, he got more interested. I had no weapon on me. Nothing to defend myself with but a hose as this massive animal starts advancing on me. I'm wondering if I should turn the hose on it, or if that would just get me dead for sure."

"What did you do?"

"I didn't do nothing. Joe came out right then banging two pots together, and damned if he didn't run the animal off on foot. He didn't have a weapon either, and his leg hadn't really healed right. He couldn't run straight but he charged that tiger all the same. He ran after it shouting and hollering at the top of his lungs, and the tiger was so shocked it turned around and left. I would've been cat food if Joe hadn't come along like that. So, I guess I always felt like I owed him." He nodded again at his wall of photos. "Everything I've got, it's down to Joe."

"Did you ever feel like Joe took a strange interest in kids?"

He stopped combing and pulled back. "Strange like how?"

"Like . . ." She didn't want to destroy this guy's image of his war buddy but there was no good way to ask this. "Like he might be attracted to them."

Otis's face twisted in disbelief. "What? No. Joe was nothing but good to my kids while he was around. Jolene, my wife, she wouldn't let him inside if he'd been drinking, but during his sober times, he'd bring them little treats and play tag with them in the backyard. They called him 'Uncle Joe.'"

Annalisa knew that bringing treats sometimes amounted to grooming, softening up the child for the later predation, but she decided not to press Otis further on this point. "There was a Christmas parade the year you reported Joe missing," she said. "A little girl disappeared."

"Eve Collier," Otis said with dismay. "We prayed hard for that girl to be found safe."

"Do you know if Joe attended the parade?"

"I doubt it. Joe had fallen off the wagon back around Thanksgiving. When he was drinking, he didn't go out except to the bars or the liquor mart. I was worried when I didn't hear from him, and that's why I went around to his place looking for him. It was a wreck—beer cans everywhere, pizza boxes with a side of roaches. No Joe."

"But this was after the parade. Right?"

"Could be. Yes, I guess you're right. It was after Christmas. I know because I took a little shaving kit over to him as a gift. I got two that year and didn't need the extra one. So, I don't know if Joe was at the parade. I hadn't talked to him in a few weeks. When the landlord said Joe had skipped out on the rent, I figured maybe he was sleeping on the streets. I was worried about him freezing to death. But I guess he went to Chicago—at least that's what they tell me. How he got mixed up in a murder, I'll never know."

"Did he have to kill anyone during the war?"

"No, it was almost over by the time we got there. He always said he was glad, you know, that we missed that part. That's why I figure if Joe killed his wife's lawyer, the lawyer probably had it coming. I said as much in the letter I sent him."

"You might not be wrong on that score."

Otis went to his wall of pictures and plucked off one to show her. "That's me and Joe." The young men wore green fatigues, smiling with their arms folded as they leaned back against a jeep. The casts on their legs were mirror images—Joe's broken right leg to Otis's left. "That's what I can't figure," he told her as she studied the picture. "If we'd seen some heavy action, I could understand why Joe might have difficulty shaking it off. But all we did was walk wrong through some rice paddies. I know Joe's leg didn't heal right the first time. They had to break it again and do another surgery when he came home to put a pin in it. Maybe that's where everything went wrong for him. I know it's all connected, brain and body." He tapped the side of his head. "But all the same, it's hard to figure how a whole life can be wrecked by one broken leg."

....

NICK SAT IN THE WINDOWLESS BOXY ROOM THAT THE COPS INEXPLICABLY STILL CALLED "THE TAPE ROOM" EVEN THOUGH NO ONE USED VIDEOTAPE ANYMORE. The room now featured computers with large monitors, valuable for spending hours searching through CCTV footage for a glimpse of a suspect or a suspect's vehicle. He had three paper coffee cups stacked up next to him and he was glad no one else was in the room because he was pretty sure he was starting to take on an odor from sitting there a third day in a row, screening footage from the Chicago streets. He had already found some video of Joe Green's aimless trips around the Loop during his couple of days of freedom, including one where Joe chatted up a homeless guy and another where Joe entertained a pair of kids outside of a Potbelly Sandwich Shop. Joe bought the homeless guy a sandwich with his attorney's credit card. The kids got shepherded away by their mother. Nick did not see any indication of where Joe met his killer.

He had better luck with the footage that came in relating to Karma Bryant's incident. The cameras backed her version of the story: that the man in the bar had followed her and instigated physical contact even after Karma clearly wanted nothing to do with him. He pinned her up against the dumpster and then ran when Karma pulled the gun—although why Karma had the gun with no cell phone or identification on her remained a troubling point for Nick. He kept loading more footage, looking for another angle, hoping for some clarity. His eyes were cracked with fatigue, and when he closed them, he still saw grainy black-and-white video of cars zipping along the Chicago streets.

The door opened and Bill Dickerson entered to rummage in the box of adapters and power cords. "You're still here?" he asked Nick.

"Yeah, I live here now," Nick muttered as he clicked on the next file. Annalisa had gone to Wisconsin, she said. He knew he should probably have asked more about what she was up to, but she didn't give details, and he didn't pursue it. Truth be told, it was nice to have her off on her own instead of shadowing him on this case.

"You should go home," Dickerson told him as he retrieved the charger he'd been looking for. Nick was about to thank the guy for his concern when Dickerson gave a humor-filled snort. "I mean, that's where your wife is, right? Annalisa will give you all the answers."

"At least I have a wife. You've got what—a goldfish and a fridge full of moldy takeout?"

"Ha," Dickerson told him, still good-natured. "I'll tell you what I've got. I've got my pride."

Dickerson left, leaving Nick alone in his gloom like a troll under the bridge. *Poor Nicky.* Missed a serial killer right under his nose until his wife came along and pointed it out to him. He jabbed at the computer key to make a new video load. At least Zimmer still had confidence in him. She left him as lead on the case and Nick was determined to find something useful to show her—ideally something that did not come from Annalisa.

Nick surfed through another hour's worth of traffic cam footage, freezing and zooming in on pedestrians, to no avail. He was practically seeing double when he switched over to the files from the night of Ray Donovan's murder. If, as they suspected, they were dealing with a single killer, then solving Ray's case would also solve Joe Green's murder. Zimmer questioned him on that logic. "Green didn't have the rune symbol," she'd pointed out. "The Berkanan."

"He still ended up in the lake," Nick had replied. "Just like the others." Privately, he admitted the commander had a point: Joe Green's death felt different. More personal. More like Cyrus Merriman's, if Nick had to classify them. Like the killer knew the victim.

He was so busy focusing on the pedestrians along Lake Shore Drive that he almost missed her at first. The time stamp read 1:13 a.m. the night of Ray Donovan's death, and Nick had stopped the video to look at a figure in the shadows that he judged to be a Black male about fifty years old. Only when he leaned back in his seat, satisfied that the guy had nothing to offer, did Nick notice the car stopped at the red light. It had a stylized *R* sticker on the front bumper for Ruby's Place and Nick raised his gaze to look at the driver. Female, probably, but he couldn't make her out from the glare of the streetlights on the windshield. He did get the plate, though, and ran it through the system. The Kia was registered to Charlotte Higgins.

TWENTY-FIVE

Charlotte let Vanessa Green in the back door. The woman had a toddler with her, a girl of about three in messy pigtails. "This is Julie," Vanessa explained with a frown. "My older girl had to work and Michael has school, so I couldn't get a sitter."

"It's no trouble," Charlotte said. "Julie can play with the other children in the art room. Would you like that, honey?"

"I make good pictures." Julie was already shedding her coat and boots, eager to follow Charlotte to the crayons, paper, and watercolors. Charlotte admired the girl's confidence and ease in the world. She tried to remember if she had ever been this way, but she couldn't recall. By age three, Charlotte already knew that little girls could get snatched from a Christmas parade as quick as Julie had removed her coat. She was surprised that Vanessa had gotten pregnant again and wondered about the girl's father. *How daring,* she thought, *to believe this time would be different.*

With Julie safely coloring with some other kids at a low table, Charlotte led Vanessa Green to the office where Karma waited. "I've got Gwen on speakerphone," Karma said, gesturing at her desk. "Layla's not here yet and I don't know where she is."

"I'm here, I'm here." Layla swooped in late, a daisy in her hand and a blush on her pale cheek. The romance with Danny seemed to be going well. Maybe Charlotte was the one who was wrong and it was possible to start again. She hoped she could hold everything together long enough to give them a new beginning.

"Thank you all for coming," she said. "I thought we should meet and talk things over."

"I feel like I'm being set up," Vanessa interrupted. Her arms folded, her foot bouncing. "I run my mouth off to the cops and that PI woman about how I'd be happy if Joe was dead, and now he is."

"Yes, Joe is dead. I think that's a good place to leave things." Charlotte glanced around at the other women's faces. "Back where we started."

"I never signed on for murder." Gwen's voice was strident on the phone. "Charlotte told me Joe did kill Cyrus Merriman. I thought we did what we did to help the police get the right guy. To help Vanessa and her daughter so they wouldn't have to testify about what Joe did to Briana."

"Now it'll be for nothing," Vanessa replied, getting heated again. "That PI . . . Vega? She knows. She knows what Joe did to Briana and she knows we came here for help."

Charlotte remembered that day and how long it had taken for Vanessa to admit why she was there. When the story finally came out, when Vanessa whispered Joe Green's name, Charlotte knew it was the same man whom Jessica had fled years ago. One man, two broken women. She thought of her fifth-grade teacher, Miss Chandler, and the saga of the wounded birds. The cafeteria windows were big and bright and birds kept flying into them, knocking themselves unconscious and injuring their wings. The science teacher used it as a lesson; she had the class nurse the birds back to health—at least the ones that survived the crash—in a cardboard box at the back of the classroom. Charlotte remembered peering in at a desperate blue jay as it hopped around and tried to fly. Miss Chandler finally decided this was a ridiculous cycle and she put masking tape across the cafeteria windows in huge X patterns that upset the principal because it destroyed the view. *No more dead or injured birds,* Miss Chandler had told him. *That's a better view.*

Charlotte had told herself that's what she was doing: putting an X over Joe Green. "The police don't have any evidence on you," she told Vanessa, "and Annalisa Vega has only vague suspicions. We have to agree to stick to the original story. As long as we don't tell them anything further, this whole thing stops with Joe."

"What about Jessica?" Gwen's voice floated from the phone. "That PI, Vega, she was asking about her too."

At Jessica's name, Charlotte stiffened. Karma caught it and looked alarmed. Layla, who had been holding the flower to her nose and daydreaming, snapped to attention. "We don't need to worry about Jessica," Layla said. "She's on board with the plan."

Vanessa looked confused. "Jessica ran off years ago. What's she got to do with anything?"

"It was her idea," Gwen said. "Wasn't it? She's the one who asked me to lie about seeing Joe with Cyrus that night. I'd told her about my sister and she told me what Joe had done to her. I still have that note, by the way. The one she sent me asking me to call Charlotte at the shelter. So don't think you'll put any of this other stuff on me."

"No one is putting anything on anyone." Charlotte took it all: a sin eater. She kept calm and reiterated the plan to everyone. No one talked. Not to the cops. Not the press. Not even each other after they left here today. She would do anything to keep Jessica out of it. Jessica, who had left Joe with no prospects and nothing but the clothes on her back and a piece of paper that had little Eve's face on it. Whatever else happened after that, Charlotte accepted it as the price of the truth. If there was ever a man who deserved to have an X through him, it was Joe Green.

"So then," she said to the group. "We're agreed? Problems solved?"

Karma's chin lifted as she looked past Charlotte to the video monitor behind her. "One problem," she said. "Detective Carelli is at the door."

Charlotte turned to study the screen, bending down so she could get a good look at the detective's face. He looked haggard and rumpled, his shirt half untucked and his hair lank. He was a far cry from the slick city cop who had shown up the first time. She had done some investigating on him. Years of stalking the men before they could stalk her clients taught Charlotte all the tricks of the trade. Detective Carelli might carry a badge, but on the inside, he was one of them. "Let him in," she said as she straightened up. "I'll deal with him."

Karma protested. "You just said no cops."

Charlotte still believed in her power to control the narrative. "I won't tell him anything. But cops are like ants at a picnic. If you don't snuff out the first one, a whole line of them follows soon behind. Take Vanessa out the back door. Then carry on with business as usual."

Karma looked like she wanted to argue further, but she did as Charlotte asked and escorted Vanessa to retrieve Julie and slip out the back. Layla lingered in the room, twirling the flower absently in her hand. "If you want to find out what the cops know, I could ask Danny about it."

"What? No. Definitely do not bring Danny into this."

"He's a good guy," Layla said. "And he cares about me. He cares about the shelter and the work that we do here. I think he'd be an ally."

"I'm sure he does care. But the less he's involved in this, the better."

"But—"

"No. People are dead, Layla."

Layla blinked. "I know that. I just can't believe . . ." She looked at the screen where Henry was letting in Detective Carelli.

"What?" Charlotte prompted.

"That after everything, it's Joe Green that keeps making trouble. Even when he's dead."

"I can handle this trouble."

"Can you?" Layla's blue eyes turned probing. "We're here for you, Charlotte. You know we are."

"I said I'll handle it." Charlotte squared her shoulders. Her family had failed Eve years ago, each of them looking away long enough for one little girl to slip through the cracks. Charlotte would not look away this time. Whatever was coming for her, whatever the consequences, she was ready.

TWENTY-SIX

Annalisa saw Nick's car parked on the street outside Ruby's Place and hesitated. Was she thinking clearly? She'd slept only a few hours after her trip back from Madison. If she was right, she was about to go confront a serial killer on her own turf. The plan had seemed sensible in her head but now she worried about the consequences. Charlotte Higgins had killed a half-dozen men without leaving any evidence, so the only way to catch her was to force her to make a mistake. The only way to do that was to sacrifice Nick. *Nick*. She had a pang at the thought of him and what was to come. He'd made all the right moves years ago, dutifully calling Wisconsin to follow up on Joe's case. The only result was that it got closed—the worst possible outcome. Nick was by the book and that's how he got played. Annalisa took no pleasure in being the one to point that out to him. She took a deep breath and got out of her car.

A brown-haired woman answered the door to the shelter, looking cautious. Only her fingers peeked out from the sleeves of her enormous sweater. *Layla,* Annalisa remembered. One of Charlotte's assistants. Annalisa smiled and tried not to show the adrenaline pulsing in her veins. "Hi," she said. "I'd like to speak to Charlotte Higgins."

"She's with someone already."

"I know. He's my husband. I really need to speak with both of them."

Layla glanced once over her shoulder before opening the door to admit Annalisa. "I guess it's okay. They're in the main office. I'll show you where it is."

Layla knocked on the office door and opened it without waiting for a response. "The private investigator is here. The one who's his wife."

Annalisa moved past her into the room, which became charged at her presence. Nick's jaw tightened and his nostrils flared at the sight of Annalisa. He had something in his hand—a printout of a car, it looked like. Charlotte's posture was defensive and closed off. She clearly wanted Nick to leave. "What are you doing here?" he asked Annalisa. "You were in Madison."

"Madison?" The word slipped out of Charlotte's mouth. Her hand slapped over her mouth to take it back but it was too late.

"I was following up on that missing persons report. The one on Joe Green." Annalisa looked from Nick to Charlotte.

"Yeah, well, you want to give us a minute here?" Nick waved the paper at Charlotte, his irritation plain. "I'm in the middle of an interview."

"No, it can't wait." Annalisa gave Nick a sympathetic glance. "You don't know what you're dealing with here."

He remained irritated. "Anna, no disrespect, but you're not on the job anymore. You have no way of knowing what evidence I have or don't have. You're interfering with a police investigation and I'm going to have to ask you to leave."

"Your investigation has failed twice already." Harsh words, but true. "You arrested Joe Green for a crime he didn't do. Then you called to check on Joe Green's missing persons report but you didn't bother to figure out why he was missing in the first place." Nick flushed hard, his mouth open to argue, but Annalisa cut him off. "You don't have all the facts. Does he, Charlotte?"

Charlotte walked to her desk and sat primly behind it, like the heft of it could keep her safe. "I don't know what you mean."

"You were born in Madison, the same as Joe Green. I think that's the piece we've been missing this whole time. Joe Green wasn't a wife beater. He was a pedophile. And in 1986, he abducted a five-year-old girl named Eve Collier from a Christmas parade."

"He what?" Nick whirled on her. "You have proof of this?"

"No, but I think Charlotte does. I think one of Joe's wives, maybe Jessica, maybe Vanessa, found the truth about Joe and what he did to Eve. They fled here to the shelter. Whichever one it was told Charlotte, possibly without even realizing Eve was her sister. But Charlotte knew."

Nick's hand tightened on the paper printout. "Anna, we should talk about this privately before this conversation goes any further. There's procedure—"

"You kept your ex-husband's surname," Annalisa continued as if Nick had not spoken. "Chester Higgins. The one you ran off with at age eighteen? That's why no one put it together any sooner that you're Eve Collier's sister."

"Anna," Nick repeated, his voice more forceful. "The hall. Now." He jerked his head toward the door, but Annalisa didn't move. She ignored him, locking eyes with Charlotte. In those eyes, Annalisa saw fear but also a hunger. How long had Charlotte waited to tell the truth about her sister?

Maybe it was the fury radiating off Nick that made Charlotte speak up. "Ms. Vega is correct," she said in a hoarse whisper. "Eve Collier was my sister. She, my brother, Keith, and I accompanied our uncle Doug to the parade so my parents could get a break. Uncle Doug watched us all the time with no problems. Who knew this time would be any different?"

"Doug killed himself," Annalisa said softly. "Over what happened to Eve."

"We all felt guilt, but Doug got the worst because he was supposed to be in charge. He left Keith to look after her in a crowd of thousands. You think maybe safety in numbers will protect you, right? So many people there. It was a Christmas parade and the happiest time of year. What could go wrong? No one would dare kidnap a child in such a public place where anyone might see. And yet." She sniffed. "No one saw. So many eyes there, but no one saw anything. Eve disappeared like a puff of smoke in the wind."

"It's horrible," Annalisa agreed. "I don't blame you for being angry."

"I was naïve," Charlotte snapped. "We all were. A crowd that big—you know how many abusers were present? Dozens. Men who bloody their wives and shatter their children. Predators? Plenty of them too, and Eve was unlucky enough to draw the short straw. They are monsters everywhere, you know. The only place you're ever truly safe is alone."

"So that's why you decided to make the world safer, right? By getting rid of Joe and Cyrus and the men who prey on women."

"That's enough," Nick said, his voice sharp. He grabbed Annalisa by the elbow and tried to force her from the room, but she broke free.

"No jury would convict you," she said to Charlotte in a rush as Nick resumed trying to drag her out. "Not after what Joe did to Eve. Once you knew who he was and what he did, you couldn't let him walk free. He had to pay and so you engineered a frame-up, right? Get rid of Cyrus and Joe at the same time. It's brilliant, really. The men you killed were monsters, like you said. They deserved everything they got and more."

"You're wrong," Charlotte said, sounding distracted and upset. Her eyes were on Nick. "Let her go."

"When she stops fucking up my case."

"I'm right," Annalisa said to Charlotte. "You know I am." She slid her gaze to Nick, whose face was flushed with anger. "And you know it too."

She could imagine the headlines when the news broke, how humiliated he would be. If there were any other way to do this, she would.

"I didn't inform her of her rights," Nick said with barely contained fury. "You're accusing her of murder with no actual evidence. There's a way to do these interviews and you damn well know it. You think because you quit the force you can go off half-cocked and the rules mean nothing? That you're some superhero who's never wrong? Hell, Anna, even if you're right about everything, you just tanked my case." He stalked out of the room, slamming the door behind him.

"Oh, my." Charlotte drew a shaky breath in the vibrating tension that followed Nick's exit. "Is he always like that?"

Annalisa gave the door a worried glance. "He's been under a lot of stress lately."

"I'm sure. But that's no excuse to treat you like that."

"He'll settle down." Annalisa hoped she sounded convincing.

"I don't mean to pry, obviously, but he clearly has a temper. Are you sure you're safe at home?"

"Of course I'm safe. Nick would never hurt me." She rubbed at the sore place on her arm where his fingers had bit into her flesh. When Charlotte noticed, Annalisa stopped. "I'm fine," she repeated firmly.

Charlotte came closer, her hands fluttering around Annalisa but not quite touching. "You worked in law enforcement," she said, her words soft, "so I'm sure you know. The leading cause of death in pregnant women is homicide."

Ice crystals bloomed in Annalisa's heart. She shook her head. "No," she said. "Not Nick."

"His father shot his mother." Charlotte blurted the words then bit her lip, realizing what she'd admitted. She'd been reading up on Nick already. "There were news stories," she said, her expression contrite. "From the Florida papers."

"I'm aware of Nick's history. He's not his father."

"He has a gun," Charlotte pointed out.

"Yes, and so do I." Annalisa had to get out of there. Nick was right that the interview had gone sideways. Charlotte hadn't admitted anything yet, but Annalisa had at least put her on notice. The woman could not afford to make a mistake now. "I have to go."

"Okay, then." Charlotte put up her hands, not believing Annalisa but not arguing either. "Just know you can always come here. We're a safe place."

Safe place. "Don't think this discussion is over," she told Charlotte. "It's just getting started. Things will go better for you if you turn yourself in."

Charlotte appeared serene, a gentle smile on her face. "But I have nothing to confess."

The two women stared at each other. "Okay," Annalisa said. "If you change your mind, you can always call me." She produced a card. "I'm a safe place too."

Charlotte trailed her to the door, still clutching Annalisa's card. Annalisa halted at the threshold when she saw Nick hadn't left. He leaned against his car door, arms crossed, like he was waiting for a fight. Annalisa braced herself for the blowback. *You knew it would be like this.* Behind her, Charlotte shielded herself with the door and whispered, "Be careful."

Annalisa adjusted her coat, which was snug over her expanding belly, and went to face Nick. He spread his arms at her approach. "What the hell was that?"

"Look, I'm sorry there wasn't time to call—"

"Time to call?" His face scrunched up with incredulity. "You come in and bulldoze my investigation and that's what you say to me? You didn't have time to call? You shoot your damn mouth off in front of my prime suspect. Yes," he said when she started shaking her head. "Yes, she was already my suspect. You think I'm an idiot? That I have no idea what's going on here? God, Anna, I know half the guys at the station think I'm a numb-nuts who needs you to lead me around by the nose, but I never thought you believed it too."

"I don't," she protested, moving to stay in front of him when he tried to walk away. "I don't think that."

He bumped her. Not hard. A light shove. "Get away from me. I don't want to look at you right now."

"Nick, please."

"No! You left me, remember? You wanted out of this partnership. You wanted to strike out on your own, and I supported that. But you won't actually go away. Instead you follow along next to me, criticizing, running your own investigation behind my back and not even bothering to share what you find. What the hell do you want from me?" He shoved her again, harder this time.

She gasped and stepped back. "Calm down. I'll go, okay? I'll go if that's what you want."

"I want you to let me run my own damn case! But no, you're always interfering, showing me up, making me the butt of everyone's jokes. Leave. Me. Alone." He roared the words, his hand recoiling, and Annalisa couldn't believe it was happening. She was so shocked she didn't even duck as he slapped her. She grabbed her face as the shelter door opened behind them and Henry came out.

"That's enough," he ordered. "Step away from the woman right now or I'll call the cops."

"I am the cops." Nick swallowed as he said the words, his dark eyes trained on Annalisa. He regretted his actions; she saw it on his face. The pain didn't hurt so much as the words. Did he really think this of her, that she enjoyed showing him up? All she ever wanted was the truth. Her hand shook as she lowered it from her face.

"I'm leaving," she said in a tight whisper. She let him wonder how far she'd go.

"Anna, wait. I'm sorry." He reached for her but she pulled away. She strode down the street to her car without looking back, unsure whether she wanted him to follow or not. By the time she reached the car, her hand was shaking so badly she could barely work the lock. When she got in, she swiveled the mirror to see the red mark on her cheek. She touched her face and traced the path mark of her tears.

TWENTY-SEVEN

LAYLA LAY IN THE SHELTER OF DANNY'S ARMS. He traced his fingers lightly over her arm, across the swell of her breast and down to her hip where the tattoo sat. "What does it mean?" he murmured against her hair, and she was relieved there had been nothing of the Berkanan in the papers. Charlotte was not reassured when Layla discussed the omission with her. *It means they're holding that information back from the press. They want only the killer to know about it.*

"It's a rune," she said. "Originally meaning birch or tree. It stands for growth, rebirth . . . change." The tattoo had been Charlotte's idea but Layla gladly went along. She'd do anything for Charlotte.

"Change for the better, I hope," Danny said.

"Mm, yes," she replied, snuggling into him. She didn't want to talk to Danny about her old life. She only wanted to imagine the future. For the first time, she could envision leaving her little apartment and venturing out into the world. Maybe see the ocean. She could only leave if Charlotte was safe, though, and the visit from the police detective and his wife gave her pause. Charlotte had gotten rid of them as she'd promised, and the fight the couple had on the sidewalk suggested they had problems that went beyond the case. But Karma had been listening at the door and she said the woman had brought up Jessica's name and Joe Green's old crimes. They had agreed when Joe Green went to prison that Jessica would have to disappear, and so far, she'd remained gone. Karma was determined to keep it that way.

Annalisa knows too much, Karma had insisted. *It's a problem.*

Charlotte brooded on a different issue. *Annalisa has a problem. It's her husband. Did you see him hit her?*

We could report him, Layla suggested. She was so tired of all these preening, condescending men who resorted to violence the moment they didn't get their way. *Tell his supervisor what he did.* It would be a win-win, she thought, because maybe the supervisor would take the detective off the case.

You know how it goes, Karma argued. *Even if his boss believes us, he gets fired but then goes home to take it out on his wife.*

Danny gave her a soft squeeze. "You feel tense. Everything okay?"

"Yeah, sure." She shifted away from him and looked at the shadowed ceiling.

"Are you worried about that cop? I know he was hassling Karma." Danny scooted closer to her again.

"No, I think she's in the clear." *This time.* Charlotte had given them both the news that the CCTV footage cleared Karma of wrongdoing in her run-in near the bar, but everyone understood what she didn't say: Karma had been out looking for trouble, and she found it. Karma had only one question in reply, one that indicated she had not learned her lesson: *did they give you the gun back?*

Charlotte hadn't answered, Layla realized now.

"Are you hungry?" Danny asked. "I could whip up some omelets."

Layla seized on this as a good distraction for him so he would stop asking about the detective and Karma. "Sure, that sounds great. Do you mind if I take a shower?"

"Hey, it's your place." He got out of bed bare-assed and she paused to admire the view. Danny had more than twenty tattoos that encompassed both arms and his shoulders, including an Escher-like staircase, a lush jungle with an eye of a tiger peeking out, and a Celtic cross. But it was the broad wings across his back that had made her cry the first time she saw them. Maybe together they could fly away.

Danny tugged on his jeans and went to her galley kitchen, whistling a happy tune. She let it play in her head as she stood under the hot spray of the shower. Charlotte swore she had everything under control, and Layla chose to believe her. She wouldn't worry unless that cop detective or his wife came around again. She knew Charlotte wanted to intervene to help the woman, but she would remind Charlotte of her own terse words when they lost poor Maya Ramirez. *You can't save them all.*

Layla was still humming when she came out of the bathroom, wrapping her robe around her and anticipating Danny's fluffy omelets that she could smell cooking on the stove. "Did you find the mushrooms?" she called out. She'd bought them with him in mind. Eating for one, you never bought anything that fanciful. Something that could go bad right away.

Danny didn't reply and in that strange beat of silence Layla felt her whole future crack. Her eyes adjusted to the dim light of the studio apartment and she saw Danny by her dresser. "What are you doing?"

He turned, a confused expression on his face. In one hand, he had a piece of paper. In the other, he held his cell phone. "I was looking in your jewelry box to see what kind of stuff you had. What you liked. I thought I might buy you a necklace or something. I was just going to snap a few quick pictures to get some ideas."

He held out the paper to her, a question in his eyes.

Layla wanted to cry. She pressed her palm to her mouth and her voice wobbled when she finally spoke. "I wish you hadn't done that."

"What does it mean?" he asked.

The eggs started to burn behind her. "Nothing," she told him in a hollow voice. How stupid she'd been to think she would ever get a happy ending. She wanted to scream, to rage at the unfairness of it all, but she forced herself to remain calm for Danny's sake. She took the paper and refolded it, tucked it back in the box. She thought of what Charlotte had said about involving him, and what he might tell his family members who were cops. Charlotte would be furious with her for this slipup. Layla resolved to fix it on her own no matter how awful it would be. She tried to smile and tugged Danny away from her bedroom area and toward the kitchen. "Come on. If we hurry, it might not be too late."

....

Across town, Annalisa also lay in bed. She stared at the wall, not sleeping, waiting for the scrape of Nick's key in the lock. When it came, Jack's head shot up from where he'd been dozing against her. He leaped from the bed and raced to the door to greet the returning hero. Annalisa didn't move. She heard the familiar sound of Nick's boots on the hardwood floor, his leather jacket being draped over a chair, the low rumble in his chest as he greeted their cat. When his footsteps grew nearer, Annalisa tensed as her mouth went dry. She had her back to the door and she did not turn around when he entered the room.

Without a word, he got into bed behind her and took her in his arms. At his touch, she let loose the sob that had been building inside her and twisted so she could hold him too. "Are you okay?" he asked, repeatedly brushing her hair from her face. "I didn't hurt you too much?"

"I'm okay, I'm okay." She was crying again, not sure if she was trying to reassure him or herself. After all, it had been her idea. "You didn't hurt me."

"That was horrible," he told her. "Let's never do that again."

"Never." She shuddered in his arms. When she had first broached the idea of a fake fight to Nick, he was against it. *I don't want to be that guy,* he'd said. *Not even for a second.*

You're not that guy. It's only for pretend.

I don't want to pretend to hurt you.

Fine. Do you know another way to trap her?

Nick had relented and agreed to try it her way. She felt a twinge of guilt that she was using his conscience against him; he'd missed Charlotte the first time, missed Joe Green and the chance to interrogate him when he was alive. Nick would do anything to fix it, including becoming his own father for one afternoon. Annalisa held him close, hoping he could feel the apology in her embrace. "I think Charlotte bought the fight," she said, burrowing nearer to him. "She offered me a place at the shelter."

"Great." He sounded glum. "I'm a believable monster."

"You're not." She hugged him, rained kisses on his jaw. "You're wonderful to do this."

"I hurt you."

"Not a lot." The words hurt more than the slap. Nick hadn't wanted to get physical with her, but Annalisa had insisted that he look violent. *Charlotte won't believe it otherwise.*

"And now I'm a sitting duck."

They agreed the fastest way to get to Charlotte would be to catch her in the act. Convince her that Nick was onto her and then have him turn on Annalisa. Charlotte could now solve two problems at once by eliminating Nick, and they hoped she'd take the chance.

"You really think she'll make a play for me?" he asked, stroking her back.

"You go sit by the lake and we'll find out." She rested so she could hear his heartbeat against her ear. His breathing slowed. "You didn't really mean it, right?" she asked after a few minutes. She toyed with a button on his shirt. "You don't really think I'm out to wreck your case and make a fool of you?"

"Of course not." He didn't hesitate but the denial wasn't entirely convincing either.

She sighed and pulled back. "You got played, Nick. But then so did I."

"That's not how it's being reported in the media."

"It will be. When the full story comes out."

"If it ever does. We have zero evidence to prove that Joe Green abducted Eve Collier at that Christmas parade. Even if his wives thought it was true, even if Charlotte was convinced of the fact, it doesn't mean it happened. She was a baby back then—far too young to remember anything."

"He had that photo of the Collier kids. I'm sure he must have known the family somehow. Eve wasn't a random victim, Nick. Joe Green knew her and knew she'd be at the parade that day. He must have to have gotten away so cleanly. He waited until the precise moment that the uncle's back was turned to snatch Eve, meaning he'd been watching her for a while. Days, maybe weeks. If we can figure out how he knew the Colliers, it would go a long way toward proving he was Eve's abductor." She paused. "And then there's Jessica."

"What about her?"

"Well, we know why Vanessa left Joe. She'd found out he was abusing her daughter. But Jessica didn't have kids and she disappeared overnight. She went so far underground that we haven't been able to raise a trace of her. I think that's because she knew what Joe was really capable of." She didn't have to spell it out for him. Joe had abducted and murdered a child. "She left because she found out about Eve. Maybe if we find her, she'll have the proof we need."

Nick propped himself up on one elbow. "We don't know for sure that Jessica is alive. If she found out the truth, then Joe might have killed her."

"I think she's alive." Jessica had fled Joe and found safety at Ruby's Place. Annalisa would bet she had another escape plan lined up once Joe went to prison.

"Great. But how do you find her? And even if you find her, how do you convince her to talk? Charlotte's obviously protecting her by keeping Jessica out of it, and I would imagine Jessica would do the same for Charlotte."

Annalisa rolled onto her back. The baby rolled too. Such an odd sensation. She patted her belly and considered the problem of how to locate Jessica Green. "The shelter may have records," she suggested. "You could subpoena them."

"On what grounds?"

"Jessica is a material witness."

"To what crime?"

"Eve's abduction."

"She didn't witness anything," Nick countered. "She may have knowledge of the crime from what Joe told her, but that's hearsay and we don't even have proof of that much."

"Charlotte's right," Annalisa said after a beat. "The law doesn't protect these women and children. No wonder she felt like she had to strike out on her own."

"Yeah, well, we can't have her running around the city deciding who to execute. Even if we might agree with some of her choices."

Annalisa rubbed his arm. "You'll need to be very careful."

"I'll be fine. The other guys didn't know what to look out for. I'll see her coming. Also, Zimmer hasn't given up on the DNA angle. She thinks the partial result from Joe Green's body might be enough to buy us a warrant for Ruby's Place if Charlotte is enough of a match. We just need to get her DNA to test it."

"Did anything else turn up in Joe's autopsy?" She'd only gotten the headline results.

"Nothing useful." Nick twisted and retrieved his laptop from the nightstand. "You can look for yourself if you want. I still say the strangest part is the lack of a Berkanan. If it's Charlotte, if it's the same killer, then why no Berkanan for Joe Green?"

"Maybe she thought he's beyond a second chance."

Nick handed her the laptop with the autopsy results open. Great. She'd paid off Ed with scotch for nothing. Annalisa sat up against the headboard to scan the results. "See?" Nick said as he settled in next to her. "I'm happy to work with you. Maybe especially now. God knows I missed a ton on this case the first time around."

"We both did."

She didn't see much in Joe Green's autopsy that she didn't already know from her earlier conversation with Ed. Joe Green had been six feet tall, one hundred eighty pounds, at the time of his death. Age seventy-two. Cause of death was evident from the stab wounds, and he was overall pretty healthy for an older adult. Prison had agreed with him. Annalisa scrolled down to the X-rays, which were standard as part of the autopsy. "Wait," she said.

"What is it?" Nick leaned over her shoulder to peer at the screen.

She zoomed in on the second X-ray. "He has no break in his leg. No pin in it."

"So?"

"So, according to Joe Green's war buddy, they both broke their femurs in Vietnam. Joe's didn't heal right and he had to have an operation to put a pin in his leg. Where's the pin?"

"I don't see one," Nick admitted.

"Nick. I don't know who's lying in the morgue right now, but it isn't Joe Green."

TWENTY-EIGHT

AS FAR AS THEY KNEW, THEIR KILLER OPERATED UNDER THE COVER OF DARKNESS, SO NICK FELT SECURE IN HIS CAR AS HE WATCHED THE DOOR TO RUBY'S PLACE THE NEXT MORNING. Annalisa had told him to stay home and rest during the day because he'd be hanging around the marina that night with a target on his back, but Nick could not sleep. He tried for an hour or so but every time he closed his eyes he saw the missing persons flyer for Eve Collier. Whoever they had lying in the morgue had a picture of Eve and her siblings in his possession. Nick had arrested the man more than thirteen years ago, had even called Madison to inquire about his past, but somehow missed any connection to Eve. Who the hell was he? And did he have anything to do with Eve's abduction? Nick wondered if, like him, Charlotte had gotten the wrong man.

He watched her now as she stepped out the door into the cold January sun. She had dark glasses on and a scarf wrapped around her head, maybe to protect against the winter glare, maybe to hide her face. Nick slouched down as she paused to survey her surroundings. The way she looked up and down the block before proceeding only cemented his feeling that she had something to hide. Innocent people didn't worry about being watched or followed. She set off on foot and Nick glanced back at the front door, wondering whether to stay put or to trail Charlotte and see where she went. He was toying with the idea of speaking to some of her employees—not Karma or Layla because he suspected they were covering for Charlotte—but Henry the bodyguard or that cook, Danny Romero, might be able to give him information on Charlotte's comings and goings. He'd seen Henry show up right at eight, but Danny wasn't at work yet unless he had slipped in through the back door.

Nick made a split decision to follow Charlotte from the other side of the street. She was his suspect and he would gain the most information from her. He pulled a knit cap low over his forehead and loped off in the direction she had gone. Although she walked with quick strides, he had no trouble catching up to her. She carried a large bag over one shoulder and he trailed her to a consignment shop, where she ducked out of the wind and inside the door. Nick remained across the street behind a parked van. He angled the large side mirror all the way in so he could see the reflection of the storefront. Charlotte remained inside so long he almost went in after her, but finally, she reappeared, walking briskly down the street in the same direction she'd been headed. Not back to the shelter.

The bag looked no lighter to him. Had she been swapping clothes in there? He made a note to double back and see if he could find out which clothes she might have dropped off. Could be evidence. He hustled after her for the moment and stopped when she entered a corner market. He knew the place, and it had two exits, one on either street, so either he had to watch from the corner or follow her inside. He crossed the street and tried to spot her through the front glass windows, but the ads took up most of the space and he mostly saw his own reflection. He went inside.

He grabbed a basket and sauntered up and down two aisles before he spotted her checking out bags of grapes. Ducking behind a display of canned goods, he pretended to study the rows of tomatoes while watching Charlotte in his peripheral vision. She went to the back where the dairy case was located. After a beat, he headed that way too, expecting to find her examining eggs or milk. Instead, he saw an older Black woman reading the label on a tub of yogurt. She glanced up at him when he nearly skidded to a halt next to her.

"Sorry," he muttered. "Thought you were someone else." He checked up and down the aisle. No Charlotte. He abandoned his basket and went down the length of the store from the back, looking at each aisle. When he didn't see her, he made his way to the front in time to see her pink headscarf disappearing around the corner. *Shit.* He chased after her, crashing through the doors and surprising a man with a baby carriage. By the time Nick dodged the carriage, Charlotte had vanished from the street in front of him. He walked on in the direction she had gone, peering in storefronts for any sign of pink. Finally he glimpsed her in line at a coffee house, which was doing a blockbuster lunchtime business. Nick squeezed in the back door and hid among the crowd, his eyes on the pink-covered head near the front.

His cell phone buzzed in his pocket and he saw it was Annalisa. *Checked with all Y employees, including one who has been here twenty-five years. No one else remembers Jessica Green. Now I'm thinking of checking other Ys and similar. If she has a daily swimming habit, she'd still need a pool.*

Nick was supposed to be home sleeping. He glanced up to make sure Charlotte was still in line before typing back to Annalisa. *Good idea.* He looked up just as the woman wearing the pink scarf received her coffee and turned around. It wasn't Charlotte, and Nick did a double take. The scarf was the same but this woman was younger with darker hair.

Nick scanned the crowd once more but saw no trace of her. He exited the coffee shop and found Charlotte waiting for him by the public trash receptacle, calmly sipping her coffee. She didn't have the scarf.

"Looking for someone?" she called to him, a self-satisfied smile on her lips.

The wind picked up, chilling him. She'd managed to slip his surveillance and turn up behind him while he'd not even noticed that he'd been spotted. Annalisa had cautioned him to be careful, but it seemed he wasn't careful enough. He edged closer to Charlotte. "Just thinking about some lunch," he told her, shoving his hands into his pockets to keep them warm.

She kept her eyes on him as she sipped from her paper cup. "The caprese panini is good."

"Yeah? Maybe I'll try it."

"Try it with a side of therapy. Anger management, perhaps. I saw you with your wife the other day. I know what you are."

"And what's that?"

"A bully. An abuser with a badge. But I've seen the statistics, and you're hardly alone. Domestic violence is endemic in law enforcement. Too many men are attracted to the power of the job, of the idea of making everyone else submissive."

"That's not why I signed up."

She pursed her lips. "I know about your father."

"Yeah? Good for you. You know how to use Google."

"It must have been scary for you when he came for your mother. He murdered her while you were hiding in the closet. That's what I read." She actually sounded sympathetic. "You didn't have anyone to model a healthy relationship growing up, so it's perhaps understandable that you might fall into old patterns. But you can choose a different path. There's help available. Therapists who specialize in these generational issues. I promise if you do the work, you'll see the benefit—for you and your baby."

Nick tilted his head as he considered her words. "You didn't report me," he said. "You didn't call the cops about what you saw." He had alerted Zimmer to the possibility that Charlotte might make a report. None came.

She got impatient. "I'm trying to help you."

"No offense, lady, but I don't need your kind of help."

"Oh." She gave him a thin smile. "You think I mean to kill you."

He shrugged. "Men in your orbit, they have a way of going belly-up in the lake. Look what happened to Joe Green."

"I didn't have anything to do with that."

"Okay, Ms. Collier, we can play it that way for now if that's what you want." She stiffened at his use of her birth name. "But you should know I'm not giving up. I'm going to keep digging until I get the proof I need—even if that means hauling you and everyone else from the shelter downtown. Someone in that place knows something. They're loyal to you within the four walls of that building, but trust me, people have a way of telling the truth when they're face-to-face with me in an interrogation room."

"You'd disrupt the whole place just for your petty vendetta."

"Petty? You've murdered half a dozen men."

"I dispute that. But let's say for argument you're correct that someone has killed these men. That their deaths are the result of one person's actions. I know you have access to their criminal histories, which are long and colorful for the most part. I suppose Cyrus Merriman slipped under the radar because he knew the legal tricks to keep himself clean, but he was an abuser just like the rest of them. Joe Green? You're the ones who say he kidnapped and murdered my sister. That's a federal offense. He could have easily gotten the death penalty for those crimes alone, never mind what else he might have done to Jessica or Vanessa or that poor girl, Briana. So, someone did the dirty work. Saved everyone the expense of a trial or of housing Joe on death row until his last days. I'd say that person is a hero."

Nick squinted into the distance. Nodded once. "Only one problem with your scenario," he told her. "That wasn't Joe Green."

The color drained from her face like she'd been unplugged. "I'm sorry. What?"

"The dead guy. He wasn't Joe Green. Kind of raises some questions about who did what to whom on the day of that Christmas parade, doesn't it? Makes you wonder."

"Wonder what, exactly?"

"If you might've got the wrong guy." He met her gaze and held it.

"I'm not scared of you." She drew herself up to her full height. She was fit and reasonably tall for a woman. Nick could see how she'd won her fights.

"Right back at you, lady."

She took her cup and moved to throw it in the garbage. She sniffed as she tossed it inside. "You know, if your mother had come to a shelter like mine, we would have helped her. She would likely still be alive."

"Ruby's Place does important work," he agreed.

She gave a derisive snort. "You say that like I can be separated from it. I am Ruby's Place. It was serving a few dozen women per year before I joined on and fought for the state grants to expand our space and our services. Do you know how many women and children we helped last year? More than six hundred."

"Congratulations."

She shook her head, her eyes wounded because he plainly didn't get it. "We save lives. You only hand out punishment."

"That's right," he agreed. "You should keep that in mind when you think about who might need to be punished."

She glared at him once more before pivoting on her heel and marching off in the direction of the shelter. Twice she glanced back to see if Nick was following her, but he didn't move from his spot on the corner. He waited until she was out of sight before slipping on a pair of gloves and fishing her paper cup from the trash. He held it gingerly as he began his walk back to the car. Charlotte wanted him to think about the value of Ruby's Place, and how it could have helped his mother. She couldn't have known about Nick's real fantasy, the one he'd had since he was eight years old: that he'd found his father's gun and shot him first.

....

CHARLOTTE PAUSED AT THE DOOR TO RUBY'S PLACE TO CHECK OVER HER SHOULDER ONE LAST TIME. She did not see Detective Carelli, but that did not mean he wasn't watching. Him or someone else. Her cold cheeks flamed as she stepped into the overheated entryway; her ears stung. She had only herself to blame for that since she'd given her scarf away to the woman in line at the coffeehouse. Nick Carelli had proved to be entirely too easy to fool. She'd crushed him so hard he belonged in a cocktail glass with a little paper umbrella. Maybe she could still pull this off.

"There you are."

She startled when Henry materialized out of nowhere. He frowned down at her like he could read her troubled mind. She took off her coat and avoided his eyes as she went to her desk. "I ran a few errands. Is there a problem?"

"Danny Romero never showed for his shift. Layla and a couple volunteers are making sandwiches for lunch, but I don't know what we're going to do about supper."

Charlotte's heart pounded so hard she thought it might escape from her chest. *You knew this would happen*. She kept her voice steady. "Then I'll go see if they need some help. We'll figure out something for dinner, even if it's ordering a bunch of pizzas."

This seemed to satisfy Henry because he smiled. "Now that's what I'm talking about. Sausage and onion for me."

Charlotte paused at the threshold to her office. "Is Karma in the kitchen too?"

"No, she went to the Y for lunch. Said she had to work off some energy." Henry looked dubious. "We could use the extra hands around here, but I'm not getting in the way of that woman and whatever helps her stay straight. You know what I'm saying?"

"Very much so. Thank you, Henry." Charlotte felt a tiny bit of relief that Karma was off the premises. It would make what she had to do somewhat easier. As she walked, she checked her cell phone and saw the last text she had received from Danny—a photo, sent yesterday, with the words *Did u know about this?* A fresh coat of sweat broke out over her neck and she wiped it away with one hand as she returned the phone to her pocket, the text unanswered.

She found Layla and a couple other women in the kitchen stacking bologna sandwiches on one tray and peanut butter and jelly sandwiches on another. "Hey there," Layla said, her smile friendly like the whole world wasn't crashing down on them. "Danny would have a fit if he saw us serving this stuff, but it was all we could rustle up on short notice."

"I heard he missed his shift."

"He said he wasn't feeling well last night." Layla dumped a can of frozen lemonade into a big pitcher and began filling it with water. "I was going to take off later and bring him some chicken soup from the deli he likes up the street."

Charlotte clutched the phone in the pocket of her cardigan sweater. "I think we have some cookies downstairs in the pantry," she said to Layla. "Would you like to help me bring them up?" The other two women were taking the trays out to put on the dining tables and did not overhear. Layla glanced at them before replying.

"Sure, okay." She left the lemonade half melted and followed Charlotte to the basement. The place resembled a fallout shelter, all concrete with tiny windows. A naked bulb hung from the ceiling and Charlotte clicked it on. Shelving lined the walls, packed to the gills with donations of clothing, toys, and tools. A locked pantry sat beyond with their stock of cereal, pasta, canned goods, and other nonperishable items. Charlotte also kept a safe in there with cash for emergencies, which is the reason the room remained locked most of the time. She opened the pantry and beckoned Layla inside. She didn't want to have this conversation anywhere the others might hear.

"Where is Danny?"

Layla looked befuddled. "He's sick. I told you."

"I went by his apartment on my way in. He's not there."

"He crashed at my place. Why? What does it matter?"

"It matters because of this." Charlotte pulled out her phone and showed Layla the text Danny had sent. Layla looked at the picture of the missing child poster with dispassion in her eyes, confirming to Charlotte she already knew what Danny had found. "What's he doing with this?"

"Nothing. He's not going to do anything." Layla tried to move out of the pantry, but Charlotte blocked her.

"How can you say that? We don't know who else he might have sent this to. I told you to be careful. I told you that Danny could be trouble."

"He's not trouble. I'm handling it."

"Oh, no. I can still fix things. I can, but you have to leave me to it. You understand? You stay out."

"But—"

"It wasn't Joe Green who got murdered."

Layla snapped her mouth closed. Her blue eyes stared into Charlotte's. "What are you saying?"

Charlotte didn't know whether to hug her or slap her. *Breathe,* she reminded herself. *You can fix this.* The story Jessica Green told them when she came to the shelter all those years ago had been full of half-truths and now Charlotte wondered what she really knew. Everything she'd done, she thought she'd understood about who she was protecting and why. Now the whole thing was coming apart. Charlotte had only one play left.

"Where is Danny?" she repeated, keeping her voice soft. She advanced a step toward Layla, who backed up against the pantry shelves.

"Why? What are you going to do?"

"I am going to fix things. I am going to make sure you, Karma, and everyone else here is protected."

"Charlotte, no. You can't do this on your own. I won't let you."

There was a time, maybe, they could have talked it over, but Layla had changed the rules on her and now Charlotte had to clean up the mess—starting with Danny Romero. Charlotte reached behind Layla's head and grabbed some boxes of cookies. "Where is Danny?"

"I told you. He's at my place."

Charlotte accepted this was the truth. She spun on her heel and marched to the door. She slammed it shut and braced her body against it when Layla tried to open it from the other side. The cookies fell to the floor. Layla started yelling but the door was thick and her words were muffled. She kicked and pounded and Charlotte struggled to get the key in the lock while holding the door shut at the same time. Layla was stronger than she looked. At last, the lock clicked into place. "I'm sorry," Charlotte called to her, though she knew Layla couldn't hear. "I wish there was another way." With shaking hands, she picked up the cookies to take to the kids upstairs. Layla would be fine in the pantry for the length of time it took for Charlotte to execute her plan. She had food, bottled water, and Charlotte had placed a bucket and toilet paper in there earlier in case Layla needed to relieve herself. She had hoped it wouldn't come to this.

Charlotte paused at the top of the stairs to smooth her hair and put a smile on her face. All those years of faking it in public had taught her well. In the dining hall, the mothers and children had filtered in for lunch, filling the space with noisy chatter. Charlotte spotted Karma with the pitcher of lemonade Layla had abandoned when Charlotte took her to the basement. Karma's hair was still damp from her trip to the Y.

"I have cookies," Charlotte said. "Who needs one?"

The kids clamored and Karma locked eyes with Charlotte across the room. She looked alarmed and Charlotte had a flash of panic that Karma somehow had heard what happened in the basement. She doled out some cookies and made her way to where Karma was filling paper cups of lemonade. "Thanks for your help," she said. "We're going to be shorthanded for a while."

"Layla said Danny is sick."

"Yes, and whatever he has, now she's got it too. She's left early."

"Yeah, well, we have other problems." Karma lowered her voice. "The PI . . . Annalisa Vega? She was at the Y asking around about Jessica Green."

Charlotte didn't let her alarm show. Nick Carelli, she could deal with, no problem. Annalisa Vega was trouble because Charlotte couldn't think of a good way to stop her. Of course, they would be looking for Jessica now. They'd want to ask her the same question Charlotte had now: if it wasn't Joe Green dead in the morgue, who was it?

Karma's eyes were round and afraid. Charlotte did what she did whenever one of her girls was frightened: she reassured her with an arm around the shoulder and a tight squeeze. "It will be okay. I'll think of something. You just hold down the fort here, okay? I'll be up in my private office for a while if anyone needs me. But . . ." She tried for a cheery smile. "Try not to need me if at all possible."

Karma faltered. "How could we not?"

Charlotte made a hasty exit before Karma could catch the tears in her eyes. She lifted Layla's jacket and backpack from the hooks in the main office and took them with her to her private apartment upstairs, where she rummaged until she found Layla's keys. If Danny was at Layla's place, Charlotte would have a half-hour commute to finalize her plan. She got a pair of latex gloves from under the sink as well as a few other tools she feared she might need. At the door, she took out her cell phone to turn it off. Upon looking at the phone, she thought twice and navigated to the text Danny had sent her. MISSING CHILD. Eve's small face with its gap-toothed smile—her kindergarten picture taken only weeks before she vanished—looked back at her. Charlotte's mouth tugged in a surge of emotion for her lost sister. This was the first and last school photo Eve ever had taken. Eve had lost her whole future the day of the parade, and Charlotte understood now that she could never make it right no matter how hard she tried. She sniffed hard and drew a shuddering breath. Then she hit "delete" on the photo and shut off the phone before setting off to Layla's.

TWENTY-NINE

Annalisa visited all the local YMCAs but failed to get even a whiff of Jessica Green's trail. If it weren't for the guy who remembered her swimming at the original Y all those years ago, Annalisa might wonder if Jessica Green had ever existed. The name was common enough to generate public records—too numerous to chase—but no indication that any of them were linked to Joe Green. The most obvious public record, a marriage license, did not appear anywhere for the state of Illinois. Either Joe and Jessica had been married elsewhere or not at all. But then again, Annalisa pondered, Joe Green wasn't Joe Green. So maybe Jessica wasn't Jessica either.

Defeated for the moment, she drove past her vacant office. There was no point in sitting around there by herself. She supposed she could go visit Effie Christos and discuss the situation with the missing ring, but since she still didn't have an easy answer, Annalisa continued to put that off. Instead, she did the only sensible thing for a woman more than six months pregnant and largely unemployed: she took a nap. She would need the rest ahead of what she imagined would be a protracted battle with Nick to participate in the stakeout happening by the lake that night. Exhausted as she was, Annalisa fell asleep like a woman falling off a cliff. She dreamed of her childhood home, of Alex and Tony and Vinny around the dinner table.

Hurry up, Pops ordered them. *You don't want to be late.*

Ma's meatloaf sat on the table, not breakfast. They weren't headed to school.

Late for what? Annalisa asked.

Prison, Alex answered, and he held up his hands to show they were cuffed. He held out his wrists to Annalisa. *Help me,* he said. *Before it's too late.*

Annalisa fled the house and went out into the yard. She had to hide before Alex or the rest of them found her. When she went to where the trash cans sat stacked against the garage, she discovered the girl from her earlier dreams already hiding there. *You can't be here,* Annalisa told her. *Not now.*

Shh, the girl said, a finger to her lips. *He'll find us.*

Annalisa didn't know what the girl had to fear from Alex. *Shove over,* she told the kid, sitting down next to her. A truck started backing down the alley behind them.

The girl grabbed Annalisa's arm. *You have to help me.*

Annalisa tried to pull away. *I don't even know you.*

You do know me, the girl insisted. *I'm Jessica.*

The truck engine started making a buzzing sound as it got closer. Annalisa sat up with a gasp and realized the buzzing wasn't a truck but her cell phone, sliding across the bedside table. The caller ID said Effie. Annalisa waited a moment longer for her heartbeat to slow before picking up the call. "Hi," she said.

"You're a hard woman to reach."

"Yes, sorry about that." Annalisa eased up so her back was against the headboard. "I've been busy with another case."

"I thought I was paying you enough to have your full attention."

Annalisa flushed and rubbed her face. "I wish I had something definitive to report. I've talked to your friends, to everyone who was there the day your engagement ring went missing. None of them admits to taking it."

"Yet obviously someone did."

"The last person to have the ring was Matilda. You want my best guess? She's misplaced it somewhere in the house."

"I told you that I've checked Matilda's quarters and the ring isn't among her jewelry."

"Did you check the freezer? The fireplace? She's clearly having some memory issues and I doubt she has any conscious recollection of what she did with the ring. With luck, it will turn up soon—probably somewhere you least expect it."

"Hmm. I confess I expected more when I hired you. Ruth said you were like some sort of wizard, solving the unsolvable."

Annalisa closed her eyes. Her head was starting to throb and her mouth was dry. "Sorry to disappoint you, but I am as human as they come." She took a deep breath. "I will tell you this: your friends love you as much as your husband Theo ever did. If you wanted me to find the truth, there it is."

"That's something." Effie sounded wistful. "They are dear people and I love them. When you get to be my age, you've lost so many folks along the way that the ones left standing are that much more precious. That's why I couldn't believe one of them would betray me like this."

"Maybe they didn't."

"Yes, all right. I'll accept your word on that. I'll ask Matilda again but I'm afraid I won't get very far with that line of questioning."

"If you want, I'll come help you look when I've wrapped up my other case." The woman had paid her handsomely to find the ring; the least she could do would be to spend a few hours poking around the mansion for it.

"Maybe I'm not meant to find it," Effie mused. "Maybe it's a message."

"What kind of message?"

"Theo's really gone," she said. "And I'll never get him back."

Annalisa promised to help her search for the ring next week, when she hoped the Joe Green case would be wrapped up. For that to happen, the trap they set for Charlotte would have to work. Annalisa heard the door open downstairs and Nick's boots in the hall. She stretched and went to greet him. "That looks good," she said when she found him in the kitchen downing a watermelon seltzer. He fetched her a can from the fridge and tapped his can to hers.

"Any luck on Jessica Green?" he asked.

"Nope. She's a ghost. How did it go with Charlotte?"

"She made the tail but it turned out okay because I got her DNA. Zimmer is having the lab put a rush on it." Suspected serial killers always moved to the front of the line. "If it's even a partial match to what we found on Joe Green's body, that'll be enough for a warrant."

"You know, we should probably stop calling him Joe Green."

"You got a better name for him?" Nick asked. Annalisa could only shrug in reply. "Charlotte seemed spooked when I delivered the news. I think she's worried she got the wrong guy."

"I'm kind of worried about that too." She set the can aside and stepped closer, putting her arms around him. "I'm also worried about you."

"It's the plan, right? I draw her out. Besides, Zimmer's already beefed up patrol along the lake. I'll also have two undercover units nearby. I'm thinking that among all of us we should be able to handle one middle-aged woman."

"She has a gun," Annalisa reminded him. They'd had to give it back to her once Karma's story cleared.

"None of the victims have been shot. But," he added before she could form a protest, "I'll be wearing a vest just to be safe."

Nothing about this felt safe. "I'll be there too," she said. "Don't worry, I'll keep my distance so I won't blow your cover. Sassy's letting me borrow her minivan so Charlotte won't recognize the car. I just think an extra set of eyes couldn't hurt."

Nick thinned his lips and looked away like he was arguing with himself. "Yeah, okay."

"Okay?" She'd expected pushback.

"You stay in the van a block away." He pointed at her in a warning fashion. "Radio contact only."

"Sure, whatever you want." She folded her arms. "To what do I owe this eager agreement?"

Nick rolled his neck around to loosen it. "Charlotte gave me the slip today on the street. I had no idea she'd even made me, but she put me on someone else's trail and then doubled back behind me. The woman is crazy like a fox."

"Maybe we shouldn't do this then."

"No, no. It'll be fine. I'll be sitting on a bench with a half-dozen cops watching me." He nudged her. "And one badass private detective."

....

NICK TOOK HIS POST ABOUT NINE. No need to pretend he was out for a stroll because Charlotte wouldn't believe that anyway. He dressed in a CPD jacket and carried an obvious radio with him, but they positioned him away from the streetlamps. The hope was that she would feel brazen enough to approach him because he was ostensibly alone. He walked the sidewalk along the shore as though keeping watch and then took his post on the bench. Every fifteen minutes, he repeated the process.

Annalisa could just make out his silhouette from where she sat in the minivan, parked in a small empty lot about a hundred yards away. With binoculars, she got more detail, but the night was misty, the moon obscured, and she couldn't read his face. Her coat and gloves kept her reasonably warm inside the van, but she'd sat there so long her rear end went numb and she desperately needed to pee. She wondered idly if Sassy still kept the kiddy toilet in the way back for emergencies.

"I'm freezing my balls off out here." Nick's voice crackled over the radio, and Annalisa grinned at hearing him.

"Good thing I'm already knocked up then," she replied.

"It's been almost three hours. I don't know if she's going to show."

"Give it until one at least. We don't know her usual time of attack. Don't you have hand warmers on you?"

Nick paced in front of the bench. "Sure, but I can't feel my face." He sat back down with a sigh. "Till one," he said. "Signing off." He put the radio on the bench next to him and Annalisa stretched her arms over her head. She contemplated making a dash for the twenty-four-hour diner she'd spotted down the block but she didn't want to take her eyes off Nick. She took up the binoculars and scanned the area around him. He had trees at his back, but they lacked leaves so they didn't provide much cover. The lake was a black void to her right. So far, the only action had been the occasional passing jogger and one homeless man dragging a beat-up suitcase behind him.

Annalisa saw a shadow move in the distance. She looked again with her binoculars and saw it was indeed a person moving in Nick's direction—medium build, not tall, dressed in a beanie hat and a long black coat. Annalisa was too far away to get any more information but the person's purposeful stride sent up warning bells. "You've got company," she said into the radio. "About twenty yards to your left and closing in fast."

She sat forward, binoculars pressed against her face. Nick didn't move. This was the plan, of course. Let Charlotte come to him. He was wired for any confession she might make. But as the figure emerged from the trees and loped toward Nick, Annalisa wanted to leap from the van and run after it.

She saw the person's coat flap open and caught a flash of metal reflected at the hip. Her hand seized the radio and she croaked a one-word warning. "Gun."

....

THE COLD FROM THE BENCH HAD SEEPED INTO HIS BODY. His knees stiffened up and he wasn't sure he could run fast at this point. *Too old for this,* he thought, wondering idly how he was going to keep up with a kid. Annalisa's alert sounded over the radio, letting him know he had company. He forced himself to remain still even as adrenaline shot into his veins like heroin from a needle. He glanced as far left as he dared without turning his head around like a damn owl but he couldn't see the figure Annalisa mentioned. His foot twitched and he touched the weapon holstered at his hip. *This is it,* he thought.

He heard the footsteps approaching as his radio came to life again. *Gun*. He didn't pause to think at that point. He leaped to his feet and whirled on the intruder with his hand poised near his holster. "Stop right there."

The woman put her hands up. "Don't shoot," she said. "Think of the paperwork."

"Hammer?" In his confusion, Nick blurted his boss's nickname. He relaxed his posture and grabbed for the radio. "False alarm," he told everyone listening. "It's just Zimmer."

As Zimmer approached him, Nick couldn't hide his dismay. "You're crashing the operation," he told her. "Blowing my cover." If Charlotte was watching, she'd know now he wasn't alone.

"I'm more than crashing. I'm calling it off." Zimmer took a seat on the bench, so Nick sat with her.

"I don't understand."

Annalisa's voice came over the radio. "What's happening? What's going on?"

Nick still waited for an explanation. "You want to fill her in?" he asked Zimmer.

"DNA came back just now. Charlotte Higgins is enough of a match to the DNA recovered from Joe Green's body that we can get a warrant."

Got her. Nick wanted to get up and do a touchdown dance. "The lab boys said they only got a partial from Joe Green." The body had been underwater, so it was a wonder they got anything at all. "It was still enough for a hit?"

"Enough bands match to eliminate most of the population, yeah. We've got the warrant to search the shelter and her vehicle for anything linking her to Joe Green—or the man known as Joe Green—and his murder. Maybe we'll get some damn answers about who we've got on ice over at the morgue."

Nick clicked over to Annalisa. "Did you get that?"

"I heard, yeah," she said. "That's great."

"You didn't have to come down here with this info," Nick said to Zimmer. "You could have radioed me or one of the others." He scanned the area for the UC operation but they were still staying out of sight.

Zimmer cleared her throat, a nervous gesture he recognized. She only did it when she had bad news. "No, I came because I have to pull you out. Charlotte Higgins did finally report your little fight with Annalisa. She went over my head and straight to the chief. I gather she has video of the whole thing."

Nick bit back a curse. "She reported me?"

"You're going to be suspended with pay pending an investigation."

"Commander, it was fake." Annalisa's voice came over the radio. "We staged the whole thing."

"I know that," Zimmer said with exaggerated patience. "And we will make sure the chief gets the message too. But until we have that conversation, I'm afraid Nick is sidelined."

Nick sat back against the hard bench. Charlotte made the one move they'd predicted she wouldn't do: she'd registered an official complaint. Maybe she'd never intended to come after him. Nick let out a heavy sigh, not relishing the future conversation with the chief. With Annalisa's support, however, he'd be cleared with no problem. "Ah, well. I can get somewhere warm now."

"And I can pee," Annalisa added.

Nick grinned while Zimmer shook her head in disbelief. "What a pair, eh?" He looked at Zimmer. "Are you going to search her place right now?"

"We can wait until morning," Zimmer told him. "Maybe you'll even be cleared by then. In the meantime, go defrost already. Go home and climb under an electric blanket or something."

"I don't need one," Nick told her. "I've got a cat."

Across the way, Annalisa rolled her eyes at Nick's statement. "I'll see you at home," she told him, waving even though he couldn't see her. Normally, she'd hike the couple of blocks to the tiny diner to use the bathroom, but she had to go so badly she wasn't sure she'd make it. She fired up Sassy's minivan and drove it the short distance to the diner, where she parked in another empty lot and jogged to the door. The place was empty save for a young guy working the counter and a pair of what looked like nurses off shift, eating breakfast in one of the three booths. Annalisa ordered a decaf coffee to go and then asked to use the restroom. The young man in the apron pointed to a nondescript orange door without saying a word.

Five minutes later, Annalisa had her coffee and an empty bladder. She hustled back out to the shadowed parking lot, juggling the coffee and her gloves as she fumbled for the clicker that would open Sassy's van. It chirped as she unlocked it, and Annalisa navigated her pregnant body behind the wheel. As she set the coffee cup in its holder, the passenger door opened abruptly.

Nick, Annalisa thought, smiling already.

Instead, Charlotte Higgins climbed inside and slammed the door behind her. Her eyes were wild and bright. "Sorry to do this," she said. "But I need your help."

THIRTY

Annalisa immediately checked the woman's hands. She did not see a weapon. "Help with what?" she asked. Her own gun remained holstered at her side, not very accessible beneath her jacket.

"I think you know. I think that's why you're out here. You and the rest of them."

So much for undercover work, Annalisa thought. "I'm not sure what you mean."

"I reported him, you know. Your husband." Charlotte peered out the windshield as though Nick might be standing there. "He shouldn't treat you that way."

"You don't really know him."

"Oh, I know him." Charlotte's voice was hard. "They all think they're special little snowflakes. The world doesn't understand them. They have so much stress. They never get a break. It's not their fault they snap sometimes. If the little wifey would just anticipate their needs better, they wouldn't have to knock her around." She shifted and made a disgusted face. "I'm sitting on a juice box."

"Sorry. It's my sister-in-law's van."

Charlotte removed the squashed sticky box from under her leg. "The sister-in-law married to your murdering brother? I saw her in the papers when the story broke. I saw you too, and read what you did. You turned him in but you'll still let your husband abuse you?"

"It's more complicated than that." Annalisa eased her hand down to switch on the radio and sent a silent prayer that Nick would still be listening.

"No, it's not," Charlotte said grimly. "It's the same story every time."

"You want to help," Annalisa said. "I think that's great."

Charlotte hunched inside her coat. "I help some. Others . . ." She shook her head vaguely. "Others it's too late."

"Like it was too late for Eve?"

"Leave her out of it." Charlotte looked at Annalisa. "Leave her name out of it or I swear I jump out of here and you'll never see me again."

"Okay, but you're the one who came to me. You said you needed help."

Charlotte balled both her hands into fists. She stared at her lap for a long moment and Annalisa wondered if she should take the opportunity to run. There had to be cops still in the area. "I think you may understand," Charlotte said in a rough whisper. "You know sometimes people do things, even crazy things, that others don't understand but you know they're right. You have a moral code."

Annalisa considered how to answer. "I believe in justice."

"Yes, justice." Charlotte seized on the word. "But justice and the law, they're not always the same thing. I'm betting you understand that. You used to be a cop but now you're not. You went your own way."

This was going to be a confession, Annalisa realized. She hoped like hell Nick was listening. In the meantime, she tried to get into her zipped pocket to access her phone. Charlotte spotted her arm moving and panicked.

"What are you doing? Don't call anyone. Don't ruin this. I only want to talk to you."

Annalisa held up her palms to show her hands were empty. "It's just you and me here. Say what you need to say."

The tendons in Charlotte's neck stood out. She stared at Annalisa with pleading eyes. "I killed them all. Just me. No one else."

"Killed who?" Annalisa wanted names.

"You know who." Charlotte looked irritated now. "The men. The abusers."

"Cyrus Merriman?" Annalisa went back to the beginning.

"He was my mistake." Charlotte seemed genuinely anguished. "I brought him into the shelter thinking it would be good for the women to have an accomplished lawyer doing pro bono work for them. Instead, he took advantage. He abused them a second time. What kind of monster preys on people who are already vulnerable?"

"I'm guessing Gwen Beaufort knew what he was." They'd been in law school together, Annalisa remembered. "Is that how you got her to lie for you about what she saw the night Cyrus was killed?"

"Gwen was happy to do it. Cyrus had gotten her drunk and raped her at a party when they were in school together. She went to the police about it two days later, but by then, no one cared. Her word against his, and the cops always believe the man." She threw the words at Annalisa like Annalisa had been the one to dismiss Gwen's statement. "If someone had stopped Cyrus back then, he never would have hurt those other women. But the cops wouldn't do anything. He would have carried on forever, abusing women who came to him for help."

"But he didn't because you stopped him. Tell me how you did it."

Charlotte looked surprised. "You already know. I shouldn't have to tell you."

"Joe Green was convicted of that murder, Charlotte. If you're trying to claim credit now, you need to back it up with facts. The whole truth."

"It was Jessica's idea to frame Joe," Charlotte murmured, turning her head to look out the window. "I thought it was brilliant. Two abusers removed at one time." As if she heard herself, she shifted back around to look at Annalisa. "I won't repeat that part, not for the record. I'll say it was my idea. I don't want anyone else taking the fall for this. Not Gwen, not Jessica. It was me who killed Cyrus, and I'll tell the police everything I did. But the others stay out of it."

"Sure," Annalisa said, knowing she could promise no such thing. "Tell me then. How did you kill Cyrus?"

"I pushed him in the lake."

"He outweighed you by eighty pounds. How did you manage to overpower him?"

"He was drunk."

Plausible, Annalisa knew. Cyrus had been bar crawling the night he died. "Go on."

"I followed him from the bar. He knew me, obviously. We struck up a conversation on the street. I suggested we walk down by the lake and he agreed."

"It was snowing that night. He wanted to go for a walk?"

"I may have suggested I'd be interested in more than a walk," Charlotte replied. "The man was a horn dog, looking for sex anywhere he thought he could get it. Easy enough to lead around by his dick to a place by the water that was far from the streetlights. We stayed there a bit, making small talk, and when he bent to tie his shoe, I . . . I hit him over the head with a rock. He got woozy. That's when I pushed him into the lake."

"Interesting," Annalisa said. "What about the Berkanan?"

"Oh," Charlotte said, her chin dropping as she corrected herself. "Right. I had a little pocketknife with me. Before I rolled him into the water, I—I opened his shirt and carved the Berkanan right about here." She indicated approximately the correct spot on her collarbone.

"And Joe Green?"

Charlotte clenched her jaw. "That man was evil."

"You killed him too?"

"I told you," Charlotte said, impatience creeping into her voice. "I killed them all."

"Okay, but why come to me now? Why confess?"

Charlotte swallowed, taken aback. "I—I've done everything on my own terms so far. I wanted to do this the same way. You're not so far removed from the police department. Maybe you can steer me to someone who can help me. Someone who is not your husband."

"You misjudge him."

"No, you do. Face it, he messed this whole case up right from the start."

Annalisa could have pointed out that Charlotte was here confessing because Nick was closing in on her, but she wanted to keep the woman on the subject of the murders. "Joe Green wasn't Joe Green," she said. "Who was he?"

"I don't know. I don't care." This felt like the truth. Charlotte looked and sounded tired. "Can you help me or not?"

Before Annalisa could answer, someone pounded on the van's windows hard enough to rock it. "Out of the car. Now!" Charlotte jumped in her seat as Annalisa's car door flung open. Nick stood there, his weapon drawn but not pointed at her. Zimmer stood on the other side of the car. She opened the door and forced Charlotte to get out and stand with her hands up against Sassy's van. Sassy would love this story.

"I trusted you," Charlotte wailed to Annalisa.

"Are you okay?" Nick reholstered his gun with one hand and touched Annalisa's face with the other.

She nodded. "Fine. You heard the radio?"

"Some of it. Enough to get an idea of what's going on."

"She's clean," Zimmer reported as she finished searching Charlotte. "No weapons." She cuffed the woman nonetheless. "Seeing as how you're so chatty, let's go somewhere and talk."

"You believe me, right?" Charlotte cast anxious eyes at Annalisa. "It was me and no one else."

"She confessed to killing everyone," Annalisa told Nick in a low voice.

"Everyone?" Nick seemed as skeptical as Annalisa felt.

"Yeah, but . . ." The doubt niggling at Annalisa bubbled its way to the surface. "What was Cyrus Merriman wearing the night he was killed?"

"Lawyer clothes. Shirt, pants, all of it costing more than I make in a month. If you want more detail than that, I'd have to check the reports."

Lawyer clothes. Exactly. "What about the shoes?"

"He wasn't wearing any when we found him."

"But he was reported missing, right? A week before that?" The missing persons report would have a description of his last known clothing.

"I don't see why this matters," Nick said.

"Just check the report."

Zimmer had Charlotte waiting at the front of the minivan. "I'm going to take this one downtown and get started on the booking. Carelli, you coming?"

Nick looked up from his phone. "I thought I was suspended."

Zimmer gestured at Charlotte. "We're arresting the complainant on multiple counts of homicide. I think you'll be okay."

"Loafers," Nick said in reply. He looked to Annalisa. "Cyrus Merriman was wearing loafers when he disappeared."

"Then he couldn't have been tying his shoe."

Charlotte looked like she might cry. "Please," she said. "You have to believe me."

"I told you that you need to get your facts straight."

"I'm a murderer. I'm the one you want." She tried to get closer to Annalisa but Zimmer held her back. "I can prove it to you."

"How?" Annalisa asked.

"I can take you to a body."

Zimmer's eyes widened, a flash of white in the dark. "Whose body?" she demanded.

"Danny Romero."

"The chef from the shelter?" Nick said. "He's dead?"

"He's at Layla's place. I didn't have time to move the body. I can—I can show you where I put him." Her knees buckled and she started to fall. Zimmer hauled her to her feet again.

"Looks like we're going on a little field trip," Zimmer said, nudging Charlotte toward the patrol car.

"If there's a body at Layla's apartment, she's got to be involved somehow," Annalisa said to Nick.

"No, I swear. I swear she's not." Charlotte halted walking and turned around. "You can check for yourselves. I—I locked Layla in the basement at the shelter so she wouldn't interfere."

Annalisa and Nick exchanged a horrified look. Was Layla dead too? "I'll check it out," Nick said to Zimmer. "You go to Layla's place."

"Take backup," Zimmer told him.

He paused on his way back to his car. "What about you?"

"I'm taking her." Zimmer nodded at Annalisa. "We'll radio for help on the way."

"Me? Really?"

"You about solved this whole damn thing," Zimmer said grudgingly. "I think you've earned a look at the final reel." Annalisa was about to thank her former boss when Zimmer let slip the real reason Annalisa got to tag along. "Besides, this way the pair of you can continue your conversation," she said, walking Charlotte to the back of the squad car. Annalisa knew it had a dashcam for both inside the vehicle and out. Whatever Charlotte said next, it would be on camera.

"Right," Annalisa said as she climbed into the passenger seat. She checked the side mirror to look back at Charlotte as Zimmer pulled out into the street. Charlotte didn't seem chatty anymore. She watched the passing scenery with hungry eyes, like she knew she wouldn't see it again for a good long while. "I'm wondering," she said to Charlotte, "if you helped Jessica Green to disappear. Maybe in return for the truth she told you about Joe and what happened to your sister."

"If Jessica disappeared, it's all Joe's doing. Not mine."

"But you know where to find her."

Charlotte's gaze turned sad. "I thought I did. Now I think maybe she's been gone the whole time."

Annalisa didn't know what to make of that. "You're saying Jessica lied about Joe? The man in the morgue isn't Joe Green. You may have killed the wrong guy, Charlotte."

"Jessica lied, but not about Joe."

Zimmer had the lights on but no sirens as she navigated the mostly empty streets. "This is the place," she said as she pulled up in front of Layla's building. "We may have to get a locksmith out here to get in the door."

"I have Layla's keys," Charlotte said from the back. "They're in my coat."

Annalisa and Zimmer exchanged a look, and Annalisa began to suspect Charlotte was telling the truth about what they would find in Layla's apartment. Zimmer pulled Charlotte, still handcuffed, from the back of the car. To Annalisa, she said, "There are gloves and booties in the trunk. I'm trusting you not to touch anything you shouldn't."

"I'm only here to observe."

Layla's building didn't have an elevator so they trudged up three floors to get to her apartment. In the dim light of the gray hallway, Zimmer looked at the keys to find the right one. Charlotte said to Annalisa, "You have to understand, everything I did, I did out of love."

"And the men you killed, they probably said the same thing."

Charlotte pressed her lips together to keep from crying, but her eyes filled with tears. "Danny was different. I'm sorry about him."

“We’re in,” Zimmer said as she opened the door. She cracked it and poked her head inside. Their backup hadn’t yet arrived but the place seemed quiet. “You stay here with her,” Zimmer said to Annalisa as she drew her weapon and entered Layla’s apartment. A few minutes later, she returned, her mouth a grim line. “Place looks clean. There’s nobody here and no obvious signs of struggle.”

“The balcony,” Charlotte said. “Rolled in a blue sheet.”

Zimmer ducked back inside and reappeared with a short nod. “Found him.” The hallway chatter and Zimmer’s back-and-forth drew a curious neighbor into the hall. He wore a bathrobe and slippers, hair disheveled and glasses crooked on his face as he took in the little tableau: Charlotte in handcuffs; Zimmer’s uniform; pregnant Annalisa with a gun at her hip.

“What’s happening? What’s going on?” the man asked.

“Nothing to worry about, sir,” Zimmer told him. “Please go back into your apartment. Everything is under control.” Outside, sirens grew louder as backup arrived. The man did not seem convinced by Zimmer’s assurances, but she tucked him back inside his home and closed the door firmly. “Get out of the hall,” she said to their little group as she shuffled them inside Layla’s apartment. “Now. Stand here by the door and don’t touch anything.”

Annalisa and Charlotte stood by the door, crowded next to the coat hooks and a little side table that held a ceramic bowl that looked like it was made by a child and various pieces of mail. Annalisa noted a man’s jacket hanging on the pegs and figured it belonged to Danny. “Why was Danny here at Layla’s?” she asked Charlotte.

“Layla and Danny were seeing each other. She told me where to find him.”

Charlotte looked nervous for the first time as the other officers started trooping into the apartment. Men, Annalisa noted. All of them. Chicago PD had more than double the number of female officers compared to the national average, but the men still outnumbered the women three to one. Zimmer gave them instructions on how to search the place. “Was Danny abusing Layla?” Annalisa asked Charlotte. “Is that why he had to die?”

Charlotte looked away. “I’d better wait to talk to a lawyer now.”

Zimmer took a phone call and stepped to the side to answer it. Annalisa saw flashing lights out the window as yet more squad cars joined the fray. The coroner would have to come pronounce the death. Crime scene techs would photograph the scene and catalog any evidence. They would find the tiniest speck of blood, a fiber, a hair—anything to prove the narrative of who did what to whom in the confines of this small studio apartment. What they would not be able to answer is why, and this question concerned Annalisa most of all. She watched Zimmer on the phone and read the confusion on the commander’s face. When Zimmer finished the call, she spent another few minutes poking at her phone. She charged across the room to Annalisa and Charlotte.

“Danny Romero’s brother reported him missing this evening. He said he got a weird text from Danny yesterday. Just a picture. No words.”

Charlotte looked ill. “A text?”

Zimmer held out her phone so Annalisa could see it. “It’s a missing child poster—kind of like you used to see on the side of milk cartons. For Eve Collier.”

Annalisa took the phone with both hands and brought it close to her face for a good look. Staring back at her was the girl from her dreams, just a couple of years younger. *My name is Jessica*. For a moment, none of it made any sense, but then she remembered “Joe’s” proclivities and she nearly fumbled the phone. “Eve didn’t die when she was kidnapped,” she said to Zimmer. “Her abductor renamed her Jessica and moved her here, to Chicago.” A chill went down her back as she remembered the truck from her dream, the one Jessica was hiding from. It was the landscape truck. Joe’s truck. She’d been trying to get away.

"Wait. You're saying Eve is Jessica?" A wrinkle appeared in Zimmer's brow as she zoomed in on the photo.

"Yes. The man we know as Joe Green took her when she was five. Back then, he claimed she was his kid. Later, when she got old enough, she became his 'wife.' As long as he kept moving around a lot, no one would know the difference." Annalisa turned to Charlotte, who had tears running down her cheeks now. "That's the big secret you've been hiding, isn't it? That's how Jessica Green knew the truth about Joe—because she'd lived it. She wasn't just any old abused wife who showed up at the shelter. She was your sister."

"We've got to find her then," Zimmer said. "She's part of this."

Charlotte shook her head, mute.

"She's more than part of it," Annalisa said. "I'm betting Eve's behind it all. That's why Charlotte's here confessing to killing all those men. She's trying to protect her sister."

"Okay, but you've been tracking this woman for days with no success. How do we find her?" Zimmer cast a glare at Charlotte, knowing she wouldn't talk.

"I feel like an idiot," Annalisa said. She pulled out her phone. "I only recognized her when I saw the picture, but it's been right in front of me the whole time." She went to the tab she kept open, the one for baby names. "Nick and I have been trying to get a short list of names. This site gives the meaning behind each name." Jessica Green did disappear, Annalisa realized. She fled her captor and became someone else—reborn, like the Berkanan said. Annalisa showed Zimmer the page she'd pulled up for girls' names. "Layla means 'night.' It means 'Eve.'" She could see it now on the poster since she knew what to look for; Layla's hair was darker now, her face rounder and her teeth grown in, but this was the same person as the one in the missing child photo.

"Carelli," Zimmer said, her eyes wide. "He went after her."

"I'm calling now," Annalisa said, already on her way out the door.

She barely heard Zimmer's pleas to wait, to let the CPD handle it. Nick thought he was safe with Charlotte in custody, that he'd be able to see any kind of threat coming, but they had all missed Layla. She had an air of vulnerability to her, maybe real, maybe practiced. After all, her abductor had changed her identity at least once, and then she had turned Jessica Green into Layla McCoy. Little Eve Collier had reinvented herself so many times that she probably didn't even know who she was anymore; for the men, she could be anything they wanted, up until the end.

THIRTY-ONE

Karma did not let Nick into the shelter right away. "Leave us alone," she said through the speaker. "You have no right to harass us like this."

"I need to get inside," Nick insisted. "Your friends may be in trouble."

Karma cracked the door and peered out at him on the stoop. "Where are Layla and Charlotte? I haven't seen them for hours and they aren't answering their phones."

"Charlotte is safe with my wife, Annalisa. They went to Layla's apartment to look for her."

"Why? What's going on?" Karma didn't budge, so Nick pressed on the door, forcing her backward. "Hey, you can't just barge in like this. You need a warrant."

"Not if there is an immediate safety concern. Where's your basement?" He had no idea if Charlotte might have hurt Layla before leaving her locked up there.

"Duh. It's downstairs. But you can't just—"

"Stay here," he ordered her. "Backup units should be arriving soon. When they get here, let them in and tell them I am downstairs." He moved with caution down the hall. For all he knew, Charlotte had booby-trapped the place.

Karma scrambled to get in front of him. "No, wait. Tell me what's going on."

"I don't have time to get into it now. I swear I'll explain everything later. You need to stay here. You need to keep everyone else away from the basement. Do you understand me?"

"Not until I talk to Charlotte."

"Charlotte has been arrested." The words came out more harshly than he'd intended as he loomed over her in the narrow hall. "You get it now? All the secrets you've been keeping are going to come out, so the best thing you can do is cooperate."

"Arrested?" The fight drained out of Karma and she staggered against the wall. "What for?"

"Stay here," Nick repeated as he charged down the hallway in search of the basement door. He found it at the end on the left, the wooden stairs going downward barely visible in the inky darkness. He paused to listen for any sound below but heard none. He took two careful steps down and stopped again. "Layla?" He called her name but got no response. Slowly, he descended in the dark, feeling along the wall for any light switch. At the bottom, a chain brushed the top of his head, and he yanked on it to turn on the light.

"Layla? It's Detective Carelli." He turned in a circle and saw the place was packed to the gills with boxes, bags, toys, and other donations. He took out a flashlight for closer inspection but did not see any sign of Layla. He tried calling her name a few more times as he navigated the crowded basement. Eventually, he found a locked door. "Layla?" A scuffling sound on the other side told him he'd found her. Yanking on the door did no good and he didn't see a key anywhere. "Hang on," he told her. "I'm going to get you out of there."

He hurried back to the shelves where he had spotted a large metal toolbox. There, he found not only the typical screwdrivers, hammer, and wrenches, but an electric drill and metal crowbar. He hefted the crowbar and took it back to the locked door. It took all his strength to force the lock, but it came free with a sharp snap. He stumbled from the exertion, breathing hard. "Layla?" He stepped inside the smaller room, his eyes working to adjust to the dark again, and he saw dry goods packed along the shelves. He did not see Layla so he took a couple additional steps into the room. Just as he was about to call her name again, he felt a presence behind him. Relief flooded his veins. He'd found her. She was saved. He started to turn around to give her the good news about her rescue when something hard and metal hit him across the back of his skull.

....

NICK AWOKE TO A THROBBING PAIN IN HIS HEAD AND THE TASTE OF BLOOD IN HIS MOUTH. He lay face-down on the grimy basement floor, his hands bound behind his back. Layla stood over him, his gun in her hand. "Get up," she said. "We're getting out of here."

Nick coughed and rolled to his side, grimacing with pain as he did so. He'd bruised his shoulder in the fall. "Look, whatever you and Charlotte have cooked up, it's over. We know everything. Charlotte's at your place right now with my boss. She confessed to everything."

"Up," she said, bending down and lifting him with her free hand. She was stronger than she looked. "We're going out the back." She shoved him forward and he staggered as his vision blurred. He wasn't afraid. More confused. Layla obviously didn't understand that Charlotte had given up the game and there was no use protecting her anymore.

"I know what she did to you, locking you down here. She was trying to protect her friends."

"She's not my friend. She's my sister." She pushed in front of him to open the door to the outside, pausing at the threshold to check for anyone else who might be around. "Okay, let's go." She half dragged him into the cold and escorted him to the garage at the back of the property. "You're going to wait here with the van." She shut him inside while she disappeared, presumably to get the keys. The small van had the cheery Ruby's Place logo emblazoned on the side, mixed with road grit and salt from their ugly winter. Nick didn't know what Layla was on about but he knew he had to get out of there. He edged along the van to the door, turning backward to try to manipulate the knob with his bound hands. She'd tied him so tightly he couldn't make the knob turn.

"There," she said as she opened the door, holding the keys where he could see them. "Now we can go."

"Go where?"

"I think you know. Get in." She opened the passenger door and pushed him toward it.

Nick had only one advantage: his size. "No." He planted his feet as she tried to force him through the van's door. She couldn't budge him more than a few inches. "This is ridiculous," he told her. "It's over. Charlotte confessed. The police are on their way here right now. I came here to rescue you."

"Yeah?" She stopped pushing on him and blew her bangs out of her eyes. "You're about thirty-five years too late for that." She trained the gun at his chest. "Get in the van. Now."

"You're not going to shoot me."

"I've killed seven men already. You'll just be one more."

She seemed serious but he couldn't quite believe it. "You've killed seven men?"

"Cyrus was the first. You'll be the last. I don't care if it's here or somewhere else." She held the gun steady, her gaze determined. "At least you won't be around to beat your wife anymore. She and that baby will be free."

Nick started to sweat. "Look, there's been a huge misunderstanding here."

"I'm going to count to three," she said. "Then I'll shoot."

"They'll arrest you."

"They're going to do that anyway. I'm not letting Charlotte go to prison for my crimes. One . . ."

"Wait, let's talk about this." He could stall her a few more minutes and help would arrive. Of course, Karma would send them to the basement. "You said Charlotte is your sister. That makes you . . . Eve?" He finally made the connection.

She flinched at the name. ". . . two."

"It's true. You're Eve." Even in his predicament, he marveled at this revelation, his eyes blinking with astonishment as he drank in the sight of her. Eve was alive. "Charlotte must have been so happy to find you."

"Three."

He saw the gun rise a few millimeters as she prepared to shoot and he lurched backward away from it, bumping his legs against the car and falling sideways into the passenger seat. Layla was on him like a lion, pushing the rest of his body into the van and slamming the door. She ran to the driver's seat and started the engine, pressing the button to open the garage door. The van lumbered down the alley, where she stopped at the mouth to the main road. Nick heard sirens approaching from the west. Layla turned east.

"I get it now," he said as he struggled to sit up in the seat. The effort left him sore, sweaty, and panting. "Charlotte was protecting you. She understands why you killed those men—they were predators, like the man who took you. The law allows for killing in cases of defense. Not just defense of self. Defense of others. That's what you were doing, right? Getting bad men off the streets so they couldn't hurt anyone else. A jury will see that."

"There won't be a jury." She gripped the wheel with both hands, his gun in her lap as she barreled down the street.

"Your lawyer, then. You'll have your pick of the best. Everyone will be amazed that you're back, that you survived."

"I'm not back. I never came back. No one will miss me."

The finality in her voice chilled him to the bone and he realized they were on a suicide mission. "That's not true," he argued. "You found Charlotte. You found your sister and she loves you. That's something."

"Charlotte." She whispered the name in agony. "I'm sorry . . ."

"We could go find her," Nick urged, twisting to try to see her face. "We could go talk to her right now."

"No." Layla remained resolute, stiffening her spine. "If she's at my place, she already knows the truth. Everyone else will soon know it too. I kept a journal hidden under my bed with lots of details, so the police won't bother Charlotte anymore. They'll know it was me, not her. The most she ever did was try to help me."

"Help you cover up the murders?"

She glared at him. "She didn't know. She thought Joe killed Cyrus and that we were just helping the police put him away. She knew he was dangerous from what I'd said and what Vanessa told her about Briana. It was my idea to set him up. I'm the one who looped in Gwen."

"I don't understand why you didn't go after Joe the first time. When you first ran away."

"That's right," she said flatly. "You don't understand."

"Then help me." He fell against the door as she made a sharp turn. "Why didn't you escape sooner? Why didn't you run to the police?"

"He said he would find me and kill me. I had no reason to believe otherwise. He'd been my whole world since I could remember and I felt completely helpless against him. When I finally did go to the shelter, Charlotte wanted to report him for spousal abuse. But that was the irony, right? Once I got a woman's body, Joe didn't want me anymore. He didn't touch me. That's how I was able to get away, because he was distracted looking for a new girl. Charlotte thought he'd been beating me because that's what I told her. I thought I had to say that to get into the shelter in the first place."

"You didn't tell her Joe abducted you?" Layla said nothing, so Nick tried again. "You must have told her something about what happened to you."

Layla stuck out her chin in defiance. "I told her an evil man took me from the parade and that much later I escaped from him. I didn't tell her Joe was that man. Charlotte thought what everyone else thought—that I married a violent husband. I didn't tell her he was the same man who raised me. I didn't want her to know. I didn't want her to know how long I'd stayed with him—what he'd really done to me."

"Why not? You could have stopped him."

"I was barely eighteen and still afraid of him. Why didn't you stop him?" She fixed him with a piercing look. "You or one of the other police? There were a hundred cops marching in that parade when I got taken. *A hundred*. Not even one of them helped me." She leaned over the wheel, her jaw set. "I had to help myself."

"That's why you killed him."

"The law never would. I saw that. I thought maybe when he got arrested for Cyrus's murder you would figure out what he did and who he was. I gave you that chance. But you didn't." Rough emotion made her voice raw. "You never saw who he was. No one did."

"Who was he? Tell me."

She shook her head. "You wouldn't believe me if I said. You took the easy story we fed you and didn't ask any more questions. Just locked him up. Well, I fixed it. I got him out and then I fixed it."

"You're the one who sent Joe that note."

"I didn't really think it would work." She sounded surprised. "I thought maybe the note would torture him a little—you know, let him know that someone believed he was innocent of killing Cyrus, but that someone wouldn't help him. Your wife, though . . . she figured it out." She glanced at him. "She's amazing. You don't deserve her."

"You're right about that." He sat back with a painful grimace, thinking of Annalisa and all they had endured together. How many second chances they'd already had. He dared to hope for one more. He thought he could play to her sympathies and remind her that he was about to be a father. "We're both nervous about the baby coming."

"You should be," she said, matter-of-fact. "This world is no place for a child." She slowed the van as they turned onto a darker, more residential street. Nick looked out and tried to catch a passing street sign. Then he recognized the buildings.

The van trundled to the end of the road and Layla hit the brakes. "Where are we?" Nick asked, but she didn't answer. She didn't have to because he already knew where she'd taken him. She got out and came around to open his door, waving him out with the barrel of his gun. The wind rushed into the van, hitting his face, and he smelled the water close by. They had arrived at the lake.

....

Annalisa pounded down the steps of Layla's apartment building while calling Nick on the phone at the same time. He didn't answer and she left a breathless message on his voicemail. "Layla is Eve. We think she's the killer. Call me when you get this." Her lungs, squished deeper into her rib cage by the baby, were on fire by the time she hit the street. She remembered then that she didn't have any car. A half-dozen squad cars were parked at odd angles, blocking the street. Annalisa marched to the nearest one, prepared to commandeer it, when she heard Zimmer calling her name.

The commander had her own phone out and waved it at Annalisa. "Units are on scene at the shelter," she said as she caught up. "Carelli is not there and neither is Layla."

"What? Where did they go?"

"No idea. His car is still parked outside."

"What about hers?"

"Also at the shelter."

Annalisa remembered what Charlotte had said. "Charlotte took Layla's keys. She may not have access to her own vehicle, but what if she took someone else's?"

"We're looking into it. Try to stay calm. We don't know that Carelli's in any kind of trouble."

"Commander, Layla kills abusive men. We painted Nick as an abusive man. If she's got him, she won't hesitate to take him out—especially if she thinks she has nothing left to lose. We've got to find him."

"Sure, but tell me where to look." Zimmer spread her arms. "If she's got wheels, they could be anywhere."

There was only one place Layla would go. "The lake."

"That's still twenty-two miles of shoreline in the city alone," Zimmer replied with a frown. "We can get units over there to look but it's a lot of ground to cover."

"Get Charlotte down here."

Zimmer radioed up to the officers keeping Charlotte in custody. One of the patrolmen brought her down to Zimmer and Annalisa. She still had tear streaks on her face and snot running from her nose since her hands were cuffed and she couldn't wipe them away. "What's going on?" she asked. "Is Layla okay?"

"We think she has my husband. Nick."

Charlotte blinked. "She's not in the basement at the shelter?"

"Not anymore," Annalisa said. "She's missing and so is Nick. We think they're together and may be headed for the lake."

Charlotte paled as she grasped the meaning of this. "When I realized what she'd done, that it had to be her, I tried to keep her safe. I locked her up. There was no way for her to get out."

"She did get out," Annalisa said, impatient now. "We need to know where she's going. Where does she take the men? Where would she bring Nick?"

"I don't know." Charlotte sounded fretful. "She never told me what she was doing. I only recently put it together myself. By then it was too late to save Danny . . ." She trailed off, distracted again, and Annalisa grabbed her shoulder to focus her.

"Who made up that story about Joe Green and Cyrus Merriman?"

"Huh?" Charlotte looked confused.

"The one that Gwen Beaufort testified to, about seeing Joe with the truck at the end of that dead-end street. Did Gwen make that up or did you?"

"Layla did," Charlotte said with reluctance. "She coached Gwen on the details."

"Then that's where we start the search," Annalisa told Zimmer. At that moment, Zimmer's radio crackled with the news that the search team at Ruby's Place had discovered the van missing.

"Layla knows where we keep the keys," Charlotte said. "They're on a hook by the back door."

"Come on," Zimmer said, handing Charlotte back to the patrol officer. "I'll drive."

"Don't hurt her," Charlotte called after them, her voice desperate. "Please don't hurt her. She's just a little girl."

The plaintive cry stopped Annalisa short. Her heart pounded as she pictured the scared girl in her dreams. A memory? Had she played with Eve as a girl while her kidnapper raked up leaves around the Vegas' yard? *Let's run away,* the girl in her dreams said. Annalisa said no. She'd had a loving home right there with her. There was no need for her to run. "Let's bring Charlotte with us," she said to Zimmer.

"No way."

"If Layla has Nick, she's already way out on a ledge. Charlotte may be the only one who can talk her down."

Zimmer hesitated another beat. "Fine," she said. She jerked a nod at the patrol officer. "She's riding with us."

They put Charlotte in the back and Zimmer took off for the lake with lights and sirens on. She radioed other units to go down by the shore and look for Nick, Layla, or any sign of the van. "Suspect is to be considered armed and very dangerous," she said. "If spotted, do not confront. I repeat: do not confront the suspect. Radio your location and keep back."

Charlotte sniffled behind them. "I should have seen it earlier. But Layla was happier now than she'd been in a long time. Maybe . . . maybe that's because Joe was finally gone. She allowed herself to be with Danny. I thought she was in love."

"Some kind of love," Zimmer muttered as she drove.

"Did Danny abuse her?" Annalisa asked. "Is that why she killed him?"

"I don't think so. I think he found out the truth."

"You mean that missing child flyer. The one that showed she was Eve? Danny texted it to his uncle."

"Layla showed it to me years ago, back when she was still Jessica. She said it was the only thing she took with her when she left Joe. I thought it was hers, you know, the only link she had to her old life. I realize now Joe must have kept it as some kind of trophy. She took it because she didn't want him to have even a little part of her. But she didn't throw it away. I told her to. She said she would but I guess she didn't."

It was proof of more than her kidnapping, Annalisa thought. It was proof her family had wanted her to come home. It was proof she'd been loved. "Here," she said to Zimmer, sitting forward in her seat. "Turn here and slow down. Kill all the lights and sirens."

Zimmer followed instructions and slowed the cruiser to a crawl. "Now what?"

"We're approaching the intersection where Gwen swore she saw Joe and Cyrus. If that story originated with Layla, it probably has meaning for her. Here. This is the turn."

Zimmer turned the corner and Charlotte let out a cry. "That's the van!"

Visible in the shadows at the end of the road was the van from Ruby's Place. Annalisa did not see Nick or Layla, and she feared they'd found the right place too late.

....

THE WIND SHEAR OFF THE LAKE FELT LIKE THE ONLY THING HOLDING HIM UPRIGHT. Nick stood on the steep side of the cliff, his feet angled to prevent a total slide into the freezing water. Layla had untied his hands but they were numb and tingly still from where she had bound him for so long. She stood above him, closer to the fence line, with the gun in her hands. "You'll have to shoot me," he called up to her. "There's no way I'm going to jump."

"If you insist," she said, raising her voice over the wind. "It might be easier on Annalisa, though, to bury you whole. She probably still loves you even after what you did to her. I loved him once. Joe. Can you believe it? I loved him."

"You were a little kid. It's not fair what happened to you."

"Life isn't fair." She pointed the gun at him.

Nick could protest that he'd never really hurt Annalisa, but that would be a lie. He'd struck her for show, at her own design, but his real damage had been done years earlier during their first marriage. His chest ached at her forgiveness, at all he stood to lose. "You put the Berkanan on the victims," he said, and Layla seemed to pause. "It signifies rebirth, right? A second chance. Why would you put that there if you didn't mean it?"

"Rebirth for me. Not for them. There's no hope for those men." She looked out at the vast expanse of water. From this vantage point, it was an ocean—nothing but cold and dark as far as the eye could see. "Not in this life, anyway. But maybe the next one."

"People change," he called out as she raised the gun again. "I know I've changed. Your solution is too final. It doesn't allow for mistakes. For forgiveness and the chance to try again."

"It's too late," she said, her voice carrying on the wind.

"No, it's not." The shout came from behind them. Nick looked up to see Annalisa and Zimmer at the fence line. Annalisa waved her arms in a frantic motion, trying to get their attention. She was the one who'd shouted. Zimmer had her gun pointed at Layla.

"Drop your weapon," Zimmer hollered, but Layla didn't move.

"Please," called another voice, and Charlotte emerged from behind Annalisa. "Please, stop, Layla. If not for him, then for me."

"He's an abuser," Layla replied, her expression hardening from the surprise she'd experienced at the sight of her sister. "You saw it." She looked at Annalisa. "Why did you bring her here? She doesn't need to be here for this."

"Then put down the gun and stop," Annalisa said, moving around Zimmer to the edge of the fence. "Come up here and let's talk about it."

"You'll be better off without him."

"No, I love him. He didn't hit me out of anger. It was a show to drag you out. And look, it worked."

Layla looked uncertain. "I know what I saw."

She took a step toward Nick and Zimmer yelled again. "Stop right there!" For all her bluster, Zimmer couldn't really risk a shot from this angle in the semidarkness. If she missed Layla she could easily hit Nick who stood just beyond her. "Put down your weapon and come back up here to the street."

"You see why I had to do it?" Layla turned her attention from Nick to Charlotte. "I'm trying to fix things. I'm trying to get rid of as many of them as I can. You're amazing, the work you do at Ruby's Place, but it's picking up the debris after the tornado's gone through. These men are destroyers who wreck everything in their path. The only way to stop them is to eliminate them for good."

"Nick's not an abuser," Annalisa said, getting closer as she came around to the edge of the fence. "You're wrong about him. You're trying to kill an innocent man. A good man."

Layla looked back over her shoulder at Nick, her face distraught. "There are no good men."

"Danny was," Charlotte cried with despair. "Danny loved you. Why did you have to kill him?"

Layla's face crumpled at the mention of Danny. "I didn't want to. He found out the truth. He was going to tell."

"The truth is out now." Annalisa stretched out her hand to Layla, offering to take the weapon. "Please, give me the gun. Give me back my husband and let us be a family. You can come up here and help your sister. She's trying to put it all on her, you know. She says she's the one who killed those men."

"Charlotte would never kill anyone." Layla was crying now. The gun shook in her hand. Behind her, Nick started inching to the side, trying to give Zimmer a clearer shot. Annalisa kept Layla distracted. "Karma's the one who understands. She shot her husband before he could kill her, and if you ask her, she'll tell you she's sorry she didn't finish the job. That's what she told me. That's when I understood what I had to do."

"Layla, please," Charlotte said. "Stop this now before anyone else gets hurt."

"It's too late." Layla wiped her face with her sleeve. "I . . ." She whirled on Nick and found him not where she'd left him. In her shock, she lunged at him and Zimmer fired at the same moment, her gunshot echoing off the lake like thunder. She missed Layla, and in the chaos, Nick lost his footing on the steep edge of the cliff.

"No!" Annalisa shouted as Nick slid over the edge. She scrambled after him, but Layla was closer. Somehow, the shock of Nick dangling there seemed to snap her out of it. She threw the gun aside with a shriek and ran to grab Nick's arms from where he held onto the rocks at the edge. "Get off of him!" Annalisa went to shove Layla aside when she realized that the woman was holding him steady, not pushing him off.

"Help," Nick said through clenched teeth. He wriggled as he tried to get his footing on the slippery rocks.

"I'm trying." Annalisa was awkward and gangly as she tried to reach over her own belly to help Nick. Zimmer appeared behind them.

"Move over. I'll do it."

Annalisa collapsed backward and Zimmer took her place. Together with Layla, she hauled Nick up enough that his center of gravity shifted and he was able to crawl to safety. Annalisa retrieved the gun that Layla abandoned and saw it was Nick's weapon. Breathing hard, still on her hands and knees, Zimmer looked at Layla. "You're under arrest," she told her.

Layla sat on her haunches, looking defeated. Annalisa stared at her with wonder. "You believed me," Annalisa murmured. "You helped save him. Why?"

"Maybe he was right." She looked at Nick. "Maybe there can be forgiveness. I hope so for your sake . . . and for mine." Layla tilted her head to yell up to Charlotte, who stood on the other side of the fence. "Remember me," she cried, her voice catching with a sob. Before they could stop her, she rolled off the edge of the rocks.

Charlotte screamed like she'd been stabbed. Zimmer cursed and pulled out her radio to call for help. Annalisa crawled to the cliff's edge to peer below, the wind whipping her hair back and forcing her to squint. She could not see Layla. Nick had risen to his feet and was looking for a way down. He navigated through the trees to the right, picking a less steep route. Annalisa watched as he got down near the water's edge, the tiny beam from his flashlight just visible as he aimed it at the lapping surf. She heard him shouting Layla's name. Annalisa cupped her hands around her face and yelled too: a different name, the last time perhaps that anyone could use it. "Eve!"

THIRTY-TWO

Despite everything, Charlotte Higgins née Collier remained at Ruby's Place doing the work that sustained her. The district attorney wasn't sure what to charge her with, Nick had said. No trial could proceed unless authorities could prove what Charlotte had known and when, and it seemed no one had any appetite to figure that out. No one even wanted to charge Gwen Beaufort with perjury; her story put a man in prison for a crime he didn't commit, but everyone agreed he belonged there anyway. What everyone most wanted to know was the same question Annalisa had: who was "Joe Green" and was he the man who had abducted Eve from the Christmas parade?

Annalisa visited Charlotte at the shelter and put this question to her, but Charlotte had no answer. She served Annalisa tea at a well-worn table, cupping her hands around the mug to absorb its warmth. "I don't know who he was. Layla wouldn't tell me. She didn't say much about her time in captivity, no matter how much I asked. I think she was trying to spare me the details."

Annalisa imagined the details were horrific. "He wasn't in the system at the time of his arrest for Cyrus Merriman's murder," she said. "They would have caught him then."

"Yes," Charlotte said dully. "Imagine if they caught him then."

This kept Nick up some nights. They'd had "Joe Green" locked up once but didn't know who he really was. Annalisa rubbed his chest and tried to reassure him. *You did everything right,* she told him.

Then how did I get it so wrong?

The only place where Nick might have found the truth was if he'd somehow dug deeper on the missing persons report. The original Joe Green was now presumed dead. The man in the morgue, the one who presumably abducted Eve, either found Joe drunk to death by happenstance or murdered him with the intent of taking over his name and social security number. But the whole point of Nick's inquiry was that Joe wasn't missing anymore. He'd been found and arrested for Merriman's murder, so what would have been the purpose in mucking around further? Cops had to give up on missing persons cases all the time due to lack of resources. Only Annalisa, with the luxury of time at her PI job, could follow a trail gone decades cold.

"If I paid you, would you go to Madison to look for him?" Charlotte asked her over tea. "To find out who he was?"

The police had only a vague interest in identifying the John Doe who had been Joe Green. Joe ended the way he'd begun, it seemed: as a missing person. Their investigation concluded the man in the morgue was Eve Collier's abductor. He'd taken over Joe Green's identity and gone on the run with Eve. Who he'd been before that was a curiosity now; there would be no trial for him because Eve had seen to that.

I don't like it, Nick had said. *The loose ends. That's how we ended up with this mess in the first place. What if there are other victims?*

Annalisa thought of Briana and how Vanessa had protected her from the heat of a trial. *He's dead,* Annalisa replied to Nick. *If there are other victims, they are free now.*

I can't believe you'd let this go. You always want the full truth.

Annalisa sighed to Charlotte as she put down her teacup. "I don't know there would be much point in investigating further. I've got the baby coming in a couple of months and nothing really to go on." If she had to dig, she'd look for men in Joe Green's life around the time of his disappearance. Drinking buddies. Workmates. Anyone who might have sized him up as a convenient patsy. But that was almost forty years ago now. Who would even remember? "The man Layla killed was the man who abducted her. I'm not sure how much more there is to learn beyond that."

"But why?" Charlotte's eyes were haunted. "Why her? Why then?"

"Finding his name won't tell you that." Annalisa shifted in the wooden chair as she tried a different tack. "You could go to Madison," she suggested. "You could see your brother, Keith." The two remaining Collier siblings were all that was left of the original family.

"I tried calling him when the news broke. He won't speak to me."

"Because you kept Eve from him," Annalisa guessed.

Charlotte made a pained face. "It wasn't my choice. Layla said I couldn't tell anyone. I thought one day she'd change her mind, but she never did. I think . . ." She broke off as if searching herself. "I think maybe she had some anger at Keith. He was the oldest. He was supposed to be watching her the day of the parade."

"He was what, eight years old?"

"I didn't say it was logical. Nothing about this was logical."

Annalisa had only one question left. The one that dogged her every day. "If you had known earlier what Layla was doing, would you have turned her in?" She leaned closer, her breath caught in her chest. She'd made a hard, lonely choice for herself, turning in Alex. She wanted to hear that Charlotte would have done the same.

Charlotte gripped the mug tighter. "Part of me says yes. I would have gotten her help. I would have tried to find her a good lawyer, someone not like Cyrus Merriman. But that's the point, isn't it? You can't tell the good ones from the bad ones until it's too late. And then the bad ones always seem to get away with it."

"And the other part?"

Charlotte leaned down and touched her leg where the Berkanan tattoo sat. "The other part would have joined her."

....

On the weekend, Annalisa went to see Alex. He had saved a copy of the headline story from the *Tribune,* the one with her picture in it. "Look at you," he said to her. "In the papers again."

"Not by choice." Press coverage was more muted than it might have been. The public, it seemed, didn't know what to do with the story. The mystery of Eve Collier was solved, but it wasn't the tragedy everyone had been expecting; she had not been murdered on the day of her abduction all those years ago. But it wasn't a happy ending either. Little Eve had survived to find her sister and to become something else. A murderer? An avenger? No one was quite sure what to call her so it was easier to say nothing at all.

The paper showed the kindergarten photo of Eve, the one from her flyer, back when she was a lost innocent. Alex traced the outline with his finger. "If guys in here had known Joe was a pedo, he never would have survived."

"No one knew. That was the point."

"You figured it out." Alex eyed her with grudging admiration. "You might be as smart as they say."

"It might have helped if I could have recognized Eve back when she came to our house. She might have still had a chance then."

"You were just a kid," Alex argued, folding the paper and pushing it to the side.

Just a kid. Like he'd been, the night he snapped and committed murder. Like Eve had been the day "Joe Green" grabbed her from the parade. Kids can disappear quicker than you think. Annalisa hugged her belly without realizing she was doing it until Alex nodded at her midsection.

"Getting close now."

"Two more months."

"You got a name picked out?"

"We're still debating." Nick would be happy to go along with whatever she chose, but Annalisa felt more overwhelmed than ever. Naming dolls or a pet was one thing. This was bestowing an identity on a real person. The baby name sites told her that Eve could mean "life" or "living." Eve had survived her kidnapping in the technical sense, but her life as she knew it ended that day. The gap-toothed smiley girl who went to the parade with her uncle and her siblings never came home. She became Jessica, which meant "seeing" or "foresight." Annalisa would bet her captor didn't know this when he chose the name; he'd probably picked it because it was common at the time and someone with the name "Jessica Green" would not be memorable. Ironically, no matter how many people met Jessica, no one really saw her. Her abductor had cut and dyed her hair. He'd moved her across state lines and given her a new name. He'd been ballsy enough to do landscaping at a cop's house with his victim running around the property. Of course, this was several years after the initial abduction. Annalisa estimated the girl in her memory to be around eight or nine. *Let's hide and never be found,* the girl said. She never was.

"Sassy was here yesterday," Alex said. "She looks good." He glanced out the window, his gaze wistful. "She told me she's going to marry that guy."

"I figured." Annalisa had talked to Sassy a few days ago and Sassy said Greg finally convinced her to go up in his airplane. *He picked a really calm, sunny day and promised we could turn around if I got scared,* Sassy told her. *But once we got up there, I wasn't afraid at all. The city's so beautiful from up there . . . and the lake looks like a huge mirror. I had so much fun I couldn't even remember what I'd been afraid of in the first place.* Annalisa looked at the slump of Alex's shoulders and her heart squeezed inside her chest. "You okay?"

He gave a helpless shrug. "I'll get used to it. What choice do I have?"

"I am sorry," Annalisa said, "for wrecking your life."

He stared back at her, a long wordless look. "And I'm sorry for wrecking yours."

....

AT THE PRECINCT, SOME OF THE COPS HAD CHANGED THE *TRIBUNE* HEADLINE FROM P.I. SOLVES "CHRISTMAS EVE" MISSING CHILD CASE to "NICKY'S WIFE" SOLVES MISSING CHILD CASE. Bill Dickerson and Andy Chavez snickered together as they watched Nick pick up the altered paper and stare at it. They probably expected him to rage and tear it up. Instead, he tacked up their handiwork on the bulletin board closest to his desk. Dickerson bellied up next to him, chuckling. "Would you look at that? Vega ain't even on the force anymore but she's still showing you up."

"Heard she had to save your life," Chavez offered, sipping from his coffee mug. "Again."

"At least I have a life worth saving," Nick countered. They guffawed and elbowed each other, but Nick only frowned. "You think it's funny? You think these little jokes make you smart?"

"Aw, lay off, Carelli," Dickerson said. "We're only having fun."

"Yeah, your kind of 'fun' helped drive Vega out of here. One of the best detectives ever to do it and she's not on our team anymore. So good job, Dickerson. Way to go, Chavez. You're right she cracked this case where I couldn't. Where we couldn't. You get that it's not just me with egg on my face? It's the chief, it's Zimmer. It's all of us." He looked them over with disgust. "I'm fine because yeah, Vega saved my butt. Vega's fine because she was smart enough not to take your shit anymore. And you, Dickerson? Well, you're just a dick."

"Carelli?" Zimmer's assistant hung her head around the corner. "The Hammer wants to see you."

Nick left Dickerson and Chavez looking chagrined and stuck his head into Zimmer's office. "Commander?" She had eyes on her computer monitor and waved him in without a word. He sat in one of the two chairs in front of her desk while she finished reading whatever was on the screen.

"I'm signing off on your final report," she said at length. "It's good work."

"It's not final," he argued. "We don't know the identity of John Doe or what happened to the real Joe Green."

"That's Madison's problem," Zimmer told him. "Eve Collier's abduction is their jurisdiction. Them or the feds."

"You know as well as I do that they aren't going to pursue it. They weren't even looking into the case when Eve was still alive."

"Yeah, because no one has the money to go chasing a ghost. Look, I get it. I'd love to get his ID too—make it all pretty with a red bow on top. But the man is dead. His crimes died with him."

Nick thought of Layla, leaping into the sea. They had recovered her body two hours later. Nick had the autopsy photos as part of his official case record, and he had sat with the close-up of Layla's hip and the Berkanan tattoo she'd had branded there. He'd traced the odd B shape and considered again its meaning. Rebirth. He hoped it could be true. "Layla's crimes were his crimes," he said to Zimmer. "He made her what she was."

"That may be so, but she's dead too. It's time to move on. See Lieutenant McKenzie for a new assignment."

She dismissed him, and Nick went back to his desk but he didn't seek out a new assignment. He pulled up Eve Collier's original missing persons picture. It was the one thing Layla took with her when she fled "Joe's" capture. This meant her abductor had a copy for her to take. But why did he keep it and how did he get it? The flyers hadn't gone up until a couple of days after the kidnapping, which suggested he'd hung around the city with Eve for a while rather than fleeing the state immediately. Had he known the family, as Annalisa suggested? Had he perhaps even participated in the search? Nick knew sometimes criminals liked to insert themselves into the investigation of their crimes, both to find out what the cops knew and to relive the high of the initial event.

You didn't see him for what he was, Layla had said.

Nick dug into the old files. "I'm trying," he muttered. "I'm trying." Investigators had compiled a bunch of pictures from the parade—photos taken by the press and by parade-goers. In one, someone had circled the little family before the nightmare began. Keith, Eve, and baby Charlotte in her uncle's arms had worked their way to the sideline to watch female baton twirlers in Santa hats. The marker on the circle went through Doug's face but Nick could see he'd been smiling like the rest of them. *Poor bastard,* he thought, easing back in his seat. A single guy out with three little kids. No wonder things went sideways.

He printed out the photo on the good printer so he could get a close-up view of the crowd around the little family. Maybe he could spot Joe Green watching Eve, preparing for the moment he'd abduct her. After all, they were operating on the assumption he knew the family and had targeted Eve in particular. He had the family photo in his possession. Nick got a magnifying glass and studied the faces in the photo one by one. Everyone was happy. Everyone was smiling. He lingered again on Uncle Doug, Keith, Eve, and Charlotte, then shifted the glass to the right and back again. Wait. He squinted and put his face right down close to the photo. *Could it be?* A prickle broke out across the back of his neck as the full horror of what he was looking at registered in his brain. He went back to the computer and did another search. When the results came back, he sat gaping at them, his hands in his hair, for several long moments. He eventually rose and sprinted back to Zimmer's office.

"Boss," he said. "Give me twenty-four more hours on the Joe Green case."

She glanced up, irritated. "Carelli, I already told you—"

"I know who he is. Come on, squeeze the budget on this one, Hammer. I'm telling you with a little more time, I can prove it."

THIRTY-THREE

It was Nick's turn to go to Madison. "I won't be gone more than two days," he told Annalisa as he threw a change of clothes into an overnight bag. "Otherwise Zimmer will cut up my credit card."

"You have a lead on Joe Green?" As she said it, Annalisa realized she wasn't sure whether she meant the original Joe Green or the John Doe they still had cooling in the morgue. "I thought Zimmer closed that case. No ifs, ands, or buts."

"Turns out my butt is irresistible," he said, kissing her cheek.

She reached around and gave it a squeeze. "I'll say. Text me when you get there so I know not to worry."

"Will do." He put his hand on her belly. "Have you thought of any more name possibilities?"

"What about Alfred for a boy? We could call him Alfie."

Nick frowned. "Too *Batman*. But I was thinking in the shower earlier: what do you think of Daphne for a girl?"

She made a face. "Too *Scooby-Doo*."

He sighed. "I guess that leaves Shaggy right out the window then." He kissed her once more and whistled as he walked out the door. Annalisa repressed a faint frustration that he was following a lead now that she couldn't. She might have tried to angle an invitation to go with him, but she had a doctor's appointment and a meeting with Effie Christos to help her look for the ring. At least the weather was cooperating, all bright sunshine and soaring temperatures. It was false spring, a weird glitch that would right itself in a day or two, but Annalisa would enjoy the mild weather while she could.

She drove to the doctor's with the windows down, ignoring the scraggly, empty branches on the trees and the patches of dirty snow in the streets. This was her third appointment in as many weeks and it felt like overkill. She'd complained to Sassy that the doctors wanted to poke her what felt like every other day. *We're in the home stretch,* Annalisa said. *Everything always comes back normal. I don't know why they need to check my blood pressure and pee samples every twenty minutes.*

Because the stakes are higher now, Sassy informed her. *That's not just a fetus anymore. It's a person who could probably live on their own, so if things go bad, they want to take the baby right away.*

They could take the baby now? Annalisa panicked. She did not feel remotely ready. *I hope it doesn't come to that.*

Ooh, what about Hope? I mean, if it's a girl.

No, Annalisa said. *Hope feels like the name would be for us, not for her.*

Well, you better figure out something quick. They won't let you leave the hospital without putting something on the birth certificate, you know.

Annalisa still had time. At least she hoped so. She turned in to Effie's winding driveway for her afternoon appointment, which she dreaded even more than the blood draws at the hospital. She'd come to help Effie search for the missing ring, which she did not expect to find, and she also had to decide whether to tell Effie the truth about what she'd learned: the ring was a fake. *Persephone,* she thought, musing on Effie's full name as she rang the sonorous bell to the mansion. Pretty, but Annalisa had looked it up and Persephone was the goddess of the underworld. The name literally meant death.

Effie herself answered the door, looking not at all like death in a vibrant pink pantsuit and pearls. Maybe names weren't destiny after all. "Come in, come in," she said. "Can you believe this beautiful day? Even the birds are singing."

Annalisa had seen a pair of starlings chasing each other around the lawn when she had parked her car. "Spring is coming," she agreed as she stepped inside. Matilda arrived to take her coat, but Annalisa didn't have one because the weather was so mild. A breeze floated by and Annalisa gave it a deep sniff. "Something smells good."

"I'm making an apple tarte," Matilda said. Her delivery was stiff and a bit cool. "Effie said we should feed you in return for helping us look for the ring. I can assure you my quarters have been searched several times over and I did not steal it."

"No one thinks you stole it." Effie moved to put an arm around the woman. "Do we, Ms. Vega?"

"No, of course not. I think it's merely been misplaced."

Matilda looked at her with wet eyes. "We saw you in the newspaper. You found that missing girl, the one who disappeared from the Christmas parade."

"I don't know if it's correct to say I found her. Stumbled over her by accident, maybe."

Effie gave Annalisa an assessing look. "I think Ruth might have been right about you. Regardless, I have a good feeling about today. It's gorgeous out, the sun is shining just like it was the day the ring went missing. That's a good omen, don't you think?" She clapped her hands together like an eager child.

"Sure," Annalisa agreed. "Where would you like to begin the search?"

"Wherever you think best," Effie replied.

Matilda tensed up. "She'll say I took it. I know she will."

"She won't." Effie rubbed her shoulder vigorously like she was bucking up a soldier. "I won't let her."

"Let's begin upstairs, if that's okay," Annalisa said. The hallway outside of Effie's bedroom was the last place she could pinpoint the ring, when Matilda had caught Louise sneaking out with it.

"Of course." Effie took the steps slowly while Annalisa and Matilda trailed behind her. "Oof," she said, pausing halfway up. "To think, I used to fly up and down these stairs a hundred times per day. Now they're my Everest."

"You should take over one of the downstairs rooms," Matilda said, fussing over her. "We could fix it up nice and proper for you and you wouldn't have to worry about these stairs anymore."

"No, thank you, Mattie. I'll be sleeping in the same room, in the same bed, I shared with Theo." With determination, she resumed her ascent. When they reached the bedroom, Annalisa stopped them in the hallway.

"Louise said you met her coming out of the room with the ring," Annalisa said to Matilda, and Effie's eyebrows shot up.

"Louise took my ring. Why?"

"I'll get to that." Annalisa kept her gaze on Matilda. "Do you remember Louise and the ring?"

"I remember someone had it. They said it was for a charity auction."

"Stuff and nonsense!" Effie interjected. "I never would have auctioned off that ring, and Louise knows that."

"Please," Annalisa said. "I want to know what Matilda remembers."

Matilda chewed her bottom lip as she tried to recall. "I took that ring back. I wanted to check with Mrs. Effie that she intended her friend to take the ring."

"Good." Annalisa encouraged her. "What did you do next?"

"I . . . I must have put it back." She drifted to the threshold of the bedroom. "Mrs. Effie had it out on the dresser over yonder, and I would have put it back where it came from." She slipped her hands into her apron pockets.

"Maybe you got distracted," Annalisa said, moving to stand next to her. "Maybe you put the ring in your pocket instead."

"No. No, I wouldn't do that."

"We've done the washing several times over," Effie said with impatience. "If she pocketed the ring, it would have turned up by now."

Annalisa went to the dresser and opened all three jewelry boxes. "And you've double-checked it didn't get mixed in with some other pieces?" She could imagine Matilda might have put the ring back in the wrong spot.

"Triple-checked," Effie said firmly. "I took out each piece, one by one. My engagement ring was not among them."

Annalisa closed her eyes and tried to picture the moment Matilda took the ring from Louise. The experience with Layla had taught her that it was possible to look right at a problem and not see the solution directly in front of her. She returned to the hall to narrate her actions. "You were returning the ring to the bedroom," she said, "but maybe something stopped you."

"No," Matilda said, following alongside her. "I would have put it straight back." In her pocket, something electronic started beeping. "My timer," she said as she pulled it out. "The tarte is done."

"You were baking pies that day," Annalisa recalled.

"Blueberry," Effie supplied. "One of her specialties."

"Maybe the timer interrupted you and you detoured to the kitchen."

"We've searched there too," Effie said. "Nothing."

"Let's go anyway. After all, the tarte needs to come out." She went to find the stairs but Matilda hung back.

"I would have taken the back stairs. They go right to the kitchen."

Annalisa and Effie followed her to the narrower servants' stairs at the back of the house. Matilda managed with no issues, her feet long used to the steep pitch, but Effie slowed to a crawl. "It'd serve me right if I fell and broke my hip. Charging around this place like I'm Columbo."

Matilda stopped to help her employer. "We won't have that. Here, hold on to me."

Annalisa watched the tender way Matilda helped Effie down the stairs and had to agree with Effie's assessment that her housekeeper never would have taken the ring on purpose. The problem was unlocking her memory about what she could have done with it. When they arrived at the kitchen, Matilda bustled over to remove the apple tarte from the oven. Annalisa looked around at the huge gleaming counters. The center island was nearly as big as the kitchen in the small house she shared with Nick. The carved oak cabinets probably dated to the original house but they remained in pristine condition.

"I'm wondering if the ring could have ended up in the flour or sugar," Annalisa said.

Matilda set the pie by an open window to cool. Immediately, a curious sparrow appeared on the ledge outside, its head bobbing as it investigated the steaming pie. "Shoo now," Matilda said, waving it away. She straightened and turned to Annalisa with an affronted look. "I don't put jewelry in with my food. It's unhygienic."

"Let's look anyway," Annalisa suggested. "Just in case."

Matilda hadn't yet returned the tins of flour and sugar to the pantry, so it was easy enough to sift each of them onto two large plates. No ring. Annalisa felt discouraged as she cast around for another idea. "Maybe it landed in with the baking tins."

"They're down there." Matilda indicated a cupboard under the island. Annalisa knelt down to look while Effie fretted over her.

"Oh, I shouldn't have you bending over like that. Not in your condition."

"I'm fine." Annalisa rummaged through the baking sheets and various tins until she was satisfied that no ring was mixed among them. It took effort to rise to her feet again. Her knees and hips protested at carrying around the extra weight, and she wondered how she would make it through the next two months.

Effie leaned against the island, tapping her fingers against the smooth marble surface. "I don't understand why Louise would have my ring in the first place. She knows I never would have put it up for auction."

Annalisa couldn't have the woman thinking her friend was a thief. "Helen asked her to get it."

Effie looked alarmed. "Helen? Why ever for?"

"To prevent you from having it appraised," Annalisa said with a sigh. "The ring wasn't what Theo represented it to be. It was a brilliant fake, orchestrated by Helen at the time of your engagement. Even with his real estate deals, Theo couldn't have afforded such a grand ring on his own."

Effie looked appalled. "You think I didn't know that?"

Annalisa blinked. "You . . . knew?"

"Of course I knew. This was the man I loved more than anything, the man I hoped to marry. I knew everything about him. I figured he had gotten the money from somewhere—a loan of some sort—to finance that ring. I wouldn't have cared. I'd have married Theo with a bottle top, but he wanted to impress my father. You're saying Helen gave him the money?"

"She financed the fake."

Effie looked perplexed and she folded her arms. "It wasn't a fake."

"But—"

"I'm telling you, it wasn't. We had it appraised once before many years ago. Around the time of our tenth anniversary. I can show you the documents. Wait here." She left the room and reappeared a few minutes later with some papers in her hand. In the interim, Matilda started hand-washing the dishes in the sink, humming as she worked. Effie thrust the documents at Annalisa. "Here. You see?"

Annalisa saw that the ring had been appraised in 1968 for approximately half a million dollars. "I don't understand."

"Theo sent all of my jewelry out to be professionally cleaned and appraised at the time. Some friends of ours had a house fire and he said we should make sure all our effects were documented in case something similar happened to us."

"Theo must have used the time to switch the rings," Annalisa murmured as she scanned the documents again. "He wanted you to have the real thing."

"Theo was the real thing," Effie said as she took back the papers. "The ring is just a symbol."

"That may be what you're left with," Annalisa admitted. "A symbol of not just Theo's love, but love from your friends as well. They wanted to protect you from finding out about Theo's initial deception. They wanted you to have your great love story."

"I did have it." Effie looked dreamy. "For sixty-two wonderful years."

Matilda put the mixing bowl upside down on the drying rack. "The tarte will be ready soon. I can serve it whenever you'd like." She wiped her hands on a dish towel and reached for the rings she'd set aside while she worked.

"You may as well stay for tea," Effie told Annalisa.

"I'm sorry I couldn't find your ring." She was a little horrified now, truth be told, knowing the true cost. It was probably worth more than a million now.

"That's why I like mine cheap," Matilda said as she put on her rings. "I love trying on Mrs. Effie's fancy items now and again, but I'd be too afraid to wear them every day." A pair of grackles appeared at the window, eyeing the tarte with hunger in their gaze.

"Attention, Mattie," Effie said, pointing to the birds. "You have customers."

"Oh, for heaven's sake. Get out of here!" She waved the dish towel at the birds, who scattered in the wind. Annalisa watched them flitter into the nearby trees and she got an idea.

"The blueberry pie you made the day the ring went missing . . . did you set it by an open window like this?" She moved to where Matilda had set the tarte to cool.

"Yes, I probably did if it was warm enough to open the windows. The ladies like their tea promptly at four, and I needed the pie cool enough to serve."

"It was unseasonably warm that day," Effie added as she joined them near the window. "We talked about it while we played cards."

"So the window was open," Annalisa mused. She turned. "And you took off your rings to do the dishes, like you always do. What if . . . what if one of those rings was Effie's?" Matilda opened her mouth to protest, but Annalisa held up a hand to stall her. "Hear me out. You had the ring, and you were going to put it back in Effie's bedroom when your timer went off. So instead of replacing the ring, you kept it with you. Maybe even slipped it on without thinking about it. Then you came down here, removed the pie from the oven, and set it by the open window. You took off the rings and put them here on the counter by the sink—in view of the birds who were drawn to the smell of the pie."

Effie's eyes went wide. "You think a bird took it?"

"I think it's possible." Annalisa pointed at a door. "Does that lead to the backyard?"

"It does."

Annalisa leaned over to look at the tall trees that lined the back of the property. "I don't suppose you have a ladder."

"Of course. But there's no way I can permit you to climb it." Effie put her hands on her hips. "You'd topple over and hurt yourself."

"I've climbed many ladders before—trees too. I promise to be careful."

"Absolutely not." Effie took out a cell phone from her pocket. "I'm calling my handyman, Gabe Tucker. He'll get to the bottom of this."

They ate apple tarte on white china plates while they waited for Effie's handyman to arrive. Effie asked after Charlotte and if she should remain as the head of Ruby's Place given what happened with Layla.

"I have no idea," Annalisa replied. "I suppose the board could vote to replace her."

"I'm on the board," Effie said. "I care about your opinion. How would you vote?"

"I think I would keep her," Annalisa replied after some consideration.

"Why?"

"Because she understands better than most people what it's like to make desperate choices."

Matilda disagreed. "That's not it at all." She put down her teacup. "That woman knows evil. She saw it take her baby sister away and she's seen it ever since. Her whole life, she won't stop trying to defeat it. You need someone like that as the watchman."

"She missed her own sister as a serial killer," Annalisa pointed out.

"Exactly my point. That baby grew up to take out the man who snatched her. That's not evil. That's justice."

Gabe arrived, a broad-chested man in a plaid shirt who might have been answering a casting call for Paul Bunyan. He didn't blink when Effie explained the mission to him. So it came to be that Annalisa stood at the base of the trees, directing Gabe to various clumps that could be nests. Effie and Matilda sat on the deck chairs near the covered pool, watching the proceedings from a distance. Tree after tree failed to produce any results. Gabe poked around until the sun started to fall in the sky, lengthening the shadows and taking the spring vibes with it. Effie crossed the lawn and shivered inside her coat. "This is a boondoggle," she said. "Let's call it off."

Annalisa couldn't believe her brilliant idea had failed. "Just a few minutes more."

"No, we've checked all these trees," Effie said, gesturing up at Gabe on the ladder. "It was a good suggestion, but the ring is not here."

"Mrs. Christos?" Gabe called out from above. He pointed across the yard at the house. "You've got one more nest I can see right there over your back porch. I can try that one if you want."

"All right, yes. One more."

Gabe moved the ladder one last time. Five minutes later, he yelled with excitement. "I've got it!"

"Oh, my." Effie grew teary at the announcement, patting her flushed cheeks. She reached over and squeezed Annalisa's arm. "You're amazing. Simply amazing."

Gabe came down the ladder, the ring pinched between his fingers. "It's kind of dirty, but I bet it'll shine up nice and pretty for you." He grinned as he handed it over to Effie, who held it up to the sky.

"Here's to you, Theo."

The setting sun caught the large diamond, glinting like fire. Annalisa couldn't help feeling emotional too as she took in Effie's beaming face. "It's as beautiful as you described," she said. "Now you can have it reappraised."

Effie blew the dirt off the ring and slipped it on her hand. "No," she said decisively, her wrinkled face all smiles. "I don't want to let it out of my sight again, not even for a moment. I don't need some number cruncher to tell me what the ring is worth. It's priceless."

THIRTY-FOUR

....

Nick returned from Madison after forty-eight hours, but he ended up needing five days in total to solve the Joe Green case. Outside of the occasional suspicious look, Zimmer had remained patient with him and he rewarded her faith in the small conference room where he had set up his computer to show the results of his investigation. Zimmer entered with her forty-ounce coffee mug and lowered herself into the seat with the best view. "I'm prepared to be wowed," she said, deadpan.

"We're just waiting on two other people," he said, glancing at the door.

"It's your party." She scrolled on her phone while Nick checked the time on the wall clock. Annalisa was late. He was about to text her for an update when she came through the door with Charlotte Higgins in tow. Zimmer raised her eyebrows at Nick. "This is quite an odd guest list you've assembled, Carelli."

"They shouldn't have to read it in the papers," Nick replied.

Annalisa pulled out two chairs for herself and Charlotte, but the other woman did not sit down. "I really think I should have my lawyer here," she said, plainly nervous.

"If you want," Nick told her. "But this doesn't have anything to do with possible charges against you."

"Then what is it about?"

"The man who took your sister."

Charlotte stared at him a moment longer and he gestured for her to take a seat. She moved in a jerky fashion and sat perched on the edge, glancing at the door as if she might flee. Annalisa gave Nick an encouraging nod. He took a deep breath and launched into his case. "Layla told me she couldn't believe we didn't see who Joe Green was," he began. "Initially, I thought she meant we did not recognize him as a pedophile and a kidnapper at the time of his arrest for Cyrus Merriman's murder. But that's only half right."

He put up a picture from the Christmas parade that showed Keith, Eve, and two-year-old Charlotte with their uncle Doug at the edge of the crowd. They were not front and center in the photo. Whoever had snapped the image was aiming for a pair of elves on a float going by, but the image was clear enough for Nick's purposes. "One of the mysteries of Eve's disappearance is how quickly it happened. How her abductor knew exactly where she was and why no one noticed anything amiss. Eve didn't scream or make a scene. She simply vanished without anyone noticing. I submit to you that this is because she knew her kidnapper and went with him willingly. He knew exactly where to find her because he'd left her there himself in the care of her older brother."

He showed the photo again, this time zoomed in on Uncle Doug's face. Zimmer squinted. Annalisa sat forward with her mouth open. Charlotte shook her head. "No," she murmured. "It can't be."

"Doug Collier is the man whose body we recovered from Lake Michigan," Nick said. He showed an autopsy photo of the man's pale face. "I had the lab do the DNA tests to prove it. He comes back as an uncle to both Layla-slash-Eve and to you, Charlotte." He switched to an image showing the DNA results.

"No," Charlotte blurted. "No, he died. He took his own life a week or so after the kidnapping."

"I'm getting to that part." Nick advanced the picture to show a Wisconsin driver's license photo issued in 1984. "This is the real Joe Green. He was, as Annalisa uncovered, a bit of a drifter who struggled with alcohol addiction, possibly as a result of his botched leg surgery years ago. He worked odd jobs to keep afloat, and one of them was working construction. In November of 1986, he was part of a demolition crew on a row of houses coming down to make room for an apartment complex. Guess who was one of the electricians putting in the new wiring?"

"Uncle Doug," Charlotte whispered.

"That's right. I was able to track down the original work order and Doug Collier's signature on it." He showed them a photo of the document. "This doesn't prove for sure that Doug and Joe knew each other, but I am betting this is where they crossed paths. As you can see from the driver's license photo, Joe resembled Doug quite a bit. Both were six feet tall and reasonably heavy guys at the time Eve went missing. They have similar facial features and almost an identical hairline." He put Doug's driver's license photo side by side with Joe's. "I think Doug realized Joe would be easy to eliminate, that he had no family and no regular job. No one would miss him."

"So Doug killed Joe and stole his identity?" Zimmer said.

Nick nodded. "He was going to need it to start over when he took Eve. We're not sure when Joe Green went missing, but it was before the parade. Doug was laying the groundwork he'd need to disappear with Eve."

"But Doug's death was ruled a suicide," Annalisa said.

"No body was ever recovered," Nick said. "When Doug went missing, the family found a suicide note in his apartment and eventually authorities located Doug's car abandoned at Lake Mendota. Doug's clothes, with his wallet and keys in the pants pocket, lay in a folded pile at the edge of the lake. A diving team looked for the body, but they couldn't find one.

At the time, no one had any reason to doubt it was a suicide. Doug was openly despondent about Eve's disappearance. He left a note. More importantly, he left his wallet, his keys, and his whole life behind. Doug Collier was never heard from again. He didn't touch his credit card or his bank account. Instead, he shaved his head, got some nonprescription glasses, lost a bunch of weight and moved to Chicago with his victim. He must have planned a place to stash Eve the day of the parade and then circled back later to retrieve her. He'd clearly been working on his disappearing act for weeks, if not months."

"He had the family photo," Annalisa recalled.

"I'm betting he took it himself," Nick answered. "He was a welcome member of the family before all this happened. He had no record, which is why his fake identity held up even after his arrest for Cyrus Merriman's murder. The actual Joe Green had never committed a felony, so his prints weren't in any national database. So when we arrested Doug, no one had any reason to believe he wasn't Joe."

"I don't understand," Charlotte whispered. "Why wouldn't Layla tell me all this?"

Nick scratched the back of his head. "I can't answer that part. Maybe she felt ashamed, having been victimized by her uncle in that way. Maybe she wanted to spare you from knowing your relative is the one who did it to her. Or maybe she didn't even consciously remember it was him. The psych doctors say they've seen cases like that, where the horror of what's happened is so great that the person's mind splits in two, burying the truth from the conscious brain. Layla was only five years old at the time. She may really have decided her uncle Doug was dead and 'Joe Green' took his place. It's possible that's all she really meant when she said we didn't recognize him—that we had arrested her kidnapper after all these years and somehow missed it."

Charlotte spread her hands on the table. "Keith would have known. He was the oldest."

"That may be why she avoided him even after she found you," Nick said gently. "We just don't know."

"How can I tell him all of this? He won't even talk to me."

"I can tell him if you like," Nick replied as he closed the laptop, removing Doug's face from the screen. Charlotte continued to stare at the blank wall, looking dazed.

"This is great work, Carelli," Zimmer said as she rose. She saluted him with her coffee mug. "Well worth the extra investment."

"Yes," Annalisa said with a trace of envy. "You figured out the last piece all on your own."

"Hardly on my own."

"What will happen to him?" Charlotte asked, turning in her seat. "What will you do with the body? We had a memorial service for him once, you know. I don't remember it but my father kept the paper from the service in one of our family albums." Her eyes watered. "They forgave him. They said it could have happened to anyone out with three little kids. They said sometimes these terrible things just happen." Her voice rose shrilly on the last words.

Nick hadn't considered the fate of the man in the morgue, now identified as Doug Collier. "Usually the body is released to next of kin," he said, glancing at Zimmer. She confirmed with a nod. "That would be you or Keith."

"I don't want him. I'm sure Keith doesn't want him either."

"Well then . . . I think the state cremates the remains. If that's what you want."

"Yes," Charlotte said. "Burn him."

Nick's grandmother had done the same with Nick's father's remains. His mother was buried in Jacksonville with a headstone that read BELOVED DAUGHTER, DEVOTED MOTHER. No word of her marriage to the man who took her life. But his grandmother held on to a portion of the ashes in a little cardboard box in the basement. Nick hadn't known they were there until she gifted him the box the day he moved out at age eighteen. *You can do what you want with them,* she'd told him.

Nick hadn't known what he wanted so he toted the box around with him to seven different living spaces. Only after his divorce from Annalisa, when he moved back to Jacksonville and tried to figure out what the hell he was doing with his life, did he make the drive to the coast to scatter the ashes. He'd been surprised to see the ashes looked like plain old dirt. But then again, that's what the Bible said, right? From dirt we came, to dirt we shall return. He didn't believe in reincarnation but he did believe in second chances. He'd waded into the ocean and poured his father onto the waves, the brackish water swirling, its current trying to pull Nick along for the ride. As the water rushed backward, the receding waves sweeping away the last of Anthony Carelli, Nick remained standing on his own two feet.

EPILOGUE

Sassy married Greg in a courthouse ceremony, no muss, no fuss, followed by a large party of family and friends at Osteria Via Stato. The rustic Italian restaurant adorned its archways with roses and the wooden tables glowed with flickering white candles. Annalisa, who had been the maid of honor at Sassy and Alex's wedding, got to be a regular party guest this time, a small mercy she appreciated since she was currently as big as a house. She watched from her chair as Sassy snuggled into Greg, swaying on the dance floor while Carla and Gigi whirled together nearby, hand in hand, to a tornado tempo only they could hear. When the DJ invited everyone onto the floor, people flooded the married couple, and Sassy turned, smiling, her arms open to welcome her family.

Annalisa remained seated. Nick had to work so he wasn't there, and she was too uncomfortable to enjoy dancing anyhow. She stroked her impossibly round belly through the stretchy fabric of her dress. "Any day now," she told the little one. Her due date was ten days away but Ma had counseled last night that first babies were often late. "Not you, though," she had said, holding her palm to Annalisa's face. "You rushed into the world in about two seconds flat. We left as soon as the contractions started and I barely made it through the doors of the hospital. In a hurry to be here, I guess. Always wanting to be part of the action."

She sat out of the action now, watching with a smile as her family proved they had more enthusiasm than rhythm. Her brother Vinny seemed to be attempting the robot. She glanced over a few tables and saw her father was sitting out the mayhem as well. When they made eye contact, he heaved himself to his feet, leaning heavily on his four-footed cane as he shuffled over to her. "Pops," she protested as he dropped into the seat to her left. "I would have come to you."

He waved her off. "Y-you sit. Like a brooding hen."

"Calling me a chicken?"

"You?" He chuffed. "Never."

They watched the dancing in companionable silence. "Bet I know," he said, "wh-what you're thinking about." Before she could answer, he said, "Alex."

Her smile faded. Pops was right, of course; it was impossible not to think about Alex today—or really any day. She lived with his mistakes at all times, as did Pops, she supposed. Pops had protected Alex at the time of his crimes and paid for it with the downfall of his own reputation and a few years of house arrest. He'd never said he was sorry and Annalisa knew this was because he wasn't. He would have taken Alex's secret to the grave.

"It's Alex's fault he isn't here."

"Yes." Pops surprised her by agreeing, and she shifted to look at him. He gave a tremulous shrug. "Y-you want me to say he did wrong? He did. No ex-excuses."

"But I did wrong too," she said with heat in her voice. "That's what you think. I screwed everything up by turning him in and now his kids grow up with someone else as their father."

Pops frowned and looked at Alex's girls on the dance floor. "You're about to learn," he said, waving at her stomach, "what it's like. L-loving someone who has the power to wreck you."

Her? Did he mean her? Annalisa opened her mouth to object, but Pops kept talking.

"You're gonna make mistakes. Impossible not to do." He glanced at her, apologetic. "Sorry. It's the truth. You have to hope your kid forgives you."

"Pops." She stared at him. "Are you asking my forgiveness?"

"I made the choice to protect Alex. May-maybe I was wrong. But you'll understand when you have a kid yourself—they make you say and do all kinds of stuff you never expected. You don't know until you're in the moment how you're going to react."

"It wasn't a moment. You had literal years to come forward with the truth. Only when I forced your hand did you say anything at all."

"Yes. You're my kid too." He backed this up with a shaky nod. "When the trouble came for you, th-that was it. You wouldn't have survived the secret, so it had to come out." He took a breath. "I would s-s-sacrifice myself for my children. I wouldn't t-trade one for another."

Annalisa looked at him in wonderment. The night before, she'd dug out the photos from Sassy and Alex's wedding eleven years earlier, pictures she had not been able to look at since the day Alex was arrested. She saw Alex smiling in every shot, looking like he'd won the lottery. Sassy looked young and sweet and glowing. Someone had captured Vinny's girl, Quinn, eight years old at the time, asleep on a bench with Sassy's bouquet in her arms. Alex had already been a murderer at the time these pictures were taken, so the happiness seemed like a lie at first. Other problems lurked just below the surface. Pops's Parkinson's disease had not yet emerged at the time. He busted a move on the dance floor, beer belly and all, but the disease was in him already; the first tremors would start within a year.

Nick wasn't in the pictures. He and Annalisa had divorced already.

Annalisa remembered standing up at Alex's wedding and thinking she would never get back to the altar again. One photo caught her alone at an empty table, its festive decorations ravaged by partygoers, candlelight in her dark eyes. She looked sad and alone, which might have been true in that moment, even if it wasn't the whole story. Nick had accused her of being relentless in wanting to get to the truth even if that meant doing damage along the way, and Annalisa had accepted that damage as the truth. But when she looked again through the photos, she decided it was more complicated. Alex's confession was a time bomb in the background, as was Pops's illness. But Alex and Sassy's wedding had been a joy, with more joys to come. Two of them in particular were chasing each other around the dance floor with cake smeared on their faces. And Nick had reappeared. He had changed. Maybe that was the most hopeful thing of all. *Change.*

"How's business?" Pops asked, searching for a new subject.

"Slow," she replied with a wry smile. "Which is probably just as well right now."

"You need money?"

"Pops. Nick has a job. We've been planning for my leave. It's not like I'll be out on the streets."

Pops nodded but looked unconvinced. He tilted his head as he watched Greg dip Sassy, the pair of them laughing. Greg and Sassy looked happy together, and Annalisa wished them well. Fervently. *Please let this work out.* "I got a buddy who needs a h-hand. He's worried his lady is stepping out on him—that she may even have a second f-family. He's happy to pay to get to the bottom of things."

Annalisa rolled her eyes. "Is your friend a raccoon? A goose?" She knew with Pops there had to be a catch here somewhere.

Pops looked offended. "Marv Mayhew—He was a deputy chief for ten years."

"Uh-huh." Annalisa drummed her fingers and waited.

Pops thinned his lips. "H-his lady is a cat. But she's getting fat and he thinks she's got a second family that's feeding her. He wants to have her followed."

"Tell him to keep his lady indoors. Or take her to the vet to make sure she's not pregnant."

"Speaking of." Pops eyed her belly. "You got a name picked out yet?"

"No." Annalisa shifted to finger a white flower from the centerpiece. "How about gardenia?"

Pops snorted. "How about f-floor tile? Archway? As long as we're just naming things in the r-room."

"Hey, Archie's not bad."

"For a boy, yes. For a man?" Pops looked skeptical. "Hey, speaking of men . . . here's yours." He stuck out his chin in the direction of the front door, and Annalisa leaned over to see Nick dressed to the nines in his dark suit and purple tie. Here at last was a reason to get out of her chair.

"Save my seat," she said to Pops and went to greet her husband. Nick took her in his arms and kissed her on both cheeks. "You made it."

"I even had time to shower. Believe me, you're grateful." He looked beyond her at the dance floor. "Are you up for a twirl?"

"Twirl, no. Standing around hugging you, yes."

He led her to a corner out of the chaos and they snuggled together. "Wasn't there supposed to be a gelato bar?" he asked, his voice a rumble under her cheek.

"It's in the back behind the pillars." She smiled but did not open her eyes. "I guess we know why you really showed up."

"No, I have our baby name dilemma solved."

Now she did look up. "Really?"

"Sure. Booked a suspect today with the actual name 'Jaws.' Good for a boy or a girl."

She swatted him. "That's not funny. We are going to have to agree soon, you know."

"Yeah, but I've been thinking," he said as he pulled her against him once more. "Maybe we're putting too much pressure on ourselves. There's no perfect name. The kid can always change it later. Plus, sometimes, the name you pick out doesn't stick for another reason. Look at Sassy."

"True." Annalisa glanced over and caught Sassy's gaze, and her friend gave her a conspiratorial finger wave. Sassy had been born Cecelia but became Sassy when her brother couldn't pronounce it.

After another moment of swaying in Nick's arms, Annalisa called "uncle" when the DJ switched to an up-tempo number. "I'll get on that gelato then," he told her, giving her hand a squeeze. "Should I bring enough for three?"

"Mint chocolate for me. Raspberry for junior here." She patted her middle and took two steps toward the table before freezing in place. Nick saw her halt.

"What is it? Are you okay?"

"I think you're going to need that gelato to go."

"You're not feeling well? We can go home."

"No, I mean the hospital." Sassy was going to kill her. "My water just broke."

Sassy wasn't angry; she was overjoyed. The restaurant staff was perhaps a bit perplexed when the party shut down an hour earlier than planned and everyone without small children moved to the hospital. Sassy's kids were already set to stay a few days with Ma and Pops so she and Greg followed Nick and Annalisa to the hospital still in their wedding attire. At Annalisa's urging, Nick brought three plastic containers of gelato.

Through contractions, Annalisa argued with Nick about their short list of names. They finally agreed on Mina for a girl. It meant "love," and she could think of nothing more she would wish for her child. With the thirty-odd Vega family members crowded in the waiting room, the baby would have that love multiplied to infinity. When it finally came time for the final push, Annalisa looked up weakly from the pillow. “Well?”

Nick grinned and squeezed her hand. “It’s a boy.”

“Shit.” The word just slipped out of her mouth, and the nearby nurse looked askance. Nick didn’t miss a beat.

“Hmm, I don’t think that’s the best choice for a name, but I’m willing to hear you out.”

“No. I mean . . . he’s okay?”

“He’s perfect.” The doctor handed Nick the wriggling red infant, and he placed their son on Annalisa’s chest before coming around so he could crouch down and make goo-goo eyes at the baby. “Hello there. Hello, little guy.”

Annalisa blinked back tears as she ran a finger over the baby’s downy head. “I can’t believe he’s real.”

“I know.” Nick’s voice echoed her quiet awe.

“When I get cleaned up, let’s have Cassidy come in first. She can meet her brother.”

Nick stroked the boy’s cheek with one finger. “She’ll like that.” He paused. “We’ll need a name to introduce him.”

“What about Chance?” She blurted out the name without thinking.

“Chance Carelli,” Nick said, trying it out. “I like it. He sounds like an action hero.”

Annalisa looked down at the baby. “He’ll be whatever he’s meant to be.” The name came to her out of the blue. It hadn’t been on any of their lists, but she didn’t need an ancestry site to look up the meaning. Good fortune. Opportunity. This was what she hoped life would always give her, her child, and everyone else who needed it: one more chance.

ACKNOWLEDGMENTS

This is my tenth book! I can hardly believe it. What a marvelous, amazing milestone, and it's a time to be grateful to the folks who got me here. My thanks to Minotaur Books, and Kelley Ragland in particular, for taking a chance on me eight years ago. Thanks also to my intrepid editor, Sallie Lotz, for her thoughtful guidance and probing questions that make the manuscript stronger. Shout-out as well to Jill Schuck, whose cheerful attitude is matched by her patience, knowledge, and helpfulness. If you've heard of this book and found it somewhere, that's probably due to the hard work of Kayla Janas and Sara Eslami, whose creativity and imagination inspire me daily. I'm so lucky to have had this whole team of great people with me on this journey.

Thanks also to my wonderful agent, Jill Marsal, who has also been with me since the beginning. I really value her wise counsel in navigating the rough seas of publishing.

Readers! Readers are the best part of being a published author, as opposed to a writer . . . which you are if you write anything, even if you never share it with other people. But in sharing our stories, we find both common ground and new perspectives. Thank you to anyone who has read my work.

As ever, this writer gig is way more fun if you are a member of #TeamBump, my beloved beta reader crew. Thank you always for your advice and your good humor. I am blessed to have a crackerjack squad of betas that includes Katie Bradley, Rayshell Reddick Daniels, Jason Grenier, Shannon Howl, Julie Kodama, Rebecca LeBlanc, Suzanne Magnuson, Garrett Rooney, Jill Svihovec, Dawn Volkart, Amanda Wilde, and Paula Woolman.

Thanks as always to my wonderful family, especially Brian and Stephanie Schaffhausen and Larry and Cherry Rooney, for their love and support.

Finally, if inspiration starts at home, I am the luckiest writer on the planet because I live with two varsity-level humans: my marvelous husband, Garrett, and our phenomenal daughter, Eleanor. They are the source of all my joy.

ABOUT THE AUTHOR

Joanna Schaffhausen wields a mean scalpel, a skill developed in her years studying neuroscience. She has a doctorate in psychology, which reflects her long-standing interest in the brain—how it develops and the many ways it can go wrong. Previously, she worked for ABC News, writing for programs such as *World News Tonight, Good Morning America,* and *20/20.* She lives in the Boston area with her husband and daughter. She is also the author of *The Vanishing Season, No Mercy, All the Best Lies, Every Waking Hour, Last Seen Alive, Gone for Good, Long Gone, Dead and Gone,* and *All the Way Gone.*